also by
Laura Thalassa

THE BARGAINER SERIES

Rhapsodic
A Strange Hymn
The Emperor of Evening Stars
Dark Harmony

Dark Harmony

LAURA THALASSA

Bloom *books*

Published by Bloom Books, an imprint of Sourcebooks
P.O. Box 4410, Naperville, Illinois 60567-4410
(630) 961-3900
sourcebooks.com

Originally self-published in 2018 by Laura Thalassa.

Cataloging-in-Publication Data is on file with the Library of Congress.

Printed and bound in the United States of America.
VP 10 9 8 7 6 5 4 3

For those who dream—
Keep at your magic.

"Stars, hide your fires; / Let not light
see my black and deep desires."
—WILLIAM SHAKESPEARE, *MACBETH*

CHAPTER 1

I stare down at my hands for the fiftieth time since Des and I returned from the Flora Kingdom, looking for something that indicates I'm different. *Changed.*

Immortal.

I press my palm to my heart. Beneath the steady thump of it, I feel something else. Something magical and mysterious.

Something that wasn't there just days ago.

My connection to Des thrums under my touch like a second heartbeat, the two of us now magically bound together.

I slide him a coy glance.

Des sits along a thick stone railing, his back resting against one of the columns bolted into the rocky island. The two of us linger on the lowest balcony of Somnia, one of the six floating islands of the Night Kingdom and the capital of the Bargainer's realm.

"I'm angry at you, you know," I say, though there's no venom to the words.

The Bargainer's eyes are closed, his head tipped back against the column. "I know."

I watch him as he sits on the very edge of the world, the dark night beyond him. In the distance, the chittering laughter of pixies rides the evening wind.

"You never asked me if I wanted to live forever." My voice catches on that last word.

Technically, I'm not going to live *forever*, but it might as well be that long. Thanks to the lilac wine Des fed me, I'm now looking at a solid four hundred years of life—if not more.

What will the earth look like by the time I actually kick the bucket? How about the Otherworld?

Need to talk to Temper about how freaking long fairy life spans are.

The Bargainer's eyes open, his glittering silver gaze looking fearsome and fae.

He gives me a hint of a smile, though there's no humor in it. "Cherub, you seem to be forgetting the fact you were dying at the time."

I was dying, and he was unwilling to let me go.

He reaches out a hand to me, and his magic tugs me toward him. I frown as I'm ushered to his side.

Des taps my mouth. "Tell me, Callie," he says, his voice like honeyed wine as his hands fall to my waist, "don't you want to spend more than just a few decades with me?"

Of course I do. That's beside the point.

I'm upset that I didn't get a chance to decide my fate for myself. And now the future looms endlessly ahead of me.

Des lifts his inked arm into the air. Luminescent blue smoke coalesces from the night, solidifying more and more as it snakes its way to the Bargainer's hand. By the time it reaches his palm, it's a glowing cord. I've seen this stuff before: spun moonlight.

The Bargainer manipulates it in his hand, working the eerie substance until it's not just a cord but an elaborate necklace.

I narrow my eyes as he brings the unearthly jewelry to my throat.

"That's not fair," I say as he clasps it behind my neck, even as my fingertips reach for the necklace. "You can't just pull one of your pretty fairy tricks and buy my forgiveness."

But he can, and he has, and he will do so again. These neat little tricks of his have made me forgive a lot.

The Bargainer turns on his perch so his legs straddle mine. He pulls me in close, my hips fitting snugly between his thighs. "My pretty fairy tricks are what you like best about me," he says, his lips skimming my mouth as he talks. His gaze drops to my lips. "Well, that and my di—"

"*Des.*"

He laughs against my skin, his warm breath drawing out my gooseflesh. Slowly, the laughter dies from his features. "I lost you once, Callie," he says, "and those seven years nearly killed me. I don't intend to lose you again."

My gut clenches at the memory. Even now I can feel the ache of his absence; it's a wound that never healed.

Des presses a hand to my heart. "Besides—is this not worth it?"

He doesn't need to elaborate on what *this* is.

Beneath his palm, I feel the warmth of Des's presence—not only against my skin but *within* me. It feels like I'm being kissed by pale moonlight, like the stars and the deep night rest under my skin, and I know that makes no sense, but there it is.

His magic even has a sound. It's a low melody, the faint

notes just beyond my reach. It makes me feel the same breathless excitement I used to feel at Peel Academy when evening was coming and Des was coming with it.

We were once mates separated by worlds and magic; now we're separated no longer, thanks to the lilac wine.

The wine came with other perks. I can now make my claws and scales and wings appear and disappear at will. And I can sense fae magic in a way I never could before.

Of course, there are drawbacks too—fairy gifts *always* have drawbacks.

I'm still coming for you. Your life is mine.

The Bargainer catches my wrist, examining my bare forearm.

"Three hundred and twenty-two favors—a lifetime's worth," he murmurs.

I follow his gaze. It's weird looking down and not seeing the Bargainer's bracelet. The skin there is paler than the rest, and I admit, my arm feels naked without the weight of all those black beads. I wore that bracelet every day for nearly eight years...and overnight it disappeared.

It was a lifetime's worth of beads, but in the end, it was even more than that—it was a *life's* worth. Those beads brought me back from the edge of death. And now I have to wonder if, from the very beginning, Des's magic somehow knew it would come to this. If all that debt and all those years of waiting were its way of gathering magic so it could prevent my untimely death.

Or maybe I just got really, really lucky.

I lower my wrist so I can look the Night King in the eye. "Anger aside—thank you." My words come out rough.

Thank you is a pitifully small show of gratitude for what Des did. Because he saved me. *Again.*

For once I'd like to return the favor.

Des's hand tightens around my forearm, and he brings my wrist to his lips, then presses a kiss there. "Does this mean you forgive me for the lilac wine?"

"Don't push your luck, fairy boy."

"Cherub, hasn't anyone told you? I don't need luck. I deal in favors."

CHAPTER 2

That evening, I stand in what feels like a void, endless darkness pressing in on all sides. I glance about, unsure how I arrived there.

"Not a slave anymore, I see."

My shoulders hike up at that voice.

That *voice*.

Last time I heard it, I was in the Flora Queen's sacred oak forest, my life bleeding out of me. And now it's at my back.

"We meet again, enchantress," the Thief of Souls says.

The monster's fingertips trail like velvet up my arm.

"Your wings are gone—" He leans forward and breathes me in. "And is that fae magic I smell? Could it be that the mighty Night King gave you the lilac wine?"

"Don't act like you're surprised," I say.

The Thief had deliberately orchestrated a situation where I'd drink the wine and become fae, all so that his power could be compatible with mine. Before then, his magic didn't work on me, just as it didn't for all humans.

"What can I say?" he responds. "Fairies in love can be terribly predictable, I'm afraid."

The Thief comes around to my front, and I finally get a good look at him.

He's as I remember him from my dreams and that moment in the woods. Jet-black hair, upturned inky eyes, pouty mouth, alabaster skin.

Like all the other fairies I've met, he's beautiful. Almost unbearably so. Not for the first time, I wish evil looked as it should.

I step away from his touch. The night shrouds us on all sides, but even in the darkness, I can make out the twisted oaks that surround me.

My stomach drops. I'm back in Mara Verdana's sacred oak forest.

Could've sworn I'd left this place.

Off in the distance, I hear the faint notes of a fiddle and the snap and crackle of a bonfire. The smell of woodsmoke carries on the breeze. There's something under the smell, a scent that's somewhat sweet. If only I could place it...

The Thief of Souls walks over to a tree, and his boot scuffs a root. "This, I believe, is where you fucked the Night King."

Bile rises into my throat.

Jesus. Had he watched us?

His gaze meets mine. "How do I know that?" He glances at the tree trunk again. The normally rough bark is coated in a slick substance. "I have eyes everywhere."

As I watch, the Thief presses a hand to the glistening bark. Within seconds, whatever coats the tree trunk now spills onto the Thief's hand, the dark rivulets snaking between his fingers and down his wrist.

And now I place that strange scent.

Blood.

It drips from the tree the Thief touches, and now it's smeared across his hand.

He gives me a small smile, his eyes glinting in the darkness.

I hear the slow patter of rain. Only I'm not sure it's *rain* dripping from the trees' boughs.

As I watch, the oak in front of me starts to groan and tremble.

The Thief eyes me up and down. "Fae magic suits you well, enchantress. I confess I'm eager to see how it interacts with my own."

Around me, the trees crack and splinter, making wet popping noises.

One by one, the trunks peel open like banana skins. Nestled inside each is a sleeping soldier, all of them still as death. Blood oozes down their skin and drips from their tattered clothes.

The oak next to the Thief ruptures, revealing a bronze-skinned fairy. The Thief touches the soldier's cheek, and for an instant, his face morphs into that of the sleeping man. Then the illusion is gone, and the Thief is himself once more.

I shudder.

"I've been waiting a while for this day to come," he says distractedly, still staring at the soldier. He drops his hand from the sleeping man and turns his full attention to me. "Tell me, enchantress, can you make a man—any man—fall in love with you? Not just enchant them for a time but truly conquer their hearts?"

My skin prickles.

The Thief leaves the soldier's side, pacing toward me. Around us, the sound of wood splintering and blood dripping swells until I feel I might go mad.

All at once, the woods fall eerily silent.

Without warning, my siren flares to life, triggered by some pressing, unknown fear. My skin brightens, illuminating the Thief's face in the dark night.

His eyes take on a fascinated sheen. "*Yes*," he says, almost to himself, "I bet you could." He closes the distance between us. "I do miss the days when I thought you a simple slave. Perhaps when you are mine, I'll pretend you still are one." He catches one of my wrists. "You'll wear metal cuffs and a collar like the slaves of old. And then you'll be my *enslaved* enchantress, and together we'll see just how close you can come to making someone like me feel affection."

He dares to threaten us? Never again will we fall under anyone's yoke.

"I hope you can manage it," he continues, "more for your sake than mine. I'm not known for being gentle with my playthings. Just ask Mara."

I stare at him for a long moment, my claws sharpening, barely staying my siren's violent tendencies. Then, all at once, I release my hold on her.

My free hand moves almost without me noticing it. I strike, swiping at his face. My claw tips tear open the skin of his cheek in four evenly spaced lines.

Almost immediately, blood begins to drip from the wounds.

The Thief looks amused.

I don't get any warning before he throws me against the tree he'd been toeing only minutes before.

I let out an angry shout as I hit the bloody trunk, my

9

chest pressed against the sleeping soldier, my eyes staring at the man's bloody face. Behind me, the Thief pins me in.

"Normally, I like my women docile," he whispers against my ear, "but you—you, I'll enjoy fighting. Breaking."

His words are decidedly sexual, and I remember all those female soldiers and the children he'd forced upon them.

I grit my teeth, my nails digging into the tree trunk.

Never, my siren vows. *We will kill him first, and we will* relish *it*.

I hear a moan on the wind, and the trees shiver, their leaves falling from the branches like tears.

In front of me, the soldier's eyes snap open.

Oh *shit*.

The Thief leans into my ear again, his lips brushing the sensitive skin there. "Enjoy the carnage. I do hope you survive it…"

———

Screams rip me from sleep.

I jerk up in bed, wide awake in an instant, my breath coming in startled gasps.

Not in the queen's oak forest. Not pinned to a rotting tree.

Not in the Thief's clutches.

The dim lamps hanging above me illuminate the Bargainer's Otherworld chambers.

I'm safe. For now.

The screams filter back through my awareness.

Then again…

Des stands at the foot of the bed, his talon-tipped wings spread, looking like one of hell's angels as he stares at a point above my head. I follow his gaze, but there's nothing there.

My eyes meet his as more shrieks vibrate through the

bones of the castle. There's something about the sound…
like it's one voice coming through many mouths.

I remember my dream, the soldier's eyes opening.
Something cold skitters up my spine.

There are no sleeping men here in the Night Kingdom, I try to
reassure myself. And it's true, there are no sleeping men here
in Somnia. But a thousand feet beneath us, an army's worth
of women lie sleeping.

The screams seem to get louder.

At least, the women *were* sleeping.

I'm pretty goddamn sure they're awake now.

CHAPTER 3

All at once the screams cut off, and the silence that follows is somehow even more ominous.

What in all the worlds…?

Des and I are still staring at each other. One second passes, then two, three, four. It's so terribly quiet.

Perhaps I imagined it all.

But then a wave of shrieks start, trickling in like the beginnings of a storm. First a single alarmed shout, then another, and then several. They sound so very far away.

The Bargainer closes his eyes for several seconds, as though the sound pains him deeply. "What are the chances I could persuade you to hide somewhere safe?" he asks, opening his eyes, his voice silken.

Hide somewhere safe? What exactly does he think is going to happen?

I kick my sheets off, swinging my legs out of bed. "Zero," I say.

His throat works. "I can't lose you, cherub." For a

moment, the crafty Bargainer's pain is transparent. "Not again."

I can still see his face from when I slipped into that final darkness.

You are not leaving me, Callie.

It's so fresh.

Des shutters his expression, the softness dissipating from it as though it never was.

Black battle leathers materialize next to me. I stare at them, my mind racing to catch up with the situation.

"You remember your training?" Des's voice doesn't sound quite right. It's not mocking or teasing. He's far too serious.

There's only one reason he'd think to ask me that.

We're going to have to kick some ass.

I nod.

"Good." He stands, his brows furrowed as he takes me in. "If I can't hide you, I will simply have to *unleash* you."

Unleash me—like I'm an unstoppable force. He might believe in me a tad too much.

More screams filter in from the depths of the island, near where the sleeping women have been left to rest. In my mind's eye, I can still see those soldiers in their glass coffins, each one buried with a weapon.

I've been waiting a while for this day to come.

I suck in a breath, realizing now what Des already has.

All those women were lying at the core of the island, waiting like bombs to detonate.

And tonight, the Thief of Souls lit the fuse.

Des's magic brushes against my skin, and the skimpy nightgown I wear melts off my body, the fabric pooling around my hips and leaving me bare-breasted.

Before I can so much as cover myself, the drawer of the nearby armoire opens, and out floats an entire outfit. It drifts through the air then settles on me, the fabric parting like butter as it touches my skin, molding to my body before stitching itself back together. More of Des's magic.

Then come the battle leathers. Then my boots. Each one is slipped on with a little help from Des's magic. He watches me the entire time, his eyes fierce with resolve.

I will destroy the world before I lose you again, they seem to say.

I'm sliding out of bed when the final piece of my outfit floats over to me. The belt that holds my holstered daggers wraps itself around my waist, the labradorite hilts of my blades gleaming.

Dressed and armed within seconds.

The Bargainer isn't fucking around.

It's only once I'm ready to kick ass and take names that his own gear rushes through the air at breakneck speed, fastening onto his body faster than I can follow. His leathers, a sword, a pair of throwing knives, a dagger strapped to his ankle and another on a holster that circles his bicep.

Dressed as he is, I'm pretty sure he could make most women spontaneously orgasm with just a look.

God, now is *not* the time for my filthy thoughts.

The screams are getting louder.

"In case you missed it," Des says, "those soldiers who slept beneath my castle are now awake, and they mean to overthrow me."

My heart pounds a little faster as Des essentially confirms what I feared: the soldiers Karnon imprisoned and abused are now our enemies.

"These women aren't civilians," the Night King

14

continues. "They've defended this kingdom for decades—centuries, even. They will not hesitate to hurt you, and they will not show you or anyone else mercy. When you come across one, go for a kill shot, and do not waste your remorse on them. I assure you they won't waste theirs on you."

My wings are itching to reveal themselves as adrenaline spikes my blood.

The Bargainer turns from me, his eyes closing. He bows his head, as if in prayer, but I feel the thrum of his restless energy as it builds within him. It sings across our bond and vibrates along my skin.

Shadows billow about the room. I barely have time to register what's about to happen when Des's magic explodes out of him.

Darkness sweeps across the chamber, blanketing the world around us in an instant, shaking the very foundations of the castle. It overwhelms my senses until I'm no one and nothing more than a pinprick of thought in the vast expanse of darkness. And then I'm not even that.

I've been here once before. The last time Des's magic blasted out of him, Karnon—the Fauna King—and hundreds of other fae died.

I steel myself for that same outcome.

But when the darkness slams back into Des, the screams haven't quieted.

The Bargainer staggers back, his face incredulous.

"I can't...kill them." The sleeping soldiers, he means.

I don't know what's more shocking—that Des was ready to single-handedly end the attack, despite the soldiers being Night Kingdom fae, or that it didn't work. I've seen the power he wields. If he wanted to, he could destroy entire cities with his will alone.

What could possibly be strong enough to withstand that sort of magical attack?

My eyes move to the weaponry strapped to his body. Better yet—how are we supposed to defeat what Des's power alone couldn't?

The screams fill the night, stealing my breath.

"They're moving fast," he says, "and they're headed our way."

And we're to meet them in combat.

I take a deep breath. The last time I fought an enemy was only days ago, and that hadn't ended too well.

Here's hoping I do a little better tonight.

I shake out my hands as I move, heading for the door. Des's form flickers, disappearing for a moment only to materialize directly in front of me.

His intense eyes lock on mine. "You know I trust you, respect you, and above all else, love you. But gods give me grace, Callie, I will have a reckoning with you if you go rogue on me."

Ye of little faith. I only did that once, and that was the time the "foe" Des and I faced was Temperance "Temper" Darling, sorceress and my best friend.

"I'm not going to go *rogue* on you, Des."

"Just so we're clear." Reluctantly, he steps out of the way, and then the two of us exit his rooms.

The floor shivers as we stride down it. There's a rumbling in the distance, like a storm coming to call, and the air carries the faintest hint of something cloying and foul.

"What is that smell?" I ask Des as I follow him through the castle. Our immediate surroundings are far too quiet.

"Dark magic," he says over his shoulder.

I raise my eyebrows. "I can *smell* magic?" That's…not normal.

"Fae magic," Des specifies. "And, yeah, apparently you can."

All riiiight. I guess I can roll with that.

Footfalls pound up the hall. Des's wings flare protectively, but the individuals that turn the corner are some of Des's royal aides.

"Where's Malaki?" Des demands, clearly interested in talking strategy with his general.

The aides look at each other, perplexed. "Haven't seen him," one of them says.

"Check the sorceress's rooms," I say. Temper undoubtedly has Des's general chained to her bed.

I'm not the only one with a taste for fairies.

The Bargainer runs a hand through his white hair. "How many soldiers are stationed here on Somnia?" he asks one of the aides.

"Eight hundred and fifty. There are a few hundred more on the other islands. The rest are stationed at the Borderlands or on peacetime leave."

Des rubs his mouth. I know what he's thinking: we're outnumbered. There are easily over a thousand sleeping women beneath this castle. If they're out for blood…they're going to overtake us.

"Call in as many reinforcements as you can," Des orders. "Send all Night soldiers to the palace. The previously sleeping women are going to try to take the castle. We can't let that happen."

I glance out the nearby row of arched windows. Bursts of light wink across Somnia like camera flashes. With them come screams. So many screams.

The aides incline their heads, and then they're off, storming back through the castle to carry out the Night King's orders.

I note that none of his men tried to linger and guard

him—nor did they try to sequester him away to wait out the battle. In that regard, fairies are different from humans. Or maybe the battle-tested Des, with his war cuffs and his darkness, is just different from other leaders.

The Bargainer strides down the hall again. "Get those daggers ready, cherub," he says over his shoulder. "We're going to face the women head-on."

I reach for my weapons with shaky hands. It's one thing to spar with Des, another to prepare for true battle.

My skin shimmers as the siren bleeds into me. With the change comes a vicious sort of confidence I was missing a second ago. I pull out my blades, the etched phases of the moon glinting along the length of the metal. The daggers are a familiar weight in my palms.

Deeper in the castle, there's a rumble followed by an explosion. Then more screams.

Besides Des's aides, we see no one. That, more than anything, has my claws sharpening and my wings manifesting. We're hunting predators.

The shrieks get louder as we move down the palace hallways, heading ever closer to the main entrance.

And then we turn down a corridor that's not abandoned.

Several fairies are fleeing our way, their eyes wild and their clothes bloody.

One of them has the wherewithal to stop when he sees the king. "Your Majesty," he pants, "please don't go that way… They're slaughtering everyone in their path."

The Bargainer's gaze slides from the man to the hall. "Get yourself to safety," is all Des says, and then he's striding forward once more.

The man spares me a hasty glance, and then he takes off like a jackrabbit.

Des and I head down another hall, toward a staircase. More fairies flee past us, and the screams are getting louder. Closer.

I tighten my grip on my daggers, my tense wings hiking up behind me, my skin glittering under the wall sconces.

As we descend the staircase, the scene below us is slowly unveiled. My blood chills at the sight. There are bloody bodies scattered across the floor, their eyes glassy. Across the landing, a female soldier closes in on a palace aide, her battle axe raised above her head. Like the dead around her, she has flat, almost vacant eyes, yet she's still moving, compelled by whatever hold the Thief has on her. She's going to cleave the man in two—as it appears she has these other unfortunate souls.

In front of me, Des disappears. He materializes between the two fairies just as the soldier brings the axe down.

I swallow my scream as he catches the weapon by its handle. The aide ducks out from behind Des and runs off.

The Night King clucks his tongue, looking completely at ease as the soldier yanks the axe against his grip. "Didn't anyone tell you that it's poor taste to kill a man indoors?"

The soldier growls in frustration as she tries to dislodge the axe from Des's hold. When that doesn't work, she swings at him with her free arm, her fist closed. Des shimmers out of existence long enough for the blow to pass through where he was and the soldier to stumble off-balance.

He reappears, kicking the soldier square in the chest, the blow throwing her off her feet. She hits the ground hard, and I hear the audible *whoosh* as her breath is knocked from her lungs. Her axe slips out of her grip, skidding several feet behind her.

"It's all that blood," Des continues, prowling toward her. "Easy enough to get it out of the floor with a little magic, but spirits love to cling to the last of their lifeblood. No one wants a ghost haunting their house."

The soldier bares her teeth at the Night King, scuttling back on her forearms to grab her axe. She snatches it up just as Des closes in on her. Casually, the Bargainer steps on her wrist, the bone breaking with a sickening snap. The soldier screams, the sound more an animalistic cry of frustration than actual pain. That's the spookiest part of it all: she's so hell-bent on carnage that her pain takes a back seat to it.

Another fairy—a nobleman by the looks of his attire—sprints onto the landing from another flight of stairs, a soldier at his back. The female soldier pauses, lifting her bow and nocking an arrow, her eyes eerily empty.

I don't fucking think so.

I cock my arm back and throw one of my daggers. It flips hilt over point. With a wet thump, it lodges into the soldier's throat.

Holy shit, I wasn't expecting my aim to be *that* good.

And, oh God, I just mortally wounded someone. The thought sits like a stone in the pit of my stomach.

The woman stumbles backward, her hand going to her bloody throat while her original target, the nobleman, flees past me. With every beat of the soldier's heart, more and more crimson liquid spills from her wound. It reminds me of my stepfather, of the penchant I have for nicking that particular artery.

I expect to hear the soldier let out a pained cry or to see fear in her eyes—any indication that there's a person residing in that body—but when her gaze finds mine, there's nothing behind those eyes except cold, calm detachment.

After grabbing the hilt of my embedded dagger, the soldier rips it out of her throat.

Goddamn. That is way too hard-core for me.

Before my eyes, her wound begins to close.

Are you fucking *serious*? I mean, I know that only seconds ago, I was horrified at her death, but now the broad just needs to go.

She stalks forward, my weapon in her hand. I tighten my fist around my remaining dagger, adrenaline pounding between my ears.

Halfway to me, she hesitates, and her hand goes back to her neck wound. As I follow her movements, I realize that beneath all the blood, the wound is still open. I don't know why, but it stopped healing.

She doesn't get any more time than that. Before she or I can do anything, Des finishes off his assailant, then manifests in front of my opponent, sword in hand. In one clean motion, he skewers her.

Her eyes widen as he removes his bloody blade from her stomach, and a moment later, her knees give out. The soldier's glassy eyes stare up at the ceiling, and her mouth opens and closes until the last of her life drains out.

The Bargainer kneels and takes my blade from her hand. He vanishes, only to wink into existence right in front of me.

He hands me my blade. "You did good, cherub," he says, his eyes shining as he takes me in.

I wet my mouth, my eyes moving to the soldier. Being good at killing is no compliment. My siren preens at it anyway.

Des grabs my jaw and gives me a quick kiss, and my siren sings at the taste of my mate on my tongue and the scent of blood in the air.

Once the Bargainer releases my jaw, his gaze lingers

21

on my face a moment longer. Reluctantly, he turns away before stalking through the palace once more, heading for the sounds of screaming.

Taking a deep breath, I follow him.

We pass several more fallen fairies as we make our way through the castle, their deaths gruesome, violent. My warring natures can't decide what to make of it. Part of me feels nauseous and horrified, and part of me is filled with vindictive bloodlust.

Make them suffer. Make them pay, my siren whispers.

The next formerly sleeping soldier we come across lingers in a dim hallway, crouched over a body. I squint at her form; almost all the sconces are snuffed out in this corridor, like the light can't bear to witness this horror.

The soldier's head snaps up, her eyes glinting like a cat's. Her face is splattered with blood, and the knife she wields is doused in it, the crimson liquid coating the blade, the hilt, and most of her hand.

There's no way the fairy beneath her is alive.

The Bargainer is on the soldier in a second, sword in hand. In one clean, swift stroke, he lops off her head.

It hits the ground with a sickening *thud*, the soldier's body joining it a moment later. A pool of dark blood spills from both.

I stare at the head. Its eyes are still blinking. Oh, my sweet Lord—why are its eyes still blinking? And holy hell—its mouth is opening and closing like a fish gasping for breath.

I feel my siren pressing upon me, growing ever more excited at the sight and smell of blood. *I want it all*, she whispers. *Their pain, their power, their very lives. Mine to savor, mine to take.*

Part of me wants to wrap my siren's viciousness around

me like armor, but a larger part of me is just as disturbed by her as I am by all the carnage. I don't want any part of me to thrive on these violent deaths.

So I do what I've always done—I keep her leashed as best I can.

Forcing myself to move, I head over to the civilian sprawled on the ground and kneel at her side. Her eyes are closed, her face is slack, and her neck is a mess of bloody tissue—and then there's all the blood *outside* her body. No human could survive that much blood loss. But then, this isn't a human.

I see her chest rise and fall and hear her laborious breath, the sound broken and ragged.

Des kneels next to me, and he places two fingers against the woman's forehead. I taste a hint of his magic in the air as it settles around the injured woman.

Her eyes flutter, and she shudders out a breath.

"What did you do?" I ask.

The Bargainer stands. "I took away her pain. The rest her magic will have to fix on its own. I am no healer."

I remember the last soldier I fought, the way her wound began to close only to stop healing. If the soldier's magic couldn't heal that wound, can this woman's magic heal hers?

Unlikely.

The thought filters in from a new part of me, the part that drank the lilac wine, the part that's now a little fae. I sense the fairy's magic slipping outside her body. It lingers in her spilled blood, and it's evanescing into the air. That magic seeps into the walls and the ceiling, and then it's no longer this woman's magic but the castle's.

What had Des said?

Spirits love to cling to the last of their lifeblood. This woman's

23

magic is slipping away from her—will her soul slip out with it?

Will I be able to sense that too?

I don't stick around long enough to find out.

We leave her there, once again making our way to the main entrance of the palace. The closer we get, the more bodies stack up. Here the sounds of fighting are almost deafening. I can tell by the noise alone that a battle rages in the great entryway of the palace.

Rather than head there, Des takes us to a staircase that leads farther down.

"Where are we going?" I ask.

"The dungeons."

"The dungeons?" I echo. "Why?"

We come to a thick door made of hammered bronze. A ward hums off the thing.

He turns to me. "Wait here, love."

"Des—"

But he's gone.

CHAPTER 4

I adjust my grip on my daggers, then shift my weight from one leg to the other.

I stare at the metal door ahead of me, the sounds of fighting at my back. My heart is thundering in my chest as my adrenaline zings through me. One minute ticks away. Then another.

The battle above me is calling to my siren, luring my dark nature. My wings flutter and resettle with my agitation, and my skin still glows as bright as ever. I edge away from the door, feeling the pull to return to the fighting. The sane part of me is not all that eager to kill more people, but I can't just stand here while innocent fairies—

The Bargainer returns to my side, stopping the thought in its tracks. In his hands is a stained wooden box.

I glance between him and it.

Seriously, *what* is going on?

Des leans down and whispers to the box in what I'm assuming is Old Fae. He pauses, listening, then speaks some more. As he speaks, I sense the container's enchantments unraveling. Once they dissolve, Des stops speaking.

For a moment, nothing happens. Then the lid springs open.

I can't help myself. I lean forward and peer inside the box. It's…empty. Until, of course, it isn't.

Shadows I didn't notice at the bottom of it begin to stir. These don't look like Des's shadows, which thicken and coil like smoke. This shadow is a two-dimensional, paper-thin thing that moves.

A bony shadow hand reaches from the depths of the container, its fingers gripping the edge of the box one by one. It pulls itself out, slithers down the side, then drips from a corner onto the floor.

My breath stutters. I've seen this creature before in Des's throne room.

A bog.

I watched the creature eat a Fauna fae who thought it would be a good idea to gift the King of Night a bag of Night fae heads.

Bet the dude regretted *that* decision.

"Remember our deal," Des tells the shadow monster.

Deal? Only the Bargainer could've struck such a thing in the sliver of time he left my side. And with a bog, of all things.

"Yessss, my kiiiiing."

The hair rises on my forearms when the creature speaks. I'm staring at a living nightmare. Literally. The bog eats its victims alive, and in the long time it takes to digest them, those people are cursed to live out their worst nightmares. Only the Otherworld could be home to such a frightening monster.

And now Des has set this thing loose.

The bog begins to move, then hesitates. I still as I feel it notice me.

Not a creature I want to catch the attention of.

A tempting adversary, my siren whispers because she has no sense.

Des steps in front of me, his wide shoulders blocking out the bog.

"Better kill whatever thought is running through your head," he growls. "Look at the Night Queen again, and you'll find out why your comrades fear me."

Night Queen?

The siren in me is *dying* to be set free. *And all shall fall under my thrall...*

"Underssssstooood," the bog hisses.

I just barely catch sight of its form as it slithers back the way we came.

Des and I follow it back up the stairs. By the time we make it to the palace's main entrance, there are dozens and dozens of fairies locked in combat, their wings flared wide behind them. Some of them are civilians, but many of them are soldiers defending the palace from other soldiers, former comrades now pitted against one another.

My eyes sweep over the rest of the gilded entry hall. The place looks like a slaughterhouse. Bodies are scattered across the floor, most of them servants, nobles, or aides—essentially, fairies who weren't trained to kill. There are fallen Night soldiers as well, but in death, it's hard to tell whether the soldier defended or raided the castle.

I stare, shocked at the chaos. Among it all I see the bog slithering about, swallowing up one traitorous soldier after the next. I have no idea how it knows friend from foe, but I figure Des ironed out those details with the monster before he let it loose.

Swords are clashing, arrows are flying, blood is spraying. Dark magic fills the air. I can smell it, taste it, feel its oily nature clinging to my skin.

Des pulls me in close, stealing a quick kiss from my lips. "Stay safe, love," he says. His eyes dip to my glowing skin, and his grip tightens. I feel his hesitation, the glamour and our bond keeping him at my side.

Somewhere underneath his armor, he wears three bronze war cuffs, awarded to him for valor. The thought of those bands comforts me. There's nothing I have that will assure him I'll be fine.

Just as I open my mouth to speak, an arrow whizzes by my head.

Acting on aggression and instinct, Des withdraws his sword, the weapon ringing as it's released. He spins toward the melee, his eyes scanning the room. The moment he finds the archer, he vanishes from my side, leaving me alone.

The world has a hollow feel to it—the shrieks, the smells, the sights.

Ours to savor, the siren whispers. *Join in. Let's take part in it until there's enough blood to swim in.*

I take a step, then another, drawn by the twisted pull of the battle. Around me, several fairies' eyes catch on my shining form.

A soldier closes in on me, her eyes bright but her face impassive as she lifts her sword.

I look at the weapon, and my blades suddenly seem small and paltry. No match for this woman, with her quick reflexes and her bloodlust.

Then again, I happen to know a little someone who fits that bill pretty well...

Let her try to kill us.

Normally, I'm careful to contain my siren, even when I use my magic. Now I let that control slip just a little.

Her laughter bubbles in my chest.

This—will—be—fun.

As soon as the soldier swings her weapon, I move, bending and dipping to avoid the hits. My movements feel fluid, like water rolling down a river.

I duck, spin, and with a swift thrust, shove my daggers up into her belly. It's an impossible strike, one that even a week ago, I wouldn't have been able to make. And now I have to wonder if, along with long life and a sense for magic, the lilac wine gave me other fae attributes, such as agility and precision.

I yank my blades up her torso, cutting through muscle and softer things, before I draw back.

The soldier staggers as I withdraw. But not even the wounds I inflicted are enough to stop her. She attacks me again. I block the first blow, but I'm not quick enough to entirely avoid the second one. The blade sinks into my leathers, then bites into my skin. I cry out and spin, one of my daggers pointed out. The weapon cleanly slices open the woman's neck.

Yessss. My siren laps up the carnage.

I'm opponent-less for all of five seconds, and then another woman is on me, her curving blades glinting wickedly beneath the light of the giant bronze chandelier above us.

After bending my knees, I spring into the air, the thick strokes of my wings forcing me up. Several feet off the ground, I tuck my wings tight against my back and drop onto the soldier, burying my dagger in her neck.

Her curved blade arcs through the air, the point skewering me in the thigh before she falls limp onto the floor. I collapse on top of her, hissing at the wound.

My shaky hand goes to my thigh. I grind my teeth against the sharp pain.

I think it's deep—definitely deep enough to make walking a problem.

I push myself off the dead fairy, nearly crying out when I place weight on my leg. But just as soon as I feel the full force of the injury, it begins to close, the blood trickling off.

Fae magic at work. Another perk of the lilac wine.

Once my wound heals, I jump back into the melee.

Across the room I spot Malaki and Temper—the latter with a wicked smile on her face—as they fight the Thief's soldiers. And far above us, Des fights in midair, his enemies dropping from the sky.

The soldiers keep coming, and it takes all my focus to fight them off.

By the time I reach the door at the main entrance of the castle, the combined smell of magic and blood coats the air like perfume. I'm dappled in the crimson liquid, wearing it like another layer of armor.

Hard to believe I agonized over a single death for years. By the end of the night—if I'm still alive—my death count will be in the double digits.

The fighting spills into the courtyard, and bursts of fae magic light up the night as fairies draw on their power.

I briefly sheath my daggers as my gaze moves over the landscape. The human part of me is trying not to heave. The grounds are strewn with glassy eyes and gutted bodies.

Soldiers are killing soldiers. Civilians are getting cut down. And the formerly sleeping women are out there in droves alongside their spawn.

Now that the time has come, those creepy casket children have cast off all pretense of innocence. Their tiny bodies feast on prone fairies, their eyes glowing with unholy malice.

It's madness I can't make sense of.

Des lands next to me and grabs my hand. He looks like a fiend, his battle leathers drenched in blood and his pale hair speckled with the fluid. It's unnerving just how much the look suits him.

"You good?" he asks, his eyes bright with concern and, ironically, fae delight.

Fairies and their feral hearts, the siren whispers. *He's enjoying this almost as much as we are.*

His gaze drops to my lips, his other hand reaching for my shining skin.

I wet my dry mouth and nod. "I'm fine."

To emphasize my point, I will my wings away. They don't disappear immediately, and even once they do, it's a struggle to keep them concealed.

It's a waste of effort. The Night King's still staring at my lips, looking entranced by them.

Around us, the air thickens with static electricity, raising the hairs along my arm. I look around to figure out its source. Des tears his gaze from my mouth, his eyes moving over our surroundings.

Something bad is coming.

BOOM!

The ground beneath me trembles, and debris flies into the air as something on the other side of the palace explodes. A moment later, a wave of dark magic slams into me, knocking me off my feet. Des catches me before I hit the ground, and the two of us share an intense look.

A fresh batch of screams rises from the other side of the castle.

I was wrong—something bad isn't coming.

It's already here.

Next to me, the Bargainer's wings appear at his back before expanding ominously. "I'll be right back, cherub."

With that, he vanishes from my side.

Des! I can still feel the press of his hands against me, but he's gone.

My eyes move toward the back of the palace, where the screams are coming from. That's where he went.

I sprint toward the back of the castle, my heart pounding wildly. There's pressure near my shoulder blades from my wings fighting to reveal themselves.

Ignoring the sensation, I run down one of the cobblestone paths that wind around the palace, the stones smeared with blood. Ahead of me, a dead fairy lies sprawled across the pale grass, her arms stretched wide, her eyes glassy.

How many lives have been cut down in a single night?

Too many. We'll make our enemies pay for the slight.

Fairies flee past me, some taking to the air, and some sprinting on foot, all running from whatever caused the explosion.

When I round the back of the castle, I come up short. I have to lock my knees at the sight in front of me.

Dear God.

The circular annex that contains the Night Kingdom's royal portal is in use, its double doors obliterated. Row after row of gore-covered soldiers pour through it, their eyes vacant. They march onto the palace grounds, their uniforms carrying the symbol of the Night Kingdom.

The sleeping men.

There are dozens and dozens of them, and more are coming with every passing second.

I stagger at the sight.

I'm going to die.

I'm going to die, and it will all have been for nothing: Finding Des only to lose him. Spending an agonizing seven years without him. Enduring Karnon. Nearly dying at the Thief of Souls's hands. Drinking the lilac wine. None of it matters anymore because an army of possessed soldiers want to wipe the Night King's people from the face of the earth, and I will be just one more casualty.

Ahead of me, Des stands very, very still. Even though I can't see his face, I swear I can sense his despair. The numbers were against us when it was just the sleeping women attacking. With the addition of the men, they're *insurmountable*.

The soldiers break ranks, fanning out to attack anything that lives.

I'm one of those things. So is Des, and so are the few fairies scattered around us who've decided to stay and fight.

The Bargainer gives a rallying cry and then disappears. He reappears in the middle of the enemy soldiers long enough to dole out death before disappearing and reappearing again elsewhere.

He glances over his shoulder at me, his eyes wild. "Hide yourself, Callie!" he cries as soldiers close in on all sides.

I don't have the will to move or flee. Even my siren is quiet. She won't whisper the truth.

We can't possibly win this.

There are a handful of soldiers for every one of us, and

those odds are only worsening as more sleeping soldiers spill out from the portal. And once they're done with us, they'll move on to other fairies, perhaps until none are left standing.

This is no battle; it's a butchery.

And I don't want to bear witness to it anymore.

"*Stop*," I whisper, my voice harmonizing as the battle unfolds. I blink as my vision blurs. Already, soldiers have caught sight of my glowing skin; they're sprinting toward me, weapons brandished, as though I'm some great and terrible threat.

The sleeping men hack into what loyal soldiers and civilians remain standing, cutting them down in seconds.

"Stop," I say, louder.

No one's listening. Of course they're not. They have more important things to do—like try to stay alive.

But I can't leave it alone. I'm coming apart, and this might be the time that does me in for good.

"*STOP!*" I shriek like a madwoman.

To my wonder, they do exactly that.

Weapons stop clashing, fairies stop moving—everything goes utterly and absolutely still.

I touch my throat.

Nah.

I look at the Night fairy nearest to me, only yards away. His foot is lifted as he stands frozen midstride, blade in hand, his face intensely focused on me. Even from here I can smell the foul odor coming off his clothes, the scent like Death decided to go dumpster diving.

"You," I say, pointing to the soldier. "Give me your sword," I demand, opening my palm.

The fairy unfreezes and sedately walks over before handing me his weapon.

My fingers close over the sword's hilt, and a wicked smile blossoms on my face.

I can fucking glamour *fairies*.

Hold on to your tits, world. Callie. Is. Back.

CHAPTER 5

I can freaking glamour fairies.

Before I drank lilac wine, that wasn't the case. I should've realized the elixir reconfigured this aspect of my magic as well as the others.

My eyes move to my mate. To my shock and horror (and maybe a smidge of delight)—he's also frozen.

"Des!" I call, my voice melodic with my power. "Come here."

The Bargainer vanishes before reappearing at my side an instant later, an eyebrow arched. Other than that, he's placid—all except for his eyes. His silver eyes sparkle in a way that is wickedly excited.

"I release you from my glamour," I say.

I've clearly gotten rusty on this whole glamour thing, because it's not just Des who follows my command. A few sleeping soldiers, including the one who just handed over his blade, now jump back into action.

Honestly, Callie, newbie mistake right there.

Des is on the soldiers in an instant, cutting them down with his sword before they get a chance to strike.

Once they've been dealt with, the Night King rolls his shoulders, as if to shake off my magic. "So *that's* how it feels to be glamoured by a siren," he says, the corner of his mouth curving up just the slightest bit. "Like I've been caught by my balls." He comes in close, his smirk growing. "The whole thing was horribly invasive. I rather enjoyed it."

The conversation is so vastly inappropriate and out of place that I let out a laugh, the sound melodic.

His eyes move over my glowing features. "Beautiful creature," he murmurs. "You were irresistible before." He reaches out with a hand, grazing my jaw with his knuckles. "I don't quite know what to do with myself now."

Des leans in and kisses me, his lips lingering.

The sound of heavy footfalls breaks the spell.

I draw away from the Bargainer, turning toward the portal. More sleeping soldiers are marching through.

"Soldiers, stop!" I say, my magic thick in my voice.

The sleeping soldiers halt in place, their bodies filling the doorway.

"You've done it, cherub," Des says, surveying the frozen fairies. "You've become someone to fear."

CHAPTER 6

It takes several hours, but eventually, I manage to incapacitate all the psycho sleeping soldiers and the casket children who were wreaking havoc on Somnia.

By the looks of it, the soldiers were staging a political coup. Excuse me, *attempting* a political coup.

Thank you, glamour.

We round the guilty up, remove their weapons, and lock them in the dungeons. Right now, my glamour is making them placid, but once it wears off in a day or two, their bloodthirsty tendencies will return.

Now Des and I head through the palace toward the dungeons. I open and close my palms as we go. I'm a little nervous, which is ridiculous. What I'm about to do was my idea.

The fairies we pass stare at me. My skin has long since stopped glowing, so I know it's not the siren drawing their eyes.

"Why are they looking at me?" I finally ask Des.

He pauses to glance at me, then at the *fairies* in question.

"You really don't know?" Des asks, raising an eyebrow, his gaze returning to mine.

I shake my head.

"*Cherub,*" he says, a small smile playing at the corners of his lips, "you're the enchantress who stopped an army. The human with the power to ensnare their will should she choose to. They are awed and afraid of you, which is the highest compliment a Night fae can give you."

Eventually, we leave the curious eyes behind, descending the same staircase we took only hours ago, back when Des released the bog.

The two of us stop at the familiar hammered bronze door.

With a brush of Des's magic, the door swings open, revealing a long hallway that disappears into darkness, the wall sconces not quite able to beat back the shadows.

Inside, armed soldiers (ones not possessed by the unholy desire to bash in as many brains as possible) somberly escort us down the hall.

By the time we arrive at the dungeon proper, we're deep beneath the castle. I can feel the walls of this place pressing in from all sides, the sensation reminding me of when I was Karnon's prisoner, trapped in one of his many subterranean cells.

I take a deep breath. Pretty sure that experience has given me claustrophobia for life.

The formerly sleeping soldiers are crammed into dozens and dozens of cells, and even though hundreds of them were killed, there's almost not enough room for the ones that remain.

As we pass the cells, I note that the fairies are still

caught in my glamour. They stare straight ahead, their faces impassive.

Don't know what's creepier, their true nature or this catatonic state they've fallen into.

In the last cell, a single soldier is housed.

She stands inert in the middle of the chamber, her flame-red hair falling in spirals down her back.

Des, our escorts, and I all pause in front of the cell, taking in the fairy. She's oblivious to our attention.

The Bargainer's hand falls to the back of my neck. His face is impassive, but I can tell he's not thrilled with this little plan of mine. He doesn't, however, try to talk me out of it.

"Open the door," Des commands the guards, not looking away from me.

The iron bars screech as the door opens. The red-haired soldier doesn't so much as glance at the door when I slip inside.

I stare at her for a long moment before I let my siren surface.

"I release you from my glamour."

I expect the soldier to attack me, but she doesn't. For several long seconds, *nothing* happens.

Then the redhead's eyes slide to me.

My muscles tense; I'm waiting for her to strike. Instead, she begins to pace, back and forth, back and forth, her gaze growing distant.

"What is your name?" I ask, my voice melodic.

"I don't have a name," she responds.

"Everyone has a name," I insist.

"I don't. Not anymore."

Losing a name is such a tiny injustice compared to

everything the Thief has done, and yet, it's what gave her an identity, and he took that from her.

"What did it used to be?" I ask.

She pauses for so long, I'm sure she'll never speak.

"Mirielle," she finally says, the magic coaxing the answer out of her.

"And do you know who I am?"

Mirielle pauses, then slowly nods. "You're the enchantress. We are allowed to hurt you, but we are not to kill you. Not yet. He wants you alive."

My claws sharpen at that. They weren't allowed to kill me? I remember how hard I fought and how vicious my assailants were. None of them seemed like they were holding back.

"Who wants me alive?" I ask, even though I damn well know.

"My master."

Fucking Thief.

The cell darkens. Apparently, the King of the Night is not too happy about that either.

"And is...your master...the one who woke you from your sleep?"

"He called and we answered," she says, continuing to pace back and forth, back and forth.

"Why did you attack your comrades, Mirielle?" I ask, my voice lilting.

She frowns when she hears her name on my lips.

"I don't know." She keeps pacing.

"What do you mean you don't know?" I get that this woman's mind has been fucked three ways to Wednesday, but surely she has a better explanation for all this carnage than "I don't know."

"We do our master's bidding," she says. "Nothing more."

"And what does your master want?" I probe.

"I don't know," she says distractedly.

Getting nowhere...

I start again. "Who kidnapped you?"

Can she remember that far back? Some of these women have been sleeping for *years*.

"My older brother," she replies coolly, still walking back and forth, back and forth.

Her *brother*?

I don't think I heard that one correctly.

"He's been dead for well over a century," Des says from the other side of the cell.

I raise my eyebrows and spare my mate a glance. He knew this woman's brother?

The soldier's eyes wander to the Bargainer, and there they rest. Slowly, she tilts her head, like recognition is upwelling from the depths of her memory.

"*You*," she breathes. "You held me once...long ago."

Come again?

My skin flares with agitation. I glance between the two of them. Is this broad seriously admitting to what I think she is?

"You made love to me then, under the stars..."

My claws elongate.

She *is*.

Let's eviscerate her slowly, my siren says. *It will be fun.*

It's a strange feeling, to be jealous of a woman who, in all probability, slept with your mate centuries before you existed. A woman who's now nothing more than a shell of herself, her mind and body commandeered by the Thief of Souls.

42

And yet I still feel the hot burn of it.

Des folds his arms, looking unamused. He doesn't try to explain himself to me, which is probably a good thing—doing so would make him look guilty as fuck, and it wasn't like he cheated on me—but damn it, I want a little groveling. Is that wrong?

He will *grovel*, the siren insists.

All right, if she thinks groveling is kosher, it's probably wrong. But that doesn't mean I disagree with her.

I force myself to refocus on the task at hand.

Des had mentioned that Mirielle's brother died a little over a hundred years ago. It takes me a moment to do the math (not my strong suit), but once I do, I realize the timeline doesn't work. Soldiers started disappearing a decade ago, not a century.

"How could your brother have kidnapped you if he was dead?"

Janus had a twin, a twin who died, the Thief had told me in the Flora Queen's woods. *The first time you met him, you were really meeting me.*

Mirielle's vacant eyes focus on the ground. "I don't know."

This vexing answer again.

"I had hoped..." Mirielle begins. Then she falls to silence.

"Speak to me freely," I command her.

Slowly, her eerie gaze shifts to meet mine. "It's dark here. Very dark."

The back of my neck pricks. "Are you in the Night Kingdom?" I ask.

"Yes and no."

I wait for her to say more, but she doesn't. "What do you mean by that?"

43

"It is very dark here," she repeats. "I want to rest. Why can't I rest?"

"Do you know where the Thief is?" I press.

"You'll never find him."

So everyone keeps saying.

"Is there anything else you can tell me?" I ask.

"Secrets are meant for one soul to keep."

I sense rather than see Des stiffen at her words.

The corner of Mirielle's mouth curves up. "He's watching you, enchantress, always watching you. My master has developed a taste for slaves."

My siren pushes through. "You can tell your master I've developed a taste for killing evil fuckers," I breathe, the words harmonic as they roll off my tongue. "Have him come find me. I'm eager to see him again. I'll teach him then what it means to be my bitc—"

I wrangle my siren into submission and regain control of myself. I walk a fine line, using my glamour and trying to keep her worst tendencies at bay.

The cell darkens again, and suddenly, Des is in the cell with us. "Interrogation is over," he says.

Before I can protest, the iron door swings open, and I'm whisked out. I swivel back to face Mirielle just as it clangs shut.

One final question. "If I let you out now, what will you do?"

Her eyes fall on me. "Conquer."

CHAPTER 7

Des broods next to me, the hallway we walk down darkening with his presence.

"You could've let me finish the interrogation," I finally say. I mean, he's not the only one in a ripe mood. I have blood caked in my hair, I'm running on half a night's worth of sleep, my bones want to give out from post-battle exhaustion, and I needed coffee *hours* ago.

"You walk on thin ice right now, Callie," the Bargainer growls.

I swivel to face him, his words riling me up. "*I'm* the one on thin ice?" I say, my voice rising. "*You're* the one who screwed the prisoner."

Brought that up sooner than I intended.

"Two centuries ago," Des says. "Do you expect me to give you a formal apology for every person I've slept with? Because if so, I damn well better receive the same from you."

"You are insane."

The Night King disappears from my side only to reappear

in front of me, his body blocking the way and forcing me to stop.

"You *goaded* him," he growls. "You goaded the Thief of Souls to find you." He runs an agitated hand through his hair, the movement exposing one of his pointed ears. "Can you not see? This is the same reason I stopped taking you on my bargains when you attended Peel Academy."

I'd glamoured a man back then too…a man who, ironically enough, knew information on the Thief of Souls. He'd been willing to die rather than share his knowledge, and still I made him talk.

I still flush at the memory. And now the Bargainer is essentially saying that in all this time, I haven't changed.

I take *issue* with that. "I'm already in the Thief's line of sight. I will *not* let that monster provoke me without provoking him back."

A muscle in the Bargainer's face ticks. He steps in close. "You want to know a secret, cherub?" he asks, his voice dropping low. "Earlier this evening, when I tried to stop all those sleeping soldiers back in our chambers—it didn't work."

There was that moment in his bedroom when I thought he'd bleed into the darkness and end those sleeping soldiers just as he had Karnon and his men. But he hadn't been able to.

"Do you want to know why that didn't work?" Des asks. He doesn't wait for me to answer. "The darkness is loyal to its own—it won't hurt another fairy that wields its power."

I feel the first thread of unease at his words.

"That means the Thief is one of my kind—he's a Night fae."

My knees go a little weak. A Night fae? One who's impervious to Des's magic?

He is not impervious to ours, my siren whispers, her voice seductive.

The King of the Night cups my face. "I am *mad* with fear for you," he says, his voice pitched low. "It feels like the wheels of fate are pushing you closer and closer to the Thief, and nothing I do can prevent it. That *terrifies* me."

To hear Des admit to being afraid...it's like that moment as a child when you see an adult cry for the first time. Like the person you depended on to have their shit together really doesn't. It's the kind of thing that shakes your world.

"I *am* sorry you had to hear about my...past...the way you did," he says hoarsely.

I think this is an apology.

He leans in close, his lips a hairbreadth from mine. "But I will admit, I greedily drank up your reaction." With that confession, he presses his lips against mine.

It's stupid how fast his kiss can banish my frayed nerves. He kisses away our discussion, his taste and touch consuming my thoughts. And even though the day is a mess, and I'm a mess, and the Otherworld has gone to crap, for a few blissful seconds, everything is as it should be.

―――――――――

All I want right now is a shower, coffee, and bed—preferably all at the same time. Don't tell me it can't happen; I'm in the Otherworld, *impossible* is this place's middle name.

But am I going to get what I want?

Nope.

Instead, I have to freaking adult it, which means hauling my butt into some random room in the castle and making sense of the clusterfuck that is the present state of affairs.

"Well, well, well, look what the cat dragged in,"

Temperance Darling, my best friend, colleague and fellow troublemaker, calls out as soon as we enter.

She sits alongside Malaki and several fae officials, her ankles propped on the table in front of her. Her eyes move over me. "Though it looks like the cat didn't just drag you in—it had a little fun with you too."

My relief at seeing Temper alive is quickly eclipsed by annoyance at her words. I spare my bloody battle leathers a glance before I take in Temper. She wears a white jumpsuit, which is *pristine*.

Next to her Malaki looks stern, his scar especially stark beneath his eye patch. He keeps opening and closing his hands, and I get the distinct impression that he wants to hurt something.

As soon as he sees Des, Malaki stands and crosses the room in a few quick strides. He brings his friend in close, slapping him on the back.

I move to the seat next to Temper. "You could take a few tips from him," I say.

She waves the comment away. "I'll give you a hug after you bathe."

I let out a little snicker before grabbing the cup of coffee in front of her and taking a sip from it.

"Hey, that was *mine*."

"Awww," I say, giving her a look like she's precious, "does someone have trouble sharing?" I take a long drink from it.

Temper's eyes narrow. "Careful I don't hex that coffee to splash you in the face every time you drink it," she says.

I smile over the rim of the cup. "Careful I don't glamour you to tell Malaki how you really feel about him."

To be honest, I don't even know *if* my magic works on humans anymore. But she doesn't need to know that.

Temper's eyes widen. "That's low, Callie."

The two of us fall to silence, watching Des and Malaki grip each other's shoulders and make all sorts of manly oaths about dying by the blade to protect each other and yada yada.

"Malaki is just being excessive," Temper says. "We heard hours ago that you two were okay." She nudges my shoulder with her own. "Heard you can glamour fae now." She puts her fist out, and I bump my knuckles against hers. "That's freaking awesome."

Des and Malaki speak in low tones for a little longer. Something the Night King says causes Malaki to chuckle, and something the general says draws Des's eyes to me, his gaze intense enough to make my stomach flutter.

He pulls away from his friend and heads over to the table before taking a seat next to me. His hand falls to my thigh as he nods at each of the advisers who've also been waiting for us at the table. A few of the advisers cast me and Temper curious looks. I doubt they're used to having humans (former or otherwise) at these meetings.

"I'm glad to see everyone alive and well," Des begins as Malaki takes a seat. "Let's get straight to the matter: the Night Kingdom fell under siege tonight at the hands of our own people. What do we know about the situation?"

And thus, the talks begin.

The group of us rehashes what we already know—a bunch of sleeping soldiers woke up from their long slumber, each possessed by the need to kill and maim and conquer. Then we tally up the dead and wounded, then note the damage wrought on the kingdom.

"We were not alone," one of the advisers says. "We received reports from the other three kingdoms that they too were attacked."

My dream floods back to me in all its vividness. Of the Thief standing among those poisoned oaks as they splintered open.

"The Kingdom of Flora fell," the adviser continues.

The Kingdom of Flora...*fell*?

The phrasing conjures up images of those giant cedar trees toppling to the ground, of the earth swallowing up the palace whole. It doesn't do the truth justice—

An entire city was likely cut down. All those people just...gone.

I can't process that sort of devastation. Not when we were just there. I danced and drank and reveled alongside Flora fairies. They might not be my favorite people, but now knowing the deadly task those sleeping soldiers set out to accomplish...

"How many died?" I ask.

The room is silent, and the adviser looks helplessly at me while another shakes her head.

Too many.

All those sleeping soldiers... The kingdom never stood a chance.

Malaki tosses a sheet of parchment into the middle of the table. "We've heard rumors that Mara got out in time, but the same cannot be said for the rest of Flora's citizens."

Des flicks his wrist, and the parchment slides his way. The Bargainer's eyes skim the notes.

"Fauna is gone as well," Malaki continues. "Though from our reports, few died. There was no resistance for the soldiers to crush."

There wouldn't even be a palace to invade. All that was wiped clean when Des rescued me from Karnon.

"The Kingdom of Day has defeated its foes for the time being," another adviser adds.

My gaze moves to the table in front of us. Painted onto it is a map of the Otherworld.

The mainland has been completely captured. The only places left unconquered are the Kingdoms of Day and Night, those that float in the sky.

Temper leans forward. "How did that pretty boy king manage to defeat them?"

Malaki frowns, and it might be my imagination, but I'm fairly sure it bothers him that Temper thinks Janus, the King of Day, is in fact, pretty. Particularly when it's so obvious Malaki *isn't* pretty, with his eye patch and scar.

Clearly, he doesn't realize his ferocious beauty is just as appealing.

But now's not the time to tell Malaki that *pretty* was never Temper's type or that Des's general should be more worried about Temper ravaging his man bits to death than her having a wandering eye. She's loyal to a fault.

"I imagine we'll find out soon enough," Des says, tapping his fingers on the table. His gaze moves from person to person. "The sleeping soldiers in the conquered kingdoms will regroup, and then they'll turn their sights on us," he says grimly. "My mate's glamour can't save us all. We need to figure out another strategy. This time, I want to be ready for them."

After Des deals out official orders, he dismisses his advisers, leaving just himself, Malaki, Temper, and me in the room.

"If we're going to defeat the Thief of Souls," the Night King says, "we need to do more than simply have a good defense against his forces. We need to figure out once and for all who and what he really is and where he's hiding."

"What if we went after Galleghar?" I say.

Galleghar Nyx, the formerly dead Night King, is somehow decidedly no longer dead. Back in the Flora Kingdom, he'd been responsible for luring soldiers into the woods, and he'd been there the night I nearly lost my life.

"If we find him," I continue, "we might find the Thief."

Temper swings her legs off the table. "One problem with that little plan of yours: we don't know where he is either. I mean, it isn't like he's outside, flashing his tits and begging us to capture him."

I give my friend a look. "I guess it's too bad we aren't PIs who specialize in finding people."

Temper gives me a considering look. "You do have a point..."

Des stands, leaning heavily against the table. His eyes meet mine, and he gives me a slight nod. "We should check Galleghar's crypt at the very least."

"Cherub," Des says, his silver gaze raking me over, "care to pay my father's tomb a visit?"

So I can kick that fucker's corpse in the balls?

"Love to."

———————

We don't visit the tomb right away.

Instead, the two of us return to the King of the Night's chambers.

I feel the weight of this long evening settling on my shoulders.

Silently, Des comes up behind me and begins to unfasten my battle leathers.

"I'm sorry," he says softly, loosening buckles and untying

straps. "For this war, for putting you in the Thief's cross-hairs, for making you endure this night."

"None of that is your fault," I say over my shoulder, my words quiet.

"Maybe…" he muses.

His quick wit is gone for the moment, and I see another side of Des, one that feels old and wise and battle weary. He pulls my leathers off my left shoulder and places a kiss there.

Despite the solemn circumstances, goose bumps break out along my skin. He removes my top, and his hands skim down my arms.

The Bargainer's touch moves farther down my body, and his magic peels away the last of my clothes and the last of his.

"Let me take care of you, cherub," he says from behind me.

For the life of me, I don't honestly know what he means by that. He's taken care of me every single day he's been in my life. But I nod anyway because being taken care of sounds really, really nice right now.

Without another word, the Bargainer scoops me up and carries me into the bathroom.

The tub is already filled to the rim with water. Scattered around it are lamps that flicker with starbursts of light. A balmy night breeze flutters in through the arched windows.

Des walks the two of us into the tub, sitting us in the warm bathwater. I swallow as the liquid turns pink. All the while the King of Night holds me close, cupping my head against his chest.

I don't know why, but this is the moment all my bravado falls away. So many people died tonight, all victims in one way or another. Some of them I killed myself. The proof of it discolors the bathwater.

The Night King must sense my shifting mood because he says, "It's all right, Callie. It's all right. We're just going to rinse off the blood and dirt."

I close my eyes, and my shoulders begin to shake, and it's stupid, stupid, stupid, but I begin to cry against him.

I feel sixteen all over again. Sixteen and broken and desperate for the Bargainer to fix me, even though that was never his job to begin with. But he *did* fix me; he picked up each broken piece of me and put me back together, and he loved my cracks in a way that only he could.

And then seven years passed, and I grew up. I believed all those fragile parts of me were gone, but here we are again, me with blood on my hands and thoughts of dead fae and that fucking Thief filling my head.

I lean my forehead against Des's chest and silently cry against him. He doesn't need a confession from me to know what's wormed its way under my skin. He cradles the back of my head and holds me to him. I sit there in his arms, keeping my eyes closed so I can't see the water. Des begins to hum.

I pause for just a moment, recognizing the melody. He used to sing the same song under his breath back in my dorm room. At the sound, my sobs quiet. Because Des is here, comforting me as he used to, and even as I mourn the evening's horrors, I savor this.

He holds me a little longer, and then he grabs a washcloth and scrubs my skin, raking the cloth up and down my back then moving to my arms. He carefully runs it down my wrist and over each finger, all the while humming that same song.

I take in a shuddering breath and watch his ministrations.

"You don't have to clean—"

"Cherub." With one word, he stops my weak protest in its tracks.

It's quiet for a few minutes as my breath evens, the only sound the slight splash of water as Des scours my body.

"This is…" Des begins, then starts again. "In my imaginings, we did this. I scrubbed the world's filth off you, until you were just you in my arms."

"Stop," I say, my voice breaking. I had almost put myself back together, but Des's words are going to pull me apart again.

The washcloth gets to my face, and he tilts my chin up. "You saved my people tonight, Callie. You *saved* them. Who knows how many more would have died if you hadn't been there?"

I stare into his moonlit eyes.

"I've never seen anything more beautiful or fearsome than you beguiling those fae. You are a force of nature."

I swallow. "You're no longer immune to it." I saw firsthand what my glamour can now do to Des.

"I'm delightfully terrified of the prospect. Our sex life has just gotten ten times kinkier."

He has no idea.

I glance at the water. I don't know what magic the Bargainer is doling out, but the bath is now crystal clear. Whatever blood once sullied it is no longer visible.

Des sets the washcloth aside and brushes his thumb along my lower lip. "Give me a wish," he says, out of the blue.

"Why?" I ask.

"Because I want one."

Demanding fairy. I raise my eyebrows. "And what's the cost?" I ask.

He taps my nose. "So jaded. I wish you had a little more faith in me."

I hike up my eyebrows farther. "So you're giving me a free wish?"

"Hmm. Perhaps *free* is not the right word."

That's what I thought.

He plays with my hair. "But you'll like the repayment. That, I promise."

I don't doubt it. "Fine. I want coffee."

"Out of all the wishes in the world, that's the one you go for?" Des looks distinctly unimpressed.

I really want a cup o' joe, all right? So sue me. My brief taste of Temper's wasn't enough.

I tilt my head back and forth, weighing his words. "You're right, on second thought, maybe I should wish for another boyfriend—"

A cup manifests out of the ether and into Des's hand. "All right, baby siren," he says. "I see how you're going to play your hand." He presses the mug into one of my palms.

I grin at him, the last of my earlier sadness vanishing with the action.

"Have to remind you later of why there will only ever be me..." he murmurs.

My grin widens, and the Bargainer leans in and steals a quick kiss, the action causing some of the blessed coffee in my mug to slosh into the water. As always, Des tastes like sin and wicked thoughts, and I'm almost more interested in drinking him up than I am the coffee.

Almost.

Once the kiss ends, I lean back against the rim of the tub and gather my knees to my chest.

"What was that song?" I ask, taking a sip of my coffee.

Des is appraising me like he wants to eat me for lunch. "What song?"

"The one you were humming just now."

Recognition sparks in his eyes. "Ah, 'For My Lost Love, I Dream of Thee.'"

I set my mug next to one of the glowing lanterns. "I like it," I admit.

He gives me a soft smile. "I'm glad you do. My mother used to sing it to me when I was little."

That confession—freely given, I note—sends a pang through me. There's a soft spot in Des's heart that belongs to his mom and his mom alone, and for the hundredth time, I wish I could've met her.

"What's the song about?" I ask.

The Bargainer's expression turns a little melancholic. "A man loses the love of his life, and he yearns for night because in dreams, they're reunited," he says.

The two of us are quiet for a moment.

"Well, that's a fucking bummer," I finally say.

That's the song he's been reassuring me with this whole time? That's like chasing away a nightmare by telling someone a ghost story.

There's a beat of silence, and then Des's laughter fills the chamber. "Yeah, cherub, it really is."

CHAPTER 8

I glance around me at the sun-scorched earth.

This is...not what I'd been expecting. I mean, I'm not sure what I *had* been expecting when it came to Galleghar Nyx's resting place, but I think I assumed it would be somewhere in the Night Kingdom—and that a cemetery would be involved.

To be fair, the place feels about as morbid as a cemetery.

After I'd had coffee, a bath, and a wink—er, okay, a fuck ton—of sleep, Des and I headed off to visit his father's tomb.

Which, apparently, is this wasteland of a place.

My eyes sweep over the landscape again. The dry, dusty earth stretches out for miles and miles around us, only interrupted here and there by a boulder. Off in the distance, some craggy cliffs rise, looking as barren as the land. The wind whistles a lonesome, loveless tune as it tugs at my hair.

It's more than just the austere look of the place. There's something about this land...like color is seeping away and my senses are dulling—it feels as though the earth itself is sucking the life out of me.

"What is this place?" I ask.

"The Banished Lands," Des says, squinting at our surroundings. "It's a section of land that divides the Flora and Fauna Kingdoms. This is where exiled fae go."

I didn't even know fae could be exiled. I assumed fae rulers just made their criminals *disappear*.

I guess you learn something new every day.

"And you buried your dad here," I say, putting the pieces together.

The Bargainer stares at the landscape, a troubled expression on his face, before his gaze meets mine. "This is as close to desecrating his body as I could get," he says.

The admission sends a shiver through me. Des is so good to me that I often forget how ruthless he can be.

Night's falling here, and for once since I met Des, the darkness doesn't feel welcoming.

I take the Bargainer's hand. "Show me where your father is buried."

We cut across the landscape, Des leading me toward an unassuming cluster of stones, the biggest of which is as large as a car. When we get to them, Des lifts his hand, his expression grim. Through our bond, I sense the pull of magic, and then I feel it around us, saturating the parched air.

With a groan, the massive stone in front of us drags itself aside, revealing a small and crudely made pit.

For a while, the Bargainer simply stares down into the inky darkness, his face expressionless.

I lick my parched lips. "Is this…?"

"My father's resting place," Des says, his eyes never wavering from that hole in the ground.

As far as burials go, this one is pretty much the equivalent of giving the dead the middle finger—a final *fuck you* to send them off to the afterlife with.

So I guess it's fitting for his a-hole dad.

"Why give him a tomb at all?" I ask. I would've thrown his carcass to the wolves.

"Believe me, I didn't want to." Des takes a deep breath then tears his gaze away from that hole. A sardonic smile pulls the corner of his mouth up. "After Galleghar died, I left his body out for carrion to eat," he says, "but no creature would touch it. When that didn't work, I threw his body into the sea—but the waves returned it to me."

I stare at him as he talks, sensing his restlessness. My own unease is growing.

"I tried burning his body." He rubs his lower lip. "It was impervious to flame. I tried to vaporize his remains, but they resisted my magic."

My eyes dip to that hole in the ground, trying not to get spooked by Des's words.

"There are only three types of souls whose bodies can resist returning to the earth: those too powerful for it, those too pure for it, and those too corrupted for it."

One guess which category Desmond Flynn's father falls into.

"Eventually, I brought him here." The Bargainer's eyes return to the pit. "It killed me to give him even this—a hole in the ground. He deserved so much worse."

From the stories I've heard—that Galleghar slaughtered all his heirs in a bid to keep his throne—I can't help but agree.

Des releases another breath and steps up to the edge of the hole. He kneels, studying its depths. Then, in one smooth motion, he lowers himself into the darkness.

Oh, sweet Jesus, we're going down there.

Of course we are.

Really don't want to…

Maybe I can just linger topside…

"Don't tell me you've developed a fear of the darkness now, cherub," Des calls from below, his voice echoing.

Ugh. *Fine.*

I move up to the hole before sitting at its edge and letting my feet dangle into it. I squint into the shaft, trying to gauge how deep it is.

From the shadows, two hands wrap around my ankles, and with a swift jerk, I'm yanked into the darkness. Before I have a chance to shriek for dear life, Des catches me, and I'm sure he can feel the drum of my heart pounding against his chest.

"Oh my God," I say, breathless, my skin brightening seconds too late, "*why* would you do that?"

Des laughs into the darkness. "You are *much* too tempting to toy with"—his eyes drop to my lips, caught in the glow of my glamour—"and to resist."

He leans in, but before he can kiss me, I press a hand to his mouth.

"Uh-uh," I chastise him, glamour in my voice. "You don't get a kiss for that."

At my words, he pulls away a little, his eyes bright. "What *do* I get?" he says, the corner of his mouth curving into a mischievous grin.

A spanking, my siren whispers. *Let's make him give himself a spanking. He's been a bad boy.*

I almost laugh at the thought.

"You get the pleasure of avoiding my siren's wrath. She wants you to spank yourself."

The appropriate reaction is to be horrified at the thought. Too bad the Bargainer is decidedly *in*appropriate.

His face fills with gleeful surprise. "Naughty thing," he chastises. "And right here in my father's grave too." Now he does give me a quick kiss. "Maybe later I'll appease your dirty thoughts." In the dim light cast by my skin, I see him wink at me.

It's enough to mollify my siren.

With that, Des releases me. "Watch your step," he advises. "There's a tricky staircase you'll need to maneuver—on second thought, it'd probably be best if I carried you…"

Before I can say or do anything else, his magic curls like smoke low in my belly. The tug of it draws me close to him.

"This is repayment for the coffee, isn't it?" I say as the magic courses through me.

That or Des really likes stirring my siren into action. Because while a second ago she was settling back down, now she's pressing against my skin, eager to take over completely.

"I told you repayment would be fun," Des says, a smirk in his voice.

Ha! "This is not really what I had in mind when I made that wish…"

"Consider this foreplay, baby siren."

And still his magic tugs at me, getting more insistent with every passing second.

"All right, but I want to ride piggyback," I state.

"I didn't realize you called the terms of repayment," he says smoothly, scooping me up. Now that I'm in his arms, the magic relaxes. "Of course, if you want to ride me from behind"—his tone is undeniably sexual—"I won't protest *too* much. Though it's not my favorite position."

God, he's in rare form today.

He moves me to his back, and I wrap my arms around his neck, breathing in his smell as his hair tickles my cheek. His hands hook beneath my legs, and he carries me down the winding stairway and deep into the ground.

The air down here is thick like molasses, heavy with protective wards meant to keep intruders out. It's a shock to feel so much magic concentrated here when the land itself seems parched of it.

Des utters a phrase in Old Fae, and within the snap of one's fingers, the magic parts, letting us through.

Ahead of us, mounted torches flare to life, illuminating a small chamber. The walls, ceiling, and floor of it are nothing more than packed dirt. Right in the middle of the room, sitting on a natural bed of rock, is a rough-hewn stone sarcophagus.

Maybe it's the spells that still thicken the air, or maybe it's the sight of the stone coffin, or maybe it's simply the fact that this is the tomb of a man so evil, the earth won't consume his body, but a wave of vertigo washes through me. If it weren't for Des's hold on me, I would slide off his back.

Gently, Des sets me down so he can lift his hand toward the sarcophagus. His magic briefly thickens the air, and then stone grinds against stone as the lid begins to slide off the coffin.

An old, sour-tasting terror like I used to feel whenever I thought about my father now rushes back. But it's not my stepdad who's frightening to me. It's the possibility of what's beneath that stone slab. A body that cannot decay, a man who's back from the dead.

The lid comes off, hovering in the air before slowly lowering itself to the ground. It lands on the dirt with an echoing thump, dust billowing out around it.

From where I stand, I can't see into the coffin. I creep forward, Des at my side.

I hear the Bargainer's sharp exhale, and then my eyes land on the inside of the coffin.

And I get firsthand confirmation of what we'd both assumed and feared.

There's no rotting corpse, nor is there a perfectly preserved body. There's nothing here at all.

Galleghar Nyx might've once rested here, but he no longer does.

The sarcophagus is empty.

CHAPTER 9

I stare up at the stars, my body stretched out along the thin pallet resting on the dry earth. The night here in the Banished Lands is so clear, the heavens sparkle above us.

Next to me, Des leans against a boulder, one of his knees bent in front of him, ruminating. He's not angry or surprised, just...lost in his own mind.

Ahead of us, our fire crackles. Its flames flicker from rosy pink to pale green to lilac then to buttery yellow, and the smoke that rises into the night sky is cast in dusty pastels. The whole thing is a kaleidoscope of color captured in heat and light, and it's putting out a shit ton of magic.

Why it looks like that is a secret Des hasn't divulged—yet.

"How long do you think your father's body has been missing?" I ask.

Des shakes his head. "No more than a decade or so."

I raise my eyebrows.

"I've checked many times over the two centuries since his death," he explains. "I've been perversely curious whether the earth would one day accept him. I should've known some other sort of fuckery was afoot."

Resurrected kings, possessed soldiers, and a body-snatching Thief. It sounds nonsensical.

Perhaps if I wrote it out, I would understand it all better.

"Do you have a notebook and a pen?" I ask the Bargainer.

In response, he snaps his fingers, and from the ether, he produces a pen and a pad of paper.

I take both from him and smooth the paper on the ground. Uncapping the pen, I begin to write.

Des peers over at what I'm scrawling. When I don't say anything, he asks, "What are you writing?"

I pause, my eyes moving to his. "A time line."

I say, "Here is what we know: your father and the Thief are somehow connected. If we start from the beginning, your father was once simply a king with a lot of consorts and kids; he probably wasn't the best dude out there, but he wasn't *always* murdering his young."

I pause, just to make sure I have the story straight so far.

Des gives me a nod, looking vaguely entertained.

"Then, at some point," I say, moving my pen down my time line, "he heard a prophecy about losing his throne, and he murdered his children as a result." I scribble the note in.

"You, his remaining son, then overthrew him." I pause to write in the facts. "And shortly thereafter you discovered his body wouldn't decay, so you put him in a tomb." I draw a long line to show the time elapsed. "Over a decade ago, his body was still entombed." I fill that out on my sheet. "Now his body is gone, and he is very much alive."

Once I've written it all out, I stare at the sheet.

And…I'm not sure this exercise produced a single answer. Except that—

The Thief of Souls began kidnapping soldiers roughly a decade ago, essentially during that shadowy period when Galleghar Nyx might or might not have been entombed.

There could be something to that.

My gaze moves back to the beginning of the time line, around when Galleghar Nyx heard a prophecy and began killing his kids. That was the first domino flicked, the one that set into motion everything that led to us sitting here in the Banished Lands, an empty tomb only a stone's throw away.

"Have you heard the prophecy yourself?" I ask.

The corners of Des's lips pull down. "It's been…lost to time."

Well, there goes *that* potential lead.

A flask materializes in the Bargainer's hand. He takes a deep swig of it, then wordlessly passes it to me.

Des is not usually this open to sharing alcohol with me. Before he can reconsider the offer, I take the flask from him and bring it to my mouth. I wince as soon as the spicy spirits hit my tongue. There's magic in the drink, magic that strokes my throat and tickles my stomach.

I pass the flask back.

"It's too quiet here," he admits, his gaze skimming our surroundings. "Something is amiss."

Something is more than amiss. A man came back from the dead.

"Des, why *are* we still here?" I ask softly. I haven't pressed the issue up until now because I wanted to give my mate time to work through whatever emotional turmoil is in his head.

And yeah, I get that an empty tomb is not a huge surprise, given that Des fought his dad back in Flora's forest, but between keeping me alive and then defending his kingdom from an army of possessed soldiers, the King of Night has probably been a little too preoccupied to actually process that event.

That said, this was supposed to be a quick adventure—see Galleghar Nyx's resting place then go. But now we're lingering, and maybe that wouldn't be a problem except that, despite the drink, I can feel this place sapping away my strength bit by bit. And Des has a distant, troubled look on his face like each second, he's moving further out of my reach.

He takes another swig from his flask before passing it back to me. "Someone here must've seen what happened to the body," he replies. "I'm going to have a little chat with them."

A little chat. *Right*. That's a Bargainer euphemism if I've ever heard one.

I swallow a shot's worth of Otherworld spirits—oh, that sits *well* in the stomach—before handing the flask to Des and glancing around us.

There's not a single spark of life anywhere within eyesight. Not an animal, not a plant, and certainly not a fairy. Besides us, there's no one here right now, just as there likely was no one here the day Galleghar's body disappeared from its tomb.

But even if there was…

"Shouldn't we be looking for them?"

"They will come to us."

I'm seriously not following.

Des smirks at me, no longer looking so distant. "Have you been feeling a little parched?"

"Yes…" I say slowly. What does that have to do with anything?

"There's a reason we banish fae here. This place is devoid of magic. A long-ago battle reaped every drop from the land. And magic, cherub, is a fairy's lifeblood."

With his flask, the Bargainer points to the bonfire, which is doing such an excellent job of shoving off the cold that I scoot away from it. "That right there is putting out magic in spades—magic any fae will be drawn to."

The smoke gives off a perfumed scent—like burning rose petals—and I suddenly get it. The fire was literally sending out a smoke signal, carrying magic off along the wind, coaxing magic-starved fae toward us.

"So we're bait," I say. "You decided to make us bait."

The Bargainer's gaze sharpens on me, his pale eyes reflecting the colorful flames. "You're not bait, love. The fire is the bait. You're an iron-manacled trap set to crush willful fairies."

Yessss, my siren says. *He understands.*

Des's eyes move to the fire, and his gaze unfocuses. I think he's going to add something else, but the seconds tick by, and soon it becomes obvious his thoughts have returned inward.

I don't think I've ever seen the big bad Bargainer fall into himself. Not like this.

"Des."

We all have roles we play. I'm used to being the vulnerable one, the lonely one, and the Bargainer is used to being the tough, secretive one. The problem is we aren't actors, and this isn't a play. We're flesh and blood, and even a fairy as strong and capable and old (and I mean *old*) as Des sometimes needs to be weak.

And it's okay to be weak and upset. I've stared down those emotions at the bottom of many a bottle.

I think that's where the Bargainer is, even though

his stoic expression gives away nothing. His kingdom is compromised, and his father is alive, and maybe all sorts of old emotions he thought he'd buried are now resurfacing. I don't know, maybe I'm wrong, but in case I'm not—

I get up and close what little distance there is between me and Des. I sink onto his lap, my thighs on either side of his hips. His gaze sharpens, and he stares at me with those intense pale eyes of his. He's hard to look at because even after all this time, he's still so ridiculously pretty.

He closes his eyes, and when he opens them, there's so much turbulence in them. So much. An immortal's worth. I touch the corner of his eye.

"I've got you," I say. And then I kiss one of his cheeks and then the other.

Wordlessly, he pulls me to him.

"Cherub." He brushes my hair back and cups my face. "I'm not sad. I'm so very, very *angry*."

Now that he says it, I can feel the emotion like it's some sort of magic unto itself. It vibrates beneath his skin and along our connection. It makes his hands shake.

"This is the part of me I don't want you to see," he says softly.

His wrathful side.

"I really hate to break it to you, Des, but I've already seen you angry."

Several times. He's always fearsome to behold.

"Not like this." He shakes his head. "Not like this."

His hands glide up my waist, and that's all it takes for me to realize that even when he's angry—maybe especially then—I want him.

His rage and his touch stir the siren within me. I denied her earlier. I'm not sure she'll be denied again.

I roll my hips against his. Beneath me, he hardens.

Des's hands tighten on my flesh. "Careful," he says in a tone that should set my teeth on edge.

I lean forward, my breath against his lips. "Or else *what*?" I challenge.

Des's eyes narrow even as his mouth curls into a smile. He hooks one of his arms around me and flips us so my back is now on the ground and his hips are nestled tightly between my thighs.

"Tonight I have especially little control," he warns. It's only now that I notice the shadows at his back. They gather into the shape of his wings, then dissipate. Gather then dissipate. Again and again.

He really is on the knife-edge of control.

"You've never been with me when my fae side comes out to play," he says. There's a note to his voice that's not human.

"I'm not scared of your fae side," I say defiantly. I never was.

He clicks his tongue. "Callie, Callie," he admonishes.

As he speaks, my clothes melt off me, like they were made of hot wax and not fiber. It's a nifty little trick of the Bargainer's.

His clothes follow, and now I feel the hard length of him pressing against my pelvis.

He drops down to take a breast into his mouth. That's all it takes for my skin to brighten and my siren to surface.

I feel a slight shudder work through him, and I'm not entirely sure if that's because he can sense my magic through our connection or if my siren simply has that effect on him.

"Sweet siren," he says between kisses, "you better sharpen those claws. Tonight I don't plan on being nice."

71

He spreads my legs wide. It's almost lewd how open I am to him. The entire time, he watches me greedily.

"Aren't you precious to think I'm worried," I openly taunt him. "I have my own tricks." I tap his lips with my finger. "Tricks that you are no longer...*immune to*," I say, glamour filling my voice.

Des's eyes flicker and his wings manifest, spreading wide behind him. They are backlit by the flames, and the thin membranes of them glow with pale warmth.

"I *dare* you, siren." The Bargainer's features seem to sharpen.

So the little fairy *has* come out to play.

This is truth or dare all over again. Only now I'm the one who holds all the cards.

How utterly exquisite.

"Do your worst, Desmond Flynn," I command him.

Something dark and obsessive and distinctly fae shines in his eyes as he pins me down to the ground, his body like living shackles. I wantonly grind myself against him.

I feel through our bond this strange need to capture and cart me away. To *claim* and *keep*.

I want it all—all his twisted, dark parts.

Without another word, he lifts my hips and savagely thrusts into me. I nearly gasp as the girth of his hard cock slides through my wetness. He takes my mouth as he pulls out, only to slam back into me, again and again.

This is no sweet claiming. This is need. This is possession. It's everything Des so assiduously fights against displaying.

Damn me, I love every second of it.

"Harder," I demand.

His lips curve up as he obliges.

It feels like more than just his cock is inside me, like all of him is surging forward and laying siege. And still I could stop him if I wanted.

If I wanted.

What I want is for him to screw me senseless and then screw me some more.

He takes my hands and presses them into the ground, holding me hostage as he pounds into me, his broad chest already slick with sweat.

"Confess," I command. "Confess to me what you're thinking."

He stares down at me, a lock of hair dangling between us.

"I want to fuck you until you're mindless with want. I want to feel you squeeze my dick as you come around me. I want to die buried inside you."

"Is this all you've got?" I say. "I'm disappointed."

It's a battle of wills at this point: His fae side pitted against my siren. His magic versus my own.

He flips me over and presses me into the ground. Leaning in close to my ear, he whispers, "We can't have that now, can we?"

Des hikes one of my legs up and shoves his cock into me from behind. My eyes flutter at the force of the intrusion. He's rougher than I'm used to—much rougher—and yet, *my God*, this is everything I never knew I wanted, and I can't seem to get enough.

The ground chafes at my knees and breasts. Couldn't fucking care less.

"Touch yourself," the Bargainer orders, his magic riding the words. I'm a prisoner to them.

Of its own volition, my hand slips between my thighs, right where I'm already soaking wet. And then my fingers begin to stroke my clit.

It's almost too much.

I arch back into Des, deepening his thrusts. I feel the slick slide of his skin against mine. In and out, in and out. I'm being rubbed in all the right places.

And then one of his hands skims my ass.

This is new. Is he going to…?

His hand stops when it finds my other opening. He touches it, circles it, puts just the slightest pressure against it until the tip of his finger teases its way in.

"Oh my *God*."

Des leans in close. "Leave God out of this, cherub. He has nothing to do with it."

Sinful, sinful man.

He keeps thrusting, I keep touching myself, and he keeps probing. It's that last one that's driving me mad.

"Deeper," I say breathlessly. It's more the siren who demands it than me.

I've never done this before. Not with any of the men I've been with. Not that they hadn't tried; I just hadn't wanted it then.

I want it now. Oh, how I want it now.

I let out a wanton moan at the sensation of having Des in me twice over.

His finger continues to press in, and this—feels—*amazing*. More, more, *more*.

"Tell me, siren, are you disappointed now?"

"God, no," I gasp out.

"There's that word again." His finger presses in deeper.

Is that touch supposed to be punishing? It's not. Another husky moan slips out of me as my body thrums with pleasure.

"Perhaps you'd better find a synonym," he says.

Des's magic winds around my windpipe, and I'm prisoner to it.

"*Des*—" I give a strangled cry.

"Much better," he says, the devil in his voice.

All this stimulation, all this sensation of being pressed and prodded and filled to the brim, it's nearly too much.

And still I hold out. This is too intense, too exquisite, too enticing, and I can't bear the thought of it ending.

So I hide from my release.

I don't know how long the two of us stay locked in our strange, taboo lovemaking. Only that at some point, Des's white hair brushes against the skin of my shoulder and his lips are in my ear.

"Am I not servicing my queen well enough?"

My siren merely purrs.

He shifts against me, and I shamelessly gasp at the exquisite feel of him.

"Surely you should've come by now—or am I losing my...touch?" He tweaks his finger, and I let out a choked cry, nearly climaxing then and there. "But perhaps you need a little more persuading."

Never want this to end.

He breathes against my cheek. "Come for me, siren."

I feel magic and darkness in those words. They settle into me, and through my haze of pleasure, I register that this is all going to come to a swift end.

I manage to squeeze one final order out. "Give me... *everything.*"

He does. Des drives into me as I shatter, his flesh pounding against mine harder and harder and deeper and deeper. The pleasure is so extreme, so acute, I can barely hold on to it. It washes over me, unnatural, consuming, addicting.

His body was meant for this—screwing and claiming and twisting my will into his own. Just as mine was meant to allure him and seduce him and ultimately bend his desires to fit my own.

With a groan, he comes, his hips slamming into mine as he fills me up. Each stroke of Des's hips sends another wave of pleasure through me.

We come down slowly, our bodies sweaty and dusty.

Des collapses next to me before dragging me onto his chest. He holds me captive in his arms, stroking my flesh softly, his lips trailing over my shoulder. He playfully bites the skin there. "Stay in my arms, cherub. Stay here and never leave."

"All right," I say, settling in against him, blissfully uncaring about the chill creeping in with the evening.

For a little while, we lie there in silence. Then, slowly, a laugh bubbles low in my belly. "I can't believe I let you stick a finger up my butt," I finally say.

I'm such a smooth pillow talker.

I sense rather than see him smirk. "Says the girl who once got me to come in my pants."

Now it's my turn to smirk. Then my thoughts circle back. "I can't believe I *liked* it."

"My saucy little siren? I can. I have the feeling that by the time the sun sets on our lives, you'll be the naughty one to my virginal, saintly soul."

I outright guffaw at that. "As *if*."

A grin spreads across his face. "You're probably right." He smooths a hand down my spine, making my skin pucker. "I have more tricks up my sleeve. All you have to do is say the word. Or challenge me again. I rather enjoyed pitting my magic against yours."

I can't contain the excited shiver that courses through me. I don't think I realized just what being mated to Des means. He rules over *sex*; everything we've done together so far—that's all the tip of a very large iceberg.

And I probably still won't fully understand what being mated to him means until I've seen and savored every one of his perversions and witnessed every one of his horrors. Only then will I fully grasp this force of nature I'm mated to.

We're quiet for a time.

"It's not enough," Des eventually says, his hand rubbing up and down my arm. "Having you. I always assumed that once you warmed my bed, it would be." He cups my pussy as he speaks, and I swear to God, I am *this close* to jumping him all over again.

"But I'm a greedy bastard, and I want more. Always more."

My fingers glide over his arm, where his tattoos seem to leap and dance in the firelight. I lift my head and rest it on his chest.

"Tell me a secret," I whisper.

He traces the curve of my cheek. "Secrets are meant for one soul to keep."

I tense at his words.

"My mother used to say that all the time," he explains. "It's one of those formative lessons of hers I've carried with me since childhood."

My brows furrow. Some of my sex-induced haze is slipping away. "And now the formerly sleeping soldiers say it."

"Up until now, I hadn't figured out how exactly they knew it." Des's finger traces my lips. "And then I fought my father, who's in league with the Thief of Souls."

His finger drops from my mouth. "You wanted to know a secret, so here's one, Callie: some time, long ago, my

77

mother whispered those same words to Galleghar Nyx. She, a spy set on escaping from him, said them as a taunt. And now Galleghar is taunting us both with them.

"I need to understand the nature of his undeath to understand the rest of this mystery."

Undeath. There should be simply life and then death, but in the land of supernaturals, both earthly and Otherworldly, there are a whole range of beings that somehow fall outside this dichotomy.

"Perhaps then I can understand how he learned that phrase. And so we wait."

Des pulls me to him and kisses me deeply, tasting like salt and sex and the night in all its secretive goodness—and then our clothes peel themselves off the ground and slide back onto us.

The two of us break apart, and whatever moment we were having is over.

I sit up and gather my legs to my chest, wrapping my arms around them. "Tell me about him," I say softly.

Des has already told me the short version of Daddy Dearest's life, but there's so much I still don't know.

Those silvery eyes are on me in an instant.

"He's not worth wasting any more breath on."

"We're already wasting breath searching for him," I say. "Tell me something about him—something I don't already know."

The Bargainer beckons his discarded flask with his fingers, calling it back to him like it's a wayward soldier. It's not until he's caught the thing and taken a sip from it that he speaks again.

"He had hundreds of concubines," Des finally says. "*Hundreds.* Just take a moment to imagine that."

Hundreds? That's like having a wife for every day of the year.

"I don't know how many of them he fathered children with, but the number is large—large enough for the killing to get a name in our histories. It became known as the Royal Purge—the Purge, for short.

"And when Galleghar died and I first walked the halls of his former castle, I saw firsthand the women he'd taken in.

"They had this look about them." Des gestures to his eyes. "Soldiers get that look when they've lived through too much. Many of them had it. And yet…and yet dozens of those women cried for him when he died." Des scoffs to himself. "He killed babies—*their* babies—and they still cried for him."

I don't say anything. There aren't words for this kind of atrocity.

"That's not to say that everyone in his harem loved him. In the years after his death, I started to uncover the details of their lives. In the ledgers, we found evidence that some of his wives died untimely deaths—usually after they openly mourned their dead children or objected to the Purge.

"Someone had also diligently recorded the dozens of suicide notes from Galleghar's various concubines. I later discovered that those who survived their suicide attempts were then brutalized by the king. He took it as a personal slight that they dared try to leave him.

"And, of course, there were other escape attempts by other wives, and those too were violently punished. Hell was a kinder place than my father's court. To think my mother dared to escape under these circumstances…"

Brave, brave woman.

The fire snaps and pops between us. Des is still lost in the past.

"Did you know that when I executed my father, I was expected to inherit the harem he left behind?" He gives a humorless laugh. "Doesn't that make your skin crawl? To inherit a lover like some sort of heirloom?"

It's sickening. But then, this entire story has turned my stomach.

"I broke with tradition when I sent them all away." His eyes move to me. "I knew about you even then," he admits, a soft smile spreading across his face. But then it disappears. "As did my father," he adds.

A chill slides over my skin. In front of me, the iridescent fire dims as the Bargainer's shadows close in on it.

"To answer your question, cherub, I never knew much about Galleghar Nyx. Only that he was a mean sonuvabitch, he tyrannically ruled over the Night Kingdom, and he killed my mother in cold blood. And now, somehow, he's alive."

CHAPTER 10

"Still no closer to finding me—or Galleghar—it appears."

The Thief stands on the other side of the fire, peering down at me with his onyx eyes.

I sit up so fast, a wave of vertigo washes through me.

"That was a neat trick you did there, back in Somnia," he says, circling around the fire as he approaches me.

I scoot backward, but there's nowhere to go out here in the Banished Lands. I look for Desmond, but other than the Thief, I'm utterly alone.

He crouches next to me and tilts his head, studying me. There's something detached and reptilian about him.

"So you can glamour fairies after all," he says.

I can glamour fairies—I can glamour him.

My skin brightens. "Get away from me."

He continues to stare at me, his eyes inky. Slowly, he smiles. "Enticing, but no. I think I'll stay right here."

It doesn't work on him.

Dear God.

"Shame your wiles don't affect me." He reads my face. "Don't fret, enchantress. I *am* tempted."

"Why did you wake them?" I ask as my skin dims.

"Why did I wake them? That's your most pressing question? Don't you want to know why I kidnapped them in the first place? Or why I put the women in caskets and the men in trees?"

Of course I do.

He sits next to me, and it takes a great amount of willpower not to recoil at his nearness.

The Thief sighs. "Because I wanted to."

He leans in. "I put the men in trees because, as the Green Man, I could. I took the women savagely and caged them like I have been caged." I feel the sick heat of his anger and his excitement as he talks. "I hid the men and showcased the women," he continues, "and oh, how I enjoyed watching all those fairies fear the unknown. It's been so long since any of them felt true fear, but now they do.

"So," he says, facing me more fully, "is that what you wanted to hear?"

Yes. No.

I've spent all these years hunting criminals, and the worst ones give these kinds of answers. They committed atrocities because they wanted to. Because they could.

But even as the Thief of Souls gives me this glimpse into his mind, he manages to evade the answer I really wanted to hear. I want to know what his plans are, not how his sick mind works.

"Enough about me," he says softly. "I know, enchantress, that if you're scared or excited enough, your baser nature will expose itself." He reaches out and strokes my cheek with the back of his knuckle.

I flinch at his touch, my nostrils flaring. I should be sprinting far away from the Thief, but my muscles are locked up. I couldn't move if I tried.

"The question is"—his hand slides to my lower jaw, and he drags my face to meet his—"which route do I explore— your passion or your fear?"

His eyes dip to my lips. God save me, I might as well be back in the Fauna Kingdom's prison because right now, I'm staring at Karnon. It's a different body but the same eyes.

My breath hitches at the reminder, and a few seconds later, my skin illuminates as the siren unfurls, stretching beneath my flesh like a stiff muscle.

A fierce fury rises in me, eclipsing my fear.

This barbarian thinks to intimidate us? Scare us?

I grab his wrist and pull it away, leaning into his space. "Whatever you think to do to me, I *dare* you to try." I take my other hand and press it to his chest, tapping a clawed finger against him. "But you should know that, if given the chance, I will gut you and make a necklace of your innards."

Not going to lie, my siren is a real piece of work. But it's times like this that I appreciate her brand of wild.

The Thief smiles at me, looking like his interest's been piqued. "I do hope you make good on your threat. I'd hate to see all this vehemence go to waste." He moves in closer, our faces inches apart.

His breath fans against my cheek. "Find me, Callypso. I'm eagerly awaiting our reunion."

"Cherub—"

My body startles, roused from sleep by Des's voice. My eyes sweep over our campsite.

I swear the Thief was here just a second ago.

His presence was so vivid that my mind isn't convinced I dreamed him up.

But then I'm distracted by Des's warm body and his penetrating stare.

"Everything all right, Callie?"

I swallow—an action his eyes dart to—and nod. "I'm fine."

That earns me a frown. But rather than pushing the issue, Des squeezes my hip.

"Someone's coming," he whispers.

I begin to get up, looking madly out at the darkness, but he gently presses me back down.

"If you could be a peach and pretend to be asleep, that would be wonderful. I want the fae to come closer."

Pretend to be asleep after the dream I just had? I think not.

But I do force myself to relax for Des's sake, even if I don't close my eyes. Instead, I strain my ears and eyes to hear and see anything beyond the fire. One long minute slips into another.

All at once, the Bargainer's power rushes out of him, thickening the air like darkness is a physical thing. I sense it close in on its prey like a snare, trapping them in place.

The caught fairy shrieks like a wild beast, the guttural sounds punctuated by a string of curses.

In an instant, Des is gone from my side, dissolving into vapor like he was never there. I flip over just in time to see my mate looming over a fairy in the distance. The fae is uselessly fighting the magic trapping him in place, his scythe-like weapon striking the magical barrier over and over.

Des folds his arms, appraising the man and looking as though he finds him wanting.

After a moment, the Night King takes the scythe away from the man. "You're going to answer some questions for us," Des says, "or you're going to die."

I pull the charred marshmallow from the fire, assessing the blackened crisp.

Damn it. This is the fifth one I've burned. I officially suck at this s'mores thing. To be fair, I'm pretty sure Des's iridescent fire burns hotter than the fires I'm used to.

I wait for it to cool before I remove it from my stick and grab another from the s'mores supplies Des presented me with when he returned with his captive.

Pretty sure this is his attempt to keep me occupied while he interrogates his prisoner.

I'm ashamed to say that it's totally working.

Meanwhile, several feet away, Des is well into his interrogation.

So far, he's folded the fairy's weapon into an origami horse, taken away his voice briefly, and removed the last of the items the fairy had on him (a couple of stones, a knife, some dried mystery meat, and a necklace made of fae hair— because heaven forbid we meet someone normal here).

"Who opened the tomb?" Des asks the fairy calmly.

The man spits at Des. The spittle never hits my mate. Instead, it stops in midair, then reverses its trajectory to splash against the prisoner fairy's face.

"Who opened the tomb?" Des repeats.

"Suck on my prick!"

"Mmm, tempting," Des says, cocking his head. "Is that a genuine offer?" His magic unlaces the man's crudely made breeches, and then it begins tugging the cloth down.

The fairy's eyes widen, and he yanks the material back up, fruitlessly trying to keep his pants on. "What in the bloody ferking gods' names!"

"Cherub," Des says, glancing over at me, "I think the man's shy. One moment he wants my attention, the next he's being a coy minx."

I pull my sixth marshmallow from the fire; it's perfectly golden brown. Success!

"Men give *such* mixed signals," I say.

I admit it—I like to toy with my targets just as much as Des does. That was always one of my favorite parts of the PI business.

After grabbing a bar of Hershey's chocolate and a graham cracker, I pull my marshmallow off its stick.

"They do, don't they?" The Bargainer's eyes brighten enough to let me know he likes my brand of wicked. Turning back to the fairy, Des taps on the prisoner's lips. "No need to be bashful. I'm sure your *prick* will be everything I've ever dreamed a prick could be."

Now the fairy's bucking, wildly trying to pull his pants up with his legs. He's failing abysmally at it. "You sick shite!" he shouts.

I munch on my s'more, and oh my God, it's one of the great tragedies of the world that s'mores are reserved for camping. These little bastards are delicious.

Des's good humor collapses in an instant. His magic quits tugging at the fairy's pants. Now that there's no more magical resistance, the prisoner nearly gives himself a wedgie yanking his pants up.

The night darkens. "I'm done being coy as well," Des says, his voice like polished steel. "Tell me what happened to the body resting in the cavern beneath that boulder"—he points to the unassuming grave markers in the distance—"or I'll start killing you in increments."

"I don't *know*!" the fairy yowls.

"Have you ever died in increments?" Des asks. "It's slow and—well, I don't need to tell you that it's painful."

"I never saw anything! I swear it—"

I feel the brush of magic, and then the prisoner's hand is jerked in front of him, his fingers splayed out.

"I like to start with the pinkie—start small, you know," Des says. Right now, he's 100 percent Bargainer. "I'll remove it, knuckle by knuckle..."

"Gods damn it! I don't know where the body is!"

The fairy's ruined scythe now unfolds, mending itself until it looks whole and untouched. It floats through the air, stopping dangerously close to the fairy's hand.

The fairy lets out a little whimper as the blade caresses his little finger.

"After the pinkie..." Des continues, "well, there are nine other fingers to play with.

"If that doesn't break you, there are teeth and toes. Even those are just a taster. And the pain—it's enough to drive a fairy to do almost anything. You'll feel the centuries of your life draining away with each amputation, and—if you hold out long enough—you'll beg me for death.

"Just when you think it's bound to be over, you'll realize you're still alive and aware, and you'll endure it for hours—days, if need be—but it will feel like decades by the end."

A sheen of sweat's developed on the fairy's upper lip. "You'll never get away with this," he swears, his voice high. "The king's men will come for you both before then." His eyes dart between us.

"*The king*," Des says, looking like a teacher whose pupil

finally answered a question correctly. "Now we're getting somewhere." Des sits, propping his elbows on his legs. "Would the king know where the body went?"

"The king knows all."

"Does he now?" The Bargainer raises his eyebrows.

The fairy should be worried. Des only uses that voice right before he kicks the hornet's nest.

The scythe lifts from the fairy's finger and circles the man.

Des stands. "Let me amend my terms: find me someone who can tell me who did this, and I'll let you live."

CHAPTER 11

I stare at the crevice in the ground. "This is where your king lives?" I say skeptically.

Just another hole in the earth.

"You'll see…" Des's prisoner says ominously.

Since directing us here, a flight that covered miles of arid, lifeless territory, this fairy has gained a lot more confidence.

We're probably about to get shanked.

I shift my weight from foot to foot. "So, what, are we just supposed to wait around…?" My words die off as someone blows a horn.

Just as my eyes scour the landscape for the fairy Des captured, dozens of footfalls echo from the hole. Not a minute later, armed fairies come pouring out of the opening, pointing their weapons at us and shouting orders.

"Hands at your backs! Hands at your backs!"

Des does as instructed, looking ever the compliant captive. Taking a cue from him, I move my own hands to my back.

The fairies clamor in close to us, all while ignoring our former prisoner. Not that I'm surprised. His clothes are tattered and homespun, and he looks like he's been on the wrong end of one too many fists, which is how these soldiers look. Des and I, however, are clothed in fine silks, and we're (relatively) clean.

"Found these two wandering around the plains," Des's former captive says. "King Henbane will want to see them. They've got magic in spades."

The soldiers grunt, eyeing us appreciatively. "You'll get your finder's fee."

"I look forward to it."

I narrow my eyes at our former prisoner.

He gives me a toothy smile and a two-fingered salute. "Enjoy your stay," he says, backing away. The fairy leaves us there, descending into the crevice until the earth swallows him completely.

The soldiers move to shackle us, and their metal restraints clang together. The sound fills me with no little amount of dread. For a split second, I'm vividly back in Karnon's prison.

"Cuff her with iron, and you'll lose your balls," Des says, pulling me back into the present.

One of the soldiers hesitates, then squints at Des, a mean look in his eye. "Is that a threat?"

"Nah, he's just reciting poetry to you," I say.

The fairy's glare moves from the Bargainer to me, his lips pressed together like he's tasted something bad. All at once, he swings the back of his palm at me.

He never lands the blow. His hand freezes inches from my face.

"Ah, ah, ah. Hasn't anyone told you it's impolite to hit a

girl?" the Bargainer's voice is beguiling, but at his back, his wings have appeared. They spread out menacingly.

The display is so obviously a warning, but the soldiers close in on him anyway.

In an instant, Des's magic lashes out, knocking the fairies to the ground. With another pulse of his power, the soldiers' weapons are yanked from them, the swords and cudgels turned on their owners. They lie pinned in place, held hostage by their weapons.

The only one not held up by their weapons is the soldier who tried to hit me. He lies on the ground, his eyes wide as his arm rises in front of him. As he watches, his fingers curl into a fist.

He stammers out, "W-what in all the—"

His fist strikes out, slamming into his face with a meaty slap. It pulls away only to land a second blow—then a third, fourth, fifth. The soldier cries out as blood drips from his nose.

"Aye, you fools," one of the fallen soldiers says. He's staring at Des's wings. "That's the Night King!"

The Bargainer's eyes sweep over them. "I'm done playing games." His voice drips with menace. "Take us to your king."

———

The Banished Lands actually has a society. You can almost call it a civilization, except *civil* has no business being in the name.

Since descending into the Otherworld's butt crack— a.k.a. the crevice in the ground—I've gotten a quick and thorough introduction into Maltira, the City of the Banished.

So far, I've seen six fights break out, four passed-out fairies, three couples going at it (seven if you count the very questionable dancing we walked by), and dozens of people wearing jewelry made from fae bones.

Apparently, bone necklaces are a *thing*.

Early on, a few fairies catcalled me, and another one grabbed his crotch. That all came to a fun little end when the catcallers mysteriously started confessing to having grandma fetishes and venereal diseases, and the crotch grabber began squeezing his bits until he was begging for mercy.

The entire time Des's face remained pleasantly passive, but through our bond, I felt the cool breath of his magic stirred to agitation.

Don't piss off my boyfriend, yo.

When he catches me staring, he drops the façade to flash me a devilish little smile. Then the façade is back up, and he's the cool but implacable Bargainer once more.

Around us, our guards walk stiffly, their spears and knives out and their expressions menacing. None of them, however, get too close to me or Des, lest they tempt the Night King's anger again.

I glance at the cavern ceiling high above me. All those stories about fairies living under the hill were true after all.

Our armed escorts lead us past buildings that rise from the earth into the air, looking as though they'd been formed from a single lump of clay. We pass rows and rows of these buildings, each one occupied by cagey fairies who've carved out some life for themselves.

Just like the land above, the air here is parched of magic. But it's not just magic that's missing from this place. I've come to expect a certain fae elegance with the Otherworld, yet most of the buildings are devoid of decoration; no one's attempted to carve designs on lintels or paint adornments. Just as noticeable as the lack of attention to aesthetics is the careless disrepair of the place. There are bits of litter here and graffiti there. The building across the way is stained and partially collapsed. The one next to it has been crudely patched up with mud and hide. It's all so very un-fae-like.

We leave this city center through a corridor cut into the rock. Already we've descended hundreds of feet, but judging by the passage's downward slope, we're about to head even deeper into the ground.

I glance at the wall sconces where flames flicker; the scent wafting from them closes my windpipes. It smells like burning hair and rotting flesh, and I'm seriously concerned that's what the odd candles are made from.

After a dizzying number of switchbacks and a few flights of stairs, our group comes upon two armed fairies who block the passageway. One of them is a Fauna fae, his soft fox ears poking from between his red hair. The other could be from any of the other kingdoms, his hair a bright blond and his eyes the color of moss. Both wear the same patchy, homemade uniforms.

"The King of the Night and his mate request an audience with the king," one of our escorts now says to the fae standing guard.

The one with the fox ears grunts, taking a nice long perusal of me, his gaze lingering on my tits, hips, and legs because apparently every criminal here has to act like a fucking cliché.

His attention moves to Des, and the Fauna fae's lip curls. "If the king can't drain them, he doesn't want to see them."

For a beat, nothing happens.

But then Des's magic rips across the room, throwing the banished fairies against the dank, earthen walls.

Not going to lie, it's been a real rough day for this group.

The Night King's power pins them there, and it's so obvious that if we wanted to, we could waltz right in to see this king, and none of his lackeys could stop us.

"You have to forgive your fellow soldier," Des says, stepping up to Fox Ears. "He didn't word our demands correctly. This isn't a *request*. It's an order. But go ahead, defy it. I do so *love* to hear fairies scream." He touches Fox Ear's cheek.

The fairy shakes his head back and forth, whimpering as though he can feel the first tendrils of pain.

Des assesses him for a moment. Then, with a flick of his wrist, he releases all the men.

They crumple to the floor, rubbing their formerly pinned limbs.

The fairies' posturing appears to be over, but before any of them can pick themselves up, Des looms over Fox Ears. "Oh, and a word of warning: look at my mate again with anything other than respect and benevolence, and you'll lose your eyes."

Damn.

Fox Ears bows his head, his ears drooping, his posture turning submissive. He nods, and with that, he and the other guard step aside and let our entourage pass by.

"Got to threaten every damn grain of sand in this place…" Des mutters under his breath.

I can't help but agree with him. The only thing anyone seems to respect around here is power.

We pass three more sets of guards (two of which also need to be threatened) and descend deeper into the mountain before we finally arrive at a massive stone door.

This far beneath the earth, where the sky is only a distant memory, I feel the barest breath of magic.

So the Banished Lands haven't been reaped of *all* power. Just the vast majority of it. And now I understand why the citizens of the Banished Lands built down. Because the lower you go, the closer to magic you get. And in a world where everyone's suffocating in its absence, even the barest hint of it is precious.

The guards push the stone door open, and I get my first good look at the king's inner sanctum.

The vaulted room is packed to the brim with fairies in wrap skirts and bandeaux, leather pants and body paint.

The fairies pin us in from all sides, making our trip down the aisle slow and claustrophobic.

I take in the hordes of them, their faces ranging from curious to bloodthirsty. Beyond them, I catch sight of the top of the makeshift throne, carved from rock and fitted with bone and steel. But it's not until we're nearly at the end of the aisle that the crowd parts and I finally see him.

The king.

He lounges on the stone throne, his legs splayed. In place of a shirt, he wears dozens of bleached bone necklaces, each one strung with a dizzying number of teeth and bones. His brown leather trousers hang low on his tan hips, and strapped to them are several blades, some made from stone, others steel.

His chestnut hair is plaited back from his face, and it hangs in ropes over his shoulders. A crown of metal and bone perches high on his head. The thing is fashioned crudely, and I'm surprised a fae would wear such a thing. It looks like something I made in art class when I was five.

His glittering green eyes fall first on Des before skipping over to me. They take their time here, moving from my face to my chest, hips, and legs. Then they make a slow climb back up. As he assesses me, his fingers tap against an armrest.

I would've said he was bored, except there's far too much interest sparking in his eyes.

The fairies in front of us stop and kneel. "Your Majesty," they murmur.

"I see we have visitors." The king says this like Des and I are offending his sensibilities. *His* sensibilities. The man sitting in the I-was-drunk-when-I-made-this chair.

The kneeling fairies now stand before turning to us.

"Bow before His Eminence, Lord of the Banished, Master of the Forgotten, Protector of the Maligned, King Typhus Henbane," one of our escorts commands, though he looks a little ill while he says it.

The Bargainer saunters forward a few steps. "You have titles? How *charming*."

King Henbane stands, his chestnut hair gleaming under the torchlight and his necklaces rustling. "Forced your way into my presence without even a bow to show for it. Can't say I'm surprised at your impetuousness, Desmond Flynn."

So he knows who Des is. I also notice he dropped my mate's title. Definitely a snub there. And today is really not the day. The Bargainer seems particularly prickly.

Typhus's gaze slides my way, and again he assesses me. This time, however, there's more than a touch of scorn in them. "But for your slave lover to not show me respect..." He clicks his tongue. "Last time I endured such a grave insult, I impaled the fairy for it."

Down our bond, I feel a flash of white-hot anger. But looking at Des, you would never know it.

The King of Night gives Typhus a mocking smile. "Last time I saw a jester pretending to be a king, I actually laughed."

Oooooh, burn.

The room goes deathly silent.

96

Welp, that got their attention.

This king's wings flicker behind his back, and his face twitches. "If you came here to curry my favor, *oh, great king*, then you might want to start over."

"You are an exiled criminal still serving out your sentence. In what world would I seek your favor?"

Typhus laughs in the face of that, the crowd echoing the sentiment.

When the room quiets, he says, "Do you know how I came to be?" The king sits back down on his throne. "I was already strong before I was ever sent here some hundred and fifty years ago. And I have since imbibed countless men's magic."

Even a day here has left me with what feels like a mild hangover. I can't imagine years, decades, *centuries* of this. Typhus must be powerful, to live here for this long and still have so much magic.

"Thousands have gifted me their powers," he continues, "all in return for my protection...protection that you are now threatening."

Des raises his eyebrows. "Is that right?"

"We're not in your kingdom anymore. We're in mine."

Typhus doesn't say it, but he's implying Des and I are bound by *loi du royaume*—that we must submit to Typhus's rule and the laws of his land.

The Bargainers eyes sweep over the room. "So this is your kingdom now?" A surprised little chuckle escapes him.

King Henbane tightens his grip on his armrests.

"Forgive me," Des says, "but this is the first I've heard of anyone *wanting* this shithole."

Henbane rises to his feet again, his face flushing with anger. At his back, angular iridescent wings form.

The king motions to someone in the crowd, and in response, a fairy steps away from the gathered masses, a pair of thick iron shackles in his gloved hands. Several of the soldiers in our entourage now hesitantly grab Des. They might not want to get in another skirmish with the King of Night, but they also don't want to betray their own king.

They move my mate's hands in front of him, and Des lets them. I make a move to intercede, but two of our escorts cut me off, holding me in place.

The King of the Night flashes me a look, and unlike all his playful words, the expression is serious, though I'm not sure what unspoken message he's trying to beam at me.

The fairy with the iron manacles steps up to the Bargainer. I don't care that Des is powerful and unyielding as the fairy moves them to his wrists; I struggle at the sight of them. During my time as Karnon's prisoner, I saw exactly what iron does to the fae.

With an ominous *clink*, the soldier cuffs Des. The iron shackles are only on his wrists for an instant before they slide uselessly off to land on the dirt floor in front of Des.

The Bargainer raises his eyebrows. "That was not supposed to happen, I take it?" he asks.

Up on the throne, the king fists one of his hands but otherwise continues to watch impassively.

Frowning, the fairy picks up the iron manacles with a gloved hand and again tries to cuff Des.

And again the shackles slip off him before falling once more to the ground. This time, when the guard stoops to grab them, the Bargainer kicks them away.

"Whoops."

Typhus settles into his seat, his sharp green eyes flicking

over me. "Since our lord king won't cooperate, put a pair on the bitch he's with."

In response, the room gets a hint darker.

Once more, the fairy bends down and picks up the shackles. Only, as soon as he touches them, the cuffs clamp themselves on his wrists. His gloves slide off, exposing his bare skin to the iron. It only takes a few seconds for his screams to start.

And that right there is proof this whole kingdom is nothing but fool's gold. I was imprisoned next to enough real soldiers to know that no matter how badly iron burned them, they wouldn't give their captors the benefit of their screams. Badassery at its finest.

That was how hardened those soldiers were. These fairies are nothing but children role-playing at being soldiers.

Des takes several steps forward, his magic thickening in the air. "You really shouldn't have said that."

That's all the warning he gives. In the next instant, power explodes out of him, tearing through the room. It blasts back the crowd of fairies, knocking them down like bowling pins. Even Typhus is thrown back against his seat, the stone trembling under the force of Des's magic.

The king looks utterly shell-shocked for a moment, and I can't decide whether he's blown away by Des's power or his audacity.

When Typhus recovers, magic forms in his fist, bending the light as it takes the shape of a spear. He throws the bolt like a javelin, aiming straight for Des.

The Bargainer doesn't move, though he has time to sidestep the throw. Instead, he takes the full brunt of it as it slams into his chest.

He grunts at the impact, then touches his chest with mild interest. "I *am* impressed. How many of your subjects have you drained to amass this sort of power? Hundreds? Thousands? You must be co-bound to damn near everyone to wield this level of magic."

Another spear forms in Typhus's hand. "They've bequeathed their power willingly"—uh-huh, and cake has no calories—"so I could defend them from men like you."

Des waves a hand, and King Henbane is thrown back in his seat, his magic disintegrating in an instant.

"*Enough.*" The King of the Night says it with such finality that the room full of hardened criminals now stills.

Des steps forward. "I was told you could give me answers, and I will have them, one way or another."

Typhus grimaces in his seat, his body slightly contorted. It takes a moment for me to realize the Bargainer's magic has him pinned in place. Around us, the fairies crowding the room seem to be held back by invisible hands.

For the first time since exiting Galleghar Nyx's tomb, the air is thick with power. It slips over my arms and curls around my ankles, caressing my skin. But unlike the magic in Galleghar's tomb, Des's power is familiar and inviting; it drapes itself over me like a shawl.

Des closes in on the dais, each careful step echoing across the quiet room. He's struck us all silent.

"There's a grave in the southwestern territory of the Banished Lands," he says, his gaze trained on Typhus. "It's marked by several large boulders. The body inside it was impervious to damage. And now it's missing. I want to know how that came to be."

Typhus narrows his eyes, a calculating gleam in them. "I have no idea what you're talking about," he says, his words ringing false.

I fibbed better when I was in diapers.

"But even if I did," he continues, "why should I tell you? You don't recognize my rule."

Des studies the fairy, his head cocked to the side.

My body tenses, expecting some reaction with a good dose of panache.

But that's not what I get.

Des's expression becomes almost contemplative. He nods, like Typhus didn't just feed him a load of horseshit.

Around the room, the Bargainer's magic lifts, and the air tastes parched once more. Cautiously, fairies get to their feet.

Typhus doesn't move, instead pretending he deliberately chose to sit like a pretzel.

"There is one other matter I must attend to before we head back to my kingdom," the Bargainer says, waiting until he's sure he has the room's undivided attention. "You know as well as I do that I can't leave here with you as you are," Des says. "So either you give them"—he jerks his head to the desperate hordes bracketing us—"back their magic, *or I'll do it for you.*"

I'm thinking "*I'll do it for you*" involves sharp weapons and a dead body.

Typhus rises from his throne, his face darkening and his hands trembling with his mounting anger.

The scent of the banished king's borrowed magic saturates the air; it smells just how you'd imagine it would— like that time you idiotically sampled too many perfumes on yourself and all those potent smells clashed and gave you a mother of a headache.

"Kill him where he stands!" It's an open order, and I'm pretty sure this idiot expects all the fairies in this room to answer to it.

"*No.*"

The power of that one word ripples through the enclosed space. But it's not Des who says it.

I step away from the Bargainer, my skin illuminating.

I've had enough of this place, where the air itself feels like it's trying to squeeze magic out of you, and I've had enough of this man, who for all his years of life has learned nothing except how to be a brutish a-hole.

In response to my magic, the crowd around us presses in, none so close as our guards. As soon as their eyes fall on me, they forget they're self-respecting fairies who have duties. They move toward me, ready to touch my skin, stroke my hair, drink me up, and consume me whole. It's the way it always has been, only here, in this magicless place, my glamour is all the more alluring.

"Get out of my way," I order, my power filling my voice.

The fairies do as I say—albeit a little reluctantly.

"What are you fools doing?" their king shouts at them, even though he can't rip his gaze off me.

"Shut up," I order.

His mouth clicks closed.

The sheer outrage on his face! I savor every drop of it.

"No one move—except to breathe," I command, my voice echoing in the cavern. "Oh, and Des, ignore my commands. You can do whatever you want."

Around us, the room seems to freeze in place. If I didn't know better, I'd say I'm in a hall of statues.

The Bargainer folds his arms and leans against the nearest frozen fairy, using him like he would a wall. Des has a good deal of mirth in his eyes, and it's clear he's eager to let me steal the show.

I walk down the aisle toward Typhus's throne, my hips swaying.

I head up to the dais, where I notice Typhus's gaze is pinned in place. "You can move your eyes," I allow.

Immediately, they snap to me. It's hard to read his emotions, since the rest of him is still frozen, but I'd say I'm getting some strong anger vibes coming from him.

"I really shouldn't let you do this," Des says behind me. He sounds gleeful.

I reach Typhus's throne, and God, his chair is even uglier up close. His crudely made crown rests right there, within reach, and I just can't help myself. I reach out and lift the thing off his head, then settle it onto mine. "Look at that," I breathe. "The human you wanted to shackle is now your queen."

Now I *can* see Typhus's anger bubbling in his eyes. Still, he's powerless.

On a whim, I command him, "Stand, Typhus."

Robotically, he rises from his chair.

"Now, oh, great king, bow before me." Typhus dips low, his nose nearly touching his knees as he's forced to follow my command.

As a PI, I've seen my fair share of pissed-off looks when someone is caught in the web of my glamour. King Henbane is no exception. He stares at me like he's cursing my very existence with his eyes.

I lap it up like a cat does cream. "Sit."

He sits.

He won't recover from this. Not now that his subjects have seen how easily I took his crown and bent his will.

I tilt my head at the sight of him, sullen and powerless. There's just something about a felled man that gets to me in the most twisted way.

Giving in to my baser nature, I move forward, climbing onto the king's lap and straddling his thighs.

I feel just the thinnest thread of jealousy through my connection. That too I lap up.

I am something to envy.

Lifting a hand, I reach for one of his necklaces, enjoying the sick way the bones and teeth shiver as they brush each other.

My gaze flicks to Typhus, and his green eyes seem to darken. There's still plenty of anger in them, but now there's lust there too.

I smile. Someone probably wants to hate-bang me.

Wouldn't be the first time.

I readjust myself on his lap, shaking my hair out. Why did I think glamouring him was important...?

Oh, right.

"You will answer all my questions fully and honestly," I command. "Now, how long ago was the tomb opened?" I ask.

His upper lip twitches in distaste. "A few weeks ago."

Recent. Part of me had assumed the tomb was opened years ago.

I glance over my shoulder at Des, a self-satisfied smirk on my face. He stares back at me, and his expression is amused, but his eyes are stormy.

Swiveling forward again, I lean into this idiot king, petting his cheek. In response, the room dims a little. Apparently, my mate has some objections to me petting other men.

"And who opened the tomb?" I breathe.

"I don't know," he growls.

"What do you mean you don't know?"

"I mean it wasn't a *who* at all."

Losing patience. "Explain," I command.

Again, he hesitates. How precious. As if he can fight the hold I have on him.

After two short seconds, he gives up. "On the night the dead man rose—the night *Galleghar* rose," he clarifies, making it clear he knows exactly who lay buried in that grave, "it was a shadow that retrieved him."

CHAPTER 12

I don't think I breathe. Around me, the room darkens.

"A shadow," I repeat.

Back to this insidious shadow. I almost forgot about this aspect of the Thief of Souls. The Night Kingdom's wet nurses saw a shadow watching over the casket children, and in the Flora Kingdom, I heard about a shadow visiting the sleeping women.

I glance over my shoulder at Des, the two of us sharing a look.

"What did the shadow look like?" I ask, facing Typhus once more. My voice lilts as the glamour drips off my tongue.

Typhus glares at me, his fury still apparent. "It looked like a *shadow*. I don't know, I wasn't there. This is just what was reported to me. Gods damn idiot slave." This last part he says under his breath, only loud enough for me to hear.

The room darkens anyway. I don't need to look behind me to know Des is all but primed for an attack. I don't let him get the chance.

I click my tongue and grab Typhus's chin, squeezing his jaw the way annoying relatives love to squeeze kids' faces. I lower my voice to match his. "This 'idiot slave' has your willpower by—the—balls. Now apologize to me."

"I'm sorry."

It's the least sincere apology I've ever heard.

I shift my weight, the reaction pulling a groan from him.

Definitely in hate-bang territory with this one.

"What are you sorry for?"

He glowers at me. "Absolutely nothing, you cock-sucking whore."

My claws sharpen, and my back pricks where my wings want to manifest.

Why do men like this always revert to these insults? It's embarrassingly predictable.

"You'll pay for that," I say quietly. "After you give me what I want, you'll pay for that." I lean in to speak near his ear. "Perhaps I'll call upon this entire room to insult you. I could make you smile as they called you the worst sort of names. And once it was over, I'd have you get on your knees and kiss their feet and beg for more insults.

"Do you think your subjects would question your authority after that? Because I think they would," I say.

"Or," I continue, "if that seems too tame for you, I could simply command you to degrade yourself in front of all these fae.

"Anything I wanted you to do—and I do mean *anything*—you would have to do." I cast my gaze about the room. "I bet I wouldn't even have to ask them to laugh at you; this crowd seems as though they would do that all on their own."

These are all empty threats, but I'm sure they're enough to guarantee his cooperation.

Typhus's borrowed magic seeps into the air around us, the most obvious indicator that behind his frozen exterior is a firestorm of anger.

Someone is really unused to being at the bottom of a power dynamic.

I pat his cheek patronizingly. "Now be a good boy, and let's cooperate for a change." My hand drops to one of his necklaces, and I finger a small bone. "You said the shadow retrieved Galleghar. What was Galleghar doing while this was happening?"

"Walking." He says this so derisively, like there's no other way a previously dead body could leave a tomb. After a brief pause, he adds, "My reports said he walked out of the tomb alongside a shadow."

So Galleghar lay undying in his tomb until one night a shadow came and presumably awakened him. Then the two skipped off into the night, and the rest of us were none the wiser.

"Good," I say absently, patting his cheek once more. "Good."

I begin to climb off Typhus's lap, my thoughts racing ahead to sleeping bodies and shadows, when I pause. "Oh, I almost forgot. There was one more thing." I sit back down on the king's lap, cocking my head to the side. He doesn't know it yet, but this is how a bird sizes up a particularly juicy worm.

"How is it you're so strong?" I ask, my skin still glowing, my voice still harmonizing. I'm burning through magic like I'm a sorority girl throwing back tequila in Cabo.

"I already told you," he says between gritted teeth, "I am co-bound to my subjects."

"How does one...*co-bind* themselves to another?" I

glance over at Des, who's beginning to pose frozen fairies like they're Christmas reindeer, each position a little more compromising than the last.

I face forward again, just as Typhus replies, "Say a short oath, exchange a little bodily fluid, and briefly embrace— that's all it takes."

"All it takes for fairies to what, give you their power?"

"If that's the oath they've sworn."

"And all these fairies just happily gave you their magic?" It's hard even voicing such a ridiculous question.

"They don't just *give* me it."

It sounds like I've come close to ruffling this king's feathers. Poor little Typhus, getting accused is the *worst*.

"That's right," I say slowly, "you offer them protection in return—and I'm guessing a place to stay in your underground city. How magnanimous of you."

The air thickens with Typhus's magic.

Definitely hit a sore spot. His eyes no longer look just angry; they seem wild with panic.

Right now, he can only answer my questions, and I'm curious to see what's going on behind those eyes.

"What is it, Typhus?"

"Fairies die out here all the time."

"And I bet you have *nothing* to do with that."

Again, he looks desperate to explain himself. Too bad we're not playing this game by his rules.

We're playing it by mine.

"Do you or the fae who work for you have anything to do with the deaths of the fairies who 'die out here all the time'?" I ask, throwing his words back at him.

The panic in his eyes increases.

You made your shitty-ass bed, buddy. Now you have to lie in it.

109

Typhus holds out on responding for a whopping three seconds. "*Sometimes*," he finally hisses.

We're not talking loudly, but his words still echo throughout the room.

I swear the silence somehow just gained claws and teeth.

I lean a little closer and drop my voice. "Remember when I told you you'd pay for your words?"

He glares at me. The fucker remembers.

I swivel around. "Every fae in this room can now move their necks."

As soon as the words are spoken, the crowd of fairies focuses their attention on us.

I rotate to Typhus once more. He still can't move, but he's beginning to sweat, little beads of perspiration giving his skin a sheen.

He knows what's coming. How delightful! I do savor how they squirm in the end.

I step off him and face the room, raising my voice so everyone can hear. "You, Typhus Henbane, are going to confess to this entire room every single thing you don't want them to hear, starting with your true intentions for taking their power," I order.

His face is turning red, and he's grinding his teeth in a hopeless attempt to stop the inevitable.

"I...I..." Typhus tries to stall, until the confession is yanked from his lips. "I spent the last century and a half coming up with ways to manipulate fairies out of their powers, using whatever means I could. I—I did this so I could stay healthy and strong in this place. I trade magic for my protection even though I'm the worst thing fae have to fear out here."

He takes a breath. "I've killed hundreds, maybe thousands

110

of fairies—some outright, and some indirectly after I drained them of too much magic. I have a hidden room filled with countless fairies who are all but dead."

An unbidden shiver moves through me.

Sounds like the Thief of Souls.

He continues, "I try to keep them alive for as long as possible—"

"Why?" I interject.

"Once a fairy dies, the bond is broken, and Typhus loses their power," Des says from where he stands. "Dead men can't uphold oaths."

Typhus explains the same thing, forced by my glamour to answer my question. Once he finishes, he pauses, ever hopeful that he can skirt around my *other* order—the one where he confesses his crimes.

I raise my eyebrows, amused.

Around me, fairies flash him venomous glares. Poor little Typhus.

With a shudder, he continues, "I have blackmailed men and women into having sex with me. I've lied about how strong I really am—I cannot single-handedly stop an uprising, should one happen…"

On and on it goes.

It takes twenty minutes—twenty incriminating minutes—for Typhus to get through the impressively long list of shitty things he's done. By the end of those twenty minutes, you can feel the room silently baying for his blood.

Hell, after hearing his laundry list of dirty deeds, *I* want to rip his throat out.

This king knows it too. He's now openly sweating; it drips into his eyes and down his chin. Gone is his cockiness. I wonder how long it's been since he's felt this kind of fear.

"Apologize to all these fairies," I command Typhus. "Apologize and *mean* it."

His eyes move to the crowd. "I'm sorry for everything I've done." His voice is low and hollow with something like guilt. It's not regret, but whatever. Some people never do regret their choices, only where their choices landed them.

I walk around the throne, my skin still glowing, high as fuck off my power. I still wear his crown on my head, and I'll admit, the weight of it gives me a little rush.

When my gaze meets Typhus's, the devil is in his eyes.

"All right," I say, "enough of this." I use my sweet, cajoling voice, and the king seems to relax at the sound of it.

I can practically hear his thoughts—*almost over.*

"Oh," I say in mock surprise, "did you think I was through with you? Oh, Typhus, no, no, no." I'm shaking my head, my voice pitying.

Through my connection, I feel a whisper of Des. The sensation is so faint that it's hard to place what emotion of his slipped across our bond, but if I had to guess, I'd say it was awe. And I realize this is the first time he's truly seen me use my magic in this way. Stopping the sleeping soldiers was one thing, but playing with a man's free will? Toying with him and drawing it out as I savor the kill?

This is new territory for him. And judging by his reaction, my twisted king approves.

"No one in this room is leaving without their powers," I say.

In response, Typhus's face goes red, and another wave of his power fills the air. He's still bound by my glamour, however, only to answer my questions.

I watch him for several seconds, letting his mighty

magic fight mine. It's useless. I have absolute control over him right now.

But I will indulge him.

"Go ahead," I say, "tell me what's on your mind."

"What you're asking for is impossible!" he gasps. "I would have to break every single oath; some fairies aren't even conscious enough to agree to that."

My voice goes ice cold. "Or they could simply kill you. Dead men, after all, can't uphold oaths." I stare down Typhus, every bit the heartless creature our lore has made me out to be. "I'm sure the lot of you will figure something out."

I back up from him, a nefarious smile spreading across my face. "Typhus Henbane," I say, my skin lit, my glamour thickening the air, "I command you to return every single bit of magic you've stolen within two days' time." Much longer than that, and my glamour might wear off.

Typhus looks like I've brought an axe down upon his neck.

I'm not even done.

"You will never again exchange power for your betterment." My eyes flick around us. "May your people have mercy upon you."

I walk away from him toward Des, my footsteps echoing throughout the throne room. I touch the crown that still perches on my head and pause. I swivel one last time to face Typhus.

"Oh, and I'm keeping this."

CHAPTER 13

Water—check, dark room—check, forehead massage—check.

I've done everything within my (limited) power to kick this migraine in the nuts. Nothing's working.

I rub my temples yet again, my head pounding. "Why does everything hurt so much?" I whine. My tongue feels swollen, and my lips, parched. Even my teeth seem to ache.

Desmond comes over to where I stand in his chambers. Around us, the soft lamplight has been dimmed to the point of near darkness. It's still not enough. "It's one of the unwelcome side effects of visiting the Banished Lands."

He holds out his closed hand. His fingers unfurl, revealing what looks like a piece of candy, if candy were iridescent. "This might help more than the massage."

"What is it?" I take the strange lozenge from his palm.

"Believe it or not, fairies have medicine, just like humans do."

I let out a laugh. "This is fae aspirin?"

"Close enough," he says.

"What do you want in return?" I ask, placing the pill on my tongue. I mean, this migraine is bad enough that I'd happily sell the Bargainer one of my appendages for it…but I do still want to know what it'll cost me.

For a moment, the avarice in his expression falls away, and he looks a little sad. "Callie, you don't owe me. Not for something like this. I'm…sorry I gave you that impression."

My features soften. "Thank you—for the magical aspirin." I say it with a lisp as the pill sits between my tongue and my teeth.

It's not bitter like human medicine, nor is it sweet like the hard candy it looks like. Instead, it tastes like honeysuckle melting on my tongue.

Des kisses my forehead, and then his eyes drift up. He touches the crown I'm still wearing. "And here I thought you didn't want to be a queen," he says, eyeing the thing.

I reach for it possessively. "It's my war prize." Even if it looks like something a drunk wombat made.

"I must admit, you are delightfully cruel when you want to be."

I was "someone's nightmare" before, and now I'm "delightfully cruel." I should be mortified by these compliments, and maybe the socially acceptable part of me is, but the part of me that wants to feast on men's hearts and bathe in their dying breaths is covetously collecting them, one by one.

Des's gaze is heavy and hungry when it drops to me. "Do you take war prizes from all your victims?"

I shiver a little. "They're not my victims."

"Hmm."

"They're *not*."

"Will you answer the question?"

I take the crown off my head and study it. It truly is ugly.

"Only the really bad ones," I say. "The ones who like to break people." They're the ones I enjoy twisting to my every whim. "I take mementos from them."

Back at my house, I have a box full of mementos I've lifted over the years. On particularly bad days, days when not even Johnnie or Jack or Jose could numb my pain away, I'd steal away to my guest room, where I kept that box, and I'd sit there for hours, taking out item after item, holding each in my palm. And I would remember how I broke a few of the great villains of the world.

If my confession freaks Des out, he doesn't show it. In fact, his expression is hungrier. The fae side of him is positively delighted to hear this perversion of mine.

"I...learned about that box one of the times I visited your house," Des admits.

I wrinkle my brow. He knew? I think I'm alarmed.

"Then why did you ask?" I say.

Des backs me up, directing me with his body to his chamber's balcony. "I wanted to hear you say it."

Behind me, the cool evening breeze stirs my hair. I turn and step outside, my skin pebbling.

Unlike the Banished Lands, Somnia is awash in magic. It radiates from every night-blooming flower, every pixie zipping around like a gust of wind. It laces each decadent cloud plume, and it drips like rain from the heavens. And now I'm a part of it, from my fae magic to the bond that connects me to this white-haired king.

I stare at Des as I take a seat on the stone floor of the balcony.

He has no idea just how in love with him I am. It would be impossible for him to understand.

I must be making a strange face, because he says, "What is it, cherub?"

This is the point in the conversation where we barter for secrets. He gives me something I want, and I confess some coveted truth. Our typical give-and-take.

I remember Des's sad eyes. *Callie, you don't owe me. Not for something like this.*

He doesn't owe me for something like this either.

I shake my head. "I love you so much. You'll never really know."

His features sharpen, and the look in his eyes intensifies. "The way fairies love… It's the same way we live. It's immortal, violent, irrational, and unbendable.

"I understand your words, cherub, because there are aspects of my love for you that are, simply put, *unfathomable.*"

My heart gallops as we stare at each other, our connection singing to me. I can feel Des beneath my sternum, even as I stare at him. He's always in me, always part of me. It's the uncanniest sensation.

Never breaking eye contact, Des lifts a hand. From deep in his chambers, a bottle of something pink and bubbly floats into his open palm. A few seconds later, two elaborate flutes slip into his other hand.

The Bargainer settles himself next to me, his back leaning against the wall. He sets the items down, and then the bottle uncorks itself and pours.

"What's the occasion?" I ask, watching the rosy liquid foam as it fills the flutes.

"My soul mate survived a day in the Banished Lands— and managed to walk away with the kingdom's crown. I'd say that's an occasion worth celebrating."

Even though a tiny part of me continues to fear we're

playing into the Thief's hands, warmth still blooms low in my stomach. Warmth that feels a lot like happy, stupid love—and maybe a little pride too. I helped chip away at the mystery of Galleghar's awakening.

When the champagne flutes are filled, one floats over to me.

I take it and peer at the drink. "This is safe to drink, right?" I ask. "It isn't like the rosé version of lilac wine?"

"You caught me, love. I'm hoping to grow you a set of pointy ears," Des says, taking his own glass.

I stare down at my drink, swirl it, and wonder if I should drink it after having a migraine then a magical pill with who knows what side effects.

Des doesn't look over at me when he says, "I wouldn't let you drink that if I thought I was putting you at risk."

I glance sharply at him. "H—"

"Please tell me you're not asking how I knew that. I'm not entirely sure my ego would recover from that sort of slight."

Heaven forbid I wonder how Des knows an unknowable thing.

"Your ego could probably use being knocked down a peg or two," I say.

He presses a finger to my mouth. "Shhh, cherub. You don't know what you're talking about."

I nip at his finger. In response, Des's eyes become like sultry little sluts.

"Fae wine doesn't interact with the body quite the same way human wine does," he says distractedly. "Now do that again."

If I do *that* again, I'll be in serious threat of turning this into a bangfest (which is always fun). Right now, I kind of just want to savor this thing between us. It's our friendship aged by eight years—with a little bit of sex thrown in.

I draw his finger away and bring the wine to my mouth. "So."

"So," he repeats, his gaze trained to my lips.

He's excruciating to look at, with his pale eyes and even paler hair. If I keep drinking him in, I'm going to cave and let him carry me inside so I can have my way with him.

I gather my legs to me and look out over his kingdom, desperate to hold on to this moment.

"I never thought I'd be here," I say before taking a steadying breath as my gaze sweeps over Somnia. "All those years ago. I mean, I always hoped you'd take me, but I never really thought I'd be here one day."

Des's gaze falls heavy on me. *I did*, it seems to say.

After several moments, he turns his attention to the night. "I never imagined it would be under these circumstances."

My wing roots prick at his words, drawing my attention away from the ominous note in his voice to the fact that I am a part of this world, with all its horror and injustice, and I fit in here as I never have on earth. I have scales and wings and claws and fae power running through my veins. I feel... suitably magical for this place.

"Think Typhus is still alive?" I ask, changing the subject.

The Bargainer huffs out a laugh. "Unlikely."

Is that a pang of guilt I feel?

"Callie, don't feel bad for the man."

I make a face into my wine (the shit is super good). "Ugh, you're like a mind reader tonight."

"I'm serious."

"That's easy for you to say. You've been making people disappear for decades." I've seen it firsthand.

Des looks at me like I'm cute and odd and exasperating all at the same time. "Have you forgotten all the terrible things that the fairy admitted to?"

Things like rape and coercion and murder and twenty minutes of other terrible deeds.

I take a drink and shake my head.

"And you still feel bad?"

Nod. The rim of the champagne flute rattles between my teeth as I play with it. "No—yes. Maybe?"

I killed fairies only a couple of nights ago; dooming a man to death doesn't top that. So it's ridiculous to feel bad for this when I haven't shed a tear for the poor souls I killed not so long ago…

I don't know why I feel this way. Nothing makes much sense anymore.

Des leans his head against the wall, staring up at the stars. "The devil is in the details, you know. Those teeth and bones Typhus wore, he took each of them from his victims—some while they were still living, some shortly after they died."

If that's supposed to make me feel better, it doesn't. My soul mate has pulled plenty of teeth of his own. He's a bad man too. It doesn't make him deserving of death—at least not in my book.

"And all that borrowed magic?" Des continues. "The process is called co-binding, and though Typhus made it sound cavalier and impersonal, it's not like that," Des says.

I stare down at my fae wine. "Then how is it?"

"Remember those horcruxes in Harry Potter?"

I begin to smile in spite of myself. "Are you seriously dropping an HP reference right here, right now?" I ask, glancing over at Des.

"I have your undivided attention, don't I?"

"And all my love."

I mean, I knew he was soul mate material before, but this pretty much just sealed the deal.

Des's face grows serious. "Essentially, when you exchange magic, you're transferring more than raw energy. You're moving a piece of yourself as well."

That's massively creepy.

"It's not to be taken lightly. Most fairies, if they decide to do to such a thing, spend centuries picking out the right individual—even then, it's a tricky business. Lovers quarrel, families divide, friends deceive. It happens. You can never fully guarantee the person you share magic with will always be your ally.

"For a fairy to give away their power to a stranger—and in the Banished Lands, where the earth itself drains away a fairy's magic shockingly fast—such an exchange is akin to suicide.

"Typhus did that to everyone there. By forcing him to return the magic he coerced from those fairies, you helped right a wrong."

I take a ponderous sip of my wine. "Have you ever done it?" I ask. "Have you ever...co-bound yourself to someone?"

The Bargainer gives me a look that should melt the panties from my body. "I bound myself to my soul mate. Would you say that counts?"

I smile into my drink. "Are you admitting I have a piece of your soul?"

His eyes dip to my curving lips. "More than a piece, cherub."

"Hey, babe, have a nice trip?" Temper asks the next day when she waltzes into the library where Des and I have spent the morning.

As soon as she enters, a dozen different paintbrushes drift away from the enormous canvas Des is working on. He's not nearly finished with it, but I already know what image he's bringing to life. There's the Flora Kingdom's ballroom, decorated with a thousand blooming plants, and in the center of it all, there I am, my black wings folded behind me, my hair twinkling with the night sky. I'm looking directly out at the viewer, my dark eyes troubled and impish all at once.

He's capturing the night he put the stars in my hair.

I don't tell the Bargainer that I get a little thrill looking at the painting, that for once I feel like I belong somewhere.

"It was interesting," I say, taking a sip from my mug of coffee. "Have fun in my absence?"

"I got by," Temper says, her fingers running over a nearby shelf of books. "I went back to that tailor to get more fae outfits." She smooths a hand down her front, and holy shit, why am I only now noticing what she's wearing?

The gown—yes, my best friend chose to put on a gown before noon—looks like woven rainwater, each individual droplet glistening as she moves. Cascading down the skirt are what look like water lilies, the flowers artfully placed so they hide all her incriminating bits. The neckline of the dress plunges down to her navel.

It's extra as fuck.

"Did you threaten the tailor again?" I ask. Last time we'd gotten fitted for outfits, she'd been a little huffy.

Temper clears her throat. "I call it *incentivizing.*"

Oh geez.

Temper's eyes move to the painting, and she whistles. "Desmond, I didn't know you painted."

He lifts a shoulder. "When I'm restless."

Malaki comes in right then, his imposing frame filling the doorway. Immediately, my eyes home in on the hickeys ringing his neck. He could've removed them—it would only take a pinch of magic—and yet there they are. In fact, not only did Malaki *not* remove the hickeys, he's also pulled his hair into one of those little buns, further displaying them.

Someone should tell him hickeys were only cool in middle school.

When Temper catches me staring, she waggles her eyebrows.

I bite my lower lip to keep my laugh in check. Joke's on her because every day she strings this fairy along, he's less likely to let her slip through his clutches. And Temper does *not* do commitment.

"So?" Malaki says, taking a seat next to Des, his bronze eye patch catching the light. "How was your visit to the Banished Lands?"

Temper sits next to me. The sleeve of her dress brushes against my arm, dampening a patch of my clothes.

"All the tomb's enchantments are still in place, there's no sign of forced entry, and yet the body is gone," Des says.

I suppress a shiver at the memory of that empty tomb. For the past month, Galleghar Nyx has been gallivanting about.

"How is that possible?" Malaki asks.

Des rolls a paintbrush between his fingers. "The best information we got was that a shadow retrieved him."

Malaki's brows furrow. "A *shadow*? Is this the Thief we're dealing with?"

"Probably," I say.

He curses. "Of course, the two worst fairies in the world have decided to team up." He shakes his head and rubs a hand over his eye. "How the hell did this happen?"

"Fuck if I know," Des says, throwing the paintbrush aside. "Are you in the mood for a bit of reconnaissance?"

Malaki's face is grim. "This has to do with your asshole father?"

Des inclines his head.

The general's eye glitters. "I'd love nothing more." His scarred face and eye patch look a little sinister in the light.

The Bargainer smiles. "Good. I'd like you to meet with some of our old connections back on Barbos. Tell them the dead king has risen, and anyone who has knowledge of his whereabouts will be handsomely compensated."

"And if someone can lead me to him?" Malaki asks.

"Report back to me first. I don't want to chance losing him. Oh, and by the way"—Des's eyes land on Temper—"be discreet."

"Why are you looking at me?" Temper's voice rises.

The Bargainer arches an eyebrow.

"I'm as discreet as they come," she says.

I'm trying really, really hard not to laugh, but the struggle is *real*.

Malaki manages a sharp nod. "We will be discreet," he assures Des.

The sorceress blows out a breath. "I am *not* the problem." She turns on Malaki. "And *you* don't need to go making promises for me. I never even said I was coming along."

"And you don't need to." The Bargainer stands. "But if you imagined staying behind so you could have fun with Callie, then you'll be sorely disappointed. The future

Night Queen has official business that will take her away from the palace."

It takes me a second to realize Des is referring to me.

"Wait," I say, "I haven't agreed to be queen."

"Yeah," Temper agrees, "Callie hasn't agreed—*what?*" She turns on me. "Have you lost your mind? Take that crown, then wear it like it's your birthright."

Ignoring Temper, Des turns his gaze to me, his features sharp. "I apologize, the Night King's *consort* has official business that will take her away from the palace."

I narrow my eyes at my mate. I might not have jumped on board with this whole queen business, but I sure as hell don't want to be known simply as someone else's *consort*.

Temper laughs gleefully. "Oh, you better sleep with one eye open, Desmond. I've seen this girl make men pay for less."

He's still staring intensely at me. "That's odd. For as long as I've known Callie, she's the one who's *paid* for my services. I admit, it'll be nice to owe her for a change."

Temper snickers, appraising Des all over again. "Screw what I said about keeping one eye open. You better not close your eyes at all."

I shake my head at Des as I stand, my eyes still narrowed. "It's time to go."

We give curt goodbyes to Temper and Malaki, then slip out of the library.

"You do realize how close you were to getting glamoured, don't you?" I say as we head down the hallway.

Des seems to be laughing at me with his eyes. "You say that like I'd mind."

Most men do. Then again, Des isn't most men.

"So what is this official business?" I say, changing the subject.

The Bargainer's face turns grim. "Now that the kingdoms of Flora and Fauna have fallen, the Day Kingdom is our one remaining ally. You and I are going to pay them a visit."

CHAPTER 14

I smell the bodies before I see them.

Des and I have barely stepped off the ley line and entered the Kingdom of Day when the scent of burnt flesh assaults me.

I don't know what I was expecting from the Day Kingdom when Des told me we would be visiting, but this isn't it.

I shield my eyes against the blindingly bright overhead sun until they adjust to the sight before them.

All around us, the world is on fire. Pyres as large as houses stretch as far as the eyes can see, and they roar as they burn. Thick, oily smoke billows off them, twisting into the air and turning the sky into a reddish haze.

We skirt around them, one by one, the smoke coating my skin. I sweat from the heat wafting off them. It's stifling, suffocating.

Around us, the flames reach high into the sky, as though trying to touch the very sun itself. As blazing as each inferno is, I can still make out the bodies within. There are dozens of them piled on one another, their forms blackened to a crisp. Their uniforms have long burned off, but I don't need to see them to know these are the formerly sleeping soldiers who invaded the Kingdom of Day.

So this is how Des's final ally defeated the enemy. They simply set them all on fire.

My eyes sweep over the landscape again. Des and I have arrived at the edge of a large floating island. Here, where the land gives way to sky, the pyres sit like grim sentinels. Beyond them, I can only make out the hazy outline of a tangle of flora and what appears to be a looming mountain range.

The sun glares down at us through the haze, and on any other day, I'm sure this kingdom is a glorious sight, but right now, the place is like spoiled wine.

Next to me, the Bargainer squints up at the sun, which now burns bloodred through the haze of smoke.

"I've always hated this place," he says. "Too bright for my taste. But this…" He shakes his head. "This makes me wish for those insufferably bright days." He takes my hand, and with that, the two of us head toward the looming mountains.

———————

"We're not walking the entire way, are we?" I glance above us as we pass under a bright green tree, violet flowers growing from its branches. Around us, the vegetation presses in from all sides. I can only see about fifty feet ahead, and it's *all* jungle.

"Cheer up, cherub, you have me as company, and I am an *excellent* conversationalist."

Crap, we are totally walking the entire way. That sucks extra balls when the air smells like a graveyard.

I wince. "The smell might legit kill me first."

Des plucks a deep blue flower from a nearby vine before sliding it behind my ear. "We can't have that," he says.

He leads us to a stairway I almost miss because it blends in with its surroundings so well. It's woven from vines and leaves, and it winds up a tree trunk and ascends high into the air. Once we're level with the tree canopies, the stairway levels, turning into a bridge that sways as we walk along it.

"What's with the bridge?" I ask.

"What about it?" Des asks, disappearing only to reappear yards away at the end of the bridge, arms crossed.

"Ugh, you never 'walk' to the palace, do you? You simply pop into existence there."

Des's eyes twinkle. "Sometimes—okay, *most* of the time, but that's because Janus hates it so much."

Just as I reach him, he disappears, winking into existence farther along the bridge, where it twists between trees.

"Are you going to do this the entire way?" I complain.

"Maybe."

"Well, can you make me disappear with you at least?" I ask, waving away some of the hazy smoke hanging in the air.

"It doesn't work like that—not unless we co-bind our power."

"But I thought that being bonded meant we shared magic." As I speak, I reach down our bond and tug on Des's power.

"We do, cherub, but it doesn't quite work the same way and—" I see his teeth set on edge even as he lets out a little laugh. "You're trying to use my magic."

Can you blame me? I mean, the dude can teleport. I want to do that. The rope bridge is cool and all, but I don't want to *walk*.

I pull on our bond one final time, feeling Des's magic slip into my veins and travel down to my fingertips. For the briefest of moments, the air subtly darkens. Then it dissipates, along with my mate's powers.

"Fine," I say. "I'll stop, but I'm not thrilled to be walking."

"Duly noted."

"We could fly."

"We could," Des agrees, which is fairy speak for *yeah, no.* Since I don't know where our destination precisely is, I'm stuck following his ass. On foot.

Boo.

I toe the woven walkway. "I still don't understand this bridge," I mutter.

I get having bridges when there are rivers and chasms that make walking impossible, but the forest floor looks perfectly fine to walk on. "I mean, if my feet touch the ground, is the earth going to rip apart and swallow me whole?"

"If it has any taste in women, then yes, that would *definitely* happen."

"*Des*," I say, trying not to laugh.

He vanishes before reappearing even farther away.

"Where are you going? I thought you were supposed to be this amazing conversationalist," I complain as I run my hands over the knotted vine railing.

He smirks at me from where he stands five million miles away.

"Or maybe," I say, my skin beginning to glow, "I should just make you walk alongside me—or carry me the entire way."

He raises an eyebrow, his glee obvious. "Is that an order?"

"It depends."

Even with the distance between us, I see him smother

a smile. "My, my, you're awfully bossy for a woman who doesn't want to be queen."

"Walk with me, Des," I say, my voice melodic.

Immediately, the Bargainer appears in front of me, his hands braced on the rope.

I saunter forward, my body swaying. My scales ripple to life along my forearms, and my claws sharpen.

Des backs up, his gaze never leaving mine. "So is this what we're going to do? You glamour me until I submit to you?" His silver eyes gleam, his white hair hanging loose around his face. He looks like the kind of rogue I want to defile and be defiled by.

I catch his shirt before he can back up more, my claws inadvertently shredding it in the process. I reel him in before pressing a kiss to his lips. "*Yes*," I whisper against him.

With that, I release him, my skin gradually fading back to its normal color.

The two of us walk, making our way across the suspended walkway.

I touch my lips, the taste of Des still sharp on my tongue. "Is this feeling between us ever going to go away?" I ask. "In three thousand years or whatever—"

"Cherub," Des interrupts, "where are you getting your information from? Fairies don't live *that* long."

"—is this thing between us one day going to fade?"

The King of Night stops to take my hand, cupping it between his own. Then he backs up, pulling me along with him. "There are certain things in life that fade with time," he says, his gaze locked on mine. "What we have, Callie, isn't one of those things. Our bond will only strengthen over the years."

He pulls me along, the muted sunlight dappling across

his skin. "I will always be here for you—when you turn thirty and when you turn three hundred."

"Don't forget three thousand," I say.

"If you defy the odds and live until then, then so will I." He gives my hand a squeeze, his face getting serious. "I will be with you on your best day, and I will be with you on your worst day. I will be there to hold our children—"

I raise an eyebrow at that.

"We're going to have *many* children," he informs me.

"Oh, are we now?"

"And I will be there for them all. I will be there when the last of your mortal friends draws their final breath. I will be there through it all, and I will tease you and infuriate you and lavish you with whatever it is your heart desires because the only thing mine desires is you."

I give him a shaky smile, trying not to show just how deeply his words have moved me. "Yay," I say.

Lamest response ever.

Only rather than cringe, Des laughs and steals a kiss from me. "And now I'll walk by your side the rest of the way because I finally, *finally* goaded you into being naughty and using your glamour."

That was him *goading* me?

He gives my knuckles a kiss, then releases my hand so he can walk in front of me. The two of us are silent for a ways after that.

At some point, I hear the thud of footfalls—lots and lots of footfalls. In the distance, trees shake violently, and for a moment, I'm back in Mara's oak forest, watching the trees writhe and split open.

The memory dissolves as the Day soldiers come into view, their golden armor glinting as they storm toward us.

Des steps in front of me, his wings flaring behind him. They stretch wide, the razor-sharp talons looking particularly menacing.

The Day soldiers close in on us, their swords brandished.

Jesus. Their motto might as well be Slash First, Ask Questions Later.

Des crosses his arms. "*This* is the welcome you give your kingdom's last remaining ally?" He clicks his tongue. "Janus *did* inform you he was expecting a visit from the Kingdom of Night?"

The soldiers' weapons lower just a fraction, but they're still eyeing the two of us—particularly me—with suspicion.

"Where is your retinue?" one of them demands.

"Recovering from battle," Des says. "I thought it wise not to bring more soldiers to your doorstep, seeing as how... *warmly* your kingdom welcomed the last batch that visited."

Even here I catch whiffs of those blazing pyres.

The soldiers begrudgingly lower their weapons the rest of the way, and one begins to speak. "By decree of the King of Day, Lord of Passages, King of Order, Truth Teller, and Bringer of Light, Janus Soleil of the Isles of Light, you are now in this kingdom's custody until such a time as His Majesty—"

"I don't think so," Des cuts in. "You'll treat us as the royal guests we are, or we leave. It's as simple as that." His wings fold behind his back. "Now, you all don't want to be responsible for derailing these talks, do you?"

When the soldier doesn't respond, another one muscles his way to the front.

"Please, Your Highness, we're sorry for the misunderstanding. Our good king is eager to meet with you. This way, please."

And with that, we resume our trek.

It takes an annoyingly long time to get to the palace. I mean, the walk is scenic and all, the forest lush with life, the ground sprinkled with glittering pools and rippling creeks and blah, blah, blah—lots of pretty shit. But it's still a stupidly long walk, and now that Des and I have five billion guards hemming us in, our conversation is next to nonexistent.

To be fair, I *have* been entertained. Des has spent most of the past hour plaiting one guard's hair into at least fifty braids—he hasn't yet noticed—and moving branches into another guard's way.

"Motherfucking trees," the fairy mutters under his breath. "I swear they're moving in my way."

"Lay off the spirits, Sythus," another says.

Ahead of us the forest parts, and—

My God.

The palace rises like a golden mountain from the jungle. The Day King's castle is brilliant, blinding gold. Just as staggering is the waterfall that cuts straight through it, plunging into a basin hidden by scores of other buildings that cluster around the palace.

"Wow," I breathe.

One of the soldiers smiles at me. "Welcome to Avalon."

CHAPTER 15

For all the Day Kingdom's opulence, Avalon is a ghost town. The city streets are all but abandoned, though there's still the lingering unholy scent of dark magic. But there are no bodies and no blood—the unpleasantries of battle have been moved to the outskirts of the island.

Even when we enter, the castle proper seems abandoned, our footsteps echoing in the cavernous space.

I glance around, looking for servants, aides, nobles, soldiers—*anyone*—but we're seemingly alone.

Our group enters a grand ballroom, the air touched with the lingering smell of blood and burnt magic. I glance up just as a shadow leaps from the golden banister high above us before swooping down in front of me and Des.

The fairy lands hard, a fist to the ground. The wings at his back are unfurled, his white feathers tinged with gold. He looks the angel to Des's devil.

It's only once he lifts his head that I realize I'm staring into the face of Janus Soleil, the King of Day.

His hair shimmers, and his bright blue eyes shine like sapphire. It would be easy to confuse the Day King for an angel. He's everything the paintings have made angels out to be.

His pointed ears are the only tell that he's something else entirely. Well, that and the hard, cunning gleam in his eyes.

Janus doesn't have blood on him, but I would stake money that he killed dozens of those burning soldiers.

The Day King's expression eases. "Desmond Flynn, I've been eagerly awaiting your arrival." His eyes move to me. "Callypso," he says, his eyes guarded as he nods at me, "good to see you again."

His cool reception reminds me that not so long ago, I accused him of kidnapping me.

Janus had a twin, a twin who died. The first time you met him, you were really meeting me.

It was the Thief who'd captured me after all, the Thief who wore the face of Julios when he snatched me from Des's backyard.

The Green Man had been dead when the Thief wore his body. Julios had been dead when the Thief wore *his* body. And that redheaded soldier, the one I interviewed, she had mentioned being lured away by her dead brother.

Holy *shit*.

I sway a little as a pattern forms.

"Callie." Des's voice cuts through the screaming in my head.

My eyes move to him.

"What is it?" he asks softly.

My eyes move from his to Janus's. "The Thief of Souls can wear the faces of the dead."

The three of us find a secluded place to talk—correction: more secluded. Honestly, the whole thing seems unnecessary. There's no one left in the palace to eavesdrop.

We don't end up striking a conversation again until we're securely in the Day King's private quarters. By then Janus's wings are put away, but his fierce expression remains.

As for what he or Des thinks about my little revelation, it's hard to say. Neither of them *looks* surprised, but then again, fairies seem to have good poker faces. But if I assumed we were going to talk about it in private, then I assumed wrong. Neither king broaches the subject again.

I mean, I know I'm no Sherlock Holmes (don't tell my clients that), but this is something, right? Right?

Janus ushers us to a cluster of chairs. Resting between the seats is a small table with a decanter and a set of glasses.

Well, at least there's booze.

I take a seat, my attention drifting to a vivid mural on the wall to my left. Half the image is painted in gold, the other in black. On one side is a golden man, rays of light emanating from his body; he holds his kneeling enemy by the throat. The captured man wears shackles on his wrists and ankles, and everything beyond his pale form is painted in the inkiest of blacks.

"Do you like it?" Janus asks, sitting across from me. He reaches for the decanter between us before pouring the liquid into three glasses.

I stare at the mural. What am I supposed to say? That the painting is just something to look at? That the most fascinating thing about it is the cute little loincloth each man wears?

That would go over super well.

"Uh, yeah," I say.

"It's called *The Banishment of Euribios*," Janus says, handing me a glass filled with emerald liquid. He hands another to Des. "It depicts the fight between Brennus, the God of Light and Order, and Euribios, the God of Darkness and Chaos."

There's a beat of silence, then—

"I thought Fierion and Nyxos were the gods of light and dark?" I say.

Janus pours himself a glass of the same liquor. "Fierion and Nyxos came later, after the Otherworld was formed. These were protogods—the ones creation was born from," he says, turning his gaze to the wall. "This captures the moment Brennus defeated his foe and banished him to the far corner of the universe. This is the moment the Otherworld came to be."

I tap my finger against my glass. "What about the Mother and the Father?"

"They too came later. They were the children of these first gods."

"This is all vastly fascinating," Des cuts in, "but perhaps we can get to the point of the visit?" He lounges in his seat, glass in hand, his legs splayed.

Janus drags his attention from the mural. "Do my stories bore you, Night King?"

"Yes," Des says flatly.

The corner of Janus's mouth lifts. "Fine. On to the bloody battle."

"I saw you dealt with your enemies the old-fashioned way," the King of Night says, bringing the dark green liquor to his lips.

The Day King raises an eyebrow. "I hear yours are still living." He leans forward. "Tell me, Flynn, how did you manage that?"

Des moves his eyes to me, a hint of a devilish smile on his face. "*I* didn't."

Janus follows his gaze. "Your human stopped an army?" Only now does the Day King truly study me. "Pray tell, how did *that* happen?"

I narrow my eyes. Fairies as a whole think humans are beneath them. Even though I'm a siren and now a fae one at that, in many fairy's eyes, I will always be a coarse mortal.

"Cherub, perhaps you can give Janus a demonstration?"

I hesitate. I don't know what the penalty for glamouring a king is, but back on earth, that shit was a no-no.

Janus takes a sip of his drink, watching me over the rim. "Seems your mate is not up to the task," he goads.

You know what? *Fine.*

I set my drink aside and uncross my legs, rolling my shoulders back and letting the siren wake.

She stretches out like a cat basking in the sun. My scales ripple to life along my forearms, and my wings itch to manifest.

As soon as my skin brightens, Janus sits a little straighter, his gaze drawn to me.

I rise to my feet, power rippling through my veins. "The great Day King," I say, my voice harmonizing. "So very cocky. Stand for me."

Janus's brows furrow as he rises to his feet. "What are you doing?"

I step up to him, taking his drink from his hand and tossing it aside. The glass shatters against the mural, spraying emerald liquid everywhere. "Giving you my demonstration," I say. "That is what you wanted from me, isn't it?"

"Yes," he says softly, quizzically. His gaze is pinned to mine.

I can sense his rising magic. It thickens the air, smelling like sandalwood and blazing like the sun.

There's one thing fairies exert particular control and restraint over. One thing that will truly prove my power.

"Show me your wings, Janus."

For a moment, nothing happens. The Day King continues to stare at me with spellbound eyes. Then he frowns and staggers a half step.

Next to me, Des sips his drink, a delighted expression on his face.

"How are you—?" Janus groans. As he bends forward, his wings burst from his back, the gold-tipped feathers shimmering.

When he glances at me next, he no longer looks dazzled. Nope, the Day King is P-I-S-S-E-D.

He stumbles toward me, his expression murderous. "How dare you—?"

"Stop," I say.

He freezes. "This is—"

"What I do," I say. I step in close as he flashes me a hateful look. "I am a siren. I glamour people—and now, thanks to the lilac wine Des gave me, I can glamour fairies as well.

"I can glamour *you*." My eyes drop to his lips. "It doesn't matter that you're a king or a powerful fairy. Even you can fall under my thrall."

He frowns at me.

"This is how I stopped an army without killing them all."

"Now," I say, "tell me truthfully: If I release you from my glamour, will you attack me?"

For several seconds, Janus works his jaw, a muscle in his cheek feathering. Finally, he says, "No."

I back up. "Too bad." I pout. "It's so much fun when my victims put up a fight."

Janus has reverted to looking at me with curiosity and no little amount of want.

I sit back down and grab my tumbler. "Is this safe to drink?" I ask, pointing to my glass.

"Yes."

"Oh good." I take a sip. "I release you from my glamour."

Janus staggers back a step. "Gods above." Hastily, his wings disappear. "That was…"

"Horribly invasive," Des says. "I know. Isn't my mate exquisite?"

Janus takes a seat, waving his hand. His shattered glass stitches itself back together, the liquid reforming in the tumbler. It floats back into his hand, and he takes a long drink.

"I could have you thrown in the gallows for what you just did," he says contemplatively.

The room darkens a touch.

"Is that a threat?" Des says, his voice calm. "It sounds awfully close to one."

"How do you even live with such a creature?" Janus asks, his gaze sliding back to me. Despite how shaken he is, he looks halfway interested.

I smile, baring my teeth at him.

"I try not to piss her off."

I guffaw at that, my skin dimming.

"All right," the Bargainer concedes, "I *do* try to piss her off, but only because she has especially twisted ideas of revenge."

Janus shakes his head. "You two are a fucked-up pair."

CHAPTER 16

We spend a painful number of hours sitting in that room, going over the battles that occurred in each respective kingdom. And just when I think we're about ready to wrap things up, we recap things all over again. And again.

In the countless hours that have passed (there's no sense of time here, just endless midday sun glaring down on the palace), I've managed to throw back an alarming amount of that emerald alcohol.

"Well, I think that's it for now," Janus says, rising to his feet. He looks at me with laughing eyes.

I give him a quizzical look, then turn to Des, who's biting back a grin as he stands.

Why do I feel like I've totally missed the joke?

I push out of my chair, staggering, then nearly falling.

Whoo. Too much alchy. Act normal.

"Cherub?" Des asks, grasping my forearm.

"Hmm?"

At least the godforsaken meeting is finally over.

"It's *gods*forsaken here," Janus says. "We have more than one god."

Whoops—I said that out loud?

"You did," Janus says.

Damn it. Shut up, mouth.

Now the Day King's lips twitch.

"I'm still thinking out loud, aren't I?" I say.

"C'mon, baby siren," Des says, escorting me out of the room. "You had fun with that liquor, didn't you?"

Janus calls out from behind us, "Why don't we meet again first thing tomorrow—?"

Ewww, no more *gods*forsaken meetings. Pleaseandthankyou.

"Callypso Lillis, your attendance is optional," he says.

Fuck on a ferry, I'm still thinking out loud.

"Desmond," Janus continues, "you'll both be staying in your usual rooms. I trust you can find your way to them?"

"We can," Des says.

"Good. Then you two have a pleasant evening—and please feel free to use any of the royal amenities while you're here. I'll see you tomorrow."

"Bye-bye," I say over my shoulder, waving to Janus. "Oh, and sorry for insulting you...and glamouring you." Even as I say it, my skin flickers, brightening and dimming at random.

Uh-oh. Just how drunk am I?

"Very," Des says, leading me out into the hallway.

I groan. "Why didn't you stop me from drinking?"

He huffs out a laugh. "I did that once, back in Malibu. Remind me again how well that went over?"

I let out a giggle that ends in a hiccup. "I was *so* mad." Mad enough to throw my entire liquor supply at him.

I lean into Des. "I smell like death. Why do I smell like death?"

"Janus is burning bodies, remember?" As the Bargainer speaks, a small smile pulls at the corners of his lips.

Oh yeah.

I subtly sniff myself again. Ew, I don't just smell like death—I smell like a corpse screwed a trash can and it didn't end well.

Des's lips quirk.

"Did I just say that out loud?"

He glances down at me, his expression mirthful. "You did."

"*Ugh*," I whine. "Why do I keep saying everything I think?"

I mean, my filter isn't the best on any given day, but this is just ridiculous.

"Callie, that dark green alcohol was aelerium liquor—it compels you to tell the truth. Or in your case…tell the world each and every little thought that crosses your mind."

Wait—*what*?

"Why didn't you say anything?"

"I'm sorry, when did I ever give you the impression I was forthcoming with information?"

I lean my forehead against Des's arm and let out another groan.

"How long have I been speaking my mind?"

"Just during the tail end of the meeting."

I don't know what constitutes the tail end of that long-ass discussion, but the longer it dragged on, the more inappropriate my thoughts became.

"So Janus knows I was sweating so much, I was worried I'd leave a butt imprint on his chair?"

"Yep."

"And that I needed to pee really, really badly?"

"Yep."

"And that I wanted to bang you?"

"Now, cherub, that one's just a given."

I howl.

"Why didn't you *say* anything?" I whine as Des leads me through the castle.

"We went over this already."

"You drank it too," I accuse him. "Why aren't you spilling your guts?"

"Because I stopped at one drink."

Unlike me.

"It's a sign of good faith to drink aelerium liquor during times of trouble," Des continues.

It's also a sign of good faith to let your soul mate know she's making an ass out of herself.

"And also," I say before Des has a chance to address that thought of mine, "unrelated but equally important: Why the *fuck* is it so miserably hot here?" I gather up my hair and use it to fan the back of my neck. "Next body of water I see, I'm hopping in. Dead serious."

Des points at a nearby archway. "That way leads to one of the royal bathhouses."

"Oh my God, take me there."

One perk of being inebriated—walking is no longer so hellacious. I mean, that *might* be because halfway to the pool, Des gets tired of me tripping over my own feet and decides to carry me, but what are details?

I lean back in Des's arms and stare up at him.

"Hi."

He glances down at me, his white hair framing his face. "Hi, cherub."

"You're kinda cute," I say.

He raises an eyebrow.

I reach up and trace his lips. "I wouldn't mind having little mini Deses running around. Someday, that is. Not today, but you know, in the future—hey, if I'm *cherub*, what would you call our kids? Is there a name for baby-baby angels?"

"Hmm," he says, assessing me with his bedroom eyes, "I'm sure I'd call them something different, love. Now, eager as I am to have this conversation, I'm not going to make any plans with you until I know you'll be able to remember them."

My head lolls a little. "You want to have baaaabies with me," I sing. "Lots and lots and lots of...baaaabies with me." I kick my legs a little as I say the words, my skin brightening and dimming.

This alcohol is really laying into me now that I'm free of that boring meeting.

I flash the Bargainer a cheesy smile, reaching up to play with his hair.

He gives the ceiling of the bathhouse a long-suffering look. You'd almost think time rewound eight years, back to when I was striking deals...

I sit up a little straighter in his arms. "Hey!" I hiccup. "Let's make a d—"

"No."

"But—"

He quiets me with a kiss. A long, drawn-out kiss that causes my toes to curl and my skin to flare to life. My siren surges through me, and suddenly the kiss has 110 percent of my focus. I wrap a hand around the back of Des's neck and fall into the taste of him.

So damn hot. Him, this room, the kiss, this kingdom in general. All of it.

Before I have a chance to turn the kiss into something deeper, it ends.

I stare up at him. "I still have to pee really, really badly."

He huffs out a laugh. "Callie, the Killer of Moments."

"Hey! You're the Moment Killer."

"Am I now?" he says.

He sounds amused.

"That's because I *am* amused," he replies.

"Ugh, *when* will this alcohol wear off?"

"Probably not for a while—you drank a lot of it."

Awesome.

Des walks us to a door, pushing it open with his body, and then he muscles us into a fancy little bathroom.

The Bargainer sets me down. "I'll be right outside."

"Wait." I catch his arm. "Will you stay in here with me?"

Des tilts his head. "There's no distance with you, is there?" he says. His eyes are totally laughing at me.

"That's a yes, isn't it?"

He sighs. "Can't deny you anything."

Yay!

"Okay, face the door," I say, while I move to the toilet. "I don't want you to see *anything*."

"Heaven forbid I catch sight of my mate's pussy—"

"Des!"

He lifts his hands. "I'm facing the door. Want me to plug my ears too?"

Yes? No? Maybe? "Plug one of them."

Now I definitely hear him laugh.

Once I'm sure he's not looking and only half listening, I lift my filmy skirt and sit—

I let out a very unladylike screech as my ass misses the toilet, and I sprawl on the floor next to it. My skirts are around my head, my unmentionables exposed.

Des turns around. I'll give him this—he doesn't laugh, though I'm sure it's taking everything in him not to.

"*Cherub.*" He comes over and helps me up, then properly sets me on the toilet. He brushes my hair back. "What happened?"

Alcohol happened. That's what.

I cover my face. "I'm so embarrassed."

The Bargainer removes my hands, kissing my knuckles. "At least you didn't start peeing."

I might've.

"Oh. Comment redacted then."

I fucking *hate* aelerium liquor.

———————

By the time the Bathroom Incident We'll Never Talk About Again is behind us, the liquor has worn off somewhat.

Des makes a disbelieving noise at the back of his throat.

All right, it's worn off just a little.

"So little that science doesn't yet have the tools to quantify such a minuscule measurement," Des says.

"Pshhh. Why do you have to be so witty all the time?"

He begins to answer, but I cover his mouth with my hands.

His eyes are still laughing at me. When I'm sure he's not going to say anything else, I remove them.

We round a corner, and the bathhouse pool comes into view. I squeal at the sight of it and skip over, tripping only a couple of times along the way.

I jump into the pool, then sigh when the cool water

slides against my skin. I was half worried the water would be oppressively hot, but it carries the perfect chill.

I linger underwater, my siren perfectly content to stay down here forever. It might not be the ocean, but it's water, and that's good enough.

When I surface, Des sits along the edge of the pool, a knee hiked up. "I'm only letting you swim while inebriated because you're a siren, and I'm ninety-nine percent sure you're incapable of drowning. Please don't prove me wrong."

"Pffft." I swim over to him. "You should come in. The water's nice. I'm even nicer," I say, grabbing his hand and tugging.

"You know, you're unbearably adorable, cherub."

Awwww.

He smiles at me.

I think he can still hear my thoughts.

"I can."

When the Bargainer doesn't slide into the water, I release his hand and sink back beneath the pool's surface. If he's content to just watch me swim, then that works too.

Oh, and neat trick—if I'm underwater, I can't blabber every single thought that crosses my mind. In fact, I'm pretty content to just lie here, at the very bottom of the pool, until the end of time. It's an improvement over the scorching midday heat I can't otherwise seem to escape.

After a minute or so, I rise to the surface once more.

"How long are we supposed to be here?" I ask.

It's already evening, but just as night never lifts from Des's kingdom, the sun never sets in the Day Kingdom.

"Ready to leave so soon?"

Does he sound pleased about that?

I nod.

"We'll leave tomorrow morning, right after I meet with Janus."

So, essentially, we'll leave three days from now, once the meeting ends.

He leans in closer. "Have I mentioned I like your sassy mouth?"

I swim over to him before folding my arms over the edge of the pool. I lean my cheek against them. The cold water is clearing my thoughts a bit.

"You know a lot of secrets," I say, looking up at him.

The corner of the Bargainer's mouth curves up. "I do."

"But you don't know anything about the Thief of Souls."

"I know *some* things," Des says, a pinch defensively.

"Not *that* many."

He presses his lips together, like he's stopping himself from arguing further. Instead, he rolls up his shirtsleeves, giving me a tantalizing glimpse of his tattoos.

Seriously, how is this guy not taking a bath in his own sweat?

"I don't get it—how can you know so much about everything *except* for the mystery surrounding the Thief of Souls?" I ask.

Des glances down at my folded arms. After reaching out, he trails his fingers over the exposed skin. "In order to answer that question, I'd have to tell you how I know so many secrets in the first place."

My brows furrow. "You bargain for them."

"Not…exactly," Des says evasively.

But I thought that was how he built a name for himself.

"I built a name for myself through my deals and my brutality."

Right. That too.

He continues to stroke the skin of my arm.

He's not going to tell me.

Des's fingers stop. He takes a deep breath. "I'll tell you—I *want* to tell you. It's just…" His eyes flick to mine. "The shadows speak to me."

I give him an incredulous look.

The shadows…can *talk*? And Des can hear them?

"Seriously?"

He taps my skin. "Mm-hmm."

Mind officially blown.

I mean, I knew fairies could spin cloth out of moonlight and wear stars in their hair, so this is technically nothing crazier than what I've already seen for myself, but still.

"That is so fucking *cool.*"

A laugh slips out of Des, and he relaxes his shoulders. Apparently, he was nervous about telling me.

"Cherub, I'm never nervous."

Okay, this freaking liquor is really starting to piss me off. Hate being this transparent.

"Tell me more," I say.

"What do you want to know?"

"Everything! I just learned shadows *talk*! That's so creepy-slash-awesome. What do they sound like? Does my shadow talk? Does yours? What do they say? Do they have personalities? I could keep going."

Des moves a wet strand of hair from my eyes. "They sound about how you'd imagine shadows to sound—like whispers—though their voices vary just like human and fae voices do. Your shadow talks. Mine, not so much. They don't really have distinct personalities, but they do have moods. And they say all sorts of things, provided they want to talk to you."

"*Wow*," I say.

I still can't get over the fact my shadow has talked to Des.

"She's told me a lot over the years."

Oh man. Not sure that's a good thing.

"So shadows have genders?"

Des looks painfully reluctant to talk about this. "It depends. Technically, they don't; they're just shadows, but some have more feminine or masculine voices."

Huh.

"Can anyone else hear them?" I ask.

He shifts a little. "Not that I'm aware of."

The Bargainer looks nervous again.

"I'm not nervous."

Oh, wait. I get it. Duh. "You know I think it's incredible that you can do this."

I mean, I guess normally when someone tells you they hear voices, that's your cue to start edging away. But I've been around Des and the impossible world of the fae for so long that learning this isn't some outlandish revelation.

In fact, it explains a lot.

"Thank you, cherub," he says quietly, taking my hand and threading his fingers between mine.

"What happens if the shadows don't want to talk to you?"

"Then they don't talk. But there are ways to cajole them. Sometimes, if I want to know something, I give them a little magic—just enough for them to hop away from their owners for an hour or two. They hate being dragged around." He shakes his head. "I can't believe I'm actually talking about this," he says.

I can't believe I got him to divulge his big bad secret.

"And what happens if you want them to shut up?"

"Same concept—a little magic for their silence."

I glance around me. There aren't many shadows in the Day Kingdom, but they do exist even here.

"Can you get them to talk right now?"

Des's eyes seem to spark with interest. His focus turns to the pool.

After a moment, he says, "Janus's father, Ignis, apparently used to hold orgies in this pool."

"Ewwww."

Des throws back his head and laughs. "Cherub, it's been well over a century since that last happened."

His laughter warms me from the inside out.

I tug on his hand again. "C'mon, let's make these shadows whisper about something else."

He stares at me for a beat. Right when I'm expecting him to shoot me down, his shoes slide off his feet, followed by his socks. He pivots where he sits, his legs swinging around so he can dip his feet in the water.

I step up between those legs and nip his chin, my hands sliding over his thighs.

More, more, more...

Des tilts his head downward. "Do you want to know a secret?"

"Hmm?"

He takes my lips in a kiss. "Sometimes I hold out on you simply because I enjoy driving you mad with need. It makes me feel less out of control from being in love with you."

"That's not nice."

He laughs low. "Whoever said I was nice?"

With that, he slips into the water, plunging beneath the surface. When he rises again, his shirt is slicked to his skin, each fold of it lovingly molding to his chest.

There are no words. He took my breath away the first

time I saw him, and it's no different now. And he still has that devilish look to him, his features a little too sharp. He screams, *Bad news.* Which, of course, is like a rallying cry to my lady parts.

His silver eyes dance.

Still hearing every damn thought that crosses my mind.

"What are the shadows saying now?" I whisper.

Des closes in on me. "They've gone quiet."

"Even mine?"

He stops in front of me, an arm sliding around my waist. "Even yours."

"The Thief of Souls?" I ask as a thought comes to me. "What do the shadows say about him?"

Callie, the Killer of Moments—it really is an apt title right about now.

The Bargainer's good mood withers away. "The shadows won't speak of him."

"Not at all?"

Des frowns. "Not a single thing. Whoever the Thief is, he has either their allegiance…or their fear."

CHAPTER 17

I wake on the ground, my eyes fluttering open.

"Ah, you're awake. I thought you'd lie there all night."

My claws lengthen reflexively at the sound of the Thief's voice, my nails scraping against the stone beneath me.

I went to bed in the Day Kingdom, and I woke…

Here. Wherever here is.

I sit up slowly and gaze around. The room is done in pale stone. Bloodred vines snake up the walls, strange flowers blooming from them. Across from me is a pool of some sort, the water luminous. And, to the left of it, the Thief reclines against a pillar.

A shudder courses through me.

"My, *what* a reaction." His onyx eyes seem to glitter in this strange place. "I take it you missed me."

"Where am I?" I ask, rising to my feet. I can't tell whether I'm inside or outside. Behind me, the walls seem to give way to open air, and the night sky shines down.

But within the walls of this place, sconces burn, the

sound muffled, like cloth snapping in the wind. And among it all is the Thief of Souls, his lips soft, his eyes cold, his attention fixed to me.

This is a dream. Just a dream. But if it's a dream, and I know it's a dream, then—

Wake up.

Wake. Up.

Nothing happens.

"Tell me, does the term *small death* mean anything to you?" the Thief asks from where he leans against that pillar.

It's just a dream. It's not real.

"No," I say, distractedly.

It's only after I answer that I process his words.

Small death. That does sound familiar.

The Thief of Souls smiles. "Come closer, and I'll tell you."

"How did I get here?" I pinch the fabric of the white shift I wear. It's all but translucent.

Not what I went to sleep in.

The Thief pushes off the pillar. "I called and you came."

I knit my brows.

His hair and eyes are so dark, they seem to absorb the light; it's a sharp contrast to his pale skin. He crosses the room, his steps echoing.

He's not real. This is not real.

That's the only thing that keeps me from running. I don't need to be frightened of a phantasm. He can't hurt me. Not here.

The Thief steps up to me. "You didn't run."

"You're not real," I say.

A creepy smile spreads slowly across his face. "Is that what you think? That I'm not real?" He searches my face.

Whatever he sees there makes him laugh. "You don't believe *any* of this is real, do you?"

The hairs on my forearms rise.

Just a dream, a really screwed-up dream.

"If none of this is real, then I guess you and I are free to do whatever we please."

He reaches out and runs a finger down the slope of my nose. "I could touch you. You could touch me—the Night King would never have to know. There are no repercussions for reveries after all."

I sidestep him. "If I touched you," I say, my claws still out, "I doubt you would enjoy it."

The Thief once again steps into my space, forcing me to back up. "That's where you're wrong, enchantress. I have... *peculiar* tastes." His eyes flick down to my throat and chest. "I've never been with a human. Or a siren. Or a mortal made into a fae. But I have been with women who fight back—I have a healthy appetite for that."

Healthy is the last word I'd use to describe the Thief's fetishes.

I go toe-to-toe with him. "That wasn't the case when you were Karnon," I say softly. "The way I remember it, you wouldn't touch a woman unless she was incapacitated."

The Thief of Souls stares at me; there's something foreign and merciless in the dark depths of his eyes. "You have me entirely figured out, don't you?" he says. "The Thief, too frightened to fuck a woman unless she's trapped."

Before I get the chance to back away, he grabs me by the throat. "Perhaps I could disprove that notion? This is just a reverie after all, just a twisted dream where a wicked man takes you against your will."

My skin brightens.

"You might even enjoy it." His eyes dip to my skin. "I know I will."

My heart quakes at his rising interest even as an insidious part of me is coming alive.

He pulls me in close.

The Thief is going to kiss me, just as he did when he was Karnon. And perhaps he'll breathe that same vile magic into me now as he did then. Only this time, I won't be immune to it.

A human would struggle against this. A siren, however…

Let him come closer. Let him think he has us.

My eyes drop to his lips. "I know you can wear the faces of the dead."

He leans in, his lips skimming my jaw. "And to think I believed you'd never figure out any of it."

He releases my throat, and I stagger back, massaging my raw skin.

"Do you want to know something?" he asks.

I gaze back at him with barely masked repulsion.

"Mara met me more than once. The first time, I was courting her sister."

Just like Janus, Mara once had a sibling. I almost forgot. I rack my brain, trying to remember her name.

Thalia. That's what it was. She was the Flora Kingdom's heir apparent, only she died before her time, falling on a sword or something like that, after, after…

My eyes snap to the Thief. "The traveling minstrel. That was *you*."

A man had come to her kingdom, and Thalia had fallen hopelessly in love with him. The way I heard it, the whole thing had ended poorly.

God, but how long ago was that? Centuries? All this time the Thief was moving his pieces into place.

His eyes seem to smile. "I was an enchanter—I just happened to have a penchant for serenading young royals. You want to know something those histories never mentioned?"

He pauses, and the silence of this strange place seems to close in on me. I never knew something as insubstantial as silence could have such weight.

"I fucked Mara then too. To this day, she has no idea I've been inside her as two separate men."

Nausea stirs low in my belly.

Just a dream.

"She was always the envious one, but especially then, when her sister had everything and she had nothing. The first time we exchanged anything more than pleasantries was after it was known that Thalia and I were together. She pulled me away at one of those frivolous parties, dropped to her knees, and well…what she lacked in power or rank, she made up for with enthusiasm. I didn't even have to enchant her—truth be told, at the time, I didn't want much to do with her, but I just couldn't resist the temptation."

I grimace.

"I remember how the story ends," I say. "You were killed."

"Do the dead ever really die?" he asks.

The same damn question he posed to me back in the Flora Kingdom.

I feel the answer right there, on the tip of my tongue. I glance from the Thief to the strange blooming vines, to the column he rested against just minutes ago, to the pool next to it.

My ears ring as I stare at that water. The longer I look, the more it seems as though it's shifting, *whispering.*

Save us…

Save...us...

Unwittingly, I take a step closer to it, my shoulder brushing against the Thief's.

"I wouldn't do that."

"What...is in that water?" I can't seem to look away.

"What does it matter? None of this *is* real."

The next morning, I do in fact skip the meeting, choosing instead to nurse my hangover. (Praise Jesus for fae medicine—that stuff totally works.)

By the time Des and Janus leave their meeting, I'm feeling loads better.

The Day King nods when he sees me, his golden hair shimmering. "Callypso," he says formally.

"Janus, may I have a word with you?" There's something I need to say to the Day King in light of all I know.

He gives me a peculiar look. "Of course," he says.

Behind him, Des slides his hands into his pockets and meanders over to a nearby guard, striking up a conversation.

I pull the Day King off to the side. "I owe you an apology," I say to Janus.

Janus looks me over, his eyes a little wary.

He's afraid of us, my siren whispers, *as he should be.*

"Actually," I amend, "I owe you several." I take a breath. "I'm sorry for acting like a fool yesterday. You and Desmond were just trying to do what was best for your kingdoms; I'm sure my thoughts on literally everything that crossed my mind were exasperating to hear.

"I'm sorry for glamouring you. I don't know how much Des has told you about sirens"—probably nothing since Des's least favorite hobby is sharing—"but...sirens enjoy violence and sex. I can't glamour someone without that aspect of my nature surfacing to some degree. I'm not nice when I use my power. I'm sorry you had to experience it yourself."

And now for the grand finale of apologies.

"Lastly, I'm sorry I blamed you for kidnapping me. I was... mistaken. I didn't understand that at the time, but I do now."

Janus gives me what might be his first genuine smile. It's unfair for anyone to be as pretty as he is, with his golden hair and bright blue eyes. He's the sun come to life—blinding in his beauty.

"I appreciate the apologies, Callypso. Despite what you may think, your commentary yesterday lightened a very solemn talk, and I am thankful for that. As for the glamour, if I remember correctly, I was the one who insisted you show me your abilities.

"I will admit, enchanters give me pause; power like that is dangerous in the wrong hands. I do, however, have reason to believe you are the right sort of person to wield such magic, regardless of your base nature.

"As for the kidnapping, I cannot imagine enduring such a trial. Of course, you are entitled to be confused and mistrustful. I don't know who or what you saw, but I do believe you."

He places a hand on my shoulder, his eyes intense. The room darkens a touch, but Janus pretends not to notice.

"Your mate and I already have a strong alliance between our kingdoms," he says, his blue eyes burning bright, "but we've never had a friendship to strengthen that unity. Perhaps, starting today, that can change."

His fingers press into my shoulder. "I personally vow that should the need ever arise, I will lend you my sword and my assistance."

It's not until Des and I are back in the Kingdom of Night that I'm truly able to breathe again.

The moment we step off the ley line and the cool evening greets us, I feel myself relax.

"God, I missed this place."

"Getting sentimental, are we?" Des says, tying his hair back into an itty-bitty bun. I try not to stare at the action, but his black sleeves bunch around his biceps, and the whole thing looks really, really good.

I lift a shoulder. "This place is growing on me," I say in all honesty.

It didn't begin that way. Originally, I wanted nothing to do with the Otherworld. But then I got kidnapped and grew wings, and going back to earth just wasn't an option.

And now… Well, let's just say the Otherworld has its perks.

The Bargainer's eyes shine in that way they do when I say something that moves him.

"You know, you're really cute when you go soft on me," I say.

"I don't know what you're talking about," he says, taking my hand and dragging me over to him. His eyes drop to my lips. "But you know what we should talk about? The fact you got a king to swear his fealty to you."

I guffaw. "I apologized to him, that's all."

"And in return he pledged you his loyalty—" Des stops speaking when he catches sight of a guard hustling over. He watches the man, face impassive.

"Your Majesty," the soldier says when he gets to us, nodding first to Des, then to me. "The sleeping soldiers, they've been talking nonstop since this morning."

Des's features harden. "About what?"

The guard's eyes slide to me. "Your mate."

When Des and I enter the royal dungeon, the noise is nearly deafening. Dozens and dozens of voices are talking at once.

"I want to speak with Callypso Lillis... I want to speak with Callypso Lillis..."

"...speak with Callypso Lillis...I want to speak..."

"Callypso Lillis."

The door slams shut behind us, and like a spell being broken, the voices quiet. In the silence that follows, my skin prickles.

I walk, Des at my heels. I could hear a pin drop in this place, it's so quiet.

As soon as we reach the first cells, I catch sight of the formerly sleeping soldiers. They all stand at attention, their bodies rigid. Only their eyes move, following me as I pass.

Malignant magic tinges the air. I can smell the evil that's settled into these soldiers. It's still residing in them like a parasite.

"Who wanted to speak with me?" I call out.

From several cells down, a low voice says, "You know who."

A chill slides down my spine. There's only one person who's poisoned this lot.

The already dark dungeon block darkens further with the Bargainer's displeasure.

"This guy's got some brass balls," he mutters under his breath.

I step up to the cell the voice came from. Inside are a dozen soldiers, all men. Their bodies are still covered in the gore they woke in…well, that and whatever blood splattered onto them during the battle.

One of the sleeping soldiers steps forward. His skin is tawny, his eyes are hazel, and his plaited hair is dark brown. He smiles at me. "Hello, enchantress."

CHAPTER 18

My siren claws at me, sensing how spooked I am.

I step up to the bars, careful not to touch the iron. "What do you want?"

The man paces the length of the cell, his gaze never leaving mine. He doesn't answer, just continues to pace back and forth, back and forth.

I let out a breath. "Come on, Des, let's go. The Thief is obviously too spineless to—"

The entire dungeon speaks as one:

*Is life but to wake
And death but to sleep?
I'd tell you, but then,
This secret I'll keep.*

*I'm not real now,
Nor was I last night,
Or perhaps I'm wrong.
Who's to say what's right?*

My blood runs cold.

The soldier who first spoke to me now smiles. He tilts his head.

Are you having fun yet?
This is our little game.
You will lose soon enough.
Then you'll be mine to tame.

My conversation with the Thief might have been a dream, but apparently it was real enough. That's what this is, a reminder that a dream is never just a dream.

My skin begins to glow very softly; it's so at odds with my heart, which is racing, racing…

I work my jaw.

No one scares us.

I step up to the cell and grab the iron bars, ignoring the pain as my skin sizzles.

"I've got a rhyme for you, fucker," I say, my voice filling with glamour. "Stop hiding behind your puppets, you stupid piece of trash. Oh, and take your lame riddles and shove them up your a—"

"Callie," Des says, prying my hands off the bars. The room's nearly pitch-black. That's the first I sense of the Bargainer's dark mood.

"Aren't I a poet?" I taunt the soldier as Des drags me away. My hands are smoking, but I can barely feel them over my rising fury.

That's about when I realize my wings have come out, the tips of them now dragging along the cool floor as the Bargainer carts me back the way we came.

"Not a poet," says one of the soldiers we pass by. "A marked woman."

He's barely gotten the words out when the darkness closes in on him. In the next moment, Des vanishes from my side. I hear steel slicing flesh and a choked cry, then nothing more.

By the time the shadows dissipate, Des is back at my side, his hand on my back.

I stare at the spot where the fairy stood a moment before. Now he lies in a puddle of his own blood, his eyes glassy.

Oh *shit*.

The Bargainer lifts his chin, his own wings arching over his shoulders. "Not in my house, Thief. Not in my house."

———————

Des wraps linen bandages around my hands, his own trembling as he does so. His wings are still out, and the room we sit in is mostly cast in shadow. His face is placid, but every so often, his upper lip ticks.

Down our bond I feel his immense rage. This is about the time when the Bargainer begins breaking bones and making his victims beg for mercy.

Only the Thief is hiding somewhere not even Des, Lord of Secrets, knows.

My own rage, by contrast, fled some time ago.

I stare at my blistered fingertips. "Can't I just heal these with my magic?" Expedited healing was supposed to be one of the perks of fae power.

Des finishes wrapping one of my hands and sets it in my lap. "Iron doesn't—" He takes a deep breath, then starts again. "Iron wounds take extra magic to heal. But you could."

"Will you show me how?" I ask.

The Bargainer cups my injured hand between his. I still feel him trembling with his anger.

"Close your eyes," he says.

"Is this—? Are you showing me how to—?"

"Close your eyes."

Reluctantly, I let mine flutter closed.

"Now breathe in and out. In and out."

My breath whooshes into my lungs, my chest expanding. I hold it in. Then I exhale, and the air rushes out of me.

"Yes, just like that," Des says.

I sense him taking his own advice, his hands steadying as they hold mine.

"Now," he says, "quiet your thoughts and focus them inward."

I'm as introspective as the next person, but I've never done this, never searched for the source of my magic. It's always just been there, and I've spent close to a decade trying to *leash* it, not to go hunting it down.

"Where is your power?"

It takes looking for my magic to truly notice where it lies within me.

"It's in the pit of my stomach." My core really. It simmers there, right at my very center. This is where the siren slumbers when she's not busy terrorizing the world. "And it's in my heart." Right where my connection to Des is anchored.

"Focus on that magic," Des says. "And now pull on it. Pretend it's a ball of yarn and you're tugging a thread of it loose."

This is so weird.

"Okay," I say.

"Now pull that thread up through your chest. Imagine it traveling past your rib cage and across your shoulders. Direct it down your arms and into your hands."

I do as he says, visualizing this power of mine as though

it were a physical thing. I imagine it moving through me. When it gets to my hands, they heat like I'm holding them close to a fire.

My eyes flutter open, even as I continue directing my magic to my palms. Des releases my hand and, unwinding the bandages, shows it to me. I stare at my fingertips. Before my eyes, the angry swelling diminishes.

"Holy crap." It's working. I'm healing myself.

As the pulsing pain of my wounds lessens, my energy drains. My siren is still there, but trying to rouse her into action would be difficult.

I release my magic, letting it retreat to my core. The worst of my injuries have healed, but my palm is still red and angry.

My gaze moves from my hand to the Bargainer. His wings are now hidden, and the shadows that cloaked the room have lifted. I glance around, surprised to see we're sitting on a veranda of sorts, a room that's not quite inside and not quite out. A row of enormous archways looks out over the city of Somnia.

Des takes my hand once more. "You did good there, cherub," he says, beginning to re-bandage it. "How do you feel?"

"Tired."

The Bargainer nods, wrapping the linen before tying it off. He brings my fingers to his lips, kissing the tip of each one. "Then we best get you to bed."

If the look in his eye is anything to go by, I'm not going to be doing much sleeping.

Before I have a chance to drag him out of there so he can properly *tuck me in*, chittering sounds come from beyond the archways.

The pleasant night air blows in through them, and riding on the draft of wind are several pixies, all chattering away. They zip across the veranda on the gust of air, only stopping when they get to me and Des. One of them hovers right in front of him. The others end up sitting on his shoulders… and mine, like they have front-row seats to a show.

"Evening, Aura," he says to the little fae.

She says something back to him, her voice high and sweet.

"Is that right?" Des says, his eyes narrowing. "Where is he?"

Aura chatters away, gesturing wildly.

The Bargainer looks at me. "Temper and Malaki have found out where Galleghar is hiding."

CHAPTER 19

I lean forward, even as the pixies on my shoulders play in my hair. (Seriously, what is with these creatures and my hair?)

"Where is he?"

The Night King's face is menacing. "Memnos." He says the word like it tastes bad coming out.

Memnos, the one island Des never took me to. The Land of Nightmares.

"Wait," I say, glancing at the pixie. "How does Aura—?" She curtsies at the mention of her name, and I nod to her. "How does Aura know this?"

The little pixies all begin chattering at once.

"Pixies are my royal messengers," Des says.

One of the pixies playing in my hair stops and says something else, her little voice demanding.

The Bargainer's mouth curves up at the corners. "Forgive me—pixies are royal messengers *and* spies."

I raise my eyebrows. "That sounds like an important job."

My words must've been the right ones because the

pixies excitedly chitter. One of them flits in front of my face and studies my features before lovingly patting my cheek.

Another one starts speaking animatedly to Des.

"I'm not going to go to Memnos *or* Barbos right now. You can tell Malaki he'll just have to wait," he replies.

Angry chittering.

"My mate is tired."

Another pixie comes over and inspects my eyes, as though looking for signs of my sleepiness.

The other pixie, meanwhile, is still arguing with Des. Eventually, she simply grabs Des's pointer finger and tugs, trying to rally him into action. It's an adorably pitiful sight. I'm pretty sure my mate shares the sentiment because the corner of his mouth lifts.

"Where does she want us to go?"

"To Memnos to slaughter the hateful tyrant Galleghar Nyx, but short of that, Malaki has requested our presence in Barbos."

I really am tired, both from healing my wounds and from the long days we've endured, and I've been dreaming of Des's bed for ages and ages. But there are two psychotic fae on the loose, and the sooner we deal with them, the sooner Des and I can get on with our lives.

I stand, and the pixies hanging on to me squeal. "Then let's go."

Des stares up at me, unconcerned that a pixie is still pulling at his finger. "Cherub, you need to rest."

"I'll rest eventually."

The Bargainer's eyes narrow. He stands, his chair scraping back. He steps in close, and his large frame fills my vision. "You don't want to go to Barbos," he says. "You want a

172

break from this madness, and I want to give that to you." His eyes have gone soft. They search my face, like my unspoken thoughts are written there.

"Des, if we wait, your father might slip away. I *am* tired, but I'll rest soon enough." I take Des's hand in my bandaged ones. "If we catch your father, he might be able to tell us where the Thief of Souls is."

A muscle in the Night King's jaw jumps. *So tempting*, his features seem to say. He glances away from me.

I give his hand a squeeze. "Let's end this."

His hand has started to tremble again. All that pent-up rage is fighting for release, and Des is a brutal enough creature that he can't deny it forever. Better to use it on his father.

Finally, he closes his eyes and nods. "We'll go to Barbos. And we'll deal with Galleghar Nyx."

Des and I soar through the clouds, the stars twinkling down on us.

God, have I missed this. There's no other sensation quite like flying.

The pixies spin around us, laughing as they ride on the wind. Des and I are a touch more somber, the two of us outfitted for battle.

These are, after all, violent times.

I ignore the exhaustion creeping through my bones; I'm pretty sure that, like a noob, I spent too much energy trying to heal my burns, and now I'm paying the piper for it.

Can't believe how much energy that took. I've never experienced a deficit of magic. Ever. Yet healing two small burns has nearly tapped me of it.

No wonder iron is so hated and feared among the fae. It's painful and magically draining.

My heart bleeds all over again for those soldiers Karnon kept prisoner; they were shackled in the stuff.

Seriously, *fuck* the Thief and all his sick deeds.

I can almost hear his laughter in my head.

This is our little game...

Only he would think of all these depravities as some sort of game.

The longer I think on it, the more my mind twists and turns, leading me back to that last strange dream.

Does the term small death *mean anything to you?* he asked me. It was the one question that seemed to be more than just posturing and scare tactics.

And of course, now that I'm levelheaded, the term *does* mean something to me. I've heard it all over the place. Somnia is the Land of Sleep and Small Death, Des used to be a member of the Angels of Small Death. And, in another dream back in the Flora Kingdom, Galleghar Nyx had mentioned small death.

Now that I look for it, it's everywhere.

I move in close to Des. "What's small death?" I ask, shouting to be heard over the gusty air.

I've never actually stopped to ask what the term means.

"Sleep," Des says, his voice amplified by his magic. I think he's misheard me, but then he adds, "Fae consider the loss of consciousness—fainting, sleep, and so on—to be a brief taste of death. The individual is caught between worlds, and so we call this *small death*."

Huh. I guess that's kind of cool. Unhelpful but cool.

"Why do you ask?"

I glance over at Des. His eyes are too keen.

Though he knows I've had nightmares about the Thief, I haven't told him the specifics about my most recent dreams.

I open my mouth to explain when a dark object manifests ahead of us. I catch a blur of white hair, hear the shrill cries of the pixies as they scatter, and next thing I know, the fae has me by the throat.

I grab the fairy's wrist, trying to pry their hand from my neck when I catch sight of the beautiful fae.

Those eyes...just like his son's.

Galleghar Nyx grimaces at me, squeezing tighter, his upper lip curling in disgust. "I could snap your neck right now and be done with it, slave."

I drop a bandaged hand from his wrist, groping along my waist for one of my daggers.

"To think you've been walking the halls of *my* palace—"

My hand wraps around the hilt of my blade.

Gotcha.

"—eating from *my* table—"

I unsheathe it.

"—sleeping in—"

I slam the dagger into his side, sinking the blade to its hilt.

Galleghar howls, his hold loosening long enough for me to suck in a grateful breath. I yank my weapon from his side.

"Bitch!" He cocks his fist just as an ominous form appears over his shoulders.

The Bargainer leans in close to his father's ear, his hands gripping Galleghar's wings. "I was hoping to run into you." With that, he snaps his father's wings, the bones making a sickening crack as they break.

Now Galleghar screams in earnest. He releases my throat before Des pulls back his fist and slams it into his father's head again, and again, and again. I feel my mate unleashing his wrath as the two men plummet from the sky.

Galleghar disappears, winking into existence in front of me again. The Bargainer follows suit, his wings flared menacingly at his back. But just as soon as Des closes in on him, Galleghar vanishes once more.

It's that night in Mara's oak forest all over again, Des and his father bleeding away into the darkness only to reform in another location. The tyrant king is having trouble though, his mangled wings bent grotesquely behind him.

Galleghar's form disappears yet again, only this time I don't see him reform—I *feel* him. His hands brace either side of my head.

He's going to snap my neck. I sense his intent in his very grip, even as gravity drags the two of us toward earth.

Frantically, I call on my siren. If I ever needed my glamour, it would be now.

She rises slowly, like she's moving through molasses. My skin begins to glow...only to dim. My siren retreats, my magic too exhausted to summon her.

I jerk in Galleghar's grip, trying to use my wings to shake him. But then Des is there and then Galleghar *isn't*, and the whole thing happens so terribly fast that I get whiplash.

I tumble through the sky, trying to right myself. The universe and all the stars in it spin around me as I fall through the sky.

And then there again is Galleghar, hand at my throat. I slash at him with the dagger in my hand, the blade catching him in the arm. Before he can retaliate, the Bargainer manifests between the two of us, his position forcing his father to release my neck. In his own hand, Des grips the sword he carries.

With one swift thrust, Des shoves his weapon into his father's gut. Galleghar's eyes go wide as his son jerks it back out of his abdomen. That's the last I see of the tyrant king as I continue to fall, a cloud swallowing me up.

I desperately try to spread my wings, fighting against wind and gravity. Before I can right myself, Des manifests next to me, scooping my body up in midair.

"We need to get back to Somnia. Now."

———————

The flight back is nothing like the previous one. Des won't release me, despite the fact that I'm fine—even if my throat is a little sore. He flies at a punishing pace, the wind howling in our ears as we speed across the sky.

"Where's Galleghar?" I ask.

"Hidden back in whatever shithole he crawled out of."

I was wrong about Des needing to release his rage. I don't think pummeling his father helped at all. If anything, he seems *more* tightly wound.

"So he's still alive."

The King of the Night's nod is barely perceptible.

Damn. Galleghar must be hurting—two broken wings and a couple of gut wounds. Not to mention the punches to the head he sustained.

The Bargainer flies us directly to his chambers and lands silently on his balcony. He sets me on my feet, his wings flaring wide around me as if to shield me from the world. Des steps into my space, his face impassive. But more than ever, I sense his tumultuous emotions, from the agitated arc of his wings to the rigid line of his shoulders.

His eyes drop to my lips, and that's the only warning I get. Reeling me in, he takes my mouth savagely.

His lips are fire, burning against mine.

Take. Claim. Keep.

Maybe he murmurs this, maybe I sense it from our connection, but those three words seem to be the driving force behind his manic energy.

I feel his wrath and his panic, his frustration and fear all tied into the slide of his mouth against mine.

I return it with equal intensity. I might be capable of living for centuries, but I can still die like a human can. I felt it there for a moment, when Galleghar was squeezing the life out of me, and again when I was falling. Just because fae consider themselves immortal doesn't mean they are.

I part Des's lips with my own, tasting his essence as my fingers delve into his soft hair.

Behind me, his balcony doors snick open. He lifts me again, wrapping my legs around his waist.

"I need to be inside you," he says hoarsely.

I nod against him, my mouth going to his again. Nothing like a brush with death to make you feel amorous. I need to feel alive, and I think Des does too.

The Bargainer steps inside, and the doors click shut behind him. Not a moment later, my clothes melt off me. Des's clothes follow suit as he moves us to the bed.

He's barely laid me on the bed and parted my thighs when he pulls me to him, thrusting deep inside me.

I gasp as his thick cock stretches me, the sensation a pinch of pain then pleasure, pleasure, *pleasure*. I revel in his muscular body pressing down on mine.

"Gods above, cherub." Des kisses the juncture between my neck and shoulder as he slides out. He pistons in again.

I lean my head back and moan as he fills me, stretches me. He's need, need, need. I can practically hear him—

Take… Claim… Keep.

The phrase echoes like a memory through my head.

"This—this won't be gentle," he warns, his entire body trembling as he dams up his wicked need.

I grasp his hair, my grip tightening as I tilt his head toward mine.

"Your warnings are wasted on me." My fingers flex against him. "You're not fucking some delicate flower. You're fucking *me*." A siren.

The King of the Night, who rules over sleep and sex, *unleashes*.

He slams into me again and again, gathering me in his arms, his gaze drinking me in. It's the oddest combo of unbridled aggression and devoted adoration.

His pace is punishing, and his strokes are deep, and I can't maintain eye contact because, Jesus, my body is pure sensation, and I need to stop looking at him, or I'm going to get an award for the world's fastest climax.

Des moves one of my legs over his shoulder, deepening his angle. I grip the blankets I lie on uselessly, my breasts bobbing from the force of each thrust.

He touches my dim skin. "This is a first."

We're deep in each other, and my siren hasn't stirred, my magic still replenishing. It's a strange sensation, not having the siren share this experience with me. I feel naked in a whole new way.

The Bargainer takes one of my bandaged hands, threading his fingers through mine. His lips skim over my forehead, then my nose, then my lips, chin, throat. There they pause—*he* pauses, his entire body drawn tight.

He kisses a trail across my neck, right where I'm sure bruises in the shape of his father's hand have appeared.

"My beautiful nightmare," Des whispers against my skin. "My beautiful, beautiful nightmare."

With that, the Bargainer thrusts into me again. I hiss out a breath as his pace picks up, his sweat-slicked chest gliding over mine again and again. I'm being lit up from the inside. It feels like there's no place he hasn't touched. We're wrapped up in each other, our bodies entwined, our hearts magically bound.

Des grips my hand tightly, as though he's afraid to let me go. "Look at me, Callie," he commands.

"Going to come if I do that."

He dips in close to kiss my cheek, all the while rocking in and out of me. "That's kind of the point. Now look at me."

I turn my gaze to his. Never has he looked so breathtaking, never has he looked so fae—like the moon come to life. His silver eyes glitter, his white hair dangling loose between us.

And it's that, not each aggressive stroke, that sets me off. I'm right there on the edge in an instant...and then I break.

Des sees the moment I climax, flashing me a wolfish smile. My gaze begins to drift as my orgasm lashes through me. I'm shattering to bits.

"Don't look away," Des orders.

I drag my gaze back to him. How to tell him it's all too much?

Des leans in, stealing a kiss from my lips as his strokes become more frantic. I catch his groan on my tongue as he gives in to his own need, his hips pumping furiously as he comes.

Take—claim—keep.

I hear the phantom words one final time, and then it's over.

"It was an ambush," Des says.

He strokes my sweaty skin, holding me close. I'm sore in all the right places—and in a couple of wrong ones too. My throat, for instance, is starting to hurt like a bitch.

"Somehow," he continues, "Galleghar knew where we were, and he intercepted us before we had a chance to locate him."

Around us, the myriad of lamps burns away, casting the Night King's chambers in low flickering light. A pleasant breeze drifts through the paneless windows. As far as nights go, this one's absolutely perfect—recent fight notwithstanding.

Des brushes a strand of my hair away from my face. "My father was going after you because we're mated."

I prop myself up, my gaze going to Des's sinful mouth. My thoughts drift for a moment to all the things I want those lips to do to me. Things besides talking.

Already, the attack seems like a dream. It happened so fast, and then it was over. And now... Well, here I am wrapped in silk sheets and a muscular fairy.

The Bargainer's eyes drop to my neck. He reaches for it with his tatted arm, his fingers trailing over the bruises that are surely there.

It's not over for him.

His hand moves from my neck, sliding over the curve of my hip. "For most mated pairs, the death of one fairy means the death of both. In some cases, like Mara's, one fairy can outlive the other, but that's surprisingly rare. Most of the time, if you kill one, you kill both." The Bargainer's eyes rise to mine. "Galleghar attacked you because he rightfully believes ending you will end me."

My heart pounds a little faster. "*Rightfully?*"

Des's fingers squeeze my hip, his eyes looking feverish for a moment. "No part of me has any intention of outliving you."

That's a bucket of ice water to the face.

I don't want to talk about this. About my death—or his. We're very much alive, and I don't really want to dwell on the alternative.

"He's going to come after you again," the Bargainer continues. "The idiot actually believes you're an easier target." The thought brings a shadow of a smile to Des's lips for a moment.

Galleghar is going to come after me again.

Suddenly, every dark corner of the room seems like it hides monsters. What's to stop Des's father from intruding on us right here, right now?

The Night King must know where my thoughts are because he says, "You're protected within the royal grounds—there are enchantments to keep out fairies like him," Des says. "That's likely why he ambushed us en route to Barbos."

Because there weren't enchantments along our flight path.

"So I'm stuck here." My stomach sours at the thought.

Des wraps his arm around my back, pulling me in close. "You're not stuck *anywhere*, cherub," he says, deadly serious. "Tell me where you want to go, and I'll take you there right now."

My brows furrow. "You're not going to try to keep me here?"

I don't touch on the fact that right now I don't want to move an inch from this bed, content to spend the rest of my long life wrapped in the King of the Night's arms.

"I will *never* keep you captive," Des vows. "Better you

happy and free than caged and safe. Besides"—he leans his forehead against mine—"Galleghar clearly hasn't heard the stories about you if he thinks you're an easier target."

"There are stories about me?" That's news.

Des crinkles his eyes and presses his lips together. "Many. What fae can resist a story about the beautiful human who beguiles fairies and escapes the Thief? They can't get enough of you. Unfortunately, my father and the Thief seem to share that sentiment."

I lift a bandaged hand and stare at Des's work. "I should've listened to you," I say thoughtfully. I drop my hand. "Back when you told me to rest."

"I happen to have great ideas," he agrees, his mouth curving fiendishly. His expression sobers. "But you made the decision a queen would, putting the kingdom's needs before your own."

"Stop using that word." *Queen*.

"It's going to happen one day or other, Queen Callypso."

Okay, I'll admit, that has a nice ring to it.

"What do you have against queens anyway?" Des asks.

I sigh. "I just want to be a normal girl with a normal job who lives a normal life." I don't want to worry about an entire kingdom.

The Bargainer rolls us so he can stare down at me. "Callie, you've never been a normal girl, and you've never lived a normal life, so I can see the appeal of wanting that. But normal is overrated. Trust me, it's overrated. I've made deals with thousands of miserable *normal* people."

I frown up at him.

"And I'm sorry," he continues, "but if you think I'm going to let you settle for normal, you've got a fight on your hands."

Damn it. Now that he's drawn lines, I'll never get him to budge. If there's one thing Des is good at, it's fighting. Oh, and deals. And secrets. And sex.

Screw it all, he's good at everything. It's annoying.

"This is just like high school," I say, remembering those days he roused or manipulated or bargained me into action. Mean but effective. "You trying to get me to do something you believe is in my best interest."

"Tell me I'm wrong, cherub. Tell me I'm pushy and bossy and don't know a thing about your deepest dreams."

See, that's the rub of it all: now that I know he can hear shadows, he's probably heard all sorts of things about my dreams that I won't willingly admit. Things that prove him right.

"You're pushy and you're bossy," I say.

He leans in and places a kiss along my sternum. "And I don't know a thing about your dreams—say it."

I feel the breath of his magic wrapping around my windpipe. Only this time, it's trying to pry the truth out of me, and the truth is that the Bargainer knows a great deal about my deepest desires.

He moves down my body, placing a kiss between my breasts. "I'm still waiting, love."

But I stay silent, and eventually his magic dissolves.

The Bargainer pauses, glancing up at me. "I love you, Callie, down to every feather and scale. I love your darkness, I love your mind, I love your humor and your most coveted dreams. And I love how you love me—wholly, deeply, passionately.

"You're not normal; you'll never be normal. I'm so sorry to tell you that. You are so blindingly extraordinary that it physically hurts me sometimes, and I'll never stop pushing you to believe this."

Des can't just say things like that. My weak heart isn't fit enough to take it.

I close my eyes and draw in a shaky breath. "Give it back."

"What is it I've taken, cherub?"

My peace of mind, my loneliness, my torment. My pain, my sanity, my dull little life.

So many things that once made me *me* are now missing, and—

"Des, I don't know who I am."

"You don't know who you are?" The Bargainer's voice drops low. "You're Callypso Lillis, plain and simple. You were her yesterday, you'll be her tomorrow. It's up to you to decide what being you actually means. No one else can do that for you. Not the man who gave you those wings, not the man who's hunting you. Not your stepfather. Not even me.

"But whatever you choose to be, cherub, make it count."

CHAPTER 20

It's late the next morning by the time I tumble out of Des's bed. The fairy is reluctant to let me go, and I'm not complaining.

A girl could get used to this kind of attention.

I stretch as I pad over to the closet, feeling the Bargainer's eyes on me the entire time.

"Creep," I say, not looking back.

"I'd have to be dead to not enjoy your backside."

I suppress a smile, then begin riffling through the pretty dresses someone's stocked in the armoire. I'm not a girlie girl by any means, but fae outfits are one exception I'll make. I grab a dress that looks like the dawn come to life, purples bleeding into pinks and oranges bleeding into yellows.

I've no more than slipped it on when the dress slips itself off.

Swiveling to Des, I raise an eyebrow. "Unless you want to break my vagina, I suggest you give it a rest."

Relentless is a great way to describe the King of the

Night's sexual appetite. Not that I'm a slacker myself, but even I have my limits—especially when my siren decides to take the night off.

Des appears in front of me, turning my healed palms up.

"Are you going to read my fortune?" I tease.

He pretends to peer at them. "You find your soul mate young. There's love—and it looks like you have a handful of kids—they take after their father, unfortunately. Brats, the entire lot of them."

I laugh and pull my hands away.

"Oh, and you live a long and happy life."

I don't say anything to that. There's so much uncertainty these days.

I pick the dress back up.

"You're not wearing that today."

"Why not?" The moment I ask it, my breath catches. I half expect battle leathers to come raining from the sky and for Des to announce that, once again, the two of us are training.

Really freaking hate training.

"I could tell you—for a price—"

I groan. "Des…"

A pile of clothes *does* come raining down, but they're not battle leathers.

"Or you could simply put the clothes on and deduce my plans like the good PI you are."

I pick up the folded clothing, recognizing a faded T-shirt I own. There's a bra, panties, and jeans. A moment later socks and white Converses join the pile. All mine, all unfit to wear in the Otherworld.

My gaze moves to Des. "What do you have planned for us?"

"Wrong question, cherub. It's not *what* I have planned, but *where*."

Oh my God. My grip tightens on the clothing. "Where, Des?"

Des gives me a wry smile. "You know the answer to that question."

I suck in a breath.

Home. Earth.

———————

Traveling on ley lines is no longer the confusing experience it used to be. Before, I couldn't make sense of these magical highways; my magic wasn't compatible with it.

But now my power recognizes these strange roads that cross worlds. The magic is thick, pulling at me from all sides. It tries to drive me in its own direction, but Des holds my hand and directs me forward, cutting through the ley line's bizarre compulsion as he leads us on.

Around me, I see landscapes fly by—hills, forests, deserts, oceans, ruins—all of it foreign and fae…until suddenly it *isn't* anymore. Gradually, it changes to recognizable cities and landmarks. I see Nepal, Cairo, Berlin, then—finally— Los Angeles.

With a powerful tug, the Bargainer leads us off the ley line.

For a moment, I feel the magic resist, eager to keep us locked away on this odd highway, cursed to forever wander. But the moment passes, the magic gives, and suddenly we're in Des's house, in the round room that contains the ley line portal.

I take a shaky step forward, my foot sinking into the soft grass. I touch the wall of the circular room, my fingers brushing against the vines of wisteria growing up it, the plants swaying against a phantom breeze.

The Bargainer leads me out of the portal room, and it's only then, only once I see the wood floors, the mounted pictures of faraway places, the mundane lines and details and colors of his Catalina home that I truly process it.

Earth. I'm really back on earth.

Dear God, never have I wanted to kiss the ground so badly. If I could bear-hug it, I totally would.

"Godsdamn, I missed this place," Des says, glancing around.

Next to me, my soul mate looks like a memory come to life. He swaggers into his hallway wearing his leather pants, his shit-kicking boots, and a faded Rolling Stones shirt, his tattooed sleeve on display.

I've been so used to him wearing fae attire that seeing him in human clothes in his human home is something out of a dream.

I release Des's hand and make my way through his house. My heart aches as I take in the furniture, the photos, the decorations on display because each one screams *Des*—at least Des as I first knew him, back when I'd never seen his life in the Otherworld.

I head through his living room and out the back door. Late-afternoon sun hits my skin, and I close my eyes, soaking it in. I might legit cry. It's not eternal night, it's not endless day; it's just your average sunny afternoon in Southern California.

Opening my eyes, I continue toward the back of the Bargainer's property, my attention drifting for a moment to the place where I was taken. Any fear the sight might've once conjured is gone, though I'm not exactly sure why.

Maybe it's because Karnon's dead or because the Thief has stopped kidnapping women. Or maybe it's not the situation that's changed but me.

I cross the last of the Bargainer's backyard, stepping right up to where the land gives way to a cliff's edge.

My skin prickles when I hear the surf crashing below. I take a deep breath, drinking in the smell of salt water.

This is where I belong.

My gaze moves to the horizon. There's a short expanse of sea that separates my house from his. On a clear day, you can make out the edges of Malibu, and if you have imagination enough, you can draw in my home among those hills.

It's the same sight the Bargainer must've stared at during all our years apart. The sight fills my heart with old agony and something sweeter, like the past and the present and the future overlay each other.

The Bargainer steps up next to me. "It's warded, you know."

I glance at him.

"Your house—my house too. They always have been, but after"—his voice catches—"after you were taken, I doubled down on the wards. I can't promise you'll be safe here," he says, reminding me of our earlier conversation, "but you won't be altogether defenseless either."

I stare at Des. The setting sun sets his features on fire. My siren stirs within me, awakening now that my magic's refueled.

We don't need defending, she whispers. *We need defending* from.

"I'm not worried."

Des flashes me a wicked smile.

People like us are not victims, he once told me. *We're someone's nightmare.*

His membranous wings appear, unfolding menacingly behind him. "Ready to go home?"

I raise my eyebrows. I assumed *this* was our destination.

"Aw, cherub, you didn't think I'd take you this far only to stop now, did you?"

I search his face, my heart expanding and expanding. He looks like something plucked from my most desperate dreams.

My own wings manifest behind me, punching through the material of my shirt. Des *tsks* at the sight. He places his hand on the clothing, and in an instant, the ripped cloth stitches itself back together.

Des smooths my shirt down. When his eyes meet mine, they dance. "Ready?" he asks, backing away.

I never get the chance to answer. Des backs right off the cliff's edge, his arms open to the world as he falls backward. My breath catches at the sight. I should know better by now. The Bargainer has wings and magic and the uncanny ability to teleport. Falling isn't going to do him in.

He twists in midair, his vicious-looking wings fanning out to catch the breeze.

He beckons to me. "Coming, baby siren?"

God, but he looks magnificent and otherworldly, bathed in the dying light of our sun.

My own wings spread. I take a running leap from the cliff, and then I'm diving, gliding, soaring. I laugh as the wind buffets me upward, catching sight of my Converses in the process.

Fucking flying over the Pacific.

The two of us cut across the sky, the ocean blurring

by beneath us. This moment could last forever, the breeze whistling through my hair, the blue water under me, the fading day above me. And Des and I, two strange birds ghosting above the world.

My body is filled to the brim with simple joy.

Inevitably, we close in on land. If we had any other destination in mind, perhaps that would be a disappointment. But up ahead I catch sight of my house, and a new sort of euphoria moves in to replace the old.

Home. Sweet, lovely, lonely home.

We touch down in my backyard.

I'm back.

Never want to leave.

I really don't. I want to drink my wine, stare out at the ocean, think deep thoughts, sleep beneath my sheets.

I want to do all that…but I want to do it with Des.

The Bargainer and I head over to my sliding glass door. Des has only to stare at the handle, and with a *snick*, the door unlocks itself and slides open. Tentatively, I step inside.

Home is a house filled with sandy floors, chipped counters, and now my soul mate. He stands in my house like he resides there—like he's *always* resided there—and the way he looks around, I have every reason to believe he intends to make this place ours.

Ours.

Not going to get over that.

"Where are all our things?" he asks.

There's that word again. *Our.*

I move through my (our?) home, expecting things to be different. It feels like ages since I was last here.

"In the attic." I couldn't bear to part with all those trinkets Des and I collected during my junior year of high school, but

I also couldn't bear to look at them. The pain of his absence always sharpened when I saw those physical reminders.

Des clicks his tongue. "Cherub, we're going to have to change that."

He lifts his hand, and I hear a few distant thumps then scraping.

Less than a minute later, a weathered box floats into the living room, scattering dust motes as it heads our way. It plops to the floor a few feet in front of me.

For several seconds all is still. Suddenly, the lid pops open, causing me to jolt.

And then the procession begins. The prayer flags, the Venetian masks, the painted gourd, and the silks, they float out of the box one by one before lining themselves up on the floor.

Once our old memorabilia have been removed from the container, my tasteful decorations are lifted from the walls, pushed off tables, and cleared from shelves. They amble through the air, then stack themselves neatly into the box. After they're all settled inside, the cardboard flaps fold over them, and the box levitates off the floor. It cants drunkenly back and forth as it returns the way it came.

I raise an eyebrow but say nothing.

Des smiles, a calculating spark in his eye.

All at once, the objects the two of us collected together— every shot glass and postcard, every drawing and note—lift into the air. For several seconds, the items hover in midair. Then, like an explosion, they scatter across the house.

Des finds a place for it all. On walls, on shelves, tucked away in cupboards, dangling from the ceiling.

I believe this is a fairy's version of peeing on his territory. And my heart is hurting so damned badly.

All these things are testaments to our friendship. Because that's what this has always been. Long before I knew Des was my mate, I knew he was my friend. And even though I wanted him in a distinctly un-friend-like way, that's all the two of us were for the better part of a year.

I'm taking in my "new" decorations when the King of the Night comes up behind me.

He kisses the juncture where my jaw meets my neck. "We'll go on more adventures," Des promises, "buy more trinkets, experience more new places together—both in this world and in the other."

I turn around. "Why did you bring me here?" I ask.

Out of all the places in all the worlds, he chose to bring me here.

Des has the universe in his eyes. "Because I love you, and this is where you're happiest."

That's not true. Happiness isn't a place, it's a person—more specifically, the one across from me.

The Bargainer leads me over to the couch. "Now, I was thinking that since we finished watching Harry Potter, we needed a new series to binge together…"

———————

I spend the evening wrapped in the Bargainer's arms, the two of us splayed along my couch as we watch TV. My coffee table is a mess of greasy pizza, popcorn, and Raisinets—all casualties of our movie night.

I trail my fingers over his inked arm. I'm supposed to be paying attention to the show, but I can't get over the joy I feel. Des is reclining here, on my couch, holding me against him as he watches a show from my living room. Earlier he ran his hands over my chipped countertops, and his boots have dragged sand across my living room. Little pieces of himself are now scattered all over the place. And he's here not because he wants me to repay the favors I owe but because he's mine.

I close my eyes and relish this. More than the Otherworld, it's this moment that seems like the dream. Everything that's been thrown at me was so much easier to accept in a world where cities floated and night reigned eternal. But a man like Des doesn't belong here in the normal world, and definitely not with a girl like me.

I want to cackle for outmaneuvering fate. Because I freaking *got* him, the bad boy who was always so out of reach.

The two of us binge-watch a couple of episodes, but somewhere along the way, the atmosphere changes.

First, it's a few light kisses Des brushes against my hairline and a few more I press to the base of his palm. Then it's the soft stroke of his fingers petting my skin, and the restless way my body reacts to the touch. But it's not until he clicks the TV off that I even realize the Bargainer is half as distracted as I've been.

"Truth or dare?" he whispers against my ear.

I bite back a smile. "Both."

Des lifts me off the couch then before turning me in his arms so I can wrap my legs around his narrow hips. I lock my arms behind his neck, playing with the ends of his hair.

He searches my face. "Truth: Tell me, sweet little siren, how many nights did you get yourself off to the thought of me when we were apart?"

I should've known Des would ask something dirty. His magic settles beneath my skin, demanding I answer this embarrassing question.

"I don't know," I say.

Not good enough. The Bargainer's magic is getting more demanding, twisting itself around my windpipe.

"Nearly every night." I glare at him.

"And what did you imagine?" His magic is still there, pressing against my throat.

"What do you *think* I imagined?" I say sarcastically.

He just waits. His power does the rest, closing in on me.

"I already gave you one answer," I say. He's already getting a two-for-one deal from this game, and now he's pressing his luck with another question.

"It's in my nature to take advantage," he says, running a finger down my cleavage. "Now, you were saying…?"

I press my lips together, though I know it's pointless. The words spill out of me anyway.

"I imagined you taking me in just about every position possible. I imagined your weight settling on me, your hips between mine. I imagined your evil-boy body fucking mine over and over and over again. I imagined it sweet and nice, I imagined it rough and kinky. I imagined you when I was alone…and when I was with other men—I even called out your name once. I imagined it all, and it still didn't hold a flame against the reality of you."

The Bargainer watches my mouth as I talk. Finally, he leans in and nips my lower lip. He rolls it between his teeth before releasing it.

He smiles in a distinctly masculine way, his wings appearing behind him. "You called out my name when you were with another?"

I flush. *Why* had I shared that?

"Cherub, I think we're going to have to make truth or dare a regular part of our days."

196

God, no. There are so many things—things like what I just divulged—that are better left unsaid.

He walks us down the hall toward the back of the house.

"What's my dare?" I ask.

"I think you'll figure it out soon enough."

We enter my bedroom, the lights flicking on.

"For seven years I yearned to enter this house of yours," Des admits. "It ate me up, needing to know what sort of life you made for yourself here."

My skin pebbles at his confession.

"That first night I returned to you," he says, "you cannot know what it felt like, lounging on your bed, knowing you slept in it. My mind was a mess."

His mind was a mess?

It was *my* mind that was a mess. The wicked, untouchable Bargainer was back from realms unknown, come to collect his debts and break my heart all over again. I was the bumbling schoolgirl, and he was the aloof, mysterious one.

"I've wanted to sleep with you here," he continues, "your body tucked against mine… Gods, how badly I wanted to insert myself into this life of yours."

The Bargainer's magic tugs at my clothes. One moment they're there, and in the next, they're a puddle on the floor.

Now I understand. *This* is the dare—sex wrapped as a game.

He lays me over my sheets but doesn't join me. Instead, he stands at the foot of the bed, feasting on my naked form.

After several seconds, the Bargainer flashes me one of his scary-as-shit grins. It's trouble in a look.

He grabs my ankles and spreads my legs wide, indecently displaying me. "I've had my own fantasies of you. Taking you right here, in your bed."

After sliding his hands under my thighs, he drags me to the edge of the mattress.

"Tonight, I'm staking a claim to this bed and everything else here." He presses a kiss to my inner thigh, his lips then dragging across my skin. "Starting with you."

CHAPTER 21

Des trails kisses along my inner thigh, moving inward until—
until—

I fist my sheets and bite back a cry, my skin flaring to life as he nips one of my outer lips then the other. I feel him smile against me, and that's almost worse. I have no defense against devilish Des.

He runs his tongue up my slit, and Jesus Christ and all the saints, this is *dirty*.

The Bargainer nips my clit, and now I do cry out.

So very, *very* dirty.

"Gods, I could eat this pussy for breakfast, lunch, and dinner," he says, right before he sucks on my clit.

I gasp out something unintelligible. If I weren't so turned on, I'd be embarrassed.

Behind me, my wings begin to form, which is unfortunate, considering they're going to be squashed beneath me.

Before I have a chance to force them back, Des's hand slides up my spine, his palm a warm pressure against my skin.

With a burst of his magic, my wings are gone, neatly taking care of that problem.

He keeps sucking on my clit, and I'm bucking against him, fighting to get away.

Too much sensation. Too, too much.

"Ah, ah, ah," he says, his breath fanning against me. "You're going to need to stay in place, cherub."

Desmond's magic rolls against me, and—

"You—are a terrible—person," I gasp, the words broken. I'm quickly losing the last of my composure.

"I am," he agrees.

He licks and sucks and rolls my clit between his teeth, the bastard only moving away when I'm close to coming. I'm pinned in place by his hands and his magic, and no amount of arching or twisting can get me out of his line of fire. So I'm left to ride out his cruel ministrations.

And they're really, really cruel. I'm caught in an endless cycle of buildup and letdown, my body winding tighter and tighter.

"Damn you, let me come," I say, glamour filling my voice.

But the order I give isn't phrased correctly, and rather than forcing the Bargainer's hand, I've allowed him to slip through mine.

Des pulls away, releasing my legs as he sits back on his haunches. He runs his tongue over his lower lip, looking like the seven deadly sins wrapped into one person, and oh my God, why isn't he finishing this?

"That's not how this works, love," he says, looking at me like a man bewitched.

After a moment, Des leans back in, but just when I think he's going to take up where he left off, he lifts me from the bed. Instinctively, I wrap my arms and legs around him, feeling his cock straining against his pants.

"Sweet thing, the night's just beginning." With that, he takes my lips in a carnal kiss.

I taste myself on his tongue, and that makes my core ache all over again.

I lock my ankles together behind him, my fingers mussing his hair. My body is on fire, my flesh raw from the way Des worked me.

Des carries me across the room until my back thuds against the wall. He breaks off the kiss before leaning his forehead against mine as he breathes heavily.

"I don't intend for this to be some easy claiming."

Claiming. He keeps using that word, and not for the first time, I sense his fae side trying to consume all that it can.

As he holds me, his clothes slide from his skin to pool beneath us. His hips pull away from mine, and keeping me flush against the wall, he thrusts into me. I gasp at the sensation, my core clutching his cock like a vise.

Yes. I bask in the exquisite pressure and fullness and his overwhelming body straining against mine.

I slide my palms over his wide shoulders, feeling the steel bands of muscle beneath. Des's presence is intimidating enough when he enters a room, but now, when he's driving into me, it's all-encompassing.

His hands slide to the backs of my thighs, angling my pelvis so each stroke of his cock slides deeper than before.

He leans his forehead against mine as he hammers me against the wall. "This is every wish, cherub, every dream of mine, actualized. I would give up all my secrets—I'd give up my very throne itself—if it meant being with you."

I want to say something eloquent, but all that comes out of my mouth is a breathy moan.

So smooth.

"And I like it when my mate moans in my arms," Des says. "Hmmm, maybe I should make you moan again…"

The first tendrils of the Bargainer's magic lick against my skin "*Don't*," I say, glamour filling my voice.

Des grins at me, looking thrilled at my response.

Our bodies make slick sounds as he pounds in and out of me, and all too soon sensation is building until I'm coiled tight. Release is right there—all I have to do is let go…

Des slides out of me, and I nearly cry out.

A woman could be driven mad by this!

The Bargainer drops to his knees before hooking my legs over his shoulders. His mouth is inches from my core, but his head is tilted up to take me in. I thought maybe this was part of his game—to withhold my orgasm as long as possible—but one look in his eyes banishes that thought completely.

He's gazing up at me like I'm something akin to his religion, something he might pray to, and right now I feel like a dark queen, my throne made of this man's flesh.

"Marry me," he says.

Time slows and my breathing stops.

Marry me.

A second ago I was mad with lust, and now…now…

"It's not enough to be mated to you," he says, "I want it all, if only you'll have me."

My hands begin to tremble where they grip him. I can barely hear my thoughts over the pounding of my heart.

"Marry me, and I will cherish you forever, cherub."

Marry me.

We're already bound by unbreakable forces. The supernatural world sees us as soul mates, as does the Otherworld.

Marriage is for humans.

Suddenly, I feel all of sixteen again, and Des is asking me to prom. Prom, marriage—all of it is for that part of me that has always been a desperate outsider, a loner. That painful part of me that wants to be *normal*.

This is Des giving me normal.

"Godsdamnit," Des whispers, "please say something, Callie."

I shake my head, beginning to smile.

Only Des misinterprets my action.

His eyes are dying, dying...

I cup his cheeks, just as I did earlier.

"*Yes*," I say, my voice hoarse with emotion. I nod, and once I start, I can't seem to stop. I smile fully, and it feels like that smile touches every inch of my face—every inch of this room. A happy laugh slips out.

I'm going to marry Des!

Life flushes through his face, brightening his features, and I'm sure the world has no use for suns with a smile as bright as his. It spreads across his whole face, his eyes crinkling from the action.

"You're going to marry me?"

I nod again, and I'm smiling so hard, my face is beginning to hurt.

"You're going to marry me," he says again, processing it. "You're going to be *my wife*." He lets out his own disbelieving laugh.

All at once, he stands, and my legs slip off his shoulders. He catches me halfway down his torso, and then he spins us, pressing me close.

Right now, it feels like the two of us are in our own little universe. He's my moon, my sun, my stars, my sky, and all that space in between them.

Des lays me down on the bed before moving up my body languidly. He takes my mouth, kissing it like he's breathing life into me.

My hands rake up his back, brushing against his wings. His wings! I didn't notice them before, but they must've emerged when I said yes. Mine are still locked away from his earlier magic.

This time when Des enters me, it's not nearly as carnal as it was minutes before. His wings splay out, shrouding the two of us as he fills me. He pulls out, the action an agony.

"Years I have waited for this," he says, "anticipated it. My *wife*."

He thrusts back into me. Again and again, he moves out and in like the tide, each deep, rolling stroke a brand, as though he wants to make it known to everyone and every-thing that we are real, we are together, we are one.

This time, when Des relentlessly pushes me toward my orgasm, there's nothing there to stop it.

"*Des*," I breathe, and then I'm moaning, arching, *coming*.

I climax in his arms, staring into those light eyes of his as I feel myself come apart.

The Bargainer pounds into me, stretching out my orgasm until he pauses, his breathing stilling for an instant. Then I feel him thickening. He groans against me.

"Callie—" he bites out. That's all he manages to say before he gives himself over to sensation, pistoning in and out of me as he rides out his own orgasm.

Eventually, his strokes gentle. Even once he's finished orgasming, he stays in me, brushing my hair back as he stares down at my face. "Cherub…there's something I'm forgetting…"

He snaps his fingers, and from the ether, a ring appears between his thumb and forefinger. "I believe this is yours."

The Bargainer's wings are still out, and beyond them, the once bright room is now dark with the Night King's magic.

Des slips off me so he can take my hand. After pressing a kiss to my ring finger, he slides the piece of jewelry on.

The stone set into the band glows faintly; it's no diamond. I'm not one to care about rings, but this one has me mesmerized.

"What is it?" I ask, staring at the glowing stone.

"I made a deal with the stars…"

A deal—of course he did. I smile a little.

"It's captured starlight," he explains, squeezing my hand. "I figured the Queen of the Night should carry a piece of her kingdom with her."

Going to cry all over again.

"You already had the ring picked out…" It's such a ridiculous statement. *Obviously*, he picked out the ring some time ago; it's not like he interrupted sex to make a deal with the stars on the spot.

Des grins, and the sight of it just slays me. "Cherub, it would frighten you how long I've carried that ring around."

Yeah, I'm sure *frightened* is not the word I'd use.

"I'm going to marry you." I get a little zing of excitement just saying the words.

"I'm going to marry the *shit* out of you," he agrees.

As I stare at him, I think about that old vow, the one that got me into trouble. "From flame to ashes, dawn to dusk, for the rest of our lives, be mine always, Desmond Flynn."

He kisses my lips. "Until darkness dies."

CHAPTER 22

The next morning, when I wake, I open my eyes and see a shock of white-blond hair. Des's head rests just above my breast, his features softened by sleep. His arms are wrapped around my waist, one of his legs thrown heavily over mine.

I can't stop the grin that spreads across my face. Des is here with me, seducing me in my home. My left hand is buried in his hair, and now I remove it to stare at my ring for the five thousandth time.

Millions of people go through this—falling in love, getting married, yada yada—and yet I can't possibly imagine anyone else being as happy as I am in this moment, as in love as I am right now.

My hand drops back to Des's white hair, and I pretend for a moment that the two of us have simple lives. That I'm just a human, and he is just my fiancé. That he has no realm to rule and that I don't have wings and scales and a fae stalker who wants my head. That we aren't embroiled in an Otherworld battle that might destroy everything fairies hold dear.

I pretend for a few minutes that we're just two long-lost lovers reunited at last. That later today we'll hold hands and stroll to the coffee shop down the street.

I hear Des's deep rumble. His face rubs against me, his arms tightening around my waist. He tilts his head up, those luminous eyes finding mine.

An easy smile slowly stretches across his face. There's nothing but love in his expression, though even that look on Des is a bit devious.

He brushes a kiss against my sternum. "You know, Callie, I've never been partial to daylight, but I definitely think I could get used to this." His hand slips down and pets my thigh. "Tell me, how do you feel about...sleeping in?"

The gleam in his eyes is hint enough. We'll be sleeping in sans the *sleeping* part.

"I think that sounds amazing."

The two of us don't slide out of bed until hours later, caught up in each other. I'm pretty sure heaven consists of endless days like this one.

Only reluctantly do I drag myself out of bed, and only because Des promised to make us breakfast.

I watch him now, my shirtless Des moving about my kitchen like this is his house and not mine. (I'm pretty sure *he* feels the place is now his.) I try not to smile as he pulls ingredients out of thin air.

Eggs dance in midair, and bell peppers chop themselves. All the while, Des whistles away, his hair tied back.

My eyes move lower, taking in his muscled body and his sleeve of tattoos. The Bargainer is a thing of beauty. A deadly, wily thing, but a beautiful one nonetheless.

It's as I'm relishing the sight of him that I notice the claw marks scouring his back.

I hiss in a breath. Apparently, unbeknownst to me, my claws came out to play earlier.

Des turns around, instantly alarmed. "What is it?"

I nod to his back. "I hurt you."

He casts a glance over his shoulder. I know he can't see the markings, but he must recall them because he smirks.

"If you're feeling truly terrible about it, Callie, I'm sure we could work out a way for you to repay—"

"Des!" That's what I get for being thoughtful.

He laughs, then turns back to my stove, where he's cooking up an omelet. I realize then that he could've simply healed himself. But much like Malaki with Temper's hickeys, he hadn't.

Never going to understand fairies.

The Bargainer flicks his spatula-wielding hand, and a mug of coffee prepares itself. Once it's finished, it floats across the kitchen to where I sit.

"For you, my love," he says, not bothering to turn around.

I catch the mug out of the air. "You're the best," I say, taking a grateful sip.

"Was there ever any doubt?" He glances over his shoulder and winks at me.

It's only a short while later that Des finishes the omelets, my dish floating over to me, his trailing after. They clatter down on the table, forks and napkins hustling through the air after them.

Des takes a seat across from me, and holy Jesus, a shirtless Des is sitting at my table. My lady parts aren't handling the situation well.

He raises his eyebrows at me and looks pointedly at the meal. The Bargainer leans back in his chair. "Stop it."

"Stop what?"

"Giving me your fuck-me eyes. I'm trying to be a gentleman and not screw you right here on your kitchen table."

I set my coffee aside. "The table can take a beating…"

This may legitimately be heaven.

"Can we do this always?" I ask.

I'm sitting cross-legged on the table, my clothing skewed. Scattered across the floor are the remnants of breakfast, the omelets splattered across the ground, the dishes shattered.

Why hadn't Des and I come back to earth sooner? It's obvious this is where we get our freak on. Honeymoon: my house…then Des's house…then somewhere in the clouds between the two.

Des steps up to me, his pants back in place. He brushes a kiss against my lips, then extends a hand. The pieces of my broken mug vibrate off the floor, then fit themselves back together. The splattered coffee funnels itself into the air and back in the mug.

The Bargainer hands it to me. "Need you even ask such a question? I'll *insist* we do this."

I take the cup of coffee from him. "Thanks."

He sits next to me on the kitchen table, a mug of his own floating into his hand. Breakfast begins to fix itself back up, the omelets reforming, the plates piecing themselves together. They clatter onto the table.

"What shall we do today?" Des sounds downright devious.

"I thought we'd already figured that one out."

"Demanding little siren. I'm nothing but your little sex doll, aren't I?"

I shake my head, blowing on my coffee. (Somehow Des managed to make it steaming hot.) "You have me all figured out."

He flashes me a mischievous smile. "I was thinking we might do a little something between shags." He snaps his fingers. "Ah, I know."

I glance over at him. He looks a little too conniving for my taste.

A minute later, a box floats out of my guest room. At first, I think we're doing Redecorating Callie's Home, Part II. But then I recognize the box heading our way.

I nearly drop my mug.

"What are you doing, Des?" This is not a part of my past I want to explore with him right now—or ever.

The box drops onto the ground in front of us.

"What does it look like I'm doing? Digging up all your dirty little secrets. Oh, look—this box isn't dusty like ours was. Someone revisits these things frequently."

I'm clenching my mug now.

The cardboard flaps of the box pop open.

I lean forward and slam a hand on them, closing the box back up. "Let's not."

"Come now, love. I want to see Callie's naughty chest."

I almost fight him on it. Even though he's seen my worst, this is not a collection I'm proud of.

But then, this is what our relationship is built on: we share our dirty little secrets with each other, things no one else might accept us for.

So I eventually lift my hand. "Fine."

The flaps pop open once more. My heart's pounding a

little faster, and my fingers are a little twitchy. No one else has seen what's in this container.

The first thing that levitates out is a gold necklace. A man's gold necklace. It pools in Des's waiting hand.

"What's the story behind this?" he asks.

If I close my eyes, I can still see the man clearly. Wiry, lean frame; mean, squinty eyes. Not all my targets look like bad people, but this one did.

"Keith Sampson. His ex wanted sole custody of their children, so she had me dig up dirt on him. Among the long list of very fucked-up shit he did in his life, he beat his wife, sold drugs to minors, and he got his daughter hooked on heroin so 'the cow could lose some fucking weight.'"

Just remembering Keith has my siren stirring with agitation.

"What did you make him do?" Des asks, curious.

Grovel. Cry. Demean himself.

"I made him turn himself in."

"Hmm," Des says, staring at the necklace.

I get the distinct impression he's listening to the shadows right now. That theory only solidifies when he smirks, then sets the piece of jewelry aside.

The next thing that comes out is a hand-drawn map.

"Arnold Mattis," I say. His girlfriend, Christina Ruiz, hired me to…deal with Arnold.

"Several years ago, Arnold beat, raped, then repeatedly stabbed his girlfriend after she tried to leave him." The crime scene photos still haunt me. "He got off with rape and assault charges, was sentenced to ten to thirty years, but was put on parole early."

When I found Arnold, he had that map on him, Christina's address written out on it. Along with the map, he had bleach, rope, duct tape, and a hammer stowed away in the trunk of his car.

"What happened to him?"

"*I* happened."

Arnold and I played a game called an eye for an eye. He didn't like it much. I did.

Next to come out of the box is an embroidered iron-on patch of a flaming skull. It lands in Des's palm, a bit of black leather still clinging to it.

"Racist biker."

The Bargainer waits for more explanation.

I shrug. "I don't know. It was a bad day, and he pissed me off."

That guy was *such* an asshole. And I had absolute power over him, despite his enormous size and his white-hot temper.

Des pulls out a tooth. He holds the incisor up. "Cherub, this looks more like my work than yours."

Now that he mentions it, it does.

I take the tooth from him before rolling it between my fingers. I close my eyes for a moment, hearing an echo of this man's screams.

"Human trafficker." I can still see his crisp white shirt and the smoke that curled from his cigarette. He looked at me like I was livestock. The memory still gives me chills.

But I'm also proudest of that case. I ended up saving over a hundred men, women, and children.

"I left him alone in a room with his victims and their families."

"Did he die?"

I shake my head. "He begged for it...but no."

I never said I'm a good person, but I came pretty close

to the devil with this one. The tooth is proof enough of that.

"I brought all these men close to death," I say, looking down at the tooth.

For several seconds, the Bargainer doesn't say anything. Finally: "How close?"

Close enough to feel that ancient power move through me, the same power that compelled my ancestors to kill.

I clear my throat. "Close enough to know I should feel ashamed."

Close enough to really enjoy it.

Des huffs out a laugh. "But you're not." It isn't a question.

"No."

Not at all. The box is full of mementos of the cruelest, most sinister people in the world. People who hurt children, who abused loved ones, who tried to get away with murder.

Not even prison or death can atone for the atrocities they've committed. I might be the closest they ever come to a true reckoning on earth.

Des shakes his head. "Gods damn it, but we're similar. Did I make you this way?"

"*You* didn't do anything"—except maybe give me a template on how to work with criminals—"I was this way before you met me."

At the reminder, the edges of the room darken. It's actually pretty heartening, seeing Des get upset for me even after all this time.

He toes the box. "Think I should pay these guys a visit?"

I doubt they'd survive it. The Bargainer doesn't have the same issue with death that I do.

Still, I smile at the thought of the King of Night in his leather pants and vintage T-shirts, dropping in on these men so he can wreak a little havoc—and all because they pissed his mate off at one point in time.

I thread my fingers through his. "Marriage with you is going to be *fun*."

CHAPTER 23

"Enchantress…"

I suck in a breath at the voice. It comes from everywhere all at once.

"Enjoying your time on earth?"

I swivel in a circle, my feet digging into sand.

Sand…?

That's when my surroundings come into focus. There's a beach, and the ocean, and a cliff—a very familiar cliff.

This is the beach beneath my house. I've been here a thousand times, usually alone. If my house is my sanctuary, this strip of land is my temple. And now it's being defiled.

"Nice view," the Thief says, his breath against my ear.

My skin flares to life as fear floods me. I spin to face him.

The Thief is clad in dark clothes—*human* clothes. I thought I saw him at his scariest before, but the Thief masquerading as a human may be the most frightening version of him.

"How did you know where I was?" I ask.

"Callypso." He runs a hand through his jet-black hair. "I know *everything*."

No supernatural is *that* omnipotent.

The Thief of Souls levels his pitiless gaze on me. For a moment we simply look at each other. Then his eyes dip lower.

"That trick you do with your skin," he says, "I quite like it." He leans in close, his mouth brushing my ear. "I imagine being inside you is like fucking a star."

The Thief straightens, running a hand down his shirt and smoothing out the imaginary wrinkles. "Speaking of stars—" Before I realize what he's doing, he captures my left hand. He angles it so he can get a good look at my ring. "The King of the Night didn't go cheap when he popped the question—and you said yes."

"What did you think I'd say? No? That I was saving myself for you?"

He chuckles at that. "What a mortal thought. I rather enjoy our talks, enchantress. No, I want you to enjoy your mate's company for as long as you possibly can. You see, life is just one long story. I don't really care how yours begins… only how it ends."

That sends a foreboding chill down my spine.

The Thief sits in the sand then, and it's so disarming. People expect evil to be obvious; they never expect it to act like anyone else might. He pats the ground next to him. "Join me."

I stare down at him. "I don't intend to stay here."

"Would you rather go back into your house? Care to see if your mate's there?" he says. "I wonder what that would be like, me cornering the two of you in your own home. Maybe we could all kiss and make up for our trespasses."

That visual physically hurts.

"Or I could just hold you down and deflower your 'virgin' cunt while the Night King is forced to watch."

This conversation is over.

I walk away from him. I haven't taken five steps when the earth violently rolls, throwing me onto my back. Beneath me the sand shifts then resettles.

I blink up at the sky, where a couple of seagulls cry out as they fly overhead.

"You are in my realm, enchantress. Here we play by my rules," the Thief says. He sits right next to me, and I have no idea whether he moved to my side or the earth deposited me at his.

My fingers dig into the sand. If I'm in his realm, a realm I only visit when I fall asleep, then...

I push myself up, studying his profile. "So you control small death, and everything that happens here." Like shaking the ground and throwing me onto the sand.

The Thief's eyes brighten. "The PI finally put it together. How very keen of you."

This asshole.

I huff out a laugh. "You know what your problem is?" I say, rotating to face him once more. "You think you're some special brand of evil, but you aren't. I've met plenty of men like you before." Men who use and break and destroy.

He gives me a sly smile, and I've never seen features so cold. It scares me—it truly does. I've caught the attention of an abominable thing, and I know the moment he really, truly gets his hands on me—not in some dream, but in the real waking world—he's going to ravage me.

"I assure you, enchantress," he says, "you've never met a man like me."

I wake in Des's arms, my body covered in a cold sweat. I'm panting, my chest rising and falling.

A moment ago, the Thief and I were sitting out on the beach beyond my backyard, and I can't shake the nonsensical belief that he's still out there, staring up at my house, debating whether he should break down the door and fuck with me and Des.

I clasp the Bargainer's forearm as he cradles my head and neck. I close my eyes and will my heart rate to slow.

When I open my eyes, the Bargainer is smoothing my hair away from my face. "We used to do this together," he says softly, "back in your dorm room. You used to get nightmares, and I'd wake you from them."

Because even when we weren't a *we*, Des was still saving me, over and over.

"Do you remember?" he asks quietly.

I nod against him.

"And now the nightmares are back, and this time I can't save you from them."

I draw a shaky breath and press a hand to my clammy forehead. "He can control dreams—the Thief. He called the place his kingdom."

Des frowns, his forehead wrinkling as his gaze searches my face. I think he's about to tell me something, but the moment passes, and his words never come.

Out my bedroom windows, I hear the surf crashing against the shore. It's one more visceral reminder of my dream.

I shudder out a breath. "I don't know why he's targeting me." I'm embarrassed by how weak I sound.

"Listen to me," Des says, gripping me tightly. "The Thief

218

of Souls may be powerful, but you are *no one's* victim. Do you understand?"

I swallow and nod.

Des searches my face, the moonlight casting his own in shades of blue. "Think you'll be able to fall back to sleep?" he asks.

And end up in another one of the Thief's sick dreams?

I shake my head.

The Bargainer lets out a breath. "Then let's grab breakfast."

I glance at the clock on my nightstand. It's 3:02 a.m.

"Where are we going to get breakfast this early?"

Des just grins.

———————

"I fucking love you, you know that, right?" I ask, pulling apart a chocolate croissant. Around us, sunlight filters into Douglas Café. It may be the middle of the night in Malibu, but it's nearly lunchtime on the Isle of Man. The place is abuzz with people chatting over coffee and pastries, life moving along the same way it did when we used to come here a decade ago.

"It's always nice to be reminded." Des kicks his booted feet up on the table, leaning back to sip his espresso. The years will pass, but watching the big bad Bargainer drink coffee from a tiny cup will never get old.

I take a sip from my coffee, watching some teenage witches gossip as they wait in line to order.

"Do you ever wish you had that when you first got to the Isle of Man?" Des asks, following my gaze.

"Had what?"

The Bargainer smirks. "Don't be coy, cherub. You know what I'm talking about."

Friends. A posse. A group of people who have your back and you have theirs. People to shop with, borrow shit from, tell all your secrets to. There were moments where I wanted all that so desperately, it hurt.

I take a deep breath, setting my mug down. "Sometimes— when I don't think about what it would've cost me." If I hadn't been so desperately lonely, I wouldn't have bartered for Des's company. And if I hadn't bartered for that…

"I would've come for you, love." He kicks his feet off the table. "I searched a hundred years for you. I would've found you, one way or another."

That confession warms me to the tips of my toes.

I take a final drink of my coffee then push it away. I glance back at the girls, who've now moved off to the side as they wait for their order. "And I did eventually get a version of that. And I still have her," I say softly.

Temper filled the gaping hole Des left in me, and I was there to fill the holes her family had left in her.

"Ah, Temper, the woman I am forever indebted to. You know, I happen to know a bit about…her situation."

My eyes widen. I know enough about her fucked-up background. I know her family betrothed her to another sorcerer when they were just kids. I know that sorcerer, Leonard Fortuna, wants to fulfill the marriage contract as badly as her family does. I know all of them are getting impatient at Temper's continued refusal to go along with their plans.

That said, there are so many more dark details about Temper's situation that she has kept from me. I never pushed because I have my own secrets, but I'd be lying if I said I don't want to learn them.

Des takes another sip of his drink. "Maybe I'll tell you sometime…for a price, of course."

Of course.

The Bargainer downs his espresso and stands. "We should get moving. We've got an appointment to make."

I brush off the cobwebs after we step off the ley line and into a condemned church.

Ley line portals occur in the eeriest places.

"Where are we?" I ask as Des leads me outside. Above us, the sky is overcast, and across the street, one building butts up against the next.

"London," Des says, taking my hand.

For a moment, I don't think that's unusual. I'm used to showing up in random cities with Des. It's what we always used to do together.

But now that Galleghar and the Thief are loose, and the Otherworld is in a war, London feels random.

"Why are we here?"

"You'll see."

With that cryptic remark, we head down the street. The two of us walk for several blocks, the Bargainer all but dragging my ass toward this mystery destination.

"Where are we going?" I ask again.

"I have an acquaintance who might be able to help us."

Help us with *what*?

"Unless you're taking me to the spa, I'm really not thrilled about this."

I mean, I will risk another drop-in from Galleghar if it means getting some spa treatment, but that's about it.

The Bargainer glances at me as we cross the street, his expression sly. "I thought breakfast bought me a little amnesty."

I grumble at that because he has a point. You ply me with sex, pastries, and coffee, and I'll overlook a lot of crap.

We finally stop in front of a sleek building.

"This is where you wanted to take me?" I ask, sizing it up. It looks like a place where fun goes to die. It's all smooth edges and modern fittings, and frankly, it looks wrong, sitting in this old city. "I'm pretty sure I'm going to hate this."

"Cherub, you don't even know what this *is*."

I snort. "Unless this place contains a themed bar, a year's worth of macarons, or fucking Santa Claus, it's going to disappoint."

All of which are also things I will risk a drop-in from Galleghar for.

"So dramatic. Maybe if you play nice, I'll take you to a themed bar after this—I might even let you take body shots off me."

I thin my eyes at Des. "That's *blackmail* right there." Completely effective blackmail, but blackmail nonetheless.

"Your deduction skills are off the charts."

I give my mate a light shove, grinning a little. "You don't have to get all mouthy on me. And I'm totally holding you to those body shots." Tequila ones. I want to lick salt off his grossly sexy abs and have him hand-feed me limes.

Why, yes, I *am* a freak.

Reluctantly, I enter the building with him. It's not until we reach the sixteenth floor and I see the metal placard that I realize what exactly the surprise appointment is.

"You're taking me to visit a *seer*?" Simply saying the name sends a wave of adrenaline through my system.

No wonder the Bargainer was being all cloak-and-dagger about our destination. I never would've agreed to come here if I knew.

"Don't you think it's about time we had someone look into your future, considering all that's going on?" Des says.

"No, I don't think so." I don't think so at all. Because *reasons*. Good ones. Ones I don't want to talk about.

I'm still staring at the sign.

Belleby & Sons, LLC
Seer
Forewarned Is Forearmed

I shiver a bit. My stepfather was a seer. He worked in a place just like this one, dealing out fortunes to the richest and most powerful people—people who were often on the wrong side of the law.

That was how I first found the Bargainer. A client had given my stepfather Des's card, and he kept it close at hand, ready to call on the Night King if he found himself in a tight situation. As fate would have it, *I* was that tight situation, and the Bargainer was my saving grace.

The floor is eerily silent, except for a distant moan. I rub my arms.

Those body shots are going to have to be the most delicious mouthfuls of tequila in the world.

Des places a hand on my back and leans over to kiss my temple. That's the closest he comes to apologizing for the rotten trick he played on me. He leads me down the hall, and the place seems all but abandoned.

"Business is really booming," I say.

Des's mouth quirks, but the rest of his face is stoic.

We stop in front of a door. Behind it, the moaning is louder.

Whoever is foreseeing futures here, it sounds like they're busy ruining someone else's life.

Maybe we should just come back later…

Without any warning, the Bargainer blasts the door open. "Knock knock."

Inside the room, a naked woman shrieks from where she lies sprawled on the desk, the man on top of her scrambling to disentangle himself.

"Oh *shit*," the man says, catching sight of Des. He rapidly tries to shove his junk back into his slacks.

Just—*ew*.

The mostly naked woman screams again, trying (pretty unsuccessfully) to cover herself.

I guess that explains the moans…

"I thought you said we had an appointment?" I whisper at Des.

My mate doesn't look at me, instead shaking his head at the man. "You know better than to mix business with pleasure, Collin."

Guess that's the seer. Color me unimpressed.

The Bargainer waves his hand idly, and the clothes the woman is trying to put on fit themselves to her body. She yelps, then scrambles from the room.

"Damn it," the man says, watching the woman leave before turning his attention to Des. "You could've called."

He has a point—after all, forewarned *is* forearmed.

"My clients always say that," Des says. "Problem is, when I call, they have a bad habit of disappearing, and I have a bad habit of finding them and adding interest to their bill. Really, this is better for all parties involved."

Collin grabs his discarded shirt and slips it back on.

"What do you want?" he asks, disgruntled. He buttons his shirt and leans back against the desk.

Going to need a Bible and some holy water to clean the deeds off that piece of furniture.

I feel the breath of Des's magic leave him. It slides the seer's shirtsleeve up, revealing two jagged tally marks.

I step forward, instantly curious. It's rare to see one of Des's clients with more than one of his tattoos. Probably means Des trusts Collin.

"Remind me again how many months you've had these?" the Bargainer asks.

The man pulls his sleeve back down, fidgeting with the cuff. I get a glimpse then of how young he really is. Midtwenties maybe? And now that I'm looking for it, there are indications he's uncomfortable in the clothes he wears.

After what we walked in on, I wasn't expecting that from this guy.

"I'm willing to pay off my debt," Collin says. "Just tell me what you want."

Now I hear Collin's rough-around-the-edges accent. A scenario takes shape: a kid with promise but not a lot of options approaches the Bargainer. The Bargainer sees something of himself in the young man, so he helps him a little more than his other clients. And thus the young seer has an inspiring rags-to-riches tale and only two debts to show for it.

Collin's eyes move to me, and there they catch.

"Who's this?" he asks with a tad more interest than is professional.

"It doesn't matter who she is. What matters is what you can do for her," Des says.

The seer's face turns cocky. He gestures for me to come forward.

"Wash your goddamn hands first," Des growls. "You're not touching her after having your fingers in some broad's pussy."

Collin raises his eyebrow but gets up. "I see our time apart hasn't made you any nicer."

Des's eyes flick briefly around the room. "I see our time apart has made you richer."

The seer grunts. Giving me a little nod, he leaves the room.

I turn to the Bargainer. "Why are we doing this?"

Really don't want to be here.

"Cherub, I personally promise that if Collin does anything you don't like—"

I open my mouth.

"—other than foreseeing your future—"

Damn it. I close my mouth.

"—I will gut him from navel to throat."

Jesus.

"Well, I'll collect my last favor from him, and then I'll gut him navel to throat," Des amends.

"No one needs to gut anyone else. I just—"

The door opens, and the rest of my words die away as Collin returns.

"All right," the seer says, "where were we?" His eyes fall to me, brightening with interest. "Oh, right, you want a reading."

"*I* don't want a reading," I say because I figure that point needs clarifying.

Collin turns to Des.

"Give her a reading."

Ugh.

The seer clears his throat. "Okay. Please, take a seat, ma'am." He gestures to a nearby couch.

I'm sure I look like a petulant child as I take a seat. I mean, I get it, just because my stepfather was Satan (that's

226

not literal—I've heard Satan is actually a lot nicer than Hugh Anders), it doesn't mean all seers suck.

But it also doesn't mean I have to be a good sport about this.

Collin sits down next to me, and Des moves to the wall across from the couch before leaning against it and folding his arms, his biceps stretching the sleeves of his AC/DC shirt.

Seriously unfair that the Bargainer can look so tasty even when I'm annoyed at him.

"I'm Collin," the seer says, drawing my attention back to him. "Figure you ought to know my name before I go peering into your future."

I'm about to clap back that I already know his name and this sucks and everything sucks, but I force out a smile. "Callie."

"Nice to meet you."

Yeah, whatever.

The seer takes my hands, his thumbs stroking my skin in a way that's not entirely professional. But maybe that's just me.

I stare down at our hands, and as I look at them, I sense his heartbeat pounding beneath his skin, moving magic with blood. His human power fills my senses.

His ability is strong, staggeringly so.

My eyes flick up to Collin.

I think I'm waiting for incense, incantations—at the very least an open flame or a shallow bowl of water to divine my future from. My stepfather had a bowl he used to carry around that was meant for scrying. He never used it on me—he never dared to face his monstrous deeds head-on—but he liked using it with clients.

This seer doesn't do any of that. He breathes in deeply, his gaze fixed on mine, his eyes searching, searching...

They unfocus.

My own gaze goes to Des, who's settled in a nearby chair. With one booted foot, he's tilted the seat so it rests on its two back legs.

When he catches me staring, he curls the edge of his mouth up. He levitates himself and the chair, entertaining me like he used to when I was a teenager.

I snicker.

"Eyes on me," the seer says gently.

My attention returns to Collin. The two of us stare at each other for a long time. Long enough to make me shift in my seat and for this to feel awkward. Long enough for me to vividly visualize those body shots.

It takes another minute, and then Collin speaks. "I see another entity shadowing you, slipping into your consciousness when it has a chance—what can do that?" the seer murmurs to himself. "This is no incubus... This is...no earthly being. It will continue to haunt you. It wants to...I'm not sure. It wants you—*enchantress*."

That name. I tense.

Des's chair lands harshly.

Now Collin closes his eyes. Seconds pass, and his breathing seems to slow.

This feels like it's going off script...

The seer's eyes snap open.

I rear back. I know the creature staring from behind those eyes.

This is no seer. Not anymore.

He speaks. "*Hurry, enchantress, you're running out of time.*"

I try to pull my hands free, but Collin's grip tightens.

"*I'll devour you slowly. Your life is mine.*"

The corner of Collin's mouth curls into a sinister smile.

"So flee from me, for once I'm through, I'll be freeing myself and coming for you."

The seer drops my hands, coughing and rubbing his throat. When he glances up again, the Thief is no longer in his eyes.

"What the *fuck* was that?" he rasps.

I'm shivering, not just from apprehension. The room's grown cold and dark.

Des steps out from the shadows. "That was a creature in need of extermination," he says, helping me off the couch. "What else did you foresee?" he asks, staring at Collin.

The seer clears his throat, still rubbing at it. "I saw darkness and death, and something about it was...*aware*. Whatever that shit was, it's closing in on her," he says, nodding to me. "If no one stops that thing...then it will get her. And in that case..." Collin looks at me apologetically. "Death is not what you should worry about."

Death is not what you should worry about. That should be the Thief's slogan. I've already seen that when it comes to this monster; there are brutally twisted things he can do that circumnavigate death.

And now my mind conjures up all sorts of impossible things worse than death.

See, this is what I mean about wanting to have a normal life. Normal people don't typically have to worry about things worse than dying.

Collin rolls his shirtsleeve up just as one of the two black lines disappears from his skin.

"That was really all you wanted?" he asks.

"Would you like me to take more?" The darkness still hasn't lifted.

"No—no," the seer rushes to say.

"Then I'll be around," Des says. "And professional tip: Try to keep your dick in your pants during the workday. It's bad for business."

Desmond puts a hand on my back. "Ready to go, cherub?" he says, his voice gentling for me.

I nod. *More than ready.*

Collin reaches a hand out, presumably to shake Des's. The Bargainer looks down at it with mild distaste.

Instead of taking the seer's hand, Des manifests a black business card between his own fingers. "You know how this works. We're not fucking chums. Give my card to a friend in a tight place, or don't, but don't forget where we stand. You still have a favor left."

I guess that's as close as the Bargainer ever gets to his nicer clients.

Collin takes the card from Des, and that should be the end of things.

It's not.

Maybe Collin is cocksure, or curious, or maybe he just wants to make a point, but at the last minute, he grasps Des's hand anyway, forcing the Bargainer into a hostage handshake.

The moment Collin's skin touches my mate's, the seer sucks in a breath, his eyes unfocusing.

Methinks someone else is getting their fortune read…

Next to me, Des's form flickers. One second Collin has him in a handshake, and in the next, Des grabs the seer by the throat.

He slams Collin back against the wall. "I'm sorry, but I don't remember asking you to fucking read my future," the Bargainer says calmly. There's nothing to give away his simmering anger—no shadows, no outline of wings—nothing.

Collin pries at Des's fingers uselessly, but the more their skin touches, the worse off the seer appears to be. Collin's eyes roll back, his breath choking. His body spasms once, twice.

I step forward. "Des, what are you doing?" I ask, alarmed.

He frowns at the seer. "Nothing." As if to prove his point, the Bargainer releases the man.

Collin crumples to the ground, his body weak and shaking. He moans, his eyelids fluttering. He coughs. "Bargainer—"

The Night King stares impassively at him. "You pull that stunt again, you'll lose those fingers one by one." Des glances over at me. "Ready, cherub?"

Uh... "Yep."

Des places a hand on my back and leads me to the door.

"Wait," Collin calls out from behind us.

The Bargainer doesn't slow.

"There's something you should know," the seer says, his voice hoarse. "The darkness...the darkness will betray you."

CHAPTER 24

We don't speak until we're a block away from the building.

"How would you like a beer?" the Bargainer finally says.

"*Des.*" It's barely a whisper.

"*I* need a beer."

"*Des.*" I stop. I feel like I can't catch my breath. "You can't just pretend the past ten minutes didn't happen."

The Bargainer mutters something under his breath. He turns to me, his hair looking like snow against the gray London backdrop.

"Callie, nothing is going to happen to me." He sounds so sure of himself. Like he's impervious to harm.

I want to shake him. "That seer said the darkness would betray you, Des!"

"The seer is a little prick who got too big for his breeches."

Why is he not listening? "He looked into your future!"

"*Callie.*" He takes my hand, rolling my engagement ring a little. (Always have to be wearing a piece of the Bargainer's jewelry.) "It's all right. I'm not discounting Collin's words. What will come to pass will come to pass, but you need to trust in me. Can you do that?"

No. Ugh, *yes*.

"It feels like I just got you back." I glance down at my feet before looking at the Bargainer again. "I can't lose you twice."

"Who said anything about losing me?" Des asks. "Don't let your mind play tricks on you now, love. Betrayal is not a death sentence."

I take a deep breath. He's right. Begrudgingly, I nod.

"You good?" Des asks.

Nope. Not really.

"I want those body shots."

Desmond finds us a themed club after all. One that offers body shots.

Alchemy, a nightclub in London, is decked out to look like a sorcerer's paradise, every decoration tied into black magic and spellcasting.

"Cherub, this is a bad idea." Des gazes up at me from where he lies, fake flickering candles encircling him. He looks like a sacrificial offering among it all, and I guess that's the point.

"You love bad ideas," I say. I hold a little vial of salt in one hand and a lime in the other.

So fucking excited.

"Normally. This one I'm not so sure of." Under his breath he says, "Would've been more fun if our roles were reversed."

I lean in close, my mouth inches from his. "I'll make *sure*

233

you enjoy yourself." I punctuate the statement by running the lime wedge around the Bargainer's navel. His eyes brighten, and through our bond, I sense the barest hint of his excitement.

He is such a liar. He's as thrilled about the situation as I am.

My attention moves from his face to his torso. I follow the lime wedge with a circle of salt.

Honestly, this is so sexy, it should be illegal.

Des flashes me a wolfish smile. "Enjoying yourself, cherub?"

"Just a little." I place the lime wedge in his mouth and flag down the waiter.

A man dressed in sorcerer's robes comes over with a handle of tequila. At my signal, he pours the amber liquid into Des's navel.

Once he's done, I lean in.

I smile at Des as I lick the salt off his abdomen.

A groan slips from between his teeth.

Pressing my lips to his navel, I swallow the tequila.

Beneath my mouth, the Bargainer's muscles flex. I place a hand against them as I rise, the alcohol burning down my throat.

I lean in again, pressing my lips against the Bargainer's, then take the lime wedge between my teeth, the citrus cutting through the bite of the alcohol.

Once I set the lime aside, Des sits up and swivels to face me, kicking over an array of candles in the process.

He places his hand between his legs on the slab. "Have you had your fill, love?"

That's a trick question, right?

I lean in. "Not even close."

Des keeps his shirt off for the rest of the night, and the entire population of this place can't handle it.

Seriously, they can't. It's a problem.

"Everyone is looking at you," I say.

Des sits *on* the bar, drinking straight from a bottle of fancy whiskey. He's really not supposed to be doing either, but when I told him that, he simply said, "Rules are meant to be broken." Then he winked and took a sip of his whiskey, and I spontaneously orgasmed.

Okay, the last one didn't happen, but it was a near thing.

I sit on the barstool like a normal, grown-ass woman… while my fairy king all but pins me in with his legs.

Not that I'm complaining about it. At all.

I mean, I'm right at eye level with his abs. There are worse views.

Des lowers his bottle of whiskey. "Everyone is looking at *you*, cherub." He shakes his head. "The years passed, but at the end of the day, you're still that high school girl woefully unaware of her own beauty."

A woman steps up to the bar next to us, her arm innocuously brushing Des's thigh.

"Sorry," she says, apologizing even though half the people in this place are touching the other half.

I give the Bargainer a pointed look. *See?*

He ignores the woman, instead leaning forward. "Your wings are starting to show, baby siren."

I'm keenly aware of that. Alcohol plus fae possessiveness plus all my lusty thoughts are making it nearly impossible to hide them.

The woman leans into Des, and this time when her arm brushes his thigh, it's no accident.

"Do you come here often?" she asks Des, ignoring me completely.

My skin brightens, and I look at the woman. "*Scoot.*"

Without another word, the woman pushes away from the bar before moving back into the crowd.

So that was technically against the law...but God, it felt good.

"Is someone *jealous*?" Des flashes a devilish smile, taking another swig from his bottle.

"Pshhh, no." *Yes.*

I glance at my skin and frown as it dims. "This is a supernatural bar, right?"

"Not exclusively." Using the hand that holds the bottle of whiskey, Des crooks a finger at me. I don't move so much as his magic presses me up against him. "Which means that, much as I love these—" He touches a wing.

Oh crap, they're out again.

"—we're going to have to put them away."

Beneath his palm, Des's magic pours into me, just as it did the last time he hid my wings, back at my house. There's a momentary pressure as the magic forces them to disappear, and then they're gone.

We stay at the nightclub for another hour, moving from the bar to the dance floor to an area where we can stand and mingle.

The entire time the patrons of this place watch me and Des, and there's so much in their looks. Lust, envy, avarice. The Bargainer does nothing but seed it; I taste his magic in the air, reckless and wild, beckoning people to make bad decisions.

Eventually, they do. They drink more, touch more, and creep ever closer to us. Fights soon break out, at least two couples appear to be participating in some *heavy* petting, and

Des and I scare off a dozen people interested in poaching on this relationship.

"Do you do this at every party you attend?" I ask.

"Do what?" he asks, appearing innocent.

"Rile people up."

He smiles. "Are you not having a good time?"

"I literally almost clawed a woman apart five minutes ago." She inserted herself between me and Des and then proceeded to flirt with my mate—at least until he conveniently sidestepped her to rejoin me.

"Shame I stopped that so soon."

Ugh. This is what happens when your soul mate is a fairy. True shows of devotion often involve spilling blood.

"But you're forgetting all the people who've approached *you*," he adds.

People who then took one look at the menacing Bargainer and rethought their game plans.

Des sets the beer he now holds on a nearby table. "Why don't we call it a night?"

The body shots were drunk, the good times were had, and everyone else here is now a sloppier mess than either of us. It's as good a time as any to get going.

The two of us leave the club, heading down a couple of blocks until we get to a local cemetery. Once there, Des leads me through a ley line entrance, the air wavering as we step through.

It takes less than a minute to travel from London back to California, and when we step off the ley line, we're back in Des's house.

The Bargainer whisks me out of the circular portal room, the door clicking shut at my back, lock after intricate lock engaging.

I glance at Des, who leans against the door for a moment. He's got the devil in his eyes when he looks at me.

"What?" I say. My blood rushes through my veins.

"You didn't think I'd let you take those body shots without repayment now, did you?" Des says.

In a blink he's in front of me.

Shamefully, his shirt is back on. It brushes against mine as he steps into my space, backing me against a nearby wall.

"How do you want it—on the floor, against the wall, or over the counter?"

Christ. My skin glows as my siren awakens, drawn by sex and magic.

His hand dips into my pants and cups my sex. "Or would you rather I choose for you?"

I gasp, my hands coming to his upper arms, my fingers digging in.

It takes little effort for him to slide my panties aside and dip a finger into my core. "I'm taking that as *choose for me*."

"*Des*."

He's feral and overwhelming and silver-tongued and so very, very fae.

A second finger dips in. I moan at the sensation.

My fingernails sharpen as I clutch him, my claws pricking his skin. My nails dig deeper, and the King of the Night grins when they pierce his flesh.

We really are a twisted pair, getting off on blood and sex.

My breath comes in pants, my legs parting wider as I urge him on.

His nose and lips brush my flushed cheeks. "Or perhaps I'll choose none of that. How I love seeing you fall apart at my touch. Perhaps my touch is all you'll get." He nips at my chin, toying with me. Clearly enjoying that I'm clay in his hands right now, ready to be molded into whatever shape he wants.

A minute ago I wasn't thinking of sex; now I'm lamenting the slow torture of him burning me up without properly filling me.

I reach for his pants, but he catches my wrist and pins it to the wall.

"Uh-uh. That's not how this works." Des kisses my neck then moves his attention to my mouth, tasting like liquor and dark deeds. All the while his deft fingers stroke me up and down.

He takes my lower lip between his teeth and rolls it around, his clever eyes particularly devious.

He releases my lip.

"Come against my hand," Des demands.

It's the same pushy order he used to give me back when I had a bracelet of beads.

And even though the bracelet is long gone, the Bargainer's magic blooms between my legs, strange and forbidden.

My knees go weak as my orgasm is pulled from me, sweeping through my system. The pleasure is violent and sudden. It seems to stretch on and on, and even once the waves of it abate, the comedown seems to last a lifetime.

I lean my head against the wall, breathless and flushed. "You are such a bastard," I murmur.

"Awww, you don't really mean that, cherub," Des says, removing his fingers from my panties. He places the two of them in his mouth, licking them clean.

Have I mentioned how dirty he is?

It only takes a minute or so for me to regroup from getting fingered within an inch of my life. My siren is riding high. Far from being satiated, she's only just gotten a taste of sex.

After pushing off the wall, I prowl over to the Bargainer. Taking his jaw gruffly, I kiss his mouth.

"For a guy who specializes in favors, your repayment plans lately could use some work," I say, tapping the side of his jaw with a clawed forefinger.

I'm sure I look just as devious as he does.

Releasing his jaw, I kneel in front of him.

"Callie..."

I unbutton his pants, glancing up at him. Des's eyes are crackling with desire; he wants to tell me to stop, but he also wants my lips around his cock—and he wants that *very* badly.

The zipper makes a hissing noise as I pull it down. "Lucky for you, when it comes to repayment, I'm willing to help."

CHAPTER 25

The world forms from chaos, blurs of color sharpening until they become things.

The first thing I notice is the tickle of wheat against my open palm. Then it's the vivid blue sky bearing down on me.

Then it's the Thief.

He walks through the fields dressed in black, looking like a reaper come to collect my soul. Like the last dream, seeing him this way is disarming. If you take the monster living under your bed and put it in broad daylight, what then?

He comes up to me, uncomfortably close. This is where I cringe away from him, where I revolt.

"You went to bed with one man and woke with another. How *very* confusing," he says.

I'm not awake. It's on the tip of my tongue, but I hesitate.

I get the uncanny feeling that this is what I'm supposed to say. That the Thief has our entire interaction choreographed, and it's all part of our little game.

Only I no longer want to play.

I'm done revolting, done being scared, done acting according to some preordained script.

Rather than respond, I squint at our surroundings.

From horizon to horizon, there are endless golden fields rippling under a painfully blue sky. The wind sings through the wheat.

"How do you choose where we meet?" I ask.

His hair stirs as he answers, "Whatever pleases me in the moment, that's what I choose."

As my eyes take in that sharp blue sky, clouds roll on the horizon. They're unnaturally swift, gathering on each other.

The Thief of Souls can build dreamscapes and wear the faces of the dead. Two staggering powers.

The clouds darken like bruises until they've shadowed the land. The sky splits open above us, and the heavens unleash. Lightning flashes and thunder booms.

Rain pelts down on me, and the wind lashes against my body, whipping my hair about. I feel like I'm at the center of some terrible vortex, and the magnitude of it all is dizzyingly beautiful.

"Does it frighten you?" the Thief asks. He watches me carefully, the wind and rain tearing at him.

No.

I turn to him, my wet hair slapping at my skin. "Do you want it to?"

An enigmatic smile crosses his face, and his eyes flash alongside the lightning.

Just as swiftly as the storm moves in, it retreats. The rain stops, the sky clears, and the sun peeks out again.

"I think you have better things to fear from me." He circles me. "Things worse than death."

I remember Karnon's prison, the women shackled in iron, raped by the Thief, slowly losing themselves to his dark magic. I think of the soldier I interviewed.

It's dark here. Very dark.

I want to rest. Why can't I rest?

He returns to my front. "I will never leave you alone, enchantress. Never. Banish the hope if you have it. You cannot ever escape my clutches. Not even in death."

I search his dark eyes. "What have I done?"

Is it being a siren? Is it as simple and as shallow as pretty skin molded over pretty bones? Or is it something specific to me, something that went wrong long ago?

There's a part of me, a long-dormant part of me, that's awakening. It should've been pulled free back in high school, when my powers blossomed, or when Karnon altered me, or even when Des fed me the lilac wine, but it wasn't.

It didn't happen then, but I feel it now, some buried strength upwelling from deep within me.

The Thief tilts his head. "What have you done?" he echoes. "You have *enlivened* me. You make me feel the blood rushing through my veins." He steps in close. "You have *aroused* me. Dirty human, beautiful woman, unlikely enchantress. You have caught my attention, and I will enjoy you for a time."

I'm not going to escape him.

This is the one simple truth I denied for so long, and now I face it.

I'm really not going to escape him. One day soon, I will have to face the Thief, not in a dream but in waking life. A reckoning is coming for us, and by the end of it, one of us will be the victor, and the other, the vanquished.

"I will break you again and again until there is nothing

left to break," the Thief says softly, running his knuckles over my cheek.

Break me?

I've been thinking about this wrong all my life. I'm not porcelain to be shattered, I'm something else entirely.

Break me?

I level my pitiless gaze on him. "You can try."

The next morning, when I wake, I'm alone in Des's bed.

I simply lie there, gathering my pillow and breathing in the Bargainer's scent.

Eventually, I sit up, running my hands through my hair. On the bedside table sits a cup of coffee. The note beside it says, *Till darkness dies.*

A little smile slips out. I take the mug and sip, letting my mind drift.

Inevitably, my thoughts move to last night's dream. For the first time since I started having them, I'm not frightened by the nightmare. The Thief of Souls and I are pitted against each other, not as hunter and hunted but as *adversaries.* And that detail changes everything.

Since Karnon's death, I've been in the business of running—so much so that I haven't truly done any *chasing.*

Setting my coffee aside, I slip out of bed and rifle through Des's things until I find a notebook and a pen. Clambering back into bed, I uncap the pen and press it to the page.

The Thief of Souls—controls dreams (small death), wears the bodies of the dead, wields dark magic, places fairies into a stupefied state, fathers children who drink blood and prophesize...

244

Most of the attributes have something to do with death, and those that don't are seemingly attributes of Night fairies. Not that this knowledge brings me any closer to answers.

Stupid mystery.

I could just glamour the Thief and force the confessions out of him.

Holy shit.

I *could* do that. Why have I not thought of this sooner?

I'm elated for two seconds before I remember I freaking already tried this trick *after* I drank the lilac wine, when he came to me in a dream. It didn't do a damn thing but excite the freak.

So much for that idea. Unless dreams have their own sort of logic to them. Maybe he's only impervious to my glamour in dreams...

I rub my forehead. I mean, who the fuck knows at this point? I'm running in circles here, and all I'm managing to do is confuse myself.

Setting my notes aside, I push myself out of Des's bed. I steal an Iron Maiden shirt from his drawer, ignoring the folded set of clothing clearly meant for me, grab my mug, then pad down the hall.

I find the King of the Night in his living room, blessedly shirtless as he paces back and forth. He stares down at an unrolled piece of parchment, his brow furrowed and his lower lip pinched between his fingers.

His eyes move from his work to me. A grin spreads across his face when he catches sight of my T-shirt. "That is a *very* good look on you, Callie."

I hold up the mug. "Thanks for the coffee."

"Anytime, love."

"What are you reading?" I ask, coming over to him.

He drops his gaze to the paper, and his frown returns. "Reports on the state of the Otherworld."

For a moment, the information is a shock. I almost managed to forget that even on earth, Des has a host of responsibilities he still must attend to.

See, this is proof I'd make a shitty queen.

"What are they saying?" I ask.

"Malaki tracked Galleghar to the Fauna Kingdom but lost him there. And, as far as the kingdoms themselves go, Flora and Fauna are suffering massive casualties.

"The wholesale slaughter in those kingdoms continues. The Thief's soldiers are moving to all the big cities and killing any fae they come across. The formerly sleeping soldiers are sustaining heavy losses themselves—Flora and Fauna fae aren't just going down without a fight—but the carnage continues."

This entire time, fairies have been dying. While I was taking body shots off Des, those soldiers were cutting through innocents.

My stomach rolls at the thought.

You've let yourself be idle, my siren whispers. *This is what happens.*

"Why would the Thief do that?" Conquering is a blood sport, but these kingdoms have already fallen. There's no reason the deaths should continue.

"Why would he indeed?" Des looks up from the paper, meeting my eyes. "You have a box of memorabilia from some of the worst humans. What would *they* do if they came into power?"

They'd kill and maim and run their kingdoms lawlessly, and no one would be safe but for them.

"This isn't a human we're dealing with," I object.

Humans have their own drives; fae have others.

"Evil doesn't work that differently between worlds,"

Des says. "Although fae *do* have a knack for creativity and flair."

Des sets the parchment aside. "Oh, by the way, I thought you should know Typhus Henbane is dead."

It takes me a minute to place the name.

The King of the Banished Lands, the one we'd come to for news of Galleghar.

The man with a city's worth of stolen magic is now dead, and I'm at least partially responsible for it.

Yesterday, that piece of information would've sat like a stone in my stomach. Today...today I'm in an odd mood.

"What happened?" I asked.

"Exactly what you feared might happen. His people rose against him and slaughtered him. They took back their magic."

The magic he'd forced them to barter away...

Bartered magic.

My eyes snap to Des.

"What?"

I run back to his bedroom, only to find the Bargainer is already there waiting for me. He stands, arms folded, watching me with curious eyes. Sidestepping him, I grab the paper I left on the bed and stare at my notes.

"Can I have my timeline?" I beckon to Des with my hand.

Wordlessly, the Bargainer produces the time line I created days ago, then drops it in my hand.

I set the two papers side by side on the mattress. Over my shoulder, the Bargainer stares down at them.

It was right in front of me the entire time.

"Galleghar and the Thief share powers."

247

CHAPTER 26

Galleghar and the Thief share powers.

I don't know how or when or why the two of them linked up, but I would stake serious money on the two being co-bound. That would explain why Galleghar keeps popping up during our search for the Thief. He's hooked on the same magical power line that the Thief of Souls is. So long as their magic is bound together, you can't have one without the other.

The proof of their strange partnership is mapped out on the time line. Centuries ago Galleghar is killed, only his body is incorruptible, defying the natural order. For two hundred years, he lay dormant—much like the sleeping soldiers—until he was awoken by a shadow—a shadow like the one that haunted the sleeping women and the casket children.

When I turn to face Des, he looks...horrified. The expression is only there for a moment before he tucks it away.

His gaze moves to mine. "*Gods.*" He takes a step closer.

"That would explain why my power wouldn't destroy the sleeping soldiers."

Because the shadows are loyal to their own. Even if the Thief isn't a Night fae, his life and magic is co-bound to a man who is one.

The darkness will betray you.

I grab my notes and read over the list of the Thief's traits. His powers obviously have something to do with necromancy, but necromancers are mortal, and the Thief is not.

"Des, can you think of any fae who can do what the Thief can?"

It's an old question, one the two of us have run around a dozen times already. So I'm not surprised when Des shakes his head. Whatever the shadows tell Des, they won't tell him this. There are some secrets not even they will give up.

Unfortunately, those are the secrets worth knowing.

I sit inside Des's kitchen and spin my engagement ring around and around my finger while he brews us a pot of coffee. For once he's not using his magic, and the domesticity of it has my throat tightening.

My time here on earth has been lovely and essential—and yet it's largely a mirage.

Neither Des nor I get to have this life—not while the Thief and Galleghar terrorize the world—and no amount of bargaining can change that. At some point, our time here will end, and then we'll have to go back to the Otherworld and deal with all the problems we left behind. I already feel them pressing in on all sides, threatening to suffocate me.

Abruptly, I stop spinning my ring as a thought comes to me.

We may have to go back soon, but there is one last thing I'd like to do before our time here is up.

My gaze moves to Des just as he turns from the coffee maker.

His brow furrows when he sees my expression. "What is it, cherub?"

I exhale. "Take me to Venice."

———————

It's been eight years since I've been to this place. Eight shockingly long years. And yet, walking next to the canals, you'd think it was only yesterday that I convinced Des to take me on one of his bargains.

Even now my heart skips a beat, remembering that first time I watched him work. His world was supposed to frighten me, but it had the opposite effect. I got a taste for his secrets, his favors, his *magic*. That was the first night I peered into his world.

So it feels only right to come back here now.

Next to me, Des studies my face. I still haven't told him my reasons for coming here.

"Secrets, cherub, are *my* thing, not yours," he says. But his eyes are bright, like he very much enjoys whatever little trick I have up my sleeve.

It's a good trick too.

"Give me an hour alone."

Des raises his eyebrows. "What mischief are you going to get into without my company?"

Awww, is someone feeling excluded? Too bad. "The kind you're not privy to."

Des narrows his eyes.

"Go find something to do for an hour," I say. "I know how to reach you."

"Hmm," he says, assessing me. His eyes rise, taking in

the glittering lights of Venice. It's late here, but the city is still alive with music, voices, laughter. The place is under its own sort of spell. "I'm supposed to just…entertain myself in the meantime? Here?" *Without you?* He doesn't say this last bit, but I hear it nonetheless. And it warms me to my toes.

"I'm sure this isn't the first night you've found yourself with time to kill."

He takes a lock of my hair and twists it around his finger. "Fine, Callie. I'll find something to do"—he says this like he's going to look for trouble—"while I wait."

I part my lips to respond, but Des disappears into thin air. The lock of hair he'd been twisting now flutters back down to my shoulder.

My heart pounds a little louder.

I've got an hour. Best make it count.

———————

I know what I want the moment my eyes land on it. I'm even surer once I run my fingers over it.

Right now, I hold the great secret I'm trying to keep from Des—

His wedding band.

I angle the ring back and forth under the light of the jewelry shop. Tiny pieces of crushed mother-of-pearl catch the light. Their iridescent color isn't as flashy as I'm used to; it looks closer to moonstone than anything else, but it isn't the moon I want Des to be reminded of. It's the sea.

My mate gave me a piece of his night sky. I'm giving him a piece of my ocean. The siren practically purrs at the thought.

I run my finger over the band again, my heart beating fast. I never thought I was the sentimental type, but here we are.

251

"I'll take this one," I tell the jeweler.

I buy the wedding band and leave the shop. I haven't even taken ten steps when I stop and pull the ring out of the small velvet case it's nestled in. I roll it between my fingers as I stare down at it.

There's one last thing I want.

I've rarely tried to tap into Des's magic, but I've had little reason to. Now I do.

I close my eyes and tug on the connection I share with the Bargainer. Down our bond I feel the pulse of his magic. I draw on it until it slips through my veins. With a little push, I send it down my fingers and into the ring itself.

When I open my eyes, I catch sight of the engraved words Des's magic bought me; they twist around the inside of the ring.

Until darkness dies, be mine always.

A combination of his vow to me and mine to him.

God, I'm really owning this whole business of being sappy.

Before I can study my work in any more detail, a familiar presence looms in front of me. I glance up at the Bargainer, startled to see him.

"You weren't supposed to come until I called," I protest.

The question falls on deaf ears. The Bargainer's eyes latch on to the wedding band, and he's looking at it like he's Gollum and I'm holding the One Ring to rule them all.

Aw, fuck.

This wasn't supposed to happen quite this way.

"You drew on my magic," Des says absently. "I was worried. What is that?"

My heart hammers at his question. I bite my lip, but it doesn't stop the words from spilling out.

"It's your ring." I take a deep breath. "Marry me, Des. Tonight. Right now."

He stares at the ring for several more seconds. Slowly, his moonlit eyes rise to mine, the silvery threads of them luminescent.

His hand closes around the ring, his other hand wrapping around my wrist like a manacle—as though I and my offer will slip through his fingers if he doesn't hold on tightly enough.

He looks…very fae. Very, *very* fae. His features seem to have sharpened, and the look on his face is rapacious.

"Are you serious, Callie?" The words are careful and clipped, like he's holding back a great deal of hope.

I nod, not daring to speak. The last of my courage slipped out with my words.

His hold on my wrist tightens, and then his wings manifest.

CHAPTER 27

I can't get over the sight of him in all his glory—right in the middle of Venice, no less.

He looks at me like he's dying, like this is agony, but then he smiles, and the sight is staggering.

His free hand threads its way into my hair, and then he's pulling me forward, and his mouth is suddenly hard against mine.

He kisses me like a man possessed, his lips laying claim to mine. I taste his magic on his tongue, like the night itself has a flavor.

Even after the kiss ends, the Bargainer keeps me close, his hand clasped behind my neck, his forehead pressed to mine.

"I would love nothing more, Callie, than to marry the shit out of you." He tilts my head so he can whisper into my ear, "You cannot know…" I feel him shake his head against me as words fail him. He holds me close, his talon-tipped wings curving protectively around us.

I reach out and touch one leathery wing, tracing a vein. "Bargainer, I would like to make a deal."

Des stiffens. "Callie…"

He doesn't need to say anything more for me to understand what he's thinking about. The last time I bargained with our relationship, we lost seven years together.

"It's a little request," I say. One that should have no lasting repercussions.

The King of the Night waits, but there's no mistaking how tense his body is.

"I want to get married somewhere special to you."

Des touches my face lightly, his expression unreadable. I think maybe he's wildly elated, but maybe that's just hope talking.

After wrapping a hand around my waist, the Night King lifts us into the air, his wings billowing about him.

"Cherub, it's a deal."

The place Des chooses to marry me is not earth, but I didn't think it would be.

We stand among the ruins of the temple of Lyra, some ancient fae goddess associated with new life. The carved marble archways and columns are now mere bones of what once must have been an extravagant building.

Time eats away at all things—not even the fae are impervious to that fate.

The wild grass has overtaken some of the fallen slabs of stone, its stalks swaying in the evening wind, the blooms of a thousand pearlescent flowers bobbing to and fro among it all.

Lyra's undying flowers, Des told me when we first set foot in this place.

Temper and Malaki arrive shortly after us. I've got to hand it to the two of them—they clean up well considering we gave them such short notice.

Short notice as in we dropped the news only a few hours ago.

"Well, well, well," Temper says when she sees me, the train of her misty blue dress dragging along behind her, "*there's* my best friend. Did you have fun boning Bat Boy while the rest of us were actually saving the Otherworld?"

I press my lips together to keep from smiling. "I wasn't just boning Des," I say. "We partied a little too."

"*Without me?*"

"Don't act like you were being held here against your will." I found her in Malaki's room, wrapped up in his sheets.

"You don't know what it's been like here." She side-eyes Malaki, who's busy thumping Des on the shoulder. Temper lowers her voice. "He's really freaking intense, which is awesome when he's drilling me, but not so much when it leaves the bedroom. I get the impression the dude wants *commitment.*"

Yeah, I'd gotten that impression too. Too bad Temper's allergic to it.

She waves the conversation off and pulls me in for a hug. "I seriously never expected this day to come," she says, holding me close. "You're giving me faith that even us wicked creatures can find love."

I laugh in her arms.

My friend pulls away to take in my glowing pale gown. The fabric is made from spun moonlight, the embroidery shining just a little bit brighter than the rest of it. At my throat is the necklace Des fashioned for me from moonbeams.

I feel like a fairy queen.

"You look beautiful," Temper says. There's no sarcasm, no joke, no usual barb to curb the sweetness of her words.

"All right, Temper, you can stop being sentimental. It's freaking me out."

Malaki comes over then, pulling me in for a hug. "Desmond is a blessed man to be mated to a woman like you. Thank you for making him happy."

Des's general and I have never talked much, and to be honest, I always worried he felt I was just some girl. So to hear him say that...

I don't have the words to tell him how that makes me feel, so I simply hug Malaki tighter.

He releases me and steps back, placing a heavy hand on the back of Temper's neck, his fingers idly rubbing her skin. She's not batting him away, which she'd have no problem doing if she didn't like the guy.

Hmm...

A mystery for another day.

Des steps up to me, clad in the same glowing silks as I am, his bronze circlet on his head. He's almost unbearable to look at; his inhuman beauty is almost painful in its intensity.

"Callie," he says, "there's something I want to show you."

Des takes my hand and leads me away from Temper and Malaki and then away from the ruins themselves. Cool night air whistles through the flowers, and it's all so very serene.

The Bargainer brings me to a small mound covered with flowers. He kneels in front of it, placing his hands on the earth.

"This might be a bit macabre, but I've wanted to bring you here for a long time," he says. "This is where I laid my mom to rest."

I start at that.

His mom, the woman who'd sacrificed everything for him in the end, was buried here?

And *Des* laid her to rest? I try to imagine that—Des carrying his slain mother to this place, digging a grave for her. Had he been alone? The possibility itself is heartbreaking.

"Why here?" I ask.

It's beautiful, but so are countless other places in the Otherworld.

"She used to tell me stories of Lyra, the Goddess of New Life." Des nods his head to the ruins.

His eyes return to the grave. "Sometimes I come here to be close to her," he admits. He glances up at me. "I'm sorry. I didn't mean to make this about the past."

"It's not." I take his hand and pull him to his feet.

The Bargainer has few important people in his life. Even in death, his mother is one of them. The first woman to care for him. It's only appropriate to be here, where she can pass that torch to me.

I give his hand a squeeze. "Let's go get married."

I begin to tug him back to Temper and Malaki, yet he resists.

"Wait, Callie, there's one more thing."

I turn just as Des reaches for the heavens. Far above us, the stars shine away, but as I watch, molten drops of starlight spin down from above before coalescing in Des's palm. He whispers something in Old Fae. In response, the starlight jumps in his hand, moving around until it forms itself into a delicate twinkling circlet.

Des grasps it in both hands and places it on my head. "There."

He steps back, the starlight reflecting in his eyes, and stares at me the same way he did all those years ago when he made me a crown of fireflies.

"In all the worlds and all the ages, there has never been another like you, Callie." He clears his throat, like he's remembering himself. "*Now* let's get married."

Des and I stand before Temper, our hands clasped. The sorceress's usual attitude is gone. Here, with Des and me before her, she's solemn. Among the oddities of the evening is that she's our officiant. Malaki stands off to the side, the witness to Temper's officiating.

Des runs his thumb over the skin of my hand as he gazes into my eyes. I'm not sure he's ever been more handsome than in his suit of spun moonlight. Standing across from him in my own glowing gown, the wind carrying my filmy train off into the night, I finally feel like this life fits.

My mate was right: I'm not normal. *This* is not normal. People don't have claws and scales and wings and Otherworldly stalkers.

But normal people also don't get to feel their soul mate's magic move in them. They don't get to be part of a fairy tale. They don't get the love that transcends time and worlds.

I squeeze Des's hands.

Normal people don't get this, but I do.

Temper reads our wedding vows, and the Night King and I recite them again to each other—with a few additions of our own.

"From flame to ashes, dawn to dusk, for the rest of our lives, be mine always, Desmond Flynn," I say. My wings have come out, exposed by my raw emotion.

The Night King brings my knuckles to his lips. "I'm yours, Callypso." His own wings are folded at his back. They've been visible ever since Temper first started reading the rites.

Des lowers my hands, his eyes searching mine. I feel his magic gathering in the air, the darkness pressing in on us.

I say, "And mountains may rise and fall, and the sun may wither away, and the sea claim the land and swallow the sky. But you will always be mine. And the stars may fall from the heavens, and night may cloak the earth, but until darkness dies, I will always be yours."

And so we get married before the ruins of Lyra, Des's mom watching us from where she lies among the undying flowers, our friends beside us, and the stars our only other witnesses.

———————

Before we leave the ancient temple, Malaki, Temper, Des, and I share a bottle of fae wine from Lephys, where the fruit itself is grown from the island's glowing waters. It tastes like hope and love and the sweetest memories.

This may be the first time the four of us have ever sat together outside a professional setting, and I find Malaki has a dirty sense of humor and that he and Des act more like brothers than best friends.

"Thank the gods you finally made an honest man of Desmond," Malaki says, leaning forward to clink my glass.

"'Honest'?" I raise my eyebrows. "Are we talking about the same man?"

Malaki laughs, and his teeth are blindingly white against his olive skin. "Aye, that's a fair point."

"Letting you two be friends might be my worst decision yet," Des says, gesturing between me and his general.

"Now you know how I feel." The only thing worse than Temper or Des on their own is getting the two of them together.

"I still can't believe you two did body shots without me," Temper grumbles.

"What's a body shot?" Malaki looks genuinely confused.

"Oh, you sweet thing." Temper pats his cheek. "I'll show you later."

After the wine's run out, Temper and Malaki return to Somnia. Des and I linger in Lyra's fallen temple a little longer, the evening breeze rustling the wild grass and making the flowers sway.

There, among the ruins, the Bargainer makes love to me, each stroke of his hips a promise. The two of us share a bond, a single life, and decades and decades of unwritten future.

Eventually, we leave the ruins, trading in Lyra's undying flowers for silken sheets and the comforts of Des's palace.

It's only in Des's chambers, my body draped over his, that the silence swarms in. I lift my head from his chest. The King of the Night is already asleep, his breathing deep and even.

I stare at his devastating features in the dim lamplight. Something thick lodges in my throat.

Husband.

It's just one more title to tuck away, one more claim I have on him.

I trace one of his pointed ears.

I'm unspeakably happy—*and yet*.

And yet I still don't get to have this life. The easy, uncomplicated one. I may be living a fairy tale, but fairy tales aren't just full of princes and fair maidens and moonlit weddings. They are full of monsters too. Monsters and violence and terror and death.

My hand shakes as I continue to trace Des's ear.

Tonight is the beginning of something…but I fear—I fear it is also the end.

CHAPTER 28

"Congratulations to the new bride."

I turn and face the Thief of Souls.

He reclines on a chair made of gold, the metal worked into strange and twisting spires that arch far above the headrest. I glance around and realize I'm back in the room made of pale stone. The same flowering bloodred vine grows up the wall, and the humming pool sits off to the side of the throne, even now vibrating with power.

All around me, the columns look like bones, and there's a faint smell here, like soured wine...

"Where are we?" I ask.

"You know, I never understood the point of small weddings. Why go to the trouble of marrying someone if no one's there to see it?"

Guess I know the Thief's answer to the question, *If a tree falls in the woods, does it make a sound?*

"Apparently *you* saw," I say.

He lifts a shoulder. "In a manner."

I narrow my eyes at him.

He leans forward, the leather he wears creaking a bit at the motion. "Have you figured out who I am yet?"

I stare at him.

"Ah." He pulls the answer from my face—or maybe he knew it already. "You may have your wiles, enchantress, but you are not one for puzzles. A shame, really"—his eyes turn sly—"when your mate so clearly is."

"What is that supposed to mean?"

The Thief looks so self-satisfied when he lounges in his seat. "He's figured out quite a bit more than you have."

It's just one more lie to add to the rest.

"What have you been doing now that you don't have women to rape and soldiers to kidnap?" I ask.

The smile he gives me is downright spooky.

"Don't you know, enchantress? I've been preparing for you."

A short while ago, a confession like that would've undone me. But now, though I feel a twinge of fear, it's eclipsed by a grim sort of exhilaration.

"That makes two of us," I say, in case he has forgotten that I too am a dangerous creature.

His eyes flicker with dark excitement. "How very intriguing. I do await our true reunion." He leans forward, steepling his fingers. "Tell me, does knowing I'm co-bound to Galleghar in any way diminish my mystery?"

I almost take a step back. *How does he know that?*

The Thief's eyes sharpen on me. "Truly, I'm disappointed at how magnificently you've underestimated me. I have spies more thorough than the Night King's pixies. I thought you would've been aware of that by now.

"I know what you ate for breakfast, how many times

you spread your pretty thighs for your mate in the past day. I know that fool Galleghar attacked you on your way to capturing him. I know he wants to do it again. I know you are not nearly so worthy of destruction as the fallen king seems to think you are. In fact, I just might keep you."

This is...*alarming*. He's been watching me like a hawk tracking prey.

I glance down at the thin shift I wear and finger the material. The dress is white and gauzy and leaves precious little to the imagination.

"It seems unfair," I say, looking up at the Thief.

He rests his chin on his fist. "What seems so?"

I walk toward him, the action causing the fairy to arch an eyebrow. Not many fae who know of his true nature would willingly approach him.

"If we're playing a game, how am I ever supposed to truly engage with you if you know so much of me and I know so very little of you?"

His fingers idly tap against his gold armrest. "Impatient human. I thought you made a career for yourself in deduction?" His fingers still. "But I *do* have an unfair advantage— and well, we can't have that now, can we?" The Thief settles back in his seat and lifts a hand. "By all means, voice your questions."

This is just another game within a game, but it doesn't stop me from asking anyway.

I glance around. "Is this a real place?"

"It's real enough."

I have a feeling sideways answers like this one are the best I'm going to get out of him.

"Where are we?"

"Three guesses," he says.

I step closer to him. I don't really want to. I'm not an idiot; this *thing* that's after me is about as evil as they come, but my siren is oddly intrigued. He makes me want to sharpen my claws and finger-paint with his blood.

"You're sitting on a throne…"

"I am."

I've now visited all the main kingdoms and seen all the palaces. This looks like none of them.

"Are you a king?" I ask.

"A king?" he scoffs. "Come now, enchantress, let's think bigger than kings."

This dude is such a megalomaniac.

"What is your real name?"

The Thief of Souls cocks his head. "And if I tell you, what then? Will you come storming my castle, seeking to batter down my doors as my soldiers did yours?"

Yes.

He glances away from me, his muscles tensing as he looks off in the distance. The corner of his mouth curls up in amusement.

The Thief relaxes and faces me once more. "One day I'll tell you my name," he says. "When it's too late."

Again, the Thief's attention is drawn away. His fingers resume tapping on his armrest. "Someone's trying to get in," the Thief says idly. "Why don't we invite them inside?"

For a moment I see him, like a mirage on the horizon.

"Malaki?"

The general's form wavers as his gaze moves in my direction. He stares blindly about.

"Callypso? Are you all right?" he asks.

"She was, until now."

One instant the Thief is sitting on his throne, and in the next, he's in front of me, lifting me by the throat.

"Callypso!" I hear the slide of steel as Malaki unsheathes his sword.

I kick out at the Thief, my claws extending. I don't bother trying to shred apart the hand choking me; instead, I swipe at the Thief's eyes, ready to gouge them out. My nails sink into soft skin, and warm *black* blood begins to pour out.

Cursing, the Thief tosses me aside.

I laugh, and I'm not ashamed to admit it sounds creepy as fuck with my glamour riding it.

"The Thief's hurting worse than I am," I call out to Malaki, who seems blind to us both.

"You're going to pay for that," the Thief says, and the surety in his voice should scare me witless.

Whatever wits I had, they're long gone now.

I get up, my skin aglow. The siren is riding me hard, and God, how we've wanted this moment.

Sword brandished, Malaki moves toward me, his eyes still unseeing. "You'll have to go through me to get to Callypso," he says to the room.

I get up as the Thief approaches Malaki.

"Dreamweaver," the Thief says, "this is no place for you. Your sentiments might be sweet, but you cannot possibly protect your precious queen. You don't even know where she *is*."

My wings come out, and my golden scales ripple to life across my forearms. I'm as Otherworldly as I ever get.

With a powerful beat of my wings, I leap into the sky, and when I land, it's in front of the general.

I flare my wings wide, blocking him from the Thief.

"This is *our* game," I say, getting a little thrill at the sight of the Thief's bloody face. "Leave him out of it."

"I intend to," the Thief says. There's malicious glee in his expression, and I can see that whatever suffering he tends to inflict, it's all for me.

"Are you trying to protect me, Callypso?" Malaki asks. I feel the brush of a hand against my wings. "Step aside. Let me gut this monster."

The Thief laughs. "And how might you do that? You are blind to us, and it is by my grace alone that you're uninjured."

As I watch, the Thief's eye repairs itself.

Jesus. How am I supposed to kill this thing if he can heal that fast?

"To think they call you Lord of Dreams," the Thief continues, his gaze focused on Malaki. "Your bloodlines are weak these days."

Behind me, the general says, "You will—"

Like a candle snuffing out, Malaki's presence is suddenly gone.

It feels colder here. I hadn't realized that even in dreams, the Thief's magic carries traces of his depravity.

"He was getting tedious, I'm afraid." The Thief dabs at his face, his fingers coming away bloody. "You got me in a mood. Don't think I'll forget this, Callypso."

"I hope you don't." I want him to remember how I hurt him.

He turns from me, heading back to his throne. When he sits and faces me again, the strange black blood is gone, all evidence of my aggression wiped away like it never was.

I fold my wings behind me and approach him once more.

"You are either very foolish or very brave to come so close to me."

Aetherial had said something similar to me once...back when we were this man's prisoners.

"What do you want?" I ask, my skin dimming. "I mean, what do you *really* want?"

The Thief lounges in his chair. "What does any creature want? To live."

Forgive me if I state the obvious, but—

"You *are* living."

He shakes his head. "No, no, no, enchantress, I am *surviving*."

If all the carnage he's wrought is his version of *surviving*, then I cannot imagine what *living* entails. Only that it simply cannot happen.

I eye the Thief up and down. He appears normal enough, but he's an oddity even among fae.

"Where are you from?"

He gives me an enigmatic smile. "Far, far away, enchantress. Far, far away."

When I wake up, Des is gone.

I sit up in bed, my hair cascading around me. For a moment, I can't place where I am. Earth or Otherworld? My house or Des's?

It's only when I catch sight of the arched windows that I remember we came back to Somnia. A balmy evening breeze blows in from outside, carrying with it the scent of flowers.

My hand slides over the empty space next to me.

"Des?" I call out.

The lamps are dimmed. I don't have a clock to go by, but I'm pretty sure this is the witching hour, a time when good little supernaturals are all fast asleep.

Probably why I'm *not* asleep.

I get up before slipping on one of the least elaborate dresses I can find. Moving from room to room, I look for the Bargainer in our chambers, playing with my wedding ring as I do so. He's nowhere to be found.

I could simply call on him. I know the words.

Bargainer, I would like to make a deal.

He'd be here in an instant.

But I don't necessarily want to pull him away from whatever he's doing.

At least, that's what I tell myself. I ignore the ball of worry in the pit of my stomach.

I'm imagining things. This is what I always do when life gets too sweet. I assume the worst—and rightfully so, the way my life's been so far.

Closing my eyes, I focus inward. Right where my heart is, I feel the glow of my bond. It's the magical tether that connects me to Des, the thing that physically makes us soul mates. I've pulled on his power through our connection, but I've never tried to simply find him through it. I know enough about supernaturals to know it can be done.

I could try.

My breathing slows. The smells and sounds and sensations all fade as I search down that magical bond.

And…*nothing.*

I open my eyes, feeling ridiculous.

Where *is* Des?

A knock on the door interrupts my thoughts. I stride over to it and, grabbing the knob, swing it open.

Malaki stares down at me, looking more ferocious than ever. "I think it's time we talk."

"Where is Des?" I ask.

The two of us are sitting in some side room I've never been in before. On the wall is an intricate mosaic depicting some great battle taking place in the heavens.

"Busy being a king." Gone is Malaki's good humor. And here I thought we'd bonded last night over that champagne.

I lean back in my chair.

"And Temper?" I ask.

"I am not her keeper."

Could've fooled me…

Just then a fairy comes in carrying a tray with an assortment of coffee and pastries on it. Malaki and I are quiet as he lays it out. It's only after the fairy leaves and the two of us are alone once more that we speak again.

"Why were you knocking at Des's door in the middle of the night?" On our wedding night, no less.

I look around, trying to figure out why I'm here, having a conversation with Malaki, instead of in bed with Des.

Seriously, where the hell is the Bargainer?

"How long have you been having dreams of the Thief of Souls?"

I focus on Malaki once more. "Since Solstice. Why?"

"You haven't talked about them," he says, leaning back in his seat.

Now that I get a good moment to study Des's friend, I realize how out of place he looks here in the palace. He's a hulking, massive man, and with that eye patch, he looks more like a pirate than some dainty fairy.

"Should I have?" I say. "They're *dreams*."

But I know better than that. Dreams are never just dreams, especially not the ones I'm having.

Malaki curses under his breath. "How long has Des known about them?"

"Since Solstice."

The general rises from his seat, looking utterly terrifying. "That *fool*," he says darkly.

I don't move, but my claws extend and my scales appear, my skin brightening just a touch. "*Careful* what you say about my mate." My voice is soft and dangerous.

A slight to our mate is a slight to us.

Malaki stares down at me, his gaze growing distracted as he takes me in. "Do you know why they call me the Lord of Dreams?" he asks.

Dreamweaver, the Thief had called him.

"It's because I am the best at what I do." He doesn't say this like he's bragging. He states it like it's a simple fact.

My skin dims back down. "And what is it you do?"

"I can spin dreams." His dark gaze pierces mine. "I design the setting, I bring in the people, I orchestrate the activities. I can pick an enemy's mind apart this way—learn his weaknesses, discover his plans.

"Last night, for the first time ever, I met a force more powerful than my own. And not just slightly more powerful. My magic was all but useless against the Thief's."

The Thief of Souls told me small death was his realm.

Malaki rubs a hand down his face. "The Thief has an unhealthy obsession with you, Callypso. I didn't understand the depth of it until tonight."

Hearing those words come out of another's mouth makes my flesh prickle.

"Desmond admitted to me yesterday that Galleghar and the Thief of Souls share power," Malaki says. "That they're co-bound."

He pauses.

I wait for him to continue. The suspense has me tensing.

"Galleghar was an extremely powerful king, but from what I understand, he could never control dreams, much less slip into them. His magic lay in more tactical areas."

I search Malaki's face. "Why are you telling me this?"

"Galleghar couldn't control dreams, he couldn't put fairies to sleep, he couldn't wear the skin of the dead. Whatever powers the former Night King bequeathed to the Thief, they don't hold a candle to the ones the Thief already has."

My heart is beating loudly. I hear it like a drumbeat.

"We already knew the Thief of Souls is powerful," I say.

Malaki shakes his head. "You're not following. The Thief's power eclipses mine—and it eclipses that of a *king*, a powerful one. And I fear—"

Commotion outside the room interrupts us. A moment later, the door bursts open, and a royal guard steps inside.

"Your Majesty, my lord," the breathless guard says, nodding to each of us. "We can't find the king, and—"

Wait, Des is not on the palace grounds *at all*?

"What is it?" the general asks, standing.

I stand too. I have a bad feeling in the pit of my stomach. At my back, my wings itch to come out.

"Sleeping soldiers," the guard says. "More of them have broken through our portal, and now they're headed for the gates."

CHAPTER 29

Malaki is already striding to the door. He points to me. "You need to bar yourself. Guards—"

He's not being serious, is he?

"I'm coming with you," I say, following the general out the doors. "I can stop them."

Malaki lets out a breath. "Desmond would want me to protect you."

Des, who's noticeably absent. "Desmond would *love* to see you try."

Malaki mutters something about stubborn human women under his breath.

The two of us head down the hallway, surrounded by guards.

"I can stop the soldiers with my glamour," I insist.

"Do you really think I've forgotten?" Malaki asks, his voice sharp. "The problem is the Thief knows that too. Whatever this is, it's most certainly a trap."

"I don't care."

Malaki grabs my upper arm before swiveling me around to face him. "Damn it, Callypso," he growls, "you will listen to me!"

My skin brightens. "Let *go* of me."

Malaki's hand drops from my arm.

"*No one* talks to me that way," I say, venom in my voice. "Not even Des, and definitely not you."

"You are thinking with your heart, not your head!" Malaki says. "I've seen hundreds of men killed for doing similar."

My voice heats. "Do you really think I'm eager to run headlong into battle? That I want to be killed or captured and reunited with that monster we've been hunting? You forget—I've been his prisoner once before. I've seen what he does to the fairies he plays with."

So long as I live, those memories will never leave me.

"What's going on now?" Temper's voice carries from down the hall.

Startled, Malaki and I turn to face her.

My friend looks sleepy and disgruntled, but despite that, her hair is on point, and she still managed to slip on a glittering black dress.

She fairies it way better than I do.

I relax at the sight of her. The thing about being best friends for as long as Temper and I is that half our conversations don't need words. All she has to do is take one look at my face and my exasperated expression, and her sharpened gaze slides to Malaki.

"What have you done to put that expression on my friend's face?" she demands.

"Temperance," Malaki says, "I don't have time for this."

"Then you better *make* time."

He hesitates, and that's all the opening I need.

I mouth *thanks* to Temper and slip down the hall.

"Hey!" Malaki shouts after me, but then I hear Temper lay into him, and let me tell you, that girl knows how to rip a man a new asshole.

A few guards have broken away from Malaki; they now trail after me. If any of them disagree with me getting involved in this situation, they keep that opinion to themselves.

I enter the entrance hall and head toward the huge bronze doors leading out.

Can't believe I'm doing this. Des wanted me to be his queen, and I fought and fought against that... And now I find myself here, eagerly taking on a threat to his kingdom.

The guards manning the main entrance open the doors for me, and then I'm passing them by, leaving the castle behind me.

I halt when I notice them.

Formerly sleeping soldiers march up the streets of Somnia, headed right for the gates, and there must be hundreds of them. These sleeping soldiers aren't from the Night Kingdom. Some have flowers sprouting from their hair; others have feathers and tails.

This is what remains of the Thief's stolen army. These are the victors, the ones who've been terrorizing the Flora and Fauna Kingdoms. The evidence of it is in plain sight—most of them are covered in gore, blood, and other bits matted into their hair or else dried and discolored on their clothing.

If there's one thing I've learned of fairies, it's that they take grooming *very* seriously. Which makes the whole thing all the ghastlier. This army looks like the risen dead.

But despite their gruesome appearance, they're not madly striking out for once. And they've come here of all places...

One of the royal aides bustles up to me. "My queen, we barred the ley line portals just like the king asked—they got through anyway."

The Thief's power…it eclipses that of a king.

"We took several of the soldiers down at the portal entrance, but they're not attacking…"

I take an audible breath, and the aide stops talking.

"I'll deal with them," I say, still eyeing the soldiers.

The aide backs away, leaving me alone. Ahead of me, the soldiers march in orderly lines, their faces passive.

The moment they reach the gates, they stop. Their final footfall echoes through the streets, and then all is silent.

I take another deep breath and cross the yard, toward the fence that encircles the palace. As I approach the soldiers, I release my siren. My skin illuminates, and my stride turns a little sensual.

"You are not to harm any of the Night King's subjects," I shout, my voice carrying through the night.

Silence. Then—

"We're not here for them," one of the soldiers says. Her voice is quiet, yet her words seem to reach every corner of this city.

"Why are you here?" I ask.

"You know why," another soldier says.

I don't. I stop several feet from the gate. "Enlighten me," I say softly.

"Your days are few, enchantress," a soldier across from me says. "We look forward to spreading those pretty thighs of yours and seeing what a king's treasure tastes like."

It tastes like your death, my siren whispers.

Around me, the night darkens.

Des.

"The next soldier to threaten my wife will be openly eviscerated," the Bargainer calls at my back, his voice ringing into the night. "And please test me."

I spin to face him.

The King of the Night paces toward me, clad in his royal regalia. His bronze circlet sits across his forehead, and his three bronze war bands are on prominent display. He even wears a cape, and it should look ridiculous, fluttering and snapping behind him, but if anything, it seems only to add to his menacing presence.

Des comes up to my side, his wings fanning out behind him. "I leave for one hour, and look what trouble my mate gets herself into," he says softly, his eyes glinting. "You're not even wearing your daggers. Have I not taught you better?" He snaps his fingers, and the daggers and their holsters manifest, fitting themselves around my hips.

Beyond him, Malaki is storming out of the palace. Temper saunters out behind him, looking pleased.

For the moment, Des and I have Somnia's attention. His people watch from windows and rooftops and the streets below. The soldiers stare sightlessly forward, though I know that behind those seemingly empty eyes lurks the Thief of Souls.

Des eyes them. "Why are you here?" he asks.

"Is it not custom for new rulers to meet?" a soldier replies.

As I stare out at the sleeping soldiers, I notice that among them are a few casket children. I bite back my horror at the sight of their sweet faces covered in gore, their eyes filled with malicious delight. Their bodies might be young, but whatever souls reside within them, they're ancient corrupted things.

"The Night Kingdom does not recognize your rule, Thief," Des says.

For a moment, the only noise is the snapping of the Bargainer's cape in the wind. Then a low laugh starts among the soldiers. It raises my gooseflesh, hearing that evil laugh ripple through the line of them.

"For now."

I step forward, my skin burning bright. "You're so eager to acquire this kingdom, and yet here we all stand. I *dare* you to make good on just one of your threats and take me."

Come for me, and I will rip you to shreds.

I'm not surprised when the air darkens. Des hates when I bait the Thief.

"Tempting," the soldier says.

I open my arms. "Take me, Thief. Right here, right now. I know you want to."

"*Cherub,*" Des warns.

I ignore the King of the Night as I step closer to the edge of the property.

A great hush has fallen over the crowd. It was silent before, but now it's as though the world is holding its breath, waiting for something to happen. I feel a thick dark magic pooling around me. Whoever the Thief of Souls is, his hunger presses down on me.

The first line of soldiers steps forward until they're right up against the fence. After grabbing their weapons, they lift them and strike out at the bronze railing.

Before their steel ever hits the fence, it collides with an invisible barrier, some strong enchantment made to ward off the enemy. The ward doesn't simply hold—it blasts the line of soldiers back like an explosion, throwing them into their comrades.

Another line of soldiers steps forward and attempts to break the enchantment, and like the first row, they're blown back. Then a third row comes forward—

"Stop," I command.

Immediately, the crowd stills.

I look over the men and women, with their empty eyes. "You might be strong, Thief, but today won't be the day you defeat the Night Kingdom."

"So confident. So strong," a soldier says. "My, haven't you grown into your role. I wonder if that will always be the case."

"Leave," I command, "before the good citizens of this place decide you are all better dead than alive."

The soldier's eyes flash as he dips his head. "Until next time, enchantress."

The lot of soldiers turns, their movements robotic.

"Oh, one last thing—" I say to their backs. "You will not harm another fae. Ever."

———

You know what the most annoying thing is about these drop-ins? There always has to be some long discussion following them. Everyone has to regroup and decide on a plan of action, but there's really no way to plan for a man like the Thief of Souls. He doesn't play by the rules, it's not clear what he wants, and there seems to be no orderly way for us to stop him.

But I sit through the meeting anyway and listen to everyone rehash the past several hours all over again. Once the meeting is over, it's clear Des and Malaki have more to talk about, the two of them moving to a corner of the room, where they continue speaking in low voices.

I turn to Temper. "Down to raid the kitchen?" *Need a drink after that meeting.*

"Do you really have to ask?"

Fifteen minutes later the two of us are sitting in some random hallway, munching on a tray of pastries and drinking fae spirits straight from the bottle.

"It's been too long since we've done this," I say.

It used to be a weekly thing. We'd go out, or we'd stay in, but it would always be together. Sleepovers, brunches, late-night movie nights, barhopping, clubbing—we were attached at the hip.

"You can say that again." Temper sighs. "That alone is reason enough to kill the Thief of Souls. He's messing with our routine."

I take a big bite of a cheese-filled pastry before washing it down with a swig of fae wine.

I pull the bottle away and stare at it. "Ever notice fairies make their liquor way too sweet?"

"*Right?*" Temper says. "Never thought I'd crave cheap scotch so much in my life, but here we are."

I turn to her. "Thanks for earlier—you know, with Malaki."

"*Anytime.* You know how it is with us."

We've been each other's wingwomen for as long as we can remember.

I set the bottle down and reach out, taking Temper's hand. "God, I love you."

"Are you drunk? You are *such* a lightweight."

"Seriously, Temper?" That's her response to me pledging my love to her? "You ingrate. I'm not *drunk.*"

She squeezes my hand. "I love you too, Callie, even if you go to earth and do body shots without me."

280

"Hey, I invited you to the wedding."

"Only because you needed an ordained minister."

She and I both know that's not the only reason.

"How did you even *manage* to get ordained?" If anyone should've been rejected, it probably should have been Temper. I mean, I love my friend, but she's not exactly a saint.

"Fuck if I know—the internet is a magical thing."

The two of us look at each other and burst into laughter.

It's Temper's turn to grab the wine bottle and throw it back. "You know, for all the battles being fought in the Otherworld, I've had hardly *any* chances to zap someone."

My mood darkens as my thoughts return to the Thief. "I'm sure your day will come."

"Oh, I *know* it will. That's why I've been hanging around this place. I love a good fight."

I give her a look.

"*What?*" Temper says defensively.

"You are such a liar," I say. "You're not here for some fight. You're not even here because I am, though I know you love me. You're here because you like shacking up with Malaki."

For a moment, Temper doesn't respond, gathering her thoughts.

"I'm here because I want a fight," she finally says, "*and* my best friend happens to be a queen. Malaki is a perk of the situation."

Yeah, I'm not buying it.

"I'm going to hex that look off your face."

"I'll stop you first," I say, my skin brightening.

"Nice try," Temper says. "Your glamour no longer works on humans." She sounds so certain of that fact, like she knows the effects of the lilac wine better than I do.

"Does it now?" I say, letting my magic fill my voice.

Temper's gaze briefly goes hazy before it clears.

"Oh, you smug siren," she says, starting to chuckle. She takes another drink of the wine, shaking her head. "You can glamour humans *and* fairies?"

I lift a shoulder. "Seems that way."

Only the Thief appears to be immune to my charms, which is unfortunate, considering he's the one I'll probably need to use them on.

"Lady, you better watch your back," I say. "Malaki gets that possessive look when he sees you." And he's annoyingly bossy, I've come to find.

Temper fans herself. "I know, isn't it fucking hot?"

Uh, that's one way of looking at it.

"Temper, he's Des's best friend. If you break his heart, shit is going to get awkward." I mean, I got a taste of Malaki when he's peeved; forgive me if I don't want to see what he's like when he's heartbroken.

"Who said anything about me breaking his heart? I'm more interested in breaking his bed."

She's not considering breaking up with him? This far into a fling, Temper is *always* considering breaking things off.

I turn to give her my full attention. "*What* is going on between you two?"

She waggles her eyebrows. "Wouldn't you like to know?"

I laugh. "Oh my God, don't hold out on me now."

"*You* don't want *me* to hold out on you? You're the one who's more secretive than your husband lately—and ugh, can we talk about the fact you're married now? You're all domestic and old."

"I'm not old. And stop changing the subject," I say. Gah, she's hard to pin down when she wants to be.

"How about we talk about the fact the Thief of Souls wants to bone you?"

"Let's *not*." I feel a shudder coming on.

"I mean, you could just give in and knock boots with the baddie."

"*Temper.*" Seriously?

"Yeah, you're right," she says. "That's too evil."

"Also, I'm married—and mated—and in love," I say slowly. "Let's not forget that either."

"Right, right, right." She takes another swig of the fae wine. A laugh slips out of her, and that's about when I realize she's teasing me.

I release my breath. "You're the *worst*."

"Suck it, Lillis. I'm the best and everyone knows it."

The air wavers in front of us, and then Des is there, an eyebrow raised as he stares down at us. "So this is why there's a pastry shortage in the kitchen."

I inconspicuously dust crumbs off my chest. Temper, meanwhile, licks her fingers.

"It's not my fault your kitchen's understocked," she says tartly.

Des's eyes flick to her. "Malaki is looking for you."

"Is he now?" Temper says, her interest piqued. She gets up, grabbing the tray of pastries, the bottle of wine still in her clutches. "Then I better go find him… See ya, Callie." She salutes me with the bottle of wine then heads off down the hall, her heels clicking.

Des turns his attention to me. "Wife." His eyes are burning. "We have some unfinished business."

CHAPTER 30

"This is not how I expected to spend the day after my wedding." The two of us walk through the castle's halls. I assume we're heading back to Des's chambers to, you know, *finish business*, but the Bargainer leads me past the halls that wind toward his suite.

"I think that's the point," Des says. "I doubt the Thief wants us to enjoy our time together."

Was that the Thief's entire reason behind that show at the gates? He told me in a dream before that he wanted me to enjoy my time with Des. So it doesn't make sense.

"Where were you this morning?" I ask.

"About."

Ugh, why can't fairies ever be straightforward?

"Your guards couldn't find you. Were you even in the palace?"

Des disappears, only to reappear a few feet away at the end of the hallway. He hooks his hands on the archway above him and leans forward, blocking my way.

"Cherub, it's precious that you should be peeved at me when *you* were the one daring the Thief to break my wards and snatch you away."

Even as he speaks, shadows thicken and coil at his feet. He sounds casual enough, but this is obviously a sore spot.

"Nuh-uh. That's not how this works. You don't get to be mad at me for how I handled the situation when you left me to do it alone," I say.

Not entirely true—he was there to witness me playing chicken with a psychopathic monster—but he wasn't there when the news reached me and Malaki.

He drops his hands and vanishes again before reappearing directly in front of me. Stepping in close, he says, "You're right." The shadows around him clear. "You were a queen this morning. I saw it, my people saw it, and the Thief saw it."

Of course, he brings this back to me being a queen.

"I also heard you outfoxed Malaki." Des's eyes practically dance at the thought.

"He wanted to hide me away like some fainting maiden."

"The *audacity*," he says.

Des takes my hand and, backing up, leads me forward again. "I forgive you for your reckless endangerment this morning—"

I raise my eyebrows. "You are *un*believable."

"—just as I'm sure you forgive me for abandoning you during such a situation."

I guffaw.

Abruptly, Des stops us in front of a bronze door, the top of it coming to a curved point.

I've been so invested in our conversation that I haven't paid attention to where the Bargainer has been leading us.

"Where are we?" I ask, eyeing the door in front of me.

Des is giving me a look, his eyes sparking. I'd say he's either particularly dangerous right now or particularly lusty—he tends to wear the same expression for both emotions. "Open the door."

I stare at him for several seconds, my brows furrowing, then grab the handle and swing the door open.

Inside, warm lamps hang from the ceiling. The far wall is nothing more than open archways. Resting half inside and half outside the columned archway is an infinity pool, filled to the brim with Lephys's glowing water. It snakes through the low-lit chambers before curving out of sight. I'm not entirely sure, but I think it might bisect every one of this suite's rooms.

Beyond the pool, Somnia is laid out before me, the lights of the city glittering amber and blue and pale green in the night.

I don't think I breathe as I take it all in. I'm used to the beauty of the Otherworld, but this truly feels magical.

"You've been holding out on me, Flynn," I say, walking deeper into the room, my gaze moving back to the pool.

I had no idea there even *was* a place like this in his palace.

"Do you like your wedding gift?" he asks from behind me.

"Wedding gift?" I turn to face him.

Des's silver eyes gleam.

I glance around again. "Wait, are these…?"

"Our new rooms."

He slides his hands into his pockets, stepping up next to me to survey the chambers. "It's no ocean—I'm afraid there are limits on what I can do—but I figured my wife needed a place for her siren to unwind."

Our new rooms. I'm still stuck on that. He did this all for me—for *us*.

The gauzy curtains blow in from the windows, the wind carrying in the evening scents. I run my hand over a column inlaid with blue tiles.

"I love it," I breathe.

"I'm glad."

When I glance back at Des, he wears a small smile on his face, his eyes soft.

Genuine happiness looks good on him.

I wander through the suite, taking in the opulent bathroom, with its iridescent turquoise tile and bronze fastenings—each detail harkening to the sea in some way. Around me, the walls of the bathroom are covered in slate-gray rock, and the sunken tub is made of the same dark stone.

"I couldn't help myself," Des admits, following my gaze. "After all this time, I miss the caves I grew up in."

Now that I look for it, I see it—the bathroom is some fusion between the ocean I love and the caverns Des misses.

"It's perfect."

I leave the bathroom and walk into our bedroom. The chamber sits under the light of dozens of lamps, their flames sparking like fireworks. The headboard of the bed is the same worked bronze as in Des's other chambers, but someone's gone to the trouble of hammering out an image of crashing waves under a star-strewn sky.

There are a thousand other details to this suite that will surely take me days to fully notice and appreciate.

I turn to face Des. "You planned all this?"

He doesn't say anything, but he doesn't need to—it's all in his eyes. Des must've spent ages putting this chamber together. I rub my chest. My heart hurts so damn much.

I shake my head. "Thank you."

Des disappears before manifesting at my side. He tucks a strand of hair behind my ear. "It's nothing," he says, his voice a little rough.

I lean into his touch, giving him a small smile. My gaze sweeps over the rooms again, and again, my eyes catch on that pool.

Really want to get in.

Before I can so much as voice those words, my clothes slip off, leaving behind a strappy bathing suit.

I touch the soft material. "How *do* you do that?" But it's not really a question, and I don't expect an answer. Des has always had his ways.

"Magic, love," he says, answering me anyway.

I back up from him. The Night King watches me with his gleaming eyes, and I feel that gaze everywhere.

"If I get in the pool, will you join me?" I ask.

"Do I have a choice?"

"Do you really want one?"

His eyes narrow, even as delight touches his features. "Answering questions with questions. You are shaping up to be an excellent fairy, Callie."

I turn to the pool to hide my grin and slowly lower myself in. The water is cool against my skin, and my siren yearns for more.

I sink farther and farther into the glowing liquid until I'm fully submerged.

Des is right—it's not the tumultuous ocean. There are no sailors to call down to their deaths, no promise of violence. But there's peace here, beneath the surface. And what's more, I think as the water shifts and Des joins me, there's *sex*.

I rise slowly from the lapping waves, my eyes meeting

the Bargainer's. He stands in the water, the glow of it illuminating all the hard planes of his bare torso. His sleeve of tattoos is on display, and his hair is tied back in a bun.

He is, in a word, *overwhelming*.

Slowly, I move over to him. As I do so, I slip one of my swimsuit straps over my shoulder and down my arm, then the other. The rest of it is quick to go. The swimsuit was a nice thought, but right now it's useless to me.

Des watches me with those silver eyes of his. When I reach him, I pause, staring up.

"I could never imagine this," I say. "Not in my wildest dreams could I imagine what life with you would be like."

He cups the side of my face, his gaze moving to my lips. "It gets to be like this; for the rest of our lives, we get to have this: the sweet moments, the confessions, the laughter, the magic—we get to have it all." His thumb strokes my cheek. "Cherub, you're every wish of mine."

Lowering my eyelids, I rise to my tiptoes and kiss him deeply, *fiercely*. After reaching for his bun, I loosen his hair, letting it fall around his face in waves. This is where I make some comment about his silly man bun, and he has some quip that keeps me on my toes.

But my humor's abandoned me. All I want is Des, and I'm pretty sure all he wants is me.

His arms come around my waist, and then he's wrapping my legs around his hips. If Des was wearing a swimsuit, it's long gone now. I feel every glorious inch of him bare against me.

I run my palms over his biceps, his tattoos catching my attention. There's that somber angel and the rose. I touch them with my fingertips. That's when I notice for the first time the ribbon of inked black beads coiling up his arm.

My fingers pause. "Is this new?"

His eyes seem to be smiling. "I wanted to wear a piece of you on me always."

I trace the string of beads to his wrist, then back up his arm to his shoulder...where they morph into inked scales. Those, in turn, transition into black feathers. The tiny inked feathers drip from his shoulder and onto his pec, a few breaking away to flutter right over his heart.

I pull my head back. "When—?"

"Last night, when I was supposed to be defending my kingdom."

So *that's* what he was doing away from the castle. My heart hurts with all I feel.

I study the tattoo again. The beads, the scales, the feathers—those things were once burdens to me.

I wanted to wear a piece of you on me always.

My throat closes. These rooms were already too much. To hear that he inked these parts of me onto himself...

He must see my throat working, must know I literally don't have the words to convey this unimaginable tangle of emotions I feel.

I'm just so unbearably, unspeakably happy.

"I love you, cherub," he says. "Till darkness dies, I will."

I rise a little, my body skimming over his hard torso. Between us, our bond throbs like a single united heartbeat. I cup his cheeks and press my mouth to his.

Like moonbeams and shadows. That's how he tastes, how he feels. As though the dark universe itself came together one day and decided to form a man. He still doesn't seem real. I hope he never does. He's my magic.

Des lowers me, or maybe I'm the one to sink back. My skin brightens as the tip of his cock presses against my opening for a moment, feeling thick, much too thick. And then it's sliding into me, and that exquisite thickness is stretching me, filling me.

I stare into Des's eyes, and I see an eternity stretched out in them. Years and years of nights like this, love like this.

He pulls his hips back, and I feel the loss everywhere. But in the next instant, he's sliding back into me, his cock throbbing.

"Love you so much, Callie," he breathes. "Would've waited an eternity if it meant finding you."

I lean my head against him, feeling him wedged deeply in me. "I would've walked through hell to find you," I whisper back.

He shudders out a breath. "You did, cherub. You did."

I don't know which experience he's referring to, and I don't really care. None of that horror gets to be a part of this moment.

I run my fingers through his white hair, the strands seeming to glow thanks to the water wetting it.

The two of us move up and down, in and out, pulling away and rushing in like the tides. We're balanced on the edge of Somnia, with the stars above and the world below.

Sometimes sex is dirty and carnal, and sometimes, like now, it's love at its most intimate.

My breasts slide over his chest as I rise and fall, the glowing water making our skin slick.

Then my breath hitches as Des's pace picks up and his strokes deepen. The whole time the two of us stare at each other. I don't know about Des, but I have the most breath-taking view. Planets have spun and stars have aligned to bring us together.

"Every wish…" Des rasps out, taking my mouth.

The taste and the feel of him—those are the triggers that send me over the edge. I cry out into his mouth, my grip tightening on Des as my orgasm crashes through me.

The kiss ends as I lap up the last of my climax. Des stares up at me, his silver eyes devouring my expression. His thrusts become frantic, almost punishing.

"My wife," he says, his voice low. His gaze drops to my lips, and his grip tightens.

With a groan, he comes. The water splashes around us as he slams into me, again and again. His gaze crawls back up, and he drinks me in as he rides out the last of his orgasm.

Even after we're finished, we stay locked together. I brush back his wet hair, trying to memorize every feature of his.

"I really love my wedding gift," I say.

He lets out a low, satisfied laugh. "So do I."

———————

I don't know what time it is, only that my body feels boneless and my siren is, for once in her life, fully sated. Des sleeps next to me, his leg thrown over mine and his heavy arm draped across my body.

I envy the King of the Night his ability to sleep. I'm sure the moment I give in to it, the Thief of Souls will be on the other side waiting for me.

Do the dead ever really die? The Thief's voice echoes through my head. I frown. I can't escape him, even now.

This is our little game—and trust me, enchantress, it's far from over.

I roll the words over and over in my mind.

He tricked Des into giving me the lilac wine the night he said that, thus making my magic compatible with his.

All so that *what*? Why would being magically compatible even matter to him?

I will never leave you alone, enchantress. Never. Banish the hope if you have it. You cannot ever escape my clutches. Not even in death.

Goose bumps bloom across my arms.

Not even in death.

The sleeping soldiers, Galleghar's incorruptible body, the Thief of Souls's ability to outlive even death...

I nearly gasp when it comes to me.

Of course. *Of course.*

All those stupid riddles, and it was right in front of me the entire time.

Not terribly long ago, Des explained the four kingdoms of the Otherworld—Night, Day, Flora, and Fauna.

But there were *two others.*

The Kingdom of Mar...and the Kingdom of Death and Deep Earth.

The Kingdom of Death and Deep Earth.

In a world at war, who would truly win?

Death would, that's who.

Do the dead ever really die?

Jesus.

This is why the Thief can wear the bodies of the dead, and this is how he can send soldiers into a sleep from which they cannot wake. All the Thief's strange, mysterious powers the Otherworld has never seen, they are powers that belonged to the Kingdom of Death.

The throne the Thief sat on, the staggering reach of his magic... He's not just any fae from the land of the dead—he must be their *king.*

This, of course, is all assuming I'm right.

I am right. I feel it in my bones.

I shake the King of Night's shoulder.

Des wakes with a smile, already reaching for me. "Insatiable wife. Want another go?"

If only.

"Des," I whisper, "I think I know who the Thief is."

CHAPTER 31

It's much, much later by the time I fall asleep. And when I do, the Thief is waiting for me in my dreams, just as I knew he would be.

"So you finally figured it out." He reclines on his golden throne, and for the first time, I see a king in him. Not the kind of king that Des is, dark and honorable and dastardly all at once. This is the kind of king you cringe away from, the kind of king you hope never notices you.

I lie on the stone floor beneath him, sprawled like I threw myself at his feet.

"Death is the one kingdom all these self-satisfied fae have forgotten," he continues.

I don't bother asking how he knows.

I remember Des's reaction when I told him my realization. His astounded expression. The disbelief that followed, then the reluctant consideration, and lastly, his horrified acceptance.

Even now I can feel the way the Night King's hands

gripped my upper arms, squeezing them as I explained my reasoning.

He was thunderstruck, but in the end, I felt the hot rush of his pride. *You figured it out, cherub. So many lives will be saved because you figured it out.*

Trouble is, I'm not sure where we go from here. Knowing who the Thief is doesn't make him easier to defeat. If anything, the fact he rules over the dead is a new conundrum.

I mean, can you really kill a thing that *lives* among the dead? Is that even possible? Des hadn't known when I asked, just as he hadn't known how to get to the land of the dead without first dying.

The Thief rises from his throne and heads over to me as I sit up. He crouches next to me on the floor. His hand goes to my neck, his flesh cold, so cold. Why did I never notice that before?

"I will tell you a story," he says, pushing me back down to the floor.

I don't try to fight him, though the siren in me wants to. "I don't really want to hear it," I say, pinned beneath his hold.

"But I think you do, enchantress." The Thief of Souls flexes his fingers, pressing lightly against my windpipe. I can tell he wants to do more, that the thought excites him. But like me, he reins in his wilder impulses.

"Many years ago a fairy hungered for power, and he did many terrible things to keep it," he begins.

The cool floor bites into my skin, and the smell of old bones is back. I swear I can smell spoiled blood rotting away somewhere nearby.

"One day, this fairy discovered his time would indeed

end—unless he took measures to ensure it didn't." Another press of his fingers. "I was one of those measures.

"I slumbered for many years before Galleghar sought me out. But then his darkness touched mine, and I *awoke*."

I knit my brows. I don't know what to make of his words. The Thief is the King of Death. I assumed that like other fae kings, he was born, he grew into a man, and at some point, he inherited the throne. Not this business of him slumbering and waking. I don't know what to do with that information.

"He gave me life so one day I might return the favor." The Thief's eyes have grown distant. "And so I did, and here we are."

I stare up at him. I feel his need to squeeze the life out of me.

"Do it," I taunt him. "Kill me. I know you want to."

This is my base nature talking. My siren wants the pain and violence. She welcomes the chaos.

The Thief thins his eyes, even as he smiles. "You are perhaps the only creature alive who dares court my violence." The Thief's fingers dig in, and he begins choking me. He leans in close. "And I'm acquiring a taste for your foolish courage."

Can't breathe.

He leans in close, his mouth only inches from mine. A lock of his dark hair brushes my cheek.

Black dots are beginning to speckle my vision.

"You and I both know I can't kill you here," the Thief says, still squeezing my neck.

Need to breathe.

It's starting to *feel* like he's legitimately killing me.

"But I *can* hurt you." To emphasize his point, his grip tightens.

297

I haven't moved, haven't struggled. I want to, I want to claw him off me, but a deeper, more insidious part of me is shaking off her own deep slumber, and she won't give this monster *anything*.

I smile at him, even as darkness creeps into my vision. *"If you want to hurt me"*—I'm mouthing the words more than saying them; my surroundings are disappearing as the darkness closes in on my vision—*"you're going to have to try harder..."*

I gasp awake, taking in a lungful of air, then another and another. Overhead, I see silvery wings spread wide.

A moment later, Des's face fills my vision. "You're awake." Relief thickens his voice.

I remember for the millionth time that when the Thief decides to commandeer my dreams, not even the King of the Night can wake me.

I can still feel the press of the Thief's hand against my neck, and I swear I can taste death at the back of my throat.

Really should stop taunting the Thief.

"Why are your wings out?" I ask, shaking away the vestiges of the dream.

"Do you know how often I fight this reaction with you?" Des says, sitting back on his haunches. He runs a hand through his disheveled hair. "A better question would be: Why aren't my wings out all the damn time? I either want to fuck you or fuck up someone for messing with you."

I give the Bargainer a small smile, and then my eyes return to his wings. I trail my fingers over them again. "Which are you leaning toward at the moment?" I ask.

The Bargainer's lips twist into a wry smile. "Both." The

expression quickly fades. He traces a knuckle along the side of my face. "You know this is almost over, right?"

I know he's talking about the Thief of Souls, but for some horrifying reason, I feel like he means us. The sheer fear at the thought—it paralyzes me.

Three abrupt raps on the door interrupt us.

"Your Majesty," Malaki calls through the door, "Galleghar has been spotted."

It must be another trap.

That's what I think when I sit in the throne room next to Des, a strange fae creature standing before us.

"I ssssaw him. The oooold king." The fae can barely speak coherent words out of its misshapen mouth. Its skin is the color of a bruise, its eyes are reptilian, and its body is thin and hunched.

I have no clue what creature this is, only that I've seen it before in one of Des's sketches.

Des leans his chin on a hand, his pointer finger tapping against his cheek. "Where?"

"Barrrrbooosssss."

My skin brightens.

"Are you working for him?" I ask, glamour dripping from my words. I don't want a replay of the last time we learned of Galleghar's whereabouts.

"Nooooo."

"Does he know you've spotted him?"

"Nooooo."

The Night King stops tapping his cheek. "What else *do* you know?"

That strange mouth twists. "He hidessss in the wildssss,

in the tunnelsssss oooof ooooold. Many hellllp him. They willlll killlll any whoooo harm the ooooold king."

"Why do they help him?" I ask.

"Theirrrr mindssss belooong toooo anoooootherrr."

I still in my seat.

Des stands, his frame imposing. "Who?"

But we already know.

"The Thief oooof Sssssoooulssss."

"We need to decide," Malaki says once the room clears. The only ones left are him, me, Des, and a handful of guards.

Desmond glances at me. "What should we do about Galleghar?"

He's asking me like I'm a coruler.

I shake my head. I don't want to make a decision like this. This is the whole reason I've been running from the idea of being a queen. It's one thing to handle a threat or interrogate a few fairies. It's another to make a decision with an outcome you cannot know, one that might have far-reaching consequences.

I'm about to say, *I don't know*, but damn it, my pride suddenly feels like it's on the line, and I don't want to disappoint Des.

Actually going to make a decision on this one. Fuck.

To go after Galleghar or not?

We know where the old king is, but we knew where he was last time, and he still got the drop on us.

However, if we do take him by surprise, then this could be the beginning of the end for both Galleghar and the Thief. The two share a bond. A bond I'm eager to break.

"I think it's time we captured your father," I say slowly.

Des stares at me for a long moment. Ever so slowly, a wicked smile spreads across his face. "The queen has spoken."

Barbos isn't as I remember it.

As Des and I descend onto the island—Malaki and Temper behind us—I get my first good look at the place since I last visited. The streets we fly over are more subdued, the sights and sounds muted. The rough crowd that usually revels out here is now largely gone. Those who remain seem to be looking over their shoulders, like they're being watched.

The whole thing gives me chills.

You're just reading into things.

At least we weren't ambushed en route. I held my breath through most of the journey, waiting for Galleghar to drop in and fight us. But he never appeared.

Either we're lucky, or the enchantments are doing their job.

I feel the spells clinging to my skin, the magic insulating me like a coat. Before we left, several of Des's men warded Temper, Malaki, Des, and I against enemy magic. Among other things, these enchantments hide us from our opponents' view, rendering us all but invisible to fairies like Galleghar.

As we fly inland, the city gives way to dense jungle. Here and there the trees are illuminated by the glowing lights of various fae. It doesn't look like a frightening place, and yet somewhere in there lurks a killer king.

Can't believe we're doing this. All because I gave Des the go-ahead. I still expect Galleghar to manifest in front of us or for the Thief's sleeping soldiers to close in from all sides. Nothing ever goes according to plan; why should this?

Yet it doesn't happen. Galleghar and what's left of the Thief's army stay away, and our group flies sedately on, the only sound the whistle of the wind against our ears.

Des dives toward the land, though this patch of jungle looks like all the others. I follow his lead, descending on the thick dark foliage until my hands and feet skim the treetops, the leaves rustling against my skin.

The tangle of dense shrubbery doesn't leave much room to land. I watch Des, seeing the way his wings tilt around trees, and I think I get it…until my wing clips a tree branch I didn't see.

I yelp at the sting of pain, and my wing closes reflexively. I tumble through the trees, hitting every branch that's ever existed. I fall to the forest floor with a heavy *thud*.

Motherfucking *ow*.

In an instant, the Bargainer appears at my side. "You're still the clumsiest siren I've ever met," he says, extending a hand to help me up.

"Yeah, yeah, yeah," I mutter, taking his hand.

Malaki drops next to me, Temper in his arms.

"Why don't you wake up the entire jungle while you're at it?" my best friend says when she steps out of the fairy's arms.

Giving Temper an annoyed glare, I dust off my battle leathers before picking branches out of my hair. At least I didn't lose my daggers; the twin blades remain strapped to my sides, their stone hilts gleaming.

I pat a back pocket. All four of us were given a pair of iron shackles, in case we happened to get in range of Galleghar. Like my knives, my set of handcuffs is right where it ought to be.

Des's eyes sweep over the thick foliage. "Follow me," he says to the group.

We walk for fifteen minutes, our footsteps silent. Around us, the jungle seems to be holding its breath.

It feels like we're wandering aimlessly until Des stops. He toes the earth in front of him. Then, at a wave of his hand, the earth in front of him clears, revealing a flat, circular stone carved with symbols in Old Fae.

He glances up at me. "We're here."

Turning his attention back to the stone, the King of the Night whispers an incantation under his breath. The Old Fae symbols glow emerald for a moment, and then the stone slides aside, revealing another freaking hole in the ground.

What is it with this dude and holes?

"No way," Temper says, eyeing it the same way I am. "No one said anything about a tunnel. I get claustrophobia."

Des's eyes briefly flick to her before landing on mine. "You can opt out too," he tells me.

I shake my head. "I'm coming with you." I go where Des goes.

His eyes glitter. "Then I'll be waiting for you at the bottom." With that, he takes a step and drops into the earth.

I glance at Temper, who is shifting her weight from foot to foot as she eyes the hole with unease, then look to Malaki. The general looks menacing in the darkness. He's not too pleased that Temper and I are here, putting ourselves in the line of fire, but he hasn't tried to stop either of us the way he tried last time.

Taking a breath, I sit at the edge of the hole, dipping my feet into the darkness. My boot bangs against a ladder set into the side of the hole, and I slide my body down until I can grab the handholds.

And then I descend.

I can't say how far down I have to climb, only that when

I reach the bottom of the hole, Des is waiting for me, his form illuminated by orbs of light.

"Brave siren," he says as I drop the last few feet to the ground.

This isn't bravery. Bravery is facing whatever lies at the end of these tunnels.

Before I respond, I hear Malaki's heavy weight as he clambers down the ladder. It's only once I step away from the hole that the general releases his hold on the ladder and drops the rest of the way to the ground before landing heavily on the damp earth.

Malaki straightens, looking back up at the opening.

As if on cue, I hear agitated muttering far above us, followed by the sound of Temper's feet against the ladder.

When she reaches the bottom, she hops off. "Let the record show that I am *not* happy about this."

"You could've waited for us above," I say.

"I'm not going to wait in some random jungle while my friends hunt a bloodthirsty king, no matter how much I hate tunnels."

Aww, she said *friends*, plural. I think we're officially forming a friend group.

Des's eyes sweep over us, and then he turns and strides down one of the tunnels. How he knows which to take is beyond me.

Overhead, tree roots cling to the curve of the ceiling, illuminated by orbs of light that bob along above us. Small fae creatures scurry along the roots, one pausing to hiss at the air in our direction, like it senses something is off. But it doesn't see us.

"What is this place?" Temper asks, staring at an orb of light as it softly bounces among the tree roots.

"The Angels of Small Death used tunnels like these to move sensitive goods," Malaki says, his voice rumbling.

Ironic that the authority they once hid from is now the criminal they're after.

I glance at our surroundings with new eyes. Des and Malaki must've worked within these tunnels for years, moving illegal items, hoarding treasure, and hiding from the king's men. The whole thing is so surreal to me—this place and all the lives Des lived long before he was mine.

He was always ours, my siren says.

I stare at the Bargainer's broad back. I know he'd say the same thing.

The tunnel seems to stretch on for an eternity, and the farther we go, the more my skin prickles. Maybe it's the close quarters, or the darkness, or being underground—or maybe it's the man we're after, but something just doesn't sit right with me.

Des stops, putting up a hand. "Galleghar is just ahead," he breathes.

Reflexively, my hand goes to my dagger.

Des begins walking again, and mechanically, I follow him.

Up ahead the tunnel opens into a room, but I don't see just how massive the chamber really is until we enter it. We must be beneath a hill, for the ceiling arcs high above us. It's as big as some of the palace ballrooms I've been in, though this one lacks all the beauty and refinement of those fae palaces. The walls here are made of plain packed earth. It's a room meant to store a warehouse's worth of goods. Now, however, it's mostly empty, save for a few bags of gold.

Well, a few bags of gold…and an undead king.

Across the room Galleghar sits on a throne of sorts. It's

the saddest sight, seeing him slouched in that silver chair, as though waiting to hear the grievances of an audience that never comes.

His storm-gray eyes are turbulent as they stare off into the distance, and I get a chill looking at that nefarious face that is so similar to my mate's.

He can't see us. The enchantments really did work. We're standing right in front of Galleghar, yet we're utterly invisible to the tyrant king.

Floating in the air in front of him is a piece of unrolled parchment, and at his side is a meal—both which he appears to have forgotten.

Is this what he does all day? Hide and ponder and plot?

My eyes move over the room again. There's a honeycomb of entrances and exits into this chamber, and I have no idea how I'm going to figure out which one to take when we leave.

A worry for later, once Galleghar is ours.

It seems so easy. He's right there in front of us. All we have to do is pluck him from his knockoff throne, slap a pair of iron cuffs on his wrists, and take him back to Somnia.

Maybe it could've played out that way, but we've only taken a few short steps toward him when the air around us wavers. Just as it does, I feel the enchantments dissolving away.

Pretty sure that wasn't supposed to happen.

In an instant, Galleghar's eyes dart to us. I catch the flicker of surprise in them, but then his face breaks into a cold, malicious smile.

"My ill-begotten son, we meet again."

CHAPTER 32

"And you brought friends," **Galleghar says casually, his eyes** flicking to us.

I suddenly feel awkward standing here, like the four of us are some gang of supernatural Avengers. Only we've been caught with our pants down.

Not how I imagined this interaction unfolding.

Des saunters forward, slipping his hands into his pockets. "I never thought I'd see the day when you were the one living in the caves, and I was the king," he says smoothly.

Ooooh, burn.

Galleghar fists one of his hands, but that's his only reaction. The piece of parchment floating in front of him rolls up and sails softly onto the floor next to the bags of gold. In one of the darkened hallways leading into the room, I see a flicker of movement.

Is that Des's darkness? Something else? It's impossible to tell.

The undead king crosses one leg over the other, raising

his eyebrows as his gaze moves over us. "I'm sorry, am I supposed to be frightened? Two slaves and a petty criminal with a title—oh, and my scheming son."

This asshole. All his atrocities aside, he must've always been a real prick to be around.

"How are your wings feeling?" Des asks. "Still broken?"

Galleghar stares up at him, settling deeper into his seat. "I imagine you remember the feeling. Your wings snapped like twigs beneath my touch."

I almost forgot the injury Des sustained back in the Flora Kingdom; so many terrible things happened that night.

"Your throne is cute," the Bargainer says, continuing forward. "I gave my servant's daughter one just like that— only I believe it was a little bigger."

Damn. Fairies don't fuck around with their insults.

Galleghar's eyes narrow. I'm waiting for his retort when he disappears.

My siren surfaces in an instant, making my skin glow.

Galleghar reappears in front of Des, fist cocked. The Bargainer vanishes just as quickly before flickering into existence behind Galleghar. Des slams a booted foot into his father's back, knocking the fairy down at my feet.

My soul mate puts a foot to his father's throat, his hand reaching for his shackles. "Is that all the fight you have? You're making this too easy."

"Why fight when the odds are so unfair?" his father rasps out.

Des tilts his head, his eyes narrowing. "You said yourself that we're just some lowly slaves and criminals; no match for the great Galleghar Nyx."

A child appears in one of the doorways leading into the room, distracting me from the face-off in front of me. The little girl looks absurdly out of place—until I see her eyes. All that anger, all that malevolence—she must be a casket child.

From the other doorways, another few children appear, followed by soldiers with glazed eyes, their uniforms bloody.

Sleeping soldiers.

"You didn't think I was talking about myself when I said the odds were unfair, did you?" Galleghar wheezes, smiling despite his windpipe getting slowly crushed.

Some of the children bare their fangs, while others growl. The soldiers methodically grab their weapons.

Enemies are coming from all directions, their bodies filling the doorways all around the room.

Des glances at the new additions, and his boot digs in a little harder. "I'd say the odds are still stacked against you, old man. But you'd only know that if you didn't live in a cave."

He's referring to me and my glamour, I realize. Sleeping soldiers are nothing more than props once I use my magic on them.

The undead king wears a malicious smile as he stares up at his son right before he disappears.

Galleghar manifests among the soldiers as they file into the room from all sides.

Within a minute, they form a ring around the four of us, their faces placid, their eyes eerily empty.

A scuffle and a choked sound come from one of the soldiers behind me. I turn just in time to see a bloody sword impaled through the fairy's abdomen. A second later, it's jerked out the way it came, making a wet sucking noise.

The bleeding soldier teeters for a few seconds then topples forward. In the darkened doorway beyond the dying fairy, a form steps out, his body rapidly brightening by the second until all I can see is a sphere of light.

When it dims again, I'm left staring at the King of Day.

Didn't know *he* was invited to the party. Apparently, Des called in his ally's help.

"I heard the Night Kingdom had a vermin problem," Janus says. His eyes alight on Galleghar. "Ah. There's the rat himself."

My mate's face remains impassive, even as he steps up to my side.

Galleghar's eyes narrow. "Did you come here to kill me too?"

"Well, I didn't come for the weather," Janus replies.

Blood still drips from his sword as he strides forward, and he makes no attempt to wipe it off. He comes over to the four of us, nodding to Des, then Malaki and Temper.

When Janus's eyes land on me, he bows. "Lady, you have my sword and shield."

My lips part in surprise. I assumed the Day King came here because he and Des are allies, but perhaps that's not the reason.

Janus swore his fealty to me not so long ago—perhaps Des told him of our plan, or perhaps this is him upholding his oath. Or perhaps it's a bit of both.

The soldiers make no move to retaliate for the death of their comrade; they just continue to watch us with those same stoic expressions.

Galleghar studies Janus for another moment, and then his eyes are drawn to me. My skin still glows, and the longer he looks at me, the more intrigued he appears.

"Slave," he murmurs. Louder, he says, "I have a message for you—"

A heavy hand falls on Galleghar's shoulder. "Enough," the soldier behind him says.

The undead king glares at the gore-stained soldier, though the fairy pays the king no heed as he saunters forward, his eyes lit with dark delight.

There's only one person who looks at me like that.

"Enchantress," the Thief says, "how you *beguile* me even now."

It's a horrible sensation to hear that mercurial spirit of his projected through someone else's body.

"I had thought to simply watch and enjoy the blood-bath, but"—he stares at me with sick fascination—"I want you to notice me as I have noticed you."

Next to me, Des's wings manifest, spreading out behind him. Around us, shadows fill the room. The Thief of Souls notices none of it.

"Baptized in blood, given over to your wildest nature—if I could touch your mind, maybe then I'd be satisfied."

The gore-stained soldier closes in on me, drawing near enough for me to smell the rot clinging to him.

Des steps in front of me, his wings shielding me from view.

"It's not my fists you need to protect her from," the Thief says. I can no longer see him, but I feel his eyes all over my skin, watching me from dozens of different soldiers. "A single secret can cause *so* much trouble. Isn't that right, Desmond?"

My mate says nothing, and unfortunately, I can't see what expression he wears. His wings, however, fold up, which is at least some indication that his emotions are steady.

The Thief continues, "And we both know you have more than just *one* secret," the Thief says. His eyes slip to me. "Has the King of the Night told you about me and Galleghar?"

What is he talking about?

I step up next to Des and take a good look at him. He's wearing his secret-keeping face. The longer I gaze at him, the more uneasy I feel.

The Thief raises his eyebrows. "I take it *he hasn't.*" He shakes his head in admonishment. "I know you have a reputation to uphold, Desmond, but one would think you'd at *least* be open with your mate."

The Bargainer's eyes move from the soldier's to mine.

"Cherub," he says, and I can tell he's choosing his words carefully, "I *have*…been dishonest with you."

He looks so foreign, so fae.

My heart beats a little louder.

"I told you I knew nothing of the prophecy of Galleghar Nyx or how he and the Thief were connected, but those were lies. I have read my father's prophecy. I know why he's after you and what he fears. I know when and how he sought the Thief out, and I know how he must be stopped."

My eyebrows pull together, even as I glance over at Galleghar. The traitor king's gaze moves to me, and I see lethal promise in them.

My siren bristles at the threat.

Come closer, fallen king, so that I might better carve you up.

"Desmond, aren't you going to tell her the rest?" the Thief chimes in. He's still staring at me, giving me that same uncanny look he used to when he was the Green Man. "Tell her how you learned of my true identity and where I lived. Tell her how you kept that knowledge from her—tell her and the rest of your friends."

Each statement out of the Thief's lips is a toxin, slowly poisoning my thoughts.

Has the Night King been deceiving me all this time?

You may have your wiles, enchantress, but you are not one for puzzles. A shame, really, when your mate so clearly is. He's figured out quite a bit more than you have.

"Desmond," Janus says, taking a step toward us, "is what he's saying true?"

Des watches me, not answering, so I answer for him.

"It is."

I feel my knees weaken as Janus and the others talk at once, voicing their frustration.

Des is smarter than this. Everything I'm learning right now doesn't align with what I know of my mate. He may be secretive and a little wicked, but he's *loyal*. Whatever's going on, whatever deception the Thief is trying to capitalize on, it must be some sort of smoke screen.

I capture Des's hand, hold it between my own. There are so many things I want to tell him. How messed up it is that he kept me out of the loop. How I swear to God, I will kick him in his fine ass if he makes a habit of lying. But more importantly—

"I trust you," I say softly.

Des's gaze is steady, but his eyes, his eyes burn like dying stars. He squeezes my hand. "You are my life, cherub."

With that, he reaches for the sword strapped to him before unsheathing it in one fluid movement. He strikes down the gore-stained soldier standing before us. Around the room, the sleeping soldiers tense.

Des backs away from me, his wicked wings spreading wide until his staggering frame seems to fill the space.

"Till darkness dies," he vows to me.

And then he disappears.

313

CHAPTER 33

Des is on his father in an instant, sword brandished. That's the cue everyone seems to be waiting for.

With a battle cry, Malaki charges at the sleeping soldiers just as they rush in to meet us. Janus takes to the air, and Temper lets out a low laugh, her power rippling along her skin.

"Soldiers, stop!" I shout, pushing as much glamour as possible into those two words.

The sleeping soldiers *should* stop, but they don't. Instead, they continue charging forward.

The hell?

Five of them close in on me at once, and I barely have time to grab my daggers before I start blocking blows.

I don't understand.

That thought runs on repeat in my head as I fight my assailants. I duck as a double-sided axe swings over my head, and then I strike out with my daggers.

I should've been able to glamour them all.

"Freeze, soldiers," I say again.

"I'm afraid they can't follow your commands," one of the soldiers says. But it's the Thief speaking. "They've been warded against your glamour," he says.

Warded against it? I go cold all over. Any advantage I thought I had is gone.

And here I thought perhaps we'd be able to pull this ambush off. But they'd been ready with their own magic—magic that stripped us of our enchantments and made them impervious to my power.

I hear the rip of fabric at my back and feel the sickening sensation of a blade sinking into my skin. I feel the cascade of blood spill from the wound before the pain sets in.

When it does set in, however—*Jesus*—it stings like a bitch.

Before I can retaliate, another blow follows the first, slicing my arm open.

I stagger forward, right into a soldier covered in dried blood and unnameable bits, my wings manifesting in response to the pain and adrenaline.

Warm blood drips from my arm and my back. And still the attack keeps coming. It's all I can do to parry most of the blows. Des might've trained me on how to fight, but I'm no match against *five* fae soldiers.

"*Callypso!*" Des roars.

Suddenly, he's at my side, cleaving through sleeping soldiers. But his father uses the distraction to appear in front of me, weapon raised.

"You will *not* be my downfall, slave," he vows.

I don't even try glamouring Galleghar. Instead, I do what any sane woman might—I kick that fucker in the balls.

Hard.

The reaction is immediate. He doubles over, releasing a choked hissing noise.

That's all I see before the sleeping soldiers close in on me again despite Des's best efforts. Blood sprays around my mate as he carves through them, but there are always more to fight, and none of them play fair.

"Thief!" Des bellows. "You and I had an understanding!"

An understanding?

The soldiers encircling me suddenly stop fighting, falling at ease.

"So we did," one of them says.

I stare around at them. Among the group, Des's dad begins to straighten. Beyond us, the other sleeping soldiers are still locked in battle, unaware that the fighting in this pocket of the room has stopped.

That thought has no sooner crossed my mind than Galleghar disappears and materializes once again in front of me, sword aimed. Before he can land a blow, a hand grabs his wrist and twists, forcing Des's father to relinquish the blade.

I follow the hand back to its owner, shocked to see it belongs to a soldier.

"*What are you doing?*" Galleghar cries.

An instant later, Des flickers into existence at his back, locking him in a chokehold. "Awww, did you think you were the only one who made deals with this monster?"

My blood goes cold. *Des, what have you done?*

Galleghar's face twists into a grimace, and then he disappears, with Des vanishing a split second after him. The two flash across the room, popping in and out of existence like fireworks.

I smell blood and dark magic filling the air as the battle rages on.

Temper's hair levitates with her power, and she wears a wild grin as her magic lashes out of her. I notice the faint shimmer of it as she eviscerates opponent after opponent, their bodies piling up on the ground. Her power is terrifying, and yet I know she's still holding back. If she fully gave in to her magic, the fight could be over in a matter of minutes. But Temper's power is unpredictable and sometimes unscrupulous; if she unleashed it all, there'd be no guarantee that we, her friends and allies, would survive it.

Malaki and Janus battle both in the sky and on the ground, using their wings to gain some advantage. The casket children have their fangs bared, their mouths bloody, and many of the sleeping soldiers have bloodstained blades.

It's not going to be a clean win for either side.

And then there's me, surrounded by a swath of docile sleeping soldiers.

I glance around at them, pointing my dagger. "Why won't you fight?" I ask, blood dripping from my wrist as I speak.

"I told you already," one of them says. "Your mate keeps many secrets."

I spin around, looking at each aggressor. From behind their eyes, the Thief of Souls smirks at me.

You and I had an understanding, the Bargainer said.

"What's the understanding you and Desmond have?" I ask, leveling the dagger at one of the soldiers' throats.

"Really now, are you going to stab me with that?" the Thief asks, smirking at the blade.

Maybe. I don't know. The threat is obviously useless on him.

"What is the understanding?" I repeat.

Around us, screams echo through the room, accompanied

by the wet sound of metal cleaving flesh. The air mists with blood. I taste the barest tang of it on my lips.

"Wouldn't you like to know."

The Thief and his games. I decided a while ago that I've had enough of them.

I push past the soldiers. If they won't fight me, I'll go help one of my comrades who's facing overwhelming odds. But as soon as I try to push my way through the crowd of them, they close off my exit.

"Get out of my way," I say, my skin brightening.

But they stand resolute.

I want to scream. Every moment that passes, my friends grow tired and more injured.

"I let my baser nature get the better of me, but your mate is right. I want to leave you whole and untouched," a soldier says at my back, "for now."

I turn to the fairy who spoke. She has long wheat-blond hair that's been plaited away from her angelic face. In her hand she holds a sickle sword.

Walking up to the soldier, I clasp her cheeks, looking deep into her seafoam eyes. The soldier remains still, the Thief's gaze lit with interest. I glance down at the woman's lips. "It's not my mind you want to touch, is it, Thief?"

The soldier studies me before lowering her eyes to my lips.

"You want what you got only a taste of in Karnon's prison," I say.

Back then all he did was kiss me. He hadn't done more.

I feel the hot rush of my power.

Kiss him. Kill him. Take it all at once.

I lean in, my lips close to the soldier's, my hands sliding up her cheeks. My fingertips brush that plaited hair of hers—

We will drag him under and make him give us everything.

That quicksilver gaze lingers on me for a second or two.

"Look up at your mate," the Thief says out of nowhere.

I frown. All my tightly coiled power is dissipating.

Not how this is supposed to play out.

"Why?" I say, my gaze unwavering.

"I want to make sure you're watching."

I feel a humming along my skin. Magic—oily dark magic—vibrates around me. It separates itself from the walls, the floor, and the ceiling, thickening in the air.

Around me, some of my allies are looking around in confusion.

I narrow my eyes at the Thief, even as the magic congeals into twisting clouds of smoke.

"What are you doing?" I ask.

"Look up."

My eyes linger on the Thief for a long moment, but eventually, I do look up, my eyes drawn to my mate.

I gasp at the sight.

CHAPTER 34
DESMOND

The years may have passed, but my father still fights the same.
Like a coward.

I chase him through the darkness, the two of us becoming one with it before we return from shadows to men. Over and over and over.

"You cannot kill me," he says as our blades clash. The two of us hover in midair, most of the fairies fighting below.

"So long as you suffer, I don't fucking care." Save for against Callie's father, I have never hungered for vengeance so badly. I want to skewer Galleghar like an animal and roast him over a spit. I want to carve him up and make him watch as I remove his organs one by one. I want to use every bit of torture I've perfected over the centuries to make him pay for my mother, for my siblings, for the threat he poses to my mate.

Galleghar parries the blow, the blades sparking at the force of the hit, and then he's gone again.

I vanish into darkness, sensing him reforming above me. I coalesce back into a man only for my father to dissipate into shadow once more. Now he's behind me; now he's across the room. I chase him, weaving through the battlefield around us. Malaki bleeds from his abdomen, and Janus is holding his arm close.

Temper might be the least hurt, but her eyes have started to glow; the sorceress is losing her mind and will to her power.

And Callie, Callie is facing off against the worst monster of them all. I have doomed her to him. Even now I quake at the thought of—

Galleghar reforms in front of me. I manifest in closer to him, my blade poised. He aims his sword for my stomach, and my swing becomes a defensive strike, knocking his weapon aside.

Galleghar laughs. "You cannot kill me. *Nothing* can kill me."

"Is that why you bound yourself to the Thief? So you could never die?"

A question hardly worth asking. Of course, the fool picked the most malevolent being to co-bind himself to.

"Secrets are meant for one soul to keep," Galleghar says.

I nearly drop my sword. My mother's words. When the sleeping soldiers began to whisper it, I wondered why.

Galleghar strikes out again, and I meet the blow with my blade.

"That bitch who whelped you said that to me," Galleghar says behind our locked blades. "Did you know that? Over and over she'd whisper that into my ear like a taunt. But the joke's on her because she's dead and the only miserable thing she cared about will die a horrible, grisly death.

"My little spy," Galleghar continues. "The Thief sees her from time to time. Has he told you that?"

Cold-pressed rage drips into my veins.

If what he says is true...

"He loves to torment the dead, and even for our kind, his attentions are uncommonly wicked."

The two of us are still locked by our blades, the metal grinding against metal.

"At least your mother will get a break soon," Galleghar continues. "Once I kill your mate, the Thief's attention will be wholly occupied. I almost pity that slave of yours. He will make her do things that would make even whores blush."

I feel my icy hatred expand.

"He might even make you watch."

I shove Galleghar's weapon back, our swords unlocking. There's nothing I'd love more than to run him through. But I haven't survived this long by giving in to my temper.

Several sleeping soldiers break away from their fighting when they notice I haven't disappeared. They leap into the air, their wings unfurling, their weapons pointed toward me. I disappear and reform only long enough to kill each one.

The soldiers' lifeless forms fall from the air, and I heave several breaths, my body bloody, as I approach my father once more.

Galleghar's eyes flick briefly to the falling dead.

"All that power," he murmurs. "I'm almost proud to see how strong my blood flows."

"You could've spared yourself all this," I say. "I'm only fighting because you wish me dead." Because he learned of his fate and made it his mission to kill every one of his offspring.

Galleghar laughs, like I'm some fool rather than a seasoned king and criminal.

"Don't delude yourself, *son*. That is not the only reason."

I scowl at him.

"Don't you feel it?" he asks. "Our brutality is right there in our magic, simmering through our veins. If I'd chosen a more peaceful path, I'd still have died by my brood's swords. We are a poisoned lot."

As if in response, the shadows begin to whisper.

I glance down at Callie and the group of sleeping soldiers that encircle her. Her wings are out, and her skin glows. My beautiful lethal siren. One of the soldiers steps toward her, a sick look in his eye.

Callie...

Dread pools in my belly, the likes of which I have *never* felt.

"What could you possibly offer that creature?" I ask Galleghar, still staring at the showdown between my mate and the monster Galleghar unleashed on this world. That ancient evil is nearly unmatched in power.

"Oh, quite a bit, my ill-conceived son," my father replies. "Freedom from his eternal bonds, power, life as we know it...and a kingdom."

A kingdom of spirits and rotten flesh. The Kingdom of Death and Deep Earth.

"How could you promise him something like that?" A kingdom to conquer. That would be like me offering another the Kingdom of Fauna.

The Thief of Souls was never Death's rightful heir.

"Surely you know this land sits right on Death's doorway," Galleghar says. "I marched my forces in, took the palace by force, and let him do the rest."

Even here, in the Otherworld, the laws of life and death are fairly rigid. To take the living into the land of the dead, then *defeat* the dead...

And now the Thief of Souls is a king. Not just a puppeteer filling the body of a dead or dying ruler, but one in his own right.

"You gave him freedom and a kingdom and some of your power, and then you let him put you to sleep, hoping he would wake you up."

"He did wake me up."

That might be the most surprising piece of this whole thing—that the Thief followed through on his end of the deal. The Thief of Souls needs Galleghar no more than I do.

I nearly laugh. "You *actually* trust him," I say, amazed.

My father was always a doomed man. No one can have that sort of ego without consequences.

I shake my head. "Surely you know you cannot control something like that," I say. Something older than us, stronger and more malicious than us.

Callie will have to face that creature.

My dread thickens.

"I don't need to," Galleghar replies haughtily. "I just need to coexist with him."

Now I do let out a cruel laugh. "You think he'll just let you be? You think he owes you *any* loyalty?"

"I freed him from his eternal bonds."

It *is* a staggering feat. Other kings wouldn't have dared. But it means nothing to a being like the Thief.

"He'll keep you around so long as you please him."

And the Thief's pleasure is a fleeting thing.

Galleghar's face twists. His age-old ego, born from centuries of pitiless ruling, shows itself. He believes too much in his own importance to see the truth clearly.

My father gives no warning. His form flickers—one moment several feet from me, the next at my back.

I sense rather than see his sword arching toward me. In an instant I'm gone, and then we're back to trading blows. For several minutes, he and I are all that exists.

He and I and Callie—always Callie. I can't *not* notice her every movement. Her power sings to me even now, that siren in her calling to me, always beckoning me back to her side. It's only time and practice that keep me focused on the battle at hand.

I nick Galleghar's arm, and he grazes my thigh. On and on it goes, blow after blow, one close hit followed by another. Never have I fought a more difficult foe—and never have I enjoyed the challenge so much.

My father is right. There's brutality in our blood. I've always been aware of it, but it's during times like this when I feel the carnage calling to me.

I can hear our labored breaths and smell the sweat and blood and magic dripping from our skin. The whole room is thickening with it…

Around me, the shadows have fallen quiet. So very, very quiet.

I feel him then. The Thief.

I parry a blow from my father and let my eyes sweep the room.

How had I not noticed?

All that vile, unnatural magic I'm choking on doesn't belong to Galleghar or any of the sleeping soldiers. It's the Thief's.

I feel his life force all around me. He's not simply an undead king or a banished leviathan—

I hadn't realized until now the true nature of darkness. It closes in on me from all sides, one with the magic.

…*We're sorry*…

…*So sorry*…

Cold, bleak certainty washes over me.

My eyes move to Callie just in time to meet her horrified gaze.

I love you, I want to say. *More than worlds can hold or words can convey. You are everything that has ever mattered to me. Have faith and strength. You'll be all right.*

The darkness closes in on me, descending on my flesh just as I saw it do to so many of my enemies.

I try to speak the words, to give Callie *something*, but the shadows sink into me, carrying dark magic with them. It feels like fire beneath my flesh, an inferno in my veins.

I'm sorry, cherub. My beautiful nightmare. You will have to save us all yourself.

CHAPTER 35
CALLIE

I watch, frozen, as Des's shadows close in on him.

His back arches, and his entire body tenses, his muscles straining against his skin.

This is what the Thief wanted me to see.

I clutch my heart. I feel his pain like a battering ram, slamming into me over and over. I nearly choke on his agony. If I'm feeling that through our connection, then what must *he* be experiencing?

And then the blackness swallows him up.

When it clears, he's gone.

Immediately, the pain in my chest cuts off. At first, I feel relief; Des is in no more pain.

But then: *Panic.* Panic like I've never known.

I can't breathe. I can't breathe, I can't breathe, I can't breathe.

My eyes scour every corner of the room. Where did Des *go*? My fingers, still cradling the skin over my heart, now dig in.

The Night King's magic, though it still dances through

my veins, now feels like a shadow of its former self. And with every exhalation, it dims and dims until I only hold a memory of it inside myself.

I grasp at the last tendrils of his power as they slide down our magical connection. Down and away from me. All the while, my gaze searches the room.

What just happened? Where did Des go?

And why can't I feel him down our bond?

In the distance, someone calls out to me.

I still can't get enough air.

Why?

Why? Why? *Why?*

My fingers tingle like they've been kissed by ice. The sensation spreads, numbing me as it goes. Putting my hands to my head, I bow over myself.

So confused…

Suddenly, I feel a presence at my back. Someone grabs a clump of my hair and jerks my head back, placing a blade to my throat. I hear Temper shout.

"Time to join your mate," Galleghar hisses against my ear.

No sooner are the words out than another burst of that sickening magic blows him back.

"I told you not to touch her," a soldier says, their voice echoing off the walls.

A second wave of magic follows the first, this one from Temper. It blasts from her palm, hitting Galleghar in the head and knocking him out.

"Eat shit, asshole," she says.

Everything happening around me barely registers. All I can focus on is the thumping of my heart and the sick certainty that something is wrong—that *I* am wrong.

Where is my mate?

Temper's footfalls echo through the room as she comes toward me, her eyes burning. "You've got about a minute to start explaining yourself," she commands a sleeping soldier, "before things get messy."

"There's only one human whose words I'll listen to," the soldier replies smoothly, "and you aren't her."

This is a dream. Of course. A *dream*.

Dropping my hands, I straighten.

"Enough with the games." I'm surprised my words come out as even as they do.

I search the room for the Thief. When I don't see his dark features, I settle on a sleeping soldier. "Where is my mate?" Glamour coats the words like syrup.

Around me, the entire room is poised, the air thick with promised violence and the Thief's dark magic.

The female soldier I stare at replies, "He's in my kingdom now."

Small death. The Thief rules over small death. That's how this nightmare is all possible. I'm asleep, and the Thief is screwing with me.

"Wake me up," I demand.

The look the Thief gives me... If I didn't know him better, I'd almost say it's pity. But he's enjoying this.

"This is no dream, enchantress. If it were, I would stand before you as myself—just as I always have."

I glance around at all the frozen faces. Malaki and Janus are sprawled on the ground, their forms unnaturally still, Galleghar hasn't moved from where Temper knocked him out, and the rest of the Thief's minions seem content to stay where they are.

The only other person who seems truly alive is Temper. My gaze falls to her just as she closes in on me.

Dear Temper, my best friend. A tear slips from her burning eyes.

I've only ever seen her cry a handful of times—when her mother told Temper she was her biggest disappointment, when her first crush called her *vile* in front of our peers, and one seemingly random evening after a night of drinks when Temper confessed that she feared she was unlovable.

Now she shakes her head. "Babe, this isn't a dream."

This…isn't a dream?

But of course it is. No one is as they seem, and nothing feels as it should.

My heart spasms, and that cold numbness, it's reached my bond to Des.

I stumble then fall to my knees.

Realization is always described as an instant of enlightenment, but that's not how it happens this time. The truth comes in icy increments.

I *wasn't* dropped into some dream. I remember the last minute and the minute before that. I remember coming here, and I remember every logical thing but that final one.

Des disappearing. Des leaving me.

Gasping out a breath, I clutch at my heart.

The darkness will betray you, the seer said.

I heave out a breath.

This is no dream.

It feels…it feels like I've fallen into an icy lake and the cold water is making my lungs seize.

Another breath shudders out.

If it isn't a dream, that means Des…Des…

My throat spasms as a cry works its way up.

I'm shaking my head.

No. No, no, no, no.

The cry is building at the back of my throat.

He can't be—can't be dead.

I scream, my siren rising within me. My wings flare wide, and my scales ripple across my forearms, my skin burning bright, so terribly bright. My fingers throb where my claws have extended.

I don't feel human; I don't feel fae. I'm losing myself, my heart and head trying fruitlessly to slip down the bond I share with Des, chasing the last echoes of his power.

But it's gone. It's gone, and I don't know if it's ever coming back.

We will get it back—or else.

I'm screaming and screaming and screaming, and the whole world is falling. My pain is darkening, deepening like the night, until I don't know where the agony ends and the anger begins.

We'll kill and kill and kill and kill and—

"Callypso."

I turn at the echoing sound of Temper's voice. Her eyes burn with her power. At her feet is Malaki, his body prone. Not too far away lies Janus, his form similarly stupefied. Victims of the Thief's dark magic.

"We're leaving," Temper says.

The sorceress's fiery gaze is focused on Galleghar's still form.

Her vengeance matches ours...

The former Night King is sprawled on the ground, unconscious from her last hit.

Temper raises her hand, her palm outstretched. She means to kill him.

"No," I say, my voice vibrating with my power. "His death is *mine* to claim."

Temper narrows her eyes on Galleghar, even as she curves her lips just the slightest. The smile is nothing but cruel. "Fine."

She turns her attention to a sleeping soldier. "You fucked with the wrong humans," she says, her voice resonating with her own magic.

Her eyes flick to me, and I see her silently asking to if she should give in to her power.

What is left to lose? I nod grimly.

A nefarious smile curves the corner of Temper's lips. In the next instant, fire flares to life at her feet. It races along the ground in a dozen different directions, heading for the sleeping soldiers. First, one alights, and then another and another. One by one, the Thief's minions get swept up by flame.

They shriek as their bodies blacken and burn, and I feel nothing at all.

The fire rages for only a few minutes, and when it's extinguished, all that remains of the soldiers are blackened bones and ash.

The only people in the room are me, Temper, Malaki, and Janus—the last two of whom are still unmoving, the Thief's magic clinging to their skin. Temper reined in her power enough to save us. Us and…

My gaze slides to the one other person she spared. Galleghar Nyx.

The root of all my suffering.

I rise from the ground, my wings fanning wide behind me. Slowly, I pace to him.

I feel so cold. Even my rage burns like ice. The only things left inside me are pain and vengeance.

Des's father is stirring, moaning a little.

Temper steps up to him, laughing low in her throat.

"You're going to wish you were dead." Her voice is inhuman, possessed by her wicked nature. For once, I wholly embrace it.

This is why no one crosses us. We are fearsomely wrought.

I close in on Galleghar, pulling out the iron shackles from my back pocket. I ignore the way the metal sizzles against my skin as I grab the former king's wrists. Dragging them behind his back, I slap on one cuff, then the other, pinning his arms behind him.

Slit his throat. Rip his heart out, then make him eat it. Disembowel him and dance on his innards.

I want it all.

Make him pay for what he did to our mate.

Galleghar's moans get louder, and his eyes flutter.

Crouching next to him, I whisper a single promise—

"Your will is mine."

All those years under the yoke of my conscience, I was running from this single sobering truth: I can do more than bend others to my will; I can utterly *bind* them to it.

All this time I hid from my true nature.

I'll hide from it no more.

CHAPTER 36

I can't feel a thing.

I didn't feel Temper's touch when she held me in her arms, her skin like fire to my ice. I didn't feel the bite of pain or gratitude when several Night fae collected us from that cavern. And I didn't feel the lashing wind against my cheeks during the long journey back to Somnia.

It's only once I'm deposited in my chambers and I take a shuddering breath that I feel *something*.

Agony like no other. It weakens my knees and chokes the breath out of me.

I squeeze my eyes shut. This is worse, so much worse, than feeling nothing. This pain is like a wound that's bleeding me out.

Temper is still at my side, her fingers threaded through mine. I slip my hand out of hers.

"Leave me," I say.

There's no way she'd ever leave me if circumstances were normal. But my skin is still glowing, and my glamour is still riding my words. My siren hasn't left me since the battle, and even a sorceress as powerful as Temper can't fight my magic.

"This is bullshit," Temper mutters as her feet carry her out of the room. She grabs the door handle and opens the door. "As soon as your glamour wears off, I'm coming back for you."

The door clicks shut behind her, and her voice gives way to silence.

My eyes sweep over the suite. Des's wedding present to me.

A sob slips out, and my chest heaves with empty, silent cries. I wander to the infinity pool, with its glowing water.

Step by step, I slip into the pool, clothes and all. My head slips beneath the surface.

This can't be real. Pain like this doesn't *exist*, and surely one can't survive this sort of suffering.

I sink to the bottom of the pool and stare up through the water. From here I hear the water rushing by my ears, and I see the suite's lamps glimmering far above me.

I could stay right here, forever, and I'd be fine with that. I don't think a siren is capable of drowning, but I'm willing to test that theory.

If I die, I'll be in the Kingdom of Death and Deep Earth. Then I'll be back with Desmond, once and for all.

My throat tightens. He's gone.

But I could join him. I could join him in the land of the dead—

That's what the Thief wants.

I let out a moan, the sound warped beneath the water.

There's no relief from this agony; not even death will be the end of it. If I die, I fall under the Thief's reign. Then the monster will wholly control me, and I doubt reuniting me with my mate is part of his plan.

So I'm stuck here, in the land of the living, all while Des—Des is dead.

Dead.

A sob slips out of me then, a burst of bubbles forming with the cry. But once I start weeping, I can't seem to stop. My sirenic voice turns the sound into music, and it's horrible that pain can sound so lovely.

He's gone, and I don't know what to *do.*

That motherfucking Thief and his sick, twisted game. I played right into his hands the moment I decided to go after Galleghar. When I set foot into that cavern, the teeth of his trap snapped shut around me.

Des is gone; Malaki and Janus are catatonic, victims of the same dark magic that compromised the sleeping soldiers.

And I am broken.

All my fault. If I hadn't made the call to go after Galleghar, Des would be here still.

I close my eyes, my tears slipping into the water.

I don't know how long I linger at the bottom of the pool. Longer than a human could withstand. Eventually, someone leaps into the pool and scoops me up before dragging me out of the water.

I cough a little, my lungs heaving in a breath.

"Your Majesty!"

I blink at the fae soldier, the water dripping down my glowing skin.

He looks panicked. "I know it's hard, but you can't die. Our kingdom needs you."

I'm not going to die.

I'm already dead.

What is death?

Do the dead ever truly die?

336

My breath catches on that last thought.

Do they? Is Des still out there?

My gaze sharpens on the soldier. Behind him, the door hangs open. Temper must've tipped him off that I'm not in a good place.

"We need you," the Night soldier repeats, shaking me a little.

His words finally register.

Our kingdom needs you.

I work my throat. He wants me to be a queen. To step up and rule now that my mate cannot.

The last decision I made killed my mate.

But there's no one else left to make decisions. Every other ruler is dead or incapacitated.

I swallow and nod. "Okay," I say, my voice hoarse.

He sets me down. I'm dripping luminous water all over the floor.

"What am I supposed to do?" I ask, my voice raw. I know nothing about being a queen.

The soldier's gaze travels over me. "Rule. Rule and save us."

———

The royal guard leaves soon after that. I don't know how I manage to convince him that I'm all right. I'm not, and I probably shouldn't be alone, even though I can't bear the thought of sharing this grief with anyone else. It feels achingly personal.

I wring out my hair and then begin the laborious task of unpeeling my clothes and dressing in something dry. Even after I do, my wet hair drips onto the clothes.

Right about now Des would've dried my hair for me. He does weird, considerate things like that all the time.

Did.

I sit heavily on my bed—*our* bed—and a piece of paper

rustles beneath me. The violent, breathless pain of my grief is slips like poison through my veins.

I cover my eyes. Ugly aching sobs rack my body.

I let it out. I let it *all* out until I feel drained dry of tears. Placing my hands on my thighs, I take a deep breath.

That's about when I finally notice the unassuming piece of parchment I'm sitting on, the paper crinkling every time I shift. It rests there like Des carelessly left it on the bed. But Des doesn't do anything carelessly.

I pull it out from under me. It's actually two pieces of paper, one a formal-looking document and the other a smaller note written by a familiar hand. I put the back of my palm to my mouth to stop another round of sobs.

Don't be frightened of yourself, cherub. You are exactly as you should be. From flame to ashes, dawn to dusk, I am yours always. Till darkness dies.

~Your Bargainer

Des knew he was going to die.

That's what this is—a postmortem love note.

Suddenly, I'm angry, brutally, grievously angry at him.

My hand shakes, the paper crinkling.

That *bastard*. How *dare* he leave me.

I almost don't read the other piece of paper, I'm so furious. But this is all I have left of him. A short note and another piece of parchment.

Grimacing, I smooth out the paper, my eyes trailing over the words written in formal stanzas.

The Prophecy of Galleghar Nyx

Mighty Nyx came,
Mighty Nyx sought
All that he could
Of his dark lot.

In the deep night,
His kingdom rose.
Beware, great king,
Of that which grows.

Easy to conquer,
Easy to crown,
But even the strongest
Can be cut down.

Raised in the shadows,
Reared in the night,
Your child will come
And ascend by might.

And you, the slain,
Shall wait and see
What other things
A soul can be.

A body to curse,
A body to blame,
A body the earth
Will not yet claim.

Beware the mortal
Beneath your sky.
Crush the human
Who'll see you die.

Twice you'll rise,
Twice you'll fall,
Lest you can
Change it all.

Or perish by day,
Perish by dawn.
The world believes
You're already gone.

So darken your heart,
My shadow king,
And let us see
What war will bring.

I stare at the words for a long time. Horror, fear, and fury all churn within me. My emotions feel like a roulette table, spinning around and around. I'm not sure which emotion will win out.

Is this supposed to mean something to me? Because it doesn't.

I set the parchment aside, my emotions spinning, spinning until eventually, they land on something like grim determination.

I *will* finish this. I will find the Thief, I will kill him and Galleghar along with him, and then I will scour the Underworld for my lost mate. I won't stop until Des is mine again.

Nothing else will do.

A knock on the door jerks me from my thoughts.

"Your Majesty?" The soldier who left me not so long ago now calls out from the hallway. I guess he doesn't trust me enough to leave me alone.

"Come in," I call. I almost don't recognize my voice. It's cool and collected, like my world hasn't just been upended.

Des is not here. Oh God, he's not here, and I have to still function.

You've functioned without him once before, back when you thought you'd never see him again. You're an old hand at this.

But back then I at least knew the Bargainer was out there somewhere in the vast universe, sipping espressos out of tiny cups and making deals with desperate people.

The heart might in fact be the shittiest organ out there because it can feel love, and love is a terrible thing.

Hate is a much better emotion.

I have plenty of hate.

I let it heat my veins as I get up and open the door.

"Your Majesty," the guard says from the hallway, "the Queen of Flora is here, and she's seeking sanctuary."

CHAPTER 37

Mara Verdana is alive—alive and here in Somnia.

For a moment, I'm so shocked, I forget my own issues.

I can picture the Flora Queen so clearly in my mind's eye. Her flame-red hair, those flowers twisted in her fiery locks. Her beautiful poisonous smile.

Brazen, wicked Mara. By the end of my stay in her kingdom, she became a tragic figure. Like me, she watched her soul mate die. And like me, she survived the ordeal.

"Get Temper," I command one of the guards as I'm led to the throne room.

I might not have wanted the sorceress's company as I fell apart, but I want her by my side for everything else.

The soldiers lead me to the throne room, and my throat bobs a little when I notice the single chair waiting for me. Someone discreetly removed the second one.

I take a seat, ignoring the room full of nobles and officials here for one reason or another. I squeeze the armrests with both hands.

I'm barely breathing; I have no clue how I'm supposed to rule when I can hardly hold myself together.

The doors at the other end of the room are thrown open, and a retinue carries an ornate velvet chair on slats. Sitting on it is the Flora Queen.

Her cheeks are gaunt, her flame-red hair has dulled, and the flowers growing in it are wilted, their edges browned. The sight of her withering away is sobering. Yet her chin is still raised in that haughty defiance I remember.

The retinue stops, their final footfalls echoing throughout the room, and the fairies carrying her chair now set it down.

In the silence that follows, one of the Flora guards trailing the procession steps forward.

"Her Majesty," he announces, "Our Lady of Life, Mistress of the Harvest, Queen of the Flora Kingdom and All that Grows, Mara Verdana."

Mara's gaze falls to me. Even her eyes, which were once so strikingly green, have now lost their luster.

If she's surprised or offended to see me—a human— sitting on a fae throne, she doesn't show it.

"I came as soon as I heard the news about Desmond," she says.

I frown at her, my claws pricking into the velvet armrests. *Word gets around fast.*

One of the side doors opens, and a Night soldier escorts Temper into the throne room before leaving her a few yards away from me. When she glances at me, she pinches her brows together with concern. Then her gaze sweeps to Mara.

She whistles. "Never thought I'd see *you* again." Temper eyes Mara up and down. "You look like you tried meth one too many times."

Mara ignores Temper and instead struggles to stand. I rise from the throne.

She puts a hand out. "I'm fine."

It takes the Flora Queen an agonizing minute to get to her feet. Once she does, her eyes flick around the room, and her gaze still has that razor sharpness I remember. Eventually, her attention moves to me.

"A moment alone?" she says.

I raise my eyebrows. "One of the last times you and I shared space, you had me whipped within an inch of my life—"

Around me some of the Night fae hiss. The sound constricts my heart. They're defensive of me. I hadn't expected that. I hadn't expected their acceptance at all.

"I believe, when it comes to discussing the fates of our mates," Mara says smoothly, "you'd prefer a little discretion."

I narrow my eyes on her. I'll give it to the Flora Queen, she has some brass balls, parading in here like some kind of rock star then demanding a private meeting.

I glance over at Temper, who's empathically shaking her head and mouthing, "Not today, Satan."

My eyes drift back to Mara, who looks exhausted but patient. She understands what I'm feeling. She might be the *only* one who understands. After staring at her a moment longer, I finally nod. "Could you please give us a moment alone?" I ask the room.

In response, it empties. Temper glowers on her way out, muttering about how useless it was for me to drag her here if I wasn't going to listen to her advice.

The last fairy leaves, and the doors bang closed, the sound reverberating along the walls.

I stare down at Mara. Is this what I'm going to become? A shell of myself?

I get up and drag a nearby chair over to the velvet one Mara entered in. "Show's over," I say, gesturing to her elaborate chair. "You can sit."

She moves over to it and all but collapses into the seat, wheezing a little.

"I know he killed your mate," she begins. I don't need to ask who she's talking about. She runs her index finger over the armrest. "I first turned to other men ten years ago. I can remember the exact day."

This is...not how I imagined the conversation going.

Mara continues, "I looked at the Green Man, and suddenly, he didn't pull me in the way he once did. In fact, if I'm being perfectly honest, I'd say I was *repulsed* by him, though seemingly nothing had changed.

"I couldn't understand why, and of course, I was ashamed of it. Never had I heard of a fairy who was disgusted by their soul mate.

"I don't know how the Thief did it, how he managed to scoop out the Green Man's spirit and insert his own." She covers her eyes for a moment. "I've only ever seen magic like that once before."

I knit my brows, then rest my forearms on my thighs and lean in closer.

"Back when I was young and my parents ruled the Kingdom of Flora, I met a man like you—an enchanter. Lazaret." Mara breathes his name. "He came to our court as a minstrel, there to entertain my family and the lesser nobility."

The Flora Queen already told me this story back when I visited her kingdom. Does she remember that, or has her mind withered along with her body?

Her eyes grow distant. "Gods, was he stunning. Golden skin, eyes like emeralds."

I try not to roll my eyes. Mara might be tragic, but she's still vapid.

"However, it was my sister," Mara says, "Thalia, who claimed his heart. I envied her then, to have the attention of such a beautiful man.

"But the longer she was around Lazaret, the weaker she became. She was convinced they were mates, even though it was ridiculous—fairies can sense that sort of magic, and it wasn't present with my sister or Lazaret. But Thalia wouldn't be swayed. She pledged her life and her heart to the enchanter...and her power.

"My parents told her to undo what she had done, that her magic belonged to the realm, not some pretty fairy, but she wouldn't listen to them.

"Even as Thalia weakened, Lazaret was having increasing sway among our people. He'd spin songs and mesmerize the audience in ways that were...unnatural." She sighs out a breath. "And the more familiar he and I became, the more he unsettled me. It was just a conversation that turned awry somewhere along the way or an inappropriate reaction to a situation."

My skin pimples. I know too well what she's talking about.

"But at the time," she continues, "we were all under his spell. Everyone but my parents, who saw him for what he truly was—a *thief.*"

That word is like a cool breath against my neck.

"They called him into court one spring morning to entertain the nobles. But it was a trap. Before he could so much as open his mouth, the court's executioner sliced off his head."

She rubs her eyes. "My sister...she didn't survive long

346

enough to see the next moon cycle. Her power was hers again, but her heart wasn't. She took my father's sword and took her own life."

Mara frowns, her hand curling into a fist. She takes a deep breath. "I was never my sister. I never wielded the same staggering magic she did. I was supposed to marry well and enjoy the fruits of court life. Instead, she died, and I inherited the throne.

"I wasn't powerful, but the land of Flora is kind; when I was most uncertain about my kingdom's future, it gave me my king.

"I found the Green Man deep in the Arcane Forest. He was born of the trees themselves; I saw it with my own eyes, the way the tree trunk's flesh parted and a fully formed man stepped forth from it."

Her words remind me of all those bloody soldiers curled up in trees. The Thief must've used the Green Man's power to put them there.

"In that instant, our bond snapped into place. Only the greatest rulers are given this sort of gift from the land itself. The Green Man was strange and magnificent, the way wild things are, but he was no normal fairy. He was a blessing, and he was mine."

She shudders out a breath. "I loved him. So much." Her eyes flick to me. "I know you probably question that, but the man you saw—"

"Was the Thief," I finish for her.

She flinches a little, her wilted flowers shifting in her hair. "How could I have missed it? I ask myself that all the time these days. I don't have any answers. I thought that perhaps the Green Man's strangeness was a sign the earth was calling him home. And when the trees started...*rotting*...I thought my magic had betrayed me."

The darkness will betray you, the seer had told Des.

I didn't know magic *could* betray its wielder, but of all people, I should know better. Des's magic tricked him into a bargain that kept us apart for seven years.

Magic is sentient.

"I was angry and jaded at my power," Mara says, "and at the mate who had begun to act odd and distant and spent long hours among my sacred oaks. I should've known. There were times when my mate seemed sinister to me.

"And then, when the sleeping women began returning to us in caskets and we began laying them out in the greenhouses, the Green Man would often visit them. I mistook his fascination for concern, never once guessing he was resp—" Her voice breaks. "Responsible.

"And so I buried my jaded emotions in warm bodies and beautiful celebrations. Even as my oaks died and my people went missing and my mate slipped away from me, I pretended everything was fine.

"I became cruel."

Her gaze holds mine captive. "And this is how my great and unlikely story ends—my soul mate dead, my lands poisoned, and an impostor in my bed who seeded his undead army in *my* sacred wood." Mara shakes her head. "*Blasphemous*," she hisses under her breath.

Grimacing, she adds, "I lived with him for ten years."

I try not to shiver at that. She spent the past decade alongside a creature who raped thousands of women and killed who knows how many more. She called him her *mate*.

"Are you going after him?" she asks me.

We will hunt him down and carve up his flesh.

I nod. Even now my vengeance surges.

"He took my sister from me," Mara says. "He took my

soul mate from me. If I could kill him myself, I would, but alas, I'm dying."

She reaches out and takes my hand, squeezing it tightly. Her eyes blaze. "Find that thing, and *end* him, once and for all."

———————

I walk away from the throne room as my audience streams back inside. Someone calls out to me, and I'm sure I'm making a mess of royal protocol.

Considering the day I've had, I'm entitled to give responsibilities the middle finger.

My emotions are hard to unravel. I didn't think I had it in me to understand Mara Verdana after everything she put me through, but I was wrong. I do understand her when it's too late for us to have any sort of meaningful relationship.

Like a ghost, I slip toward my chambers.

Once I'm inside, the door firmly shut behind me, I kick off my shoes and crawl into bed.

It's another one of those Hail Mary days, only this time, there's no Bargainer to drive my pain away.

Tomorrow won't be any easier.

I squeeze my eyes shut, my entire body heavy. I don't think I can move if I try.

Never want to leave.

It takes no more than ten minutes for Temper to find me. I hear her sure footfalls as she enters the room. She sets something aside then crawls onto the bed, sliding beneath the sheets.

Her arms snake around me, and she holds me close.

"It's all right, babe," she whispers.

I shake my head. "It's not."

Temper exhales. "You're right. It's not. But you're not alone. I'll always be here for you."

That makes a tear slip out. "Des promised me the same thing."

The liar.

My best friend brushes my hair back, leaning over me to get a good look at my face. "It's sweet that you're worried about me," she says, "but you and I both know my ass is too evil to kill."

A laugh slips out of me, and she joins in.

"I think mine might be too," I admit.

"Hell, yeah, it is," Temper agrees. "You're scary when you want to be."

Temper's arm tightens around me. "Callie, you and I have been through some shit over the past decade. You don't need to be strong with me. Just let it out."

I don't know if I needed to hear that or if Temper's words were simply the straw that broke the camel's back, but I do give in and cry—if you can call it that.

I'm not just crying—I'm sobbing and shaking and heaving.

Temper begins to cry with me, her own pain surfacing.

"I'm so sorry," I whisper when I realize that while I've been wallowing in my grief, Temper has been carrying her own. "I didn't even think about how you must be feeling." I pet her hair back, staring into her face.

She squeezes her eyes shut and shakes her head. "You don't have to apologize about that," she says hoarsely. "I understand." After a moment she whispers, "I wasn't supposed to like him."

More tears come, and the two of us hold each other as we fall apart.

We fall asleep like that, commiserating over our heartache and comforting each other just as we've always done.

CHAPTER 38

"Missing your mate?"

I spin at that voice, my skin brightening and my wings manifesting.

The Thief of Souls reclines on his throne, a self-satisfied smirk on his face.

"I will *gut* you—" I stalk toward him, my claws out in an instant.

Drink his screams. Laugh as we watch him die.

He raises an eyebrow. "I'd like to see you try."

My wings move, pulling me into the air. I descend on him like a Fury, my legs straddling his, my claws bared.

The Thief catches my wrists.

"What was it you said the last time you dreamed of me...?" He pretends to search his memory. "Oh yes. 'If you want to hurt me, you're going to have to try harder.'

"Tell me, enchantress, have I tried hard enough?"

I shriek, fighting his hold on my wrists. I want to rip away that smug smile of his. "Damn you!" My voice is raw with fury and pain. An angry tear slips out. "I will fucking make you feast on your own heart for what you did."

"That's *awfully* vivid. You're going to have to carve it out of my chest first, and"—he glances at the wrists he holds captive—"it doesn't look like that'll happen anytime soon."

I yank against his grip, my teeth gritted.

The Thief resettles himself between my legs. "My, this is intimate."

"Where is Des?" I demand. Glamour fills my voice, but it does nothing to pry the truth loose from the Thief.

"If you want your soul mate," he says, his voice low, "you'll have to come and get him." He jerks on my wrists, pulling me in close.

The Thief leans in and licks my bared throat. "*For a price,*" he says, using words he stole from the Bargainer.

I go feral in his arms, bucking wildly and scratching anything I can.

The Thief easily tosses me to the floor in front of him.

I'm back on my feet in an instant, but that's all it takes for the ground to split and a cage to literally *grow* up from the floor. The black bars rise around me, arching overhead until they meet.

"I think you've forgotten that inside a dream, I can do anything." To emphasize his point, my outfit—a wispy pale blue dress—vanishes inch by inch.

"I can humiliate you," he says, as the dress's hem climbs up my legs and the straps slide off my shoulders, revealing my breasts.

I scowl at the Thief, too angry to be embarrassed. Distractedly, I push the straps back in place, covering my chest once more.

His eyes are alight with excitement. "I can hurt you."

The metal bars bow in until they touch my skin. My flesh sizzles and smokes under the press of iron.

"This isn't even me being creative," he adds. "I could make the floor grow eyes and a mouth and swallow you whole. I could change your appearance."

He grins. "I could even make the dead come back to life."

"Cherub."

I start at that voice, my breath catching. I turn so fast that I burn myself against the bars all over again.

Stepping from the shadows, clad in leather and a faded Guns N' Roses shirt, is my soul mate.

A small sound escapes my throat. "*Des.*" My eyes scour him, taking in his sleeve of tattoos, his broad, sculpted shoulders, his ponytail.

I know he's not real, that none of this is real, and yet he looks completely lifelike.

In the Otherworld, dreams are never just dreams. They're another sort of reality.

Des told me that once.

With every step he takes toward me, his strides get longer, brisker. Des stops in front of my cage, his eyes searching my face. His gaze flicks to the Thief, his upper lip twitching. A grim smile grows on Des's features.

"She's going to kill you," he says with certainty.

"No," the Thief disagrees, "she's going to do things for me—many perverse things—over the course of her very long life, and there's nothing you can do to stop it."

My heart hammers in my chest, my pain and rage feeding the siren inside me.

I flash him a malicious smile. "If you want to taste me, Thief, then come closer," I beckon.

His face is shrewd, but his interest is piqued. "I could come to you—or you could come to me."

I knit my brows.

All at once a strong wind tears through the Thief's palace. The gust blows away the bars of my cage; it blows away the bone-like columns holding up the ceiling then the pale stone walls along with it. The wind blows away the floor, yanking on my dress.

Then, to my horror, it blows away Desmond, piece by piece. First his feet and his calves, then his chest and arms and pelvis. He stares at me with his fierce silver eyes, his irises glittering enigmatically. Those too are lost a second later, scattering like dust in the wind.

I let out a cry, but the wind snatches it away, whipping my hair as it does so. The supernatural gust is sweeping everything into inky darkness.

The last things to be wiped away are the Thief and his gilded throne.

He smiles down at me, looking like a conqueror. "*Come find your mate where oblivion lies. I'll keep you captive till darkness dies.*"

I wake with a gasp.

My hair is plastered to my face, and my skin glows. Next to me, Temper sleeps deeply, dried tracks of tears staining her cheeks. I take a fortifying breath against the sight of them and everything they remind me of.

I slip off the mattress and rummage around the room, discreetly looking for a swimsuit. When I don't find one, I settle for lingerie. After changing into the items, I head back for the pool that lingers half indoors, half out.

This time, when I enter the glowing waters, I don't sink to the bottom. Instead, I flip on my back and let myself drift along the surface. Inevitably, the water moves me to the outer edges of the pool, and I stare up at the stars.

Des…

My chest feels like it's caving in.

Even the stars seem to mock me. How can they continue to shine when the man who ruled them is gone?

Come find your mate where oblivion lies…

I glow all over again, just thinking about the Thief.

It's been a long time since I've wanted to hurt someone this badly.

Let's sing to him our sweet, strange song. He will know pleasure then—pleasure and pain. We'll remind him why sirens are known as killers.

The conundrum of it all is how to get my hands on the Thief. Dying is the most obvious way—it's a one-way ticket straight to the Thief's kingdom. But that's exactly what he wants—it's the very reason he wanted me to drink the lilac wine. Because, at the end of the day, once a fairy dies, their soul is under the domain of the King of the Dead.

At least I think he wants me under his domain… He hasn't tried very hard to kill me.

Come find your mate where oblivion lies…

Said as though I could just fucking *walk* there.

I glare up at the stars—

My breath leaves me all at once.

Holy *shit*. What if I *could* just walk to the Kingdom of Death? What *if?*

The Kingdom of Death and Deep Earth is a physical place in the Otherworld, just like the other kingdoms. Death is the most obvious route in, but…

If fairies can spin moonlight into cloth and Des can put starlight in my hair, why can't the living enter the realm of the dead *without* dying?

Even on earth, there were tales of living people entering the Underworld—some even leaving with the dead. Here in the Otherworld, a place where the impossible is made possible, perhaps I can do the same.

Or perhaps grief has made you weak in the head.

I deflate.

Then I continue to stare up at the stars, the water lapping against my skin. But the longer my thoughts wander, the more they keep coming back to the possibility of a way for me enter the Land of the Dead, one that doesn't involve dying.

I bet it's possible.

Maybe then I could face the Thief of Souls without being his subject.

After all, I wouldn't have been the first person to visit the King of the Dead and live to tell the tale. There was one other who sought him out long ago...

I sit upright in the water, the waves splashing at the movement.

God damn it, I have an *idea*.

An idea that may actually work.

CHAPTER 39

"All hail the Queen of the Night."

I stride into the throne room, Temper trailing me. A chorus of cheers rises as fairies watch me file in, their gazes drawn to my glowing skin. My power still hasn't settled down, not since yesterday. At this point, I'm not sure it ever will.

Not until I get my mate back.

I take a seat on Des's throne, with Temper stopping just off to my side. Hours ago I filled my friend in on all I know about the Thief and the kingdom he rules—and then I told her my idea. Now all that's left is executing it.

The room goes quiet, people waiting on me for further instruction.

I don't wear a crown, and I'm not here by choice, but for once, I feel…queenly.

Too late for Des to see it.

I glance at one of the Night soldiers guarding the doors at the back of the room. "Bring the traitor in."

The soldier ducks his head and slips out. In his wake, the silence seems to deepen.

We wait, the minutes ticking by.

All at once the double doors swing open, and two guards dressed in black escort a white-haired fairy down the aisle.

Galleghar smirks at me, clearly pleased at himself despite the situation—pleased his last remaining child is dead.

At the sight of him, I squeeze the armrests, my claws puncturing the velvet.

We will tear into him and make ribbons of his flesh.

The soldiers lead Des's father to the end of the aisle.

"Release him," I say to the guards.

Immediately, they step away from Galleghar, moving to take their posts nearby.

The former king glances down at his iron cuffs, a smile twisting his mouth. "How does it feel to lose what you loved most, slave?" he asks, peering up at me.

The room sucks in a collective breath at the slur.

I watch him, tapping a claw against my armrest.

Let's taste his flesh as he begs for mercy, my siren whispers. *Bring him closer.*

"All my life, I've never truly understood my power," I begin. "Why must the nature of sirens be to entice men?"

Galleghar furrows his brows. Not the response he was expecting, and he has no idea where I'm going with this.

But I do.

"I don't understand," he says, forced to answer because of the glamour in my voice.

Whatever wards protected him from my magic back on Barbos, they're gone now.

We have him in our clutches.

I study him. "You will."

Why does my power draw others in?

I always wondered about that. About how much my alluring nature was to blame for my stepfather's sick assaults. Obviously, that's incorrect thinking—my *stepfather* was to blame for his actions, not *my* power—but at the time I didn't know it. And then an instructor at Peel Academy touched me inappropriately, and the abuse felt like a pattern. I wondered all over again—*why*? Why did I have to be this way? If I blended in more, could I have escaped the abuse I endured?

No.

No, I could not have.

There will always be bad men, and they will take and take and take.

But so will I.

People like us are not victims. We're someone's nightmare.

I finally understand why my power draws others in.

"There are two kinds of predators," I say softly. "One that chases after prey, and one that coaxes its prey to it."

Galleghar hasn't lost his smug expression.

He will in a moment.

"What do you see when you look at me?" I ask.

"My mortal enemy," he says. "You must be destroyed."

"What else?"

Again, his brows draw together.

"A slave," he says, compelled to answer by my magic.

"What else?"

He frowns, but his eyes drink me in, fascinated. "An enchantress," he finally says.

"A *siren*," I correct him.

There are aspects of my magic I've unconsciously dulled over the years. The ability to ensnare my victims with a look alone—that is one of them.

The same part of me that resented my nature also feared *this* part of me. The sinister, powerful, punishing part of me. I already disliked the attention I received. I didn't want any *more* of it.

That's why, even at Peel Academy, I was a loner. I willed myself to be overlooked. I didn't realize then what I was doing, but I did it nonetheless.

And I continued doing it.

Until now.

All at once I unleash the full force of my magic on the room. My skin brightens a touch, and my power fills the air.

Dozens of fairies stand, their eyes glazing over as they look at me. Many clamber over chairs, trying to get closer to me. Even Temper cuts toward my throne.

"Everyone, stay where you are." My audience stops where they stand, binding them by my order.

I gaze down at the former Night King. Abruptly, I stand. Stair by stair, I descend the dais until I'm only a couple of yards from him.

"What do you see now?" I ask.

This is what it's like for a siren to hunt.

He sways toward me a little, his eyes bright, his gaze ensnared.

"There...aren't words," he breathes, his vendetta forgotten. He shakes his head wondrously. "In all my years, I have never beheld one such as yourself." His eyes move over me covetously. "Why should my son receive such a prize from the gods instead of me?"

A moment ago I was a slave. Now I am a prize. Always an object to be possessed.

I close my eyes, even as the former Night King murmurs promises about the future. "When I am king again, you can still live here... The Thief is not to touch this kingdom... You can be one of my concubines... I will make you my favorite... You will have everything you ever wanted..."

The only thing I ever wanted is *gone*.

Teach me again how to be someone's nightmare, I once asked Des.

My power ripples over my skin.

With pleasure, mate.

I open my eyes. "Kneel," I command.

Galleghar doesn't even have it in him to glare at me. I hold his very mind in the palm of my hand; what rules him now is *desire*.

I scowl at the former Night King. This is the seed of evil that started it all. Had it not been for Galleghar's selfishness, the entire fabric of this world's history would have been different. Des's mother might still be alive, along with his half siblings. Des might've been raised in a castle rather than a cave. He might have had a great life.

We might never have met, and he might never have died before his time.

The horrible thing about true love is that I would erase *us* if it meant keeping him alive.

Slowly, I diminish my glamour. I don't want Galleghar to mindlessly enjoy what I'm doing to him. I want it to bother him very, very badly.

Within seconds, the former king's expression goes from lustful to confused to furious.

"You *bitch*," he snarls.

"Uh-uh," I chastise him. "The next time you say anything unflattering about me—or anyone else for that matter—I will make you eat your tongue. *Literally*."

I reach out to caress Galleghar's cheek.

Ours to taste, ours to break.

He lifts his bound hands, presumably to push mine away.

"No," I say. "You won't fight me, and you won't flee. You will sit here, answer my questions, and let me touch you as I please."

His hands drop, even as he curls his upper lip. Galleghar has so much power—I sense it vibrating within him—and yet against me, it's utterly useless.

I stroke his cheekbone. "You're very pretty," I say, "in a cruel sort of way. Too bad the rest of you is useless." I grab him by his lower jaw and tilt his head back and forth, assessing him from different angles. "Then again, perhaps I *can* find some use for you. Now that my mate's gone, there's nothing stopping me from starting my own harem."

I lean closer. "You would be my concubine. I should warn you, *if* you were in my harem, there are many things I would ask of you that you may not be comfortable with. Sirens are known to enjoy both sex and blood. I *do* hope you're not squeamish."

I smile a little at the hate in his eyes. I doubt he's ever had someone turn his tricks back on him.

Releasing his jaw, I say, "Relax, asshole, I would *never* be intimate with you."

Enough toying with him. I straighten. "I want to pay the Thief of Souls a personal visit. How do I get to him?"

Galleghar laughs. "You'd have to die first."

I wait for his laughter to trail off. "Is that the only way?" I ask.

He hesitates.

"Is it?" I press.

The hateful look is back. I watch as he holds out against my glamour for one—two—three—four—five seconds.

"No," he eventually grits out.

My pulse races. I was right. There's another way in.

"Tell me everything you know about this other entrance to the Kingdom of Death and Deep Earth."

Galleghar's lips twitch as he fights my compulsion. For once, it isn't satisfying to watch him resist. Every second he holds out answering feels like an eternity.

Impatient, I unleash a little more of my power. "You *want* to answer me," I say, my voice hypnotic. "Now *tell me.*"

The mean look in his eyes dissolves; he stares at me like I'm some rare treasure. "In the Land of Nightmares, there's a forest," he says.

The Land of Nightmares... Why does that sound familiar?

Memnos, I remember. The Land of Nightmares was another name for Memnos, one of the floating islands of the Night Kingdom. It was the only island Des didn't take me to—and for good reason. It was where the creatures of nightmares live.

"Deep in this forest, there's the Pit." Galleghar's gaze never wavers from mine. "Go to the Pit and travel as deep as you dare, and there you will find the Kingdom of Death and Deep Earth and the Thief himself."

I exhale.

There it is, my sought-after answer. My heart shudders to life. I want to laugh at all the hope I feel.

I will drag Des back up to the land of the living, and no one can stop me. Not even the Thief himself. For once, I will save the mate who's saved me so many times.

I glance over at Temper. Like the fairies in the room, she's caught by the coils of my glamour, her eyes bright. Still, she manages a predatory smile.

Turning back to Galleghar, I shutter the full force of my power.

It's the most natural thing in the world, strengthening and weakening my magic. And here I thought I had poor control over my siren. I never realized I kept such a tight leash on my power this entire time, even when I had used it. At least I hadn't realized that until now, when I no longer care about reining my alluring, destructive nature.

Galleghar's expression flickers, then shifts as my hold on him lessens. His features contort with his fury. I doubt anyone has treated him like this.

I study the former king, who's still on his knees. Despite being a prisoner, he's still dressed in fine linen, and he wears several rings.

"Let me see your hands."

He fights my glamour, his hands trembling, but eventually, he extends them to me. Galleghar wears three bronze rings, one masterfully crafted to depict a crescent moon and stars, another one inset with a black stone, and the last one a simple band with the crudely carved face of a wild-haired woman, her mouth open in a scream.

My fingers land on that ring.

Beneath my touch, Galleghar's skin shivers. Ignoring his reaction, I slip the ring off.

"What are you doing?" he demands.

"Isn't it obvious?" I say, my voice lilting. "I'm taking your jewelry." A memento to remember him by—the king I brought to his knees with a look alone. The man who abused his power in so many horrific ways is powerless now, perhaps for the first time in his unnaturally long life.

His mouth moves, probably to curse my name, but then I think he remembers my warning.

I will make you eat your tongue.

Whatever he was going to say stays firmly behind his teeth. He settles on glaring at me some more, the hate in his eyes mixing with a little pain. Being powerless is a terrible, humiliating feeling. Des and I would know. We were powerless before, victims of our fathers' cruelty. Eight years ago Des dealt with mine; now I'm returning the favor.

"Tell me, fallen king," I say conversationally, "how many of your own children have you killed?"

He growls at me, battling the words. I wait, a small smile tugging at my lips. He can't hold out forever.

"I…do not…know." The words are ripped from his throat.

I raise my eyebrows. "That many." It hurts, thinking about these long-dead heirs, some who must've been children and babies when their own father came after them. "And have you ever been brought to justice for these crimes?"

The room is rapt, watching this horror show unfold.

"*No*," he grinds out from between his teeth.

"Then it's time you faced punishment."

Galleghar scowls at me, furious.

"How does the Night Kingdom repay the man who forced countless women into his harem?" I ask. "Women he took advantage of, women whose children he slaughtered. How do we repay the man who allowed the Thief of Souls to kidnap thousands of soldiers and force unspeakable cruelties on them?

"How do you collect justice for something like that?" I ask him.

It's quiet for several seconds, the two of us staring each other down.

"You cannot," Galleghar finally spits out, answering my rhetorical question.

Now I smile, just a little.

"That," I say softly, "is where you're wrong." My eyes move to the soldiers standing by the doors. "Guards, find the bog and bring him here."

Galleghar's eyes widen, and now his anger is replaced by panic. The former Night King's face reddens as he squirms against my glamour, fighting to break free. Strong as he is, he cannot.

I feel Temper's eyes on me, sense her surprise, and feel the barest breath of her approval. She might not know what a bog is, but she knows I'm about to do something bad, and she's okay with that. We both harbor monsters within us; she understands.

The sentiment in the rest of the room is a mystery. There's magic in the air, and it tastes of fear and anticipation and wicked delight, but the fairies themselves give no indication of their true feelings.

It takes an eternity for the creature to join us. The entire time I stare Galleghar down. It's the ripple of voices through the room more than the monster itself that alerts me of the bog's arrival.

Eventually, I see it creeping up the aisle.

I don't know if I'm doing right by Desmond or anyone else or if my own wickedness is overtaking me, but I do know I feel no guilt.

None at all.

"I don't know what your fears are," I say to Galleghar, "but I hope the bog savors them as much as I will."

Ours to kill, the siren protests.

But I'm saving the killing for another creature.

Galleghar curls his upper lip, though he's still pinned to the ground by my orders. "I hope the Thief makes you suffer," he says as the bog's shadowy form slips up to him.

The former king's attention moves briefly from me to the monster closing in on him. His breath hitches.

Galleghar's gaze skirts back to me. He won't beg—even now he has too much misplaced pride for that—but his eyes are imploring me for mercy.

The time for mercy has long since passed.

"I want you to know," I say, "I'm doing this for every woman you wronged, every child you killed, every person you hurt. But more than that, I want you to know I'm doing this for Desmond and his mother—and I'm doing this for *me*."

I turn to the bog. "Devour him."

CHAPTER 40

I'm going to save you, Des.

That line repeats through my head as I stalk through the Night King's palace, the gauzy dress I wear dragging along behind me.

Need to change.

"Callie, that was *cold*," Temper says at my side as the two of us put distance between ourselves and the throne room.

"You would've done the same."

She snorts. "I would've done *worse*. We all know that of the two of us, you're the good cop."

I used to be. Now…

"Des's father can't be killed," I say.

At least Galleghar can't be killed so long as the Thief continues to prolong his unnatural life. That means the bog might scare the crap out of the fallen king, but he won't die from the experience.

Temper sucks in a breath. "So you're just going to let him rot away inside that creature?"

"No."

Unfortunately.

"I still need Galleghar."

Temper gives me a questioning look.

"He's going to guide me to the Pit."

She raises her eyebrows. "You're going to try to save Des."

"Not try. I *will* save him."

She cracks her neck. "I've never been to the Underworld before. This should be fun."

"You're not coming." I don't look at her when I say it.

For a beat, there's silence. Then—

She flashes me an astonished look. "Of course I'm coming. Don't be ridiculous."

I stop in the middle of the hallway and turn to her. "Temper, I'm probably going to die."

And I can't bear the thought of putting her life at risk in the process.

"One," Temper says, "you're not going to *die*. This is not a suicide mission—otherwise, I'd be chaining you to one of the stupid marble sculptures littering this place rather than getting ready to pack my bags.

"And two, yeah, this is dangerous. You want to rescue your soul mate and kill that asshole Thief while you're at it. I'm not even sure how you're supposed to do that. What I do know is that you need a sorceress to help you out. I like frightening scary creatures and messing shit up in general. I'm coming with you."

I hem and haw as the two of us stand there in the hallway. I mean, there is no one better to have at your side than an angry sorceress when facing down an enemy of epic proportions.

But the thing is, the Thief has seemingly boundless power and influence.

"Temper, I don't know how this is going to turn out, and I don't want—"

I don't want you to die.

She raises her eyebrows. "You actually think this freak could take me out? Now I'm offended." Her eyes briefly blaze with power.

Ugh, she's impossible.

"Fine, come with me then." Not going to fight with her over this.

She lets out a low laugh, her tongue running over her lower lip. I love this lady, but right now Temper looks *sinister*.

"Callie," she says, "let's make that bastard *pay*."

"I need weapons. Lots and lots of weapons," I order one of my guards as Temper and I head toward my rooms. "And battle leathers. Bring enough for the two of us."

The sorceress, for her part, is practically glowing with her excitement. She's got a healthy appetite for revenge, this one. I only hope she doesn't get overeager with it; the more potent her power is, the more unpredictable it gets.

Temper and I enter my chambers, and I try not to shudder at the sight of the rooms. I keep expecting Des to appear at any moment, his wry voice at my back.

But I'm not going to hear him or see him—not until I save him.

Several minutes later, a couple of Night soldiers come to my chambers, their arms full of a wide variety of weapons and armor. They deposit the goods on the bed and retreat.

Once the door closes behind them, Temper and I begin to change.

Since Des isn't here to magically help, suiting up takes a good ten minutes. As the two of us fasten and buckle on the battle leathers, we arm ourselves—a sword here, a dagger there.

I slide my trusted daggers into their sheaths on either side of my hips while Temper picks up a double-headed axe.

"Look," she says, "it's lady sized for my wee woman fingers."

I snicker. The weapon *is* small. Temper slides the axe into a holster at her back. Guess its wee size works.

I finish cinching up a thigh holster and straighten.

There's no more fear. I went from sorrow to desperation, to numbness, and now this. Cold, hard determination.

Essence to essence. Breath for breath. I've chipped away my weaknesses. This is what's beneath. Dead or not, I'm getting my mate back, and so help the gods, I will bring down the universe if I have to.

Till darkness dies, Des.

Two hours later, Temper and I stand in front of a moaning Galleghar, his body coated in a clear mucus-like substance, which I can only assume is the bog's stomach acid.

The bog, for its part, is safely tucked away in the same unassuming box Des once released it from.

I frown down at Galleghar, who's holding his head.

"Get up," I command, my skin glowing.

He pushes himself up on shaky feet. When he takes me and Temper in, he lets out a cry that's somewhere between feral anger and blinding fear.

The sorceress assesses him. "You never thought two humans would fuck up your life, did you?"

Not just two humans, two *women*, which for Galleghar is somehow worse.

"I will kill you," he says, staggering forward.

"No, you won't," I say calmly. "What you *will* do is receive a shower, get some new clothes, and help us."

"You bitch—"

"I *don't* need your tongue, so unless you want to lose it, you will continue to speak to me and my sorceress friend here in the most reverential of ways."

"I want him to call me *Great Goddess*. Can you make that happen?" Temper says to me.

Staring at Galleghar, I say, "You will refer to the sorceress from here on out as *My Great Goddess of Fuckery and Other Magical Things*. Understood?"

If Galleghar could spit fire right now, he would. Instead, he nods sharply, his nostrils flaring.

"Good," I say. I motion to the soldiers posted nearby. "Please get the traitor a bath and fresh clothing—and something to eat. He'll need his strength for what's to come."

"What's to come?" he echoes, a spark of fear lighting his eyes.

"Did I not tell you?" I say. "You're taking us to Memnos."

———

Memnos is supposed to be a frightening place, but when I catch sight of the dark island on the horizon, all I feel is a cold thrill.

Getting close now.

Des's aides and his soldiers were all reluctant to let me come here with nothing but a human and a traitor. They wanted to send in the last of their army, uncaring that the Thief of Souls could put them all to sleep in an instant if it pleased him.

So I ignored their advice. In the end, they couldn't do much about it—not when I had glamour working for me.

The three of us close in on the island, Temper cradled in Galleghar's arms. The once mighty king is now nothing more than our errand boy. He wears a venomous look, but he's magically bound to my orders. And so he obediently leads us forward to the floating island.

When we reach it, we pass over a small city. The lights below us are muted, and the smell of blood and corrupted magic tinges the air. I practically feel the danger radiating off the land.

The buildings give way to thick blighted forests with shadowy trees and strange light glittering from within their depths. The woods are only broken up by the odd fortress or cottage, the structures looking downright nefarious.

The trees thin out, and those that remain look weak and warped. It's among these trees that we land.

I drop to my feet, folding my wings up as Galleghar lands ahead of me.

His arms shake as he gently releases Temper. I can tell he badly wants to throw my friend to the ground, but my glamour forbids him from harming the sorceress.

"Where's the Pit?" Temper asks, looking around.

"Up ahead...My Great Goddess of Fuckery and Other Magical Things." He mumbles the last part.

"Speak up," I command.

His eyes shoot daggers at me. "I said, it's up ahead...Oh Dark Queen Who Thinks I'm a Douchebucket of the Most Epic Proportions."

373

Temper smirks. "What's your name again?" she asks him.

He curls his lip at her.

"Callie?" Temper says, calling for a little assistance.

"Answer her," I order.

He grinds his teeth. "Galleghar O'Malleghar, King of Asshats, Killer of Boners, Wannabe Emperor Who Needs to Eat a Bag of Dicks and Die."

The titles clearly got a little out of hand.

I mean, we might not be able to kill him or bring him to justice, but we can humiliate the shit out of him.

I gesture around us. "Lead us to the Pit."

The forest is preternaturally quiet...until it isn't.

First, it's an angry yowl of some lone creature. Then the caw of a crow joins it. Within minutes, the woods are full of hisses and howls, wails and half-mad cries.

"Fucking creepy," Temper whispers next to me.

The noises aren't the worst thing about this place. I feel a dozen different sets of eyes on me as we cut through the sparsely wooded forest. I'm still glowing like a beacon, my power drawing an increasing number of fae. More malevolent magic tinges the air, and it's only getting worse the farther we walk.

The last of the trees clear, and I see it—the Pit.

The thing is massive; it looks like a sinkhole, its depths cast into darkness. The longer I stare at it, the more I realize the darkness is *moving*, writhing either with living things or magic.

Don't want to go down there.

My very bones protest getting any closer.

Two shadowy creatures separate themselves from the

darkness. They're longer and spindlier than a regular fairy, but I smell their fae magic.

I stare at them as they approach. "What are they?"

"Reaves," says Galleghar with no little amount of distaste. "They're the overseers of the Pit, Oh Dark Queen Who Thinks I'm a Douchebucket of the Most Epic Proportions."

"You can stop with the titles," I say.

"He still better call me by mine," Temper says.

"You can stop with all the titles except hers," I amend, pointing to my friend.

Galleghar glowers.

The reaves approach us, the sight of them making my arm hairs stand on end.

I don't know how they feel about me using their precious Pit to get to the Kingdom of Death and Deep Earth, but I doubt they're going to be thrilled about it.

They stop when they get close to us, one of them scenting the air. God, they're a hideous pair—their limbs gangly, their eyes beady, and their lips tight and bloodless.

"Our old king, a human, and...something halfway interesting," one of them announces, its eyes landing on me. Around us, I feel that thick, cloying magic stir.

Des's father steps up from behind me. "As rightful heir—"

"Hold your breeches, buddy," I say. "You're not to talk to these two nice reaves."

The nice reaves who look like they wouldn't mind eating us all alive.

"The King of the Night is at the bottom of that pit," I say to them, nodding to the hole. Strange inhuman noises are coming from it.

Things *live* in that place, things that don't necessarily

belong to this world or the next. I'm going to have to face them.

"All the dead end up somewhere at the bottom of the Pit," one of the reaves says from his twisted mouth.

"You misunderstand me," I say slowly. "I'm telling you your king is down there not because he's dead but because I'm going into that hole and getting him *back*."

"You can't," one of the reaves says. "It's forbidden."

The other reave's nostrils flare; I get the impression he's scenting the air again.

"I *am*, and neither you, nor anyone else will stop me," I command, my voice harmonizing with itself, my glamour thick in the air.

"You can't possibly navigate your way down," the other reave says, even as he steps out of my way.

"You better hope I can," I reply, "or else I'm dragging you down there with me."

In the darkness, some creature hisses, and the noises from the Pit ratchet up with excitement.

"*Fresh blood*," one of the voices seems to say.

Yes, my siren purrs, *there's plenty of fresh blood for us to spill*.

"Is that a threat?" the reave asks.

We're wasting time squabbling. With every moment that passes, Des is slipping away from me.

I unleash the full force of my power, my flesh throbbing with the pulse of my magic. "I'm going into the Pit, and I'm coming out with your king. No one is to stop me, and no one is to do me or my human friend here any harm."

"The white-haired fairy, you can mess with," Temper adds darkly, earning her a glare from Galleghar.

In response to my commands, the reaves fall back, their eyes glittering with malice.

I glance at Temper. "This is where I leave you."

Her attention snaps to me fast. "What do you mean 'leave you'?" she asks accusingly.

"You will not follow me into the Pit," I command.

Did she really think I'd let her enter the land of the dead?

"Don't you *dare* leave me out here." Temper's magic sparks down her skin, a sure sign that she's getting pissed. "That is *not* how this works."

How this works is I'm not going to let my friend get killed.

"I love you, Temper, but this is my battle." She isn't dying today. "I need you here in case..." *In case things go south.* "If I'm not back in a day, then you can come looking for me."

God, please don't make me eat my words.

"I'm not waiting a *day*," she protests.

I grip her arms. "I have to do this, Temper." I'm practically begging her.

She stares at me for a beat, then pulls me into her arms and hugs me tight. "You keep yourself safe—the least you can do is promise me that."

I squeeze her, holding her close. "I promise." It's a lie, but one we both need to hear.

"You kill that asshole," she adds.

I nod into her shoulder. "I will." Or at least I'll try. Not sure yet how I'm going to kill an undead thing.

Releasing her, I back up. Temper doesn't try to stop me, though the broken expression on her face nearly makes me falter.

Beyond her, I catch sight of a retreating figure. Des's father, trying to get away, that snake.

"Galleghar, stop," I command.

He pauses midstride.

"Come back to me."

Robotically, he returns, his steps halting as he fights my glamour.

They never figure out it's useless.

I tilt my head when he stops in front of me. "Did you really think I'd let you leave?"

He snarls something incoherent.

"That's cute," I comment. My heart pangs when I realize it's something Des would've said. "When I told you you'd be my guide, I meant you were leading me *all* the way down."

He glares at me but obediently steps up to the edge of the Pit.

I follow him, aware of the curious gazes of dozens of different fae, all watching what we'll do next.

Des's father stares down into the inky blackness.

"Go ahead," I say. "Lead the way to the Thief's kingdom."

"You're going to die for this," he vows.

Before I can respond, Galleghar's wings manifest again. I feel something lodge in my throat at the sight of them. They're dark and talon-tipped.

So similar to Des's.

Galleghar steps off the ledge then, diving into the darkness.

I spare a final glance at Temper, whose skin is continuing to spark, her power barely under control. She looks devastated at being left behind.

I lift a hand to her, and then I step off the ledge.

My wings unfurl behind me, spreading out to control my fall as I spiral downward.

I made a mistake thinking Galleghar could lead the way. The darkness here seems to swallow *everything*, including him. I'm the only thing illuminating this trench in the earth,

378

and the glow from my skin is shedding light on the frightening fae that live here.

Hairless, naked creatures cling to the walls, their forms emaciated, the wings at their backs shriveled with disuse. One of them snarls at me as I pass, and another sniffs the air, its mouth gaping open.

Truly, these fae are the things of nightmares.

Winged, pixie-like creatures with snapping teeth zip through the air, battering into me like bugs against a windshield, their forms drawn in by my light and my glamour.

"You are to let me pass unharmed," I command. I have to repeat the order over and over again as I descend so fae who were once out of earshot can hear my words and obey.

Down and down I go, and there's seemingly no end in sight. By all logic, the bottom of this pit should either bring me to the heart of the floating island...or it should cut straight through the island and empty out into the night sky below. Instead, this trench is supposedly going to spit us out in the Thief's kingdom.

I'll believe it when I see it.

The temperature dips, getting increasingly cold. The fae living this far down are strange sightless things, their bodies pale and fleshy, their eyes clouded from disuse.

Eventually, the air grows still, and I stop seeing fae at all. Every now and then, I hear a yowl or a piercing cry, but those too die off.

This feels like death. Silent like the grave, the air stagnant. Even the dust motes caught in my light seem frozen in place, glittering in the air.

All at once, the ground rises from beneath me.

I land hard on a pile of bones, the brittle remains

crumbling beneath my weight. A plume of dust kicks up, unfurling slowly in the molasses-like air.

I dust myself off, taking in my surroundings. I can't see much besides bones and bones and bones. There are skulls and femurs and ribs and so many other bits of anatomy that I can't identify. The longer I look, the more I notice the tarnished armor among the bones. A crescent moon is stamped onto a metal shield. Another helmet bears the same mark.

Night soldiers.

Shit.

"There you are."

My head snaps up as Galleghar steps out from the darkness. He's bloody, and his clothes are in tatters. Across his skin are bite marks and, in some areas, missing flesh. They're healing over, but each wound is a grim reminder of what might've happened to me if I didn't have my glamour to fend off all the fae living in the Pit.

I glance back down at the bones.

"Why are there Night soldiers down here?" I ask.

Galleghar kicks a bone uselessly aside.

"Long ago, I invaded the Kingdom of Death and Deep Earth."

Horror dawns on me. All these bones, they belonged to fairies Galleghar brought down here—brought down here to die.

"Illuminate this place," I command him.

Galleghar stares at me for several seconds. Then, extending his hand, he forms a ball of light. As I watch, it grows bigger and brighter before lifting off the fallen king's palm and floating into the air above us.

Now I get a good look at our surroundings. As far as the

eye can see, the ground is an ocean of bones. There must be…*thousands* of bodies.

"Why?" I ask, my eyes searching the remains.

"The Thief needed a realm to rule."

I glance sharply at Galleghar. "What do you mean the Thief needed a realm to rule?"

Des's father gives me a cryptic smile. "He was an invader."

My eyes sweep over the graveyard. "And you helped him."

Galleghar brought an army here to take over a kingdom. He allowed these soldiers to die, all so he could insert the Thief on a stolen throne.

Jesus.

Someone else used to rule this place. Someone who presumably is now under the rule of the Thief. I shiver to think what the afterlife must be like for them.

"I did." Galleghar moves away from me, the bones of his former soldiers crunching under his feet. He pays them no attention. And why should he? In his mind, fairies are only as good as their use.

"This way," he says over his shoulder. "Unless you've changed your mind."

We stride on, wading through the frightening graveyard. Among the dead soldiers are skeletons of monsters who lived and died in this place. I'm not sure I've ever seen something like this—or that I ever will again.

Galleghar's earlier light bobs along above us, illuminating a massive stone archway ahead. On our side of it lay the bones of the dead; on the other side, thick curling smoke obscures our view.

The fallen king passes under that archway without a backward glance, the smoke stirring as it swallows him.

I hesitate.

I have no game plan, no grand knowledge that could be the Thief of Souls's undoing. All I have is determination and a few weapons.

I hope that's good enough.

Taking a deep breath, I pass under the archway and officially enter the Kingdom of Death and Deep Earth.

CHAPTER 41

I wasn't expecting gardens. Gardens filled with plants that probably have names like bloodthorn and devil's bane, but gardens nonetheless. They extend to either side of me, bordering the stone pathway I stand on.

Galleghar is twenty feet ahead of me, walking up the pathway, and he doesn't even bother looking back. Far ahead of us, a palace made from pale stone reaches up toward the night sky, its towers and spires looking like the bones of a monster. The castle sits perched at the edge of an ocean.

The afterlife has an *ocean*. My siren stirs at that.

The air is still icy and motionless, but this place looks like any other in the Otherworld, with its manicured gardens and the night sky overhead. This is not at all how I'd imagine the afterlife.

I follow Galleghar up the stone path to the palace. The entire time we don't see another soul.

The Thief is somewhere in this place. I feel his dark

magic pressing in on all sides, and I sense unseen eyes on me. But if he's near, he's not making himself known.

Galleghar steps up to two enormous doors. I stop alongside him.

"What now?" I ask.

In response, the massive double doors groan open.

Galleghar gives me a chilling smile.

"After you," he says, gesturing forward.

And have him at my back? I don't think so. "You lead the way," I command.

The fallen king gives me a long look, then steps into the castle with me at his back.

Inside, our footsteps echo. There's an entryway, and side tables, and tapestries, and strange plants growing up the castle's walls. Basically, the Kingdom of Death's castle looks like every other fae palace I've been to, which makes the whole experience frighteningly real.

I've never been more certain of my own mortality than this moment, stepping inside the palace of the King of Death and Deep Earth. It feels like I've moved too far from the land of the living.

But then, my heart throbs, my bond with Des giving a soft tug, and I nearly fall to my knees. Letting out a soft gasp, I press my hand to my chest.

I feel him. It's weak, but I *feel* him.

My Bargainer. The world stopped turning the moment he disappeared. Now I can imagine it moving once more.

Desperation like I've never known takes over. Turning inward, I try to use the pull of our bond to track my mate.

I've done this once before, and it didn't work, but now I move with my instincts, leaving Galleghar's side and wandering through the castle, unaware of the rooms I'm moving through, focusing on the magical tether that's reawakened now that I'm in the Kingdom of Death and Deep Earth.

Wonder of wonders, I can *feel* my connection to Des subtly strengthening.

I'm doing it. I'm actually tracking my mate through our bond. The thought nearly takes my breath away.

My footsteps echo around me. Getting closer. I can feel it.

The next room I enter is covered from floor to ceiling with shelves upon shelves, each one crammed with jars, potions, books with gilded titles, and instruments whose use I couldn't possibly guess. Right in the middle of the room is an intricately carved marble slab, and lying on the slab is—

"*Des.*" His name, unbidden, spills from my lips.

Now I run.

He's so still. Too still.

He *can't* be dead. Not here, in the land *of* the dead. This is where fae get to spend their afterlife.

I stop when I get to that stone slab. My connection pulses once, as if to confirm this isn't some illusion. I reach out, my hand trembling. I'm almost afraid to touch him. Something thick lodges in my throat.

I thought I'd be elated, finding Des. Instead, I feel like I'm losing him all over again.

His long eyelashes kiss the top of his cheeks, and his white hair fans around him. He looks like all those bespelled people in the fairy tales, trapped in eternal sleep. He's beautiful and heartbreaking to look at.

"Des," I repeat, my voice pleading. With a shaky hand, I touch his cheek; his skin is clammy and cold. "Wake up."

He doesn't move.

My fingers trail down his face, over his chin, and past his neck before stopping at his heart. I press my palm to it. Beneath my touch, his heart beats sluggishly.

He's *alive*—whatever that means at this point.

I feel weak with relief for several seconds until I remember that the sleeping soldiers were technically alive too, suspended in a state much like this.

A bit of me dies at the thought. My Night King reduced to this.

Behind me, someone clucks their tongue. "*You* don't belong here."

My skin prickles at the familiar voice.

I turn, and it's only now that I notice the flickering torches and candelabras beating back an unnatural darkness.

The Thief of Souls stands among it all, and he's exactly as he appeared in my dreams. Inky hair and empty upturned eyes. Pale skin and a mouth that's far too soft for the rest of his face.

Finally, the two of us meet in the flesh.

He claps. "Well done, well done, enchantress. You figured out how to find me. And here I thought you were utterly useless at solving problems. I should've known you'd simply need the right"—his eyes slide to Des—"*incentive.*"

My skin is still glowing, but now I unleash the full force of my glamour.

"Wake my mate up," I demand.

The Thief's eyes shine with interest. He walks over to Des, staring down at the Night King for a moment. Lifting a hand, the Thief holds it over the Bargainer's face. I sense dark magic gathering in his palm, but then he closes his hand and withdraws it.

"I don't think I want to do that," the Thief says.

How could he defy us?

"Don't look so surprised," he says. "You didn't really think that was going to work on me, did you?" The Thief's eyes still spark, but he doesn't have the look of a glamoured fairy.

He saunters over, and I watch him with angry eyes.

The Thief stops right in front of me. "Tell me, how *do* you plan on slaying me and reclaiming your mate?" With a finger, he lifts one of my holsters. "Surely not with *these* weapons? Were you hoping to use them against me?" The Thief's mouth curves up. He pulls the blade out and tosses it aside. "I'm sorry to tell you that you can't kill me with any of the little toys you brought."

And...there go what plans I did have.

Slowly, the Thief circles me, reaching out to remove various weapons. All the while he looks bored and unimpressed.

This situation is unraveling. I came here to save my mate, and instead, the Thief has proven nothing at my disposal can harm him.

I back away from him, and he lets me, even though he hasn't finished disarming me. I still have a dagger strapped to my thigh and another holstered around my calf. For him to leave me with some weapons...they must truly be useless against him.

My attention returns to Des. The Night King is still as death itself. I could pretend like my heart isn't lying right here on this slab, but the Thief already knows what he has.

I rest my hands on my soul mate's arm; there's a frightening chill to his skin. "Why did you do this to him?"

The Thief steps up to my side. "If you knew anything about leverage, you'd know the answer to that."

I turn to the Thief, a retort on my lips. But in an instant, he disappears, vanishing just as Des and Galleghar have.

I feel his dark, cruel magic all around me. It's wild in a way not even fae magic is. It swarms in the air then slips down, toward the Night King, until it's no longer in the air but in *my mate*.

Beneath my fingers, Des's arm twitches. I start at the sensation. Then my grip tightens.

"Des?"

His eyes flutter, and his lips move, like he's murmuring something. But if anything, our connection seems to grow fainter.

Dear God, what's happening?

The wild, malevolent magic lifts from Des, and he's still once more.

I rub my chest as our bond restrengthens.

"Ah, well, it was worth a try."

I jolt as the Thief crowds in behind me.

"And here I'd hoped I'd have a few more days," he says. "Then perhaps my form"—he smooths his shirt down—"would be a bit more...to your liking."

I rotate to face him. "What are you talking about?" Even as I ask, realization dawns.

The Thief was trying to invade my mate's body.

A bolt of sheer terror courses through me.

Is that what he intends to do? To wear Des's form just like he did the Green Man's? To terrorize me with the face of my mate while he inhabits the Night King's body?

Bile rises in my throat as I stare at his dark features.

Don't, I want to warn him. There are lines that are crossed, and then there are *lines that are crossed*. Parading around as my soul mate falls into the second category.

388

But, of course, I don't say that because I have a deep-seated belief that the more I give away my fears, the likelier the Thief is to exploit them.

"Is that your real face?" I say instead.

"Who says I truly have a face?" he retorts.

A chill runs down my spine.

"This, enchantress, is the form I choose to take—for now," the Thief says.

The sound of footsteps interrupts our conversation. Then Galleghar enters the room, looking vaguely peeved. Or maybe that's his normal expression.

It's probably his normal expression.

First, Galleghar sees his son lying on the stone altar. Then he notices the Thief standing too close to me.

His eyes narrow on his partner. "How could you have left me to this human?" he accuses the fairy at my side.

The Thief of Souls steps away from me, appraising Galleghar. There's nothing behind the Thief's eyes, no camaraderie, no softness—nothing at all to indicate these two have any sort of closeness.

"What, precisely, was I supposed to do?" the Thief asks. "The Night Queen has tamed my soldiers."

"She is *not* a queen," Galleghar says vehemently.

"She is," the Thief insists.

Galleghar gives me a look that plainly says he still disagrees.

"You were supposed to *kill* her," Des's father says. "What the fuck happened to that plan?"

I still remember the attack in Barbos; the Thief wouldn't let me die there. Apparently, I'm not the only one surprised by that.

Something in the air shifts, and the Thief's magic churns. It feels violent.

"I did kill her. Back in Mara's forest," the Thief responds smoothly.

"And yet here she stands," Galleghar says. "You had a perfectly good opportunity on Barbos, but you wouldn't commit. Worse, you wouldn't let me finish what you *couldn't*."

The two stare at each other for several seconds, and I'm oddly calm about the whole thing, considering they're discussing killing me.

"You made a mistake coming here," the Thief says.

"No"—Galleghar's voice rises—"*you* made a godsdamn mistake mooning over this mortal. You let your dick make decisions when we had a plan."

The room practically crackles with power. I swear something is poised to happen.

"Kill her," Galleghar says, striding toward us. "Or let me do it."

The Thief gives him an indolent look.

"*Kill her*," Des's father repeats, insistent.

Magic floods the air. And still, the Thief makes no move. It's answer enough.

Galleghar's upper lip curls. "You swore an *oath*. Uphold your end and kill—"

"*No.*"

CRACK!

Magic splits the air, and Galleghar is blown back. His body slams into a wall of shelves, books and bones and jars all raining down from behind him. He crumples to the ground, moaning.

The Thief's form ripples like it's a mirage, the magic so intense, it bends the light. A darkness is gathering around the Thief, dimming the room.

I don't know if this is the Thief's own power or what he borrowed from Galleghar, but it's uncannily like Des's.

Des's father looks shocked as he lies there. "Oathbreaker," he whispers.

"I don't know why you're so surprised," the Thief says. "I mean, you said it yourself—I didn't kill her on Barbos when I could've."

Galleghar's voice rises. "We had a deal!"

"You thought an *oath* would bind me?" The Thief walks forward, casually surveying Galleghar. "After all you learned of my nature, you thought that would be sufficient?"

"I *freed* you," Des's father says.

The Thief flicks his wrist, and a bolt of magic slices open Galleghar's chest, cutting him to the bone.

I jerk at the sudden violence, even as Des's father lets out a shocked cry.

He turns to me. "Release me!" Galleghar begs.

"Release you?" I echo. *From what?*

"Your glamour still binds me," he explains. "Release me from it."

The Thief laughs. "You think being able to disappear will save you? I could follow you to the darkest corners of the universe. No place is safe from me."

He punctuates his words with blow after magical blow. Galleghar's body jolts at each one, the hits ripping open his flesh. The former king cries out, either in pain or anger.

He tries to get up. "Please," he implores me again.

The Thief laughs. "You're begging the slave now? How the tides have turned, my friend. And here I thought you wanted her dead."

The Thief of Souls flicks his wrist back and forth, back

and forth, cutting Galleghar apart inch by inch, a small smile on the Thief's face.

"Do you regret the price you've paid for power?" he asks.

But Galleghar is beyond words, his face a mass of wounds. Whatever regenerative powers he has, he either can't or won't use them.

At some point, I turn away. I'm as bloodthirsty as the next creature, but there's vengeance and then there's sadism. This is the latter.

I return to the stone slab, to Des, ignoring the choked sounds behind me.

Softly, I stroke his cheek. *How am I going to get us out of here?*

"Bargainer," I whisper, "I'd like to make a deal."

Nothing happens. I hadn't expected that anything would, but it's a letdown all the same.

My other hand drifts to Des's upper arm, his three bronze war bands cool against my skin. His matching circlet sits perched on his brow. He's never looked more like a king than now, lying here like the solemn dead.

Galleghar has stopped making noise, and the wet sound of skin ripping is gone. In the silence, the Thief's footfalls echo like tolling bells.

He comes to my side and unceremoniously takes my hand, pulling me away from Des.

"Come," the Thief says, "I have much to show you."

I resist. "Wake him up."

"Okay."

I spin around to face him, shocked by his response.

The Thief steps in way too close, forcing me to lean back against the altar. His arms move to either side of the slab and cage me in.

"Tell me," he says, "what would you do to wake your mate?"

392

I don't respond. I don't need to. The Thief knows.

He leans in close. "Now, enchantress, you and your mate had a little game you used to play—truth or dare. Why don't we have a go at it?"

I curl my upper lip.

This is our little game—and trust me, enchantress, it's far from over.

"So, truth...or dare?" he asks, his strange empty eyes glittering.

"Neither."

"I'm afraid that's not an option," he says. "Why don't we start with a simple dare? Touch me."

"No."

The Thief pauses, and then he smiles. It's only then that I realize he wants my disobedience more than anything else.

He glances at Des. I follow his gaze, unease coiling low in my stomach.

Suddenly, the Night King's back arches, and he begins to shout.

My knees nearly buckle at the sound. *So much pain.* I feel echoes of it through our bond.

"Stop," I whisper.

The Thief ignores me, and Des continues to shout, his eyes sightless. The sound closes my throat.

"Stop!"

No reaction.

I swallow my disgust and my anger. I imagine for a moment that I am Des, that I am dark and untouchable and nothing can ever hurt me.

I gaze up at the Thief. In all my life, I've never hungered for someone's death so badly. But instead of delivering death, I lift a hand and cradle the side of the Thief's face.

And still Des's cries carry on.

The Thief's eyes slide to mine. "More," he commands. I see the thrill in his eyes.

There are so many ways to control a person, but blackmail is, perhaps, the worst of them all.

Taking a deep breath, I close my eyes and force myself to drown out my mate's horrifying shouts. I guide the Thief's face to mine. Very softly, I brush my lips against his.

I taste the barest hint of the Thief's dark magic. It reminds me of all those other kisses he forced on me.

We're simply picking up where we left off.

When Des's shouts finally quiet, I drop my hand and end the kiss.

The Thief smiles at me. "I think I'm going to like this game very, very much."

Going to gut him for this.

"Oh, don't look at me like that, Callie. You'll learn to love it—or live with it. Because you *will* live. After all, that was part of your mate's bargain."

What?

"Des made a bargain with you?" My heart stutters. I glance over at my mate, his face placid.

You and I had an understanding, he'd said to the Thief.

"Desmond, Desmond, Desmond, *ever* the secret keeper," the Thief says. "Did he not tell you just what lengths he went to, trying to save you?"

I continue gazing at my mate's sleeping form. The flickering light makes shadows dance along his skin. Perhaps it's just my imagination, but it looks as though the darkness is grieving for him.

Des, what did you do?

It shakes me to the core to think that whatever Des

plotted and planned, it landed him here in this state. I've never known someone to get the upper hand on the Bargainer.

Not like this.

The Thief steps away from me, circling the altar. It makes me jumpy, seeing him focus on Des when my soul mate is so exposed.

"I had heard so many things about the King of the Night's infamous bargains. How shrewd he was, how calculating and unforgiving. Love seems to be his downfall.

"See, he came to me not too long ago. Did he tell you this? He came to me, and he made a deal: so long as I never killed him or his precious mate, he'd willingly become my prisoner."

The room seems to tilt a little, and I have to place a bracing hand on the altar. My eyes move back to Des.

This is not life. This is a mockery of it.

But Des must've been aware of this going in. He saw the sleeping soldiers, so he knew the Thief could keep a man alive without them ever truly living.

So why would he make such a deal?

The Thief stares down at the Night King. "What your mate missed is this: the truest pain comes with life, not death."

Des would *never* miss something like that. The question is: What am *I* missing?

"You know," the Thief continues, "he's still in there. His mind, everything. Perhaps I will wake him up…" I see the gears in the Thief's head turning.

I manage a delicate swallow. I want to see Des's eyes open—more than anything in the world, I do—but I don't want the Thief to compel them open. And I don't want Des seeing whatever it is the Thief intends.

The Thief breaks his stare. "Perhaps we'll revisit that exciting thought later."

He takes my hand again.

"I'm not leaving him," I insist. I can't. The thought of walking away from Des now that I've finally found him is unbearable.

"You are," the Thief insists, a bit of his good humor seeping away.

I bare my teeth at him. "Make me." I'm still glowing, still feral with my power.

He laughs, the sound skittering up my arms. The Thief's grip tightens on mine, chaining me to him. "Do you realize I could immobilize you just as I have your mate? I have done it to a thousand different fairies. Now that you've tasted lilac wine, you are no different from any of them."

He's right. He could incapacitate me so easily. His threat hangs over my head like a blade.

I search his face. "Is that what you're going to do? Are you going to force dark magic on me as you have every other fairy?"

He doesn't need to speak for me to pull the answer from him.

"You're *not*." Oh God, he's going to do everything *but* that. For some perverse reason, the Thief wants to watch me in a tailspin.

His hand slides to my wrist, where golden scales dust my skin. He squeezes my flesh to the point of pain.

"Do you feel that?" he asks.

For a moment, I assume he's talking about the pressure on my wrist. But then there's a stirring in my chest. What is happening? My hand moves over my heart, and then my back bows as a rush of magic floods my connection to Des.

For an instant, it feels like the bond we share is coming back to life. On the slab, Des stirs.

As quickly as the sensation comes, it passes, settling back to dying embers. My soul mate goes still again.

"That's what's at stake for you," the Thief says.

I hate him. Christ, do I hate him.

He holds Des's life in the palm of his hand, and while he may not outright kill my mate, he'll dangle our bond in front of me. That's all he needs to get my compliance.

"This is what's going to happen," the Thief says, "you're going to do everything I tell you. Otherwise, you lose Des, piece by piece." To emphasize his point, dark magic thickens the air, and Des's back arches again. Like he's stuck in some sick dream, my mate begins to cry out again.

"Stop—stop!" I'm shouting, and my glamour is everywhere and in everything, burning so brightly. It doesn't make any sort of difference.

"Understood?" the Thief says calmly, Des bellowing between us as pain continues to rack his body.

My wrath gathers in my veins, but those shouts—it's as though a part of me is dying.

"Understood," I say, my voice raw.

Des shudders, his body falling limp on the stone slab.

"You're going to regret doing that," I say, blazing with barely contained rage.

"No, enchantress, it's you who will be regretful, should you defy me again."

CHAPTER 42

The Thief leads me out of the room and through his castle, showing me this or that, all while wearing a triumphant smile on his lips. We both know he doesn't give a shit about anything in this stolen castle of his, save for the wretched souls he gets to torment. He's just savoring my pain.

We'll stab out his eyes and cut out his tongue—

Ever since the Thief started leading us through the palace, my siren has been whispering all the ways he will pay for his crimes.

We'll bring him to the point of pleasure, and then we'll destroy him as we have always *destroyed our enemies.*

Eventually, the Thief leads me out onto a balcony. From where we stand, I see the vast ocean. Under the cover of night, it looks like spilled ink, stretching out as far as the eye can see.

Next to me, I sense the Thief about to speak.

"Why am I here?" I ask, swiveling to him. "Why not just kill me or incapacitate me like all the other fairies you've come across?" That would've been easier.

The Thief pauses, assessing me.

"Why?" he finally says. "Why, why, *why*? You creatures and your need to have orderly logical answers. When someone falls in love, is it logical? And when they blindly hate, is that logical either? Your deepest drives are based on *nothing*. What you're asking for is an explanation for the unexplainable."

I didn't expect that answer. The Thief of Souls went and got philosophical on me.

He steps in close. "Stop trying to understand me. You will *never* fathom my motives. I am not like you or anyone else."

I study him. "What do you intend to do with me?"

Now that sinister smile is back. A minute ago, I could almost pretend he was civilized. I can't now.

"Whatever I please," the Thief says.

We'd like to see him try.

"Yeah, I fucking get that, but what does that actually mean?"

"Is the anticipation killing you, enchantress?" He touches a lock of my hair, his hand sliding down it. "It means I'll have you in all the most obvious ways you fear—I'll fuck you, I'll eat out that enchanting little pussy, I'll make you go down on me. But that won't be the end of it. There are many things you will do to please me, and there are many things I will do to you to please myself. It will go on and on like this until you can no longer do them."

Until my spirit is utterly broken, he means.

"The true question will be how long you survive my… attentions. Your life is now measured in centuries, not decades. That mind of yours is more resilient than it was when you were human—and of course, your bond will keep you sane and keep your priorities right where I need them to be. I have a feeling you will last a long while."

The horrible truth is that even though I'm aware the Thief's using my bond against me, I'm still going to play right into his hand. Because seeing Des in pain and feeling him slip away from me, it makes me panicked.

"You're going to find I'm not that fun of a captive." I wasn't when I was his prisoner before. I won't be this time around either.

"On the contrary, I think you'll be exceedingly pleasing."

I can't even fathom the future he intends for me. All those minutes, hours, days, years—*centuries*. All a sick, twisted horror show.

Maybe this is hell. Maybe this is hell and I'm getting my first taste of it.

I glance out at the sea, frowning. It stretches into the night, and it's not clear what—if anything—lies beyond it.

A pier juts out from the castle grounds. Tethered to it is a lone ship, its sails in tatters and its hull deep in the water. It leans severely to one side, and the ship's rigging dangles limply, and there isn't a breeze to stir any of it.

At once, I'm struck by the true oddness of this place.

Why would the Kingdom of Death and Deep Earth have a palace right next to a strange ocean? Why would there be a ship? And why would that ship fall into disrepair?

And speaking of hell and the afterlife—

I glance around. "Where are all of the dead?"

You'd think they'd be roaming these halls, either as specters or as full-blooded people, yet I haven't seen a soul other than Des and Galleghar—and the Thief, of course.

The Thief stares at me, his mind a mystery. "I'll show them to you shortly."

With that cryptic response, he takes my hand and placidly leads me back inside his palace, with its pale walls and the bloodred vines that look like gashes.

We pass through several rooms, each one looking a bit like the last. The one he takes me to should be no different, except it is. When we enter, I see someone I don't recognize.

The fairy is covered in iron shackles—his neck, his wrists, his ankles. Thick iron chains link the manacles together. I suck in a breath at the sight of his blistering skin.

The fairy is not alone either. The woman at his side has an ethereal glow to her.

She's dead, I realize with shock.

I hadn't thought the Thief was going to show me the dead so soon after his cryptic response.

If the dead look like that...

Des isn't dead. I hadn't thought he was, but I hadn't been sure. This place bends reality.

The shackled man ignores us entirely, leading the dead woman on.

"Who is he?" I ask as we pass the two by.

"Kharion, the ferryman."

The ferryman? "You mean the guy who transports the dead?" Back on earth, we had human myths about that. I hadn't realized that at least in the Otherworld, the afterlife really works this way.

"Just when I think your only redeeming quality is your face, you surprise me with your infinitesimal intellect," the Thief says.

I thin my gaze. "Why is he shackled?" I ask.

"We don't see eye to eye."

Before I can ask any further questions, the Thief drags me out of the room, and onward we go.

401

"Where are we going?" I ask.

I'm getting impatient. My siren is still whispering her dark deeds, and I'm not acting on any of them because I'm afraid nothing will stop the Thief—nothing but patience and surprise.

"I assumed you'd want to see where you will be staying."

I'm not staying. I'm leaving here with Des as soon as I see a good opportunity to do so—or else Temper is coming down here for all our asses.

The two of us arrive at a Gothic door, and I glance at the Thief, my eyebrow raised. In response, he flashes me a sly smile.

With an ominous creak, the door opens.

"Welcome to our rooms."

Our.

My blood chills as I sweep my eyes over the space. Even though I'm brave and angry, I still quake at the sight in front of me. The bed, with its crimson sheets, has iron cuffs and chains affixed to the four posts. It's obvious they're meant for me.

There's an iron maiden, a human-sized cage hanging from the ceiling, and a breaking wheel. Chains dangle from the walls and ceilings, and just about every surface has iron or leather braces affixed to it.

It looks like a BDSM dungeon met the Inquisition and they had some fucked-up kids together.

My hand edges for my thigh holster.

Kill him! Kill him now before he can chain us.

The Thief leaves my side and wanders to the wheel. "Care to test this one out?"

"That's not my kink," I say. *Watching you die is.*

"Have you ever tried it?"

Obviously not. I don't dabble in light torture on the weekends. "What do you think?" I say tartly.

"I think you won't know what you enjoy until you've tried it."

"I didn't realize my enjoyment mattered to you."

His hand leaves the wheel, and he walks over to me, stepping in close. "You better hope it matters to me, enchantress. Otherwise, the next two hundred years of your life could be very, very bleak."

I'm tense, waiting for the Thief to break this brief stretch of civility. It won't last with him—it never does. And where better to begin than in this fucked-up room?

But it never comes. His hand grabs mine, and he leads me out of the room and down the hallway.

If I thought this was the end of the palace tour, I thought wrong.

"Do you know how the Kings of the Dead have made their way?" he asks casually as we walk.

I have no idea what else he hopes to show me in this castle. The dungeons maybe? Even an asshole like him only has so many terrible surprises to share.

"They—*we*—have to kidnap our brides," he says. "This is nothing unusual for a fairy. In case you hadn't noticed, we rather enjoy snatching away beautiful youths. It's all part of the thrill.

"But Death Kings—well, they've always done things a little differently. When choosing spouses, they would wear the skin of the dead and go topside. Invariably, there's always one fae festival or another moving through the Otherworld. Those have always been a favorite hunting ground for the rulers of the dead."

My skin prickles as I think of Solstice. How the Green Man sought me out again and again.

"Surprising, really, how many fairies love the mysterious stranger. Give them enough spirits and let them dance until they are drunk on magic and wine… It is *so* easy to whisper a few promises and lure a fairy away."

Understanding is dawning on me.

"So the Death Kings would draw their unwilling spouses to the Kingdom of Death and Deep Earth. They would then baptize them in the Well of Resurrection and bind their spouses to their side—forever."

The Thief's hand drifts to my shoulder, his fingers digging in. "And then those chosen consorts lived here, just as you will."

Yeah, that's not fucking happening.

"Of course, switching skins is useful for more than just snatching spouses. One can lure just about any fairy away by wearing the face of the beloved dead."

Stealing the sleeping soldiers, that's what he's referring to.

"So I took fairy after fairy, and I fucked them and breathed my magic into their bodies until, one by one, they fell prey to it."

I already knew the lurid truth about the sleeping soldiers, but hearing the Thief of Souls recount it all makes my stomach roil.

"The men, I hid away. But the women… I took their babies and their bodies and had them delivered back to where they came from.

"They were my army, and I brought my darkness into the world above and watched it grow." He rubs his lower lip with his thumb then barks out a laugh. "To tell you the truth, it all became quite boring…until, of course, it was time to handle the Night King. That is how I discovered his oh-so-charming mate.

"The shadows couldn't stop talking about you. The prettiest human they'd ever seen. The cherished soul mate of the Night King. They're real conversationalists *if* you can get them to sing."

I stumble to a stop, the Thief's hand slipping from my shoulder. "You can talk to the shadows?"

Dear God.

The Thief smiles slyly. "You thought your mate was the only one? He isn't. The shadows whisper to me too."

That's...not good. It also happens to explain how the Thief knows so much. The shadows spy for him.

He grips my shoulder once more and forces me to walk again.

Suits of armor, displayed swords, soaring architecture—all of it barely registers as I pass it by.

"They told me everything I need to know about you," the Thief says. "I've heard all about your fucked-up life, my pretty bird. I know your stepfather raped you, over and over. I know you killed him and that our gallant Desmond Flynn swooped in and saved you. Did you know he had Daddy Dearest resurrected?"

He did?

Immediately, I doubt the Thief's words. Des would've told me something like that.

"Of course," the Thief continues, "that was only so he could torture and kill the man all over again. I do appreciate a good killing. Too bad Desmond had to then go and try his hand at honor, all so he'd keep himself from fucking you prematurely."

I distractedly notice we've entered another room, our footsteps echoing against the stone walls.

"I know the Night King's magic kept you two apart for

seven years," the Thief continues. "I know you made each other *such* ardent promises—the Night Kingdom really does know its way around romance. 'Until darkness dies'… Truly, that's a sweet sentiment.

"You know, there's only one problem with that phrase—"
He stops and turns my way.
"Me."

CHAPTER 43

I furrow my brows. "What are you talking about?" I glance around us as I ask.

I've been here before, I realize.

There are those bone-like columns, the ceiling that gives way to the dark night beyond. There's that unsettling pool, which hums with magic, and then there's the Thief's throne. This last one glints and flickers in the candlelight, its peaked spires looking especially sharp and deadly.

The Death King's throne room.

Nothing good ever happens in these throne rooms.

"I'm talking about who I am," the Thief responds.

He circles me, and my skin burns brighter than ever.

"You saw all those fallen soldiers at my doorway. We both know I was not born in this kingdom, that I invaded this place. That I have lived for centuries—that Galleghar used me to save his own life."

He finishes circling me, coming back to my front.

"So who am I?" he says. "The question everyone wants to know."

The place is ominously still, and the only sound comes from the pool on the other side of the room.

"Not a conqueror." He shakes his head. "Not a king. I come from a time before such things.

"You see, I am not a man. I'm a *god*."

A...god?

"Don't look so shocked, enchantress," the Thief says. "A woman talks to the darkness—is she really so surprised when the darkness talks back?"

I don't have time to feel disbelief or to question the Thief's claim. His body expands before my eyes, his form darkening until he's nothing more than the shape of a man. Pinpricks of light—stars, they seem to me—glitter from deep within that darkness. I can barely make out his features among it all.

I take a step back as that still air moves and churns.

Around us, candles flicker, and the hum from the pool seems to grow louder.

"All this time, you've wanted to know who I am. Enchantress, I'm *Euribios*." He breathes the name with a shiver of magic. It skitters across my skin. "I am what came *before*."

I feel that part of his magic then—not the wickedness of it, but the *wildness*. I stare up at him as he gets larger and larger. The room darkens, his form sucking away the light.

Among all that darkness, I sense his smile, and it chills me to the core.

"Once, Death and Night were the very same thing. Once, there was nothing else." The room is giving way to shadow, and the Thief is losing his form. "Back then, when the world was young, before everything came into existence, I reigned supreme."

It comes to me then, where I heard the name *Euribios*. Janus mentioned it in reference to some artwork.

He's the primordial god of darkness.

Fucking Methuselah. The Thief isn't *just* a god; he's one of the big ones.

"I will reign again," he continues. "Kingdom by kingdom, I will vanquish this world until nothing is left—no life, no afterlife. I will tear down the sun and consume the land."

My very bones quake at the thought.

What he's speaking of is annihilation.

"But don't fear, mortal, I *will* stretch the end out, for once this world is gone, there will be nothing to entertain me again."

We must end him. This is no longer about revenge. It's about preservation.

"That first evening of Solstice," Euribios says, "do you remember what Mara said?"

As he speaks, he continues to grow, his form expanding until his head touches the ceiling, his body becoming one with the darkness.

He quotes, "Deep from the womb of the night, we were born, and deep into the night do our spirits return when the body has died and the flesh has cooled."

With those words, the room goes dark.

Euribios and I and everything else in this underworld are swallowed up by the void he's created.

"I am the beginning and the end," he continues. "I am death and darkness, but I am infinitely more. I am what came before, and I am unending."

I feel...I feel as though I'm losing myself. The shadows are swallowing everything. My body, my mind, my *bond*.

409

Not losing that.

The impasse is over. My patience is spent.

I reach for the blade stashed in my thigh holster and the other strapped to my calf, the ones the Thief was too cocky to remove.

I stride toward that terrible darkness, weapons raised, my wings unfurling behind me. I can't see Euribios, but I sense him, his body the epicenter of his magic.

My wings beat, and with a leap, I rise into the air.

Blinded by the darkness, I use my other senses to close in on Euribios. Smell, sound, and my ability to sense magic.

I draw close to him, my blades poised.

In the instant before I strike, I feel my connection to Des stir, then...*awaken.*

Des.

It almost makes me pause. I want to believe Des is responsible for the sensation, but it's Euribios who's the puppet master, Euribios who holds our bond hostage, Euribios who's now taunting me with everything I have to lose.

And with this one act, I might lose it all.

Don't be frightened of yourself, cherub. You are exactly as you should be.

With a single powerful stroke, I sink the blades into that terrible darkness. They hit *something*; I feel the resistance. It's not flesh, but it's not just air either.

I withdraw my weapons. Sink them into that strange somethingness again. My body glows the entire time, and I smile viciously, my siren filling me up.

My connection to Des still burns brightly, and I should be frightened by that. This is exactly what the Thief wants—to make me understand what I have so that later I feel the ache of its loss. But the sensation gives me perverse strength.

We will defeat him.

Among the darkness, Euribios laughs. A moment later, he grabs my daggers by their blades.

"You still think you can kill me?" he asks. "I am a deity." He jerks the weapons from my grip and tosses them aside.

Heedless, I slash at him with my claws, my siren consuming me.

Euribios doesn't have flesh like I do. I'm not even sure what I'm tearing into, only that even in that darkness, he still has substance.

The entire time, my bond pulses. I feel Des on the other end of my bond.

"Enough," Euribios says.

The magic around me shifts, and I shift with it, fluidly evading the dark power.

I swoop in again and collide with magic and flesh. Immediately, I sink my claws into the substance—whatever it is. I can't see anything, except for the galaxies twinkling deep within his form, but it's enough.

Something like blood slips between my fingers as I tear into the Thief's odd form.

Behind me, I sense his magic closing in again. At once I release my hold, dropping to the ground just as his power moves overhead, stirring my hair. I hear a crack as the Thief's magic strikes my own.

"Gods could not destroy me." His voice thunders in the darkness. "It's foolish to think *you* can."

I leap back into the air, claws bared. I attack darkness once more.

Let's see if this thing has a heart.

I can't see his body, but there's something left of him in

411

the darkness. My fingers tear into his strange flesh, digging for that organ of his.

He hisses at the sensation.

We will find his heart—we will find it and rip it out.

I feel bone and blood—

Euribios's magic slams into me—or maybe it's his hand; impossible to tell when the world is so dark and he's morphed into something that's half human, half shadow.

"Enough!"

He throws me onto the ground, my bones cracking at the impact.

I moan. Things are…broken. Wing bones, ribs.

Didn't kill him. Didn't even come close.

I feel Euribios's form, his immense dark form looming over me, his power pinning me in place.

I drag myself away. My magic moves through me, mending bones and tissue as it goes. Now that I've drunk the lilac wine, my body can heal itself. Not that it's pleasant.

I grit my teeth as bones snap back into place, my body throbbing at the speedy healing.

All the while, my connection pulses.

I feel a foot on my back. A second later it kicks my side, flipping me to my back. My wings vanish, the pain and pressure of them too great.

I'm blind, and yet I feel Euribios's soulless, empty eyes staring down at me.

"I will never stop fighting you," I say.

"I count on it, enchantress."

Familiar magic—Des's magic—reaches out through our bond and brushes against me. A choked cry nearly slips out of me at the sensation.

Des?

412

...*Ssshhh*...the shadows seem to whisper.

All at once, the darkness peels back. Its smoky, shadowy tendrils fold away from the edges of the room. I can smell old bones and rot; I can see the pale walls and the Thief's stolen throne. I take in a shuddering breath. The quiet humming from the pool behind me drifts in again.

...*A trick*...

...*A clever trick*...

The whispers are coming from all around me, and I feel as though I might be going mad.

Slowly, the Thief's form becomes visible. One by one the stars on his body wink out, and then the darkness settles back into pale flesh.

...*He doesn't know*...

Euribios still looms over me, his foot resting on my chest. His own chest drips with inky black blood that evaporates into the air like curls of smoke. A few final claw marks heal over as I stare.

...*Don't tell him*...

Tell him what?

But then, as quickly as the whispers came, they're gone.

Euribios tilts his head. "How to punish you for your transgression?"

I steel myself, swallowing thickly. I don't know what's going on, but I do know trying to carve out the Thief's heart has probably earned my mate some form of punishment.

The shadows around us ripple, raising the hairs along my arms. Just when I expect to hear Des's distant screams, there's...*nothing*. No screams, no weakening of my bond.

The Thief sways, his foot leaving my chest. He glances away from me, at the doorway.

413

He turns back to face me, his furrowed eyebrows belying his confusion. "Hmm…on second thought…"

Euribios lifts his foot from my body and extends a hand to me.

I stare at it warily.

When I don't take his hand, he smiles down at me. "Fine."

With one hand, he reaches for my head, and with the other, my mouth. Taking a thick clump of my hair, he drags me toward the pool.

I scream, my cries muffled by his hand, and I claw at his wrist—anything to relieve the horrible pressure on my scalp.

"Tradition dictates that every Death King's bride must be baptized in the Well of Resurrection."

The closer we get to that pool, the more the humming becomes a soft dirge. That glowing, *flickering* water calls to my siren.

Right as we're on the very edge of it, Euribios lifts me to my feet so I can see firsthand the pool he means to baptize me in.

The surface of the water stirs, and then something from its depths *moves*.

I'm not going in there, I want to say, but my mouth is still muffled.

Something else moves, a bit of cloth catching my eye. The longer I stare, the more I see—first a delicate arm, then a face—then another face, and another. All fairies, all silently screaming in apparent agony.

Jesus.

They crowd toward the surface, their hands pressed against the water as though there were a true barrier preventing them from escaping. I suck in a breath when I see a familiar face among them. The fae woman who so recently passed through Euribios's halls is now trapped down there with who knows how many other souls.

The Thief pulls me close. "You wanted to know what happens to the dead. Look no further."

They reach for me.

My wings threaten to expose themselves, and the Thief must notice.

"Enchantress, are you frightened?" he asks, his lips brushing against my ear. "Because you should be. Once I throw you in, you will have to fight your way out."

Going to carve him up from ear to ear and wear a necklace of his entrails, the siren hisses.

With a fierce push, Euribios shoves me into the pool.

I hit the water with a hard slap, but I don't go all the way under, not right away. My head and shoulders are still above water.

Immediately, I feel them. The ghosts who live in this pool. Their phantom skin slides against me, and their spindly fingers grab at my leathers, pulling me deeper into the pool.

"Let me go," I command.

The hands holding me don't budge.

So much for that.

I begin dragging myself back to the edge of the water, toward the Thief who watches me with a treacherous smile. More and more hands grab for my legs, my ankles, and my torso.

The dead are clinging to me! I'm utterly spooked by the sensation.

They haven't tried to do more than that though. At least not yet.

I want to reach for the Thief and beg him to save me.

Anger and pride halt my hand and my voice. Instead, I settle for glaring at him.

He grins back at me, his form darkening slightly.

I can't believe he's a god. An evil, cursed god.

"You know," he says conversationally as I'm dragged backward, "I knew a siren once. She was beautiful like you. And mated, like you. But that is where the similarities end."

A hand jerks on my ankle hard, and I nearly lose my footing.

I don't really give a fuck about story time right now. I just want these dead fairies to stop groping me.

Euribios frowns, his eyes softening as they grow distant. "But that was another life," he says, still lost in his memories.

I shudder as phantom bodies swarm around me. They stare at me from below with agonized eyes. Piece by piece, they remove my gear and carry it off, leaving me in nothing but the shirt and trousers I put on back in Somnia.

Even that is not enough to satiate their interest in me. They rally around me, drawn to my life force or my glamour. I cannot imagine how many of them have been imprisoned in this pool. Not even death could release them from the Thief's torment.

Euribios leans against a nearby pillar. As he watches me, he moves his hand, murmuring under his breath.

"What are you doing?"

He pauses his chants, but his hand still twists and flicks. "Removing a ward."

Removing a ward? What ward?

"There are worlds where magic has no effect on me," he says conversationally, "and worlds where it does. This is the latter."

So he's affected by magic? And the ward in question—is

this something he placed on himself? Something he's now lifting?

If so, *that* changes things.

"Why are you telling me this?" My voice wavers midsentence as an arm winds around my torso and yanks me back.

"I want to hear you sing," he says as he finishes.

I feel the subtlest stir in the air as the ward dissolves. It was so expertly crafted that I didn't detect its presence, and now I barely notice its departure.

"No holds barred," Euribios continues. "I want to feel what all those men felt when they died at your kind's feet."

I raise my eyebrows. "You're not immune to my glamour?" I ask, my skin glowing. It's slow to process, partly because I have a horde of dead fae trying to drag me under—but *holy shit.*

He smiles a little, narrowing his eyes. "Enchant me, if you can."

The siren surges. *We can* enthrall *him.*

My wings protrude, my claws sharpen, and my scales shift and resettle along my forearms. My glamour thrums against my skin and coats my throat.

At the display, the dead around me grow frenzied, grabbing me and dragging me down with greater urgency.

I fight against them, but it's a losing battle.

And just when things were becoming halfway interesting.

Of course, that's the entire reason the Thief removed the ward. He wants to hear my glamour when I pose no threat.

If he can fall prey to us, then we'll always be a threat.

My neck slides under the water, my chin skimming the surface. I part my lips. There are only two things I want from him: one, for the Thief to release his hold on Des; two, for him to die.

He looks undaunted. "Any attempts you make on my life will be thwarted. I have my own tricks too, enchantress."

Then saving Des it is. I'm trying to piece together the correct order when the spirits of the pool jerk hard on me. My mouth slips beneath the surface, and I have to tilt my head back to speak.

Time's up.

"Come join me in the water," I breathe, and then I'm dragged under.

The blood rushes through my veins, my siren singing as I call a god to me. To *us*.

This has been a decade in the making. This is what I was born to do.

Only now am I finally listening to the siren's call.

Some of the spirits release me, swarming over to this new creature. Even with my glamour, I can tell the dead find him infinitely more interesting. He's a god, which makes him more than just alive. He's eternal.

It will make killing him interesting.

As soon as the dead's hold loosens on me, I rise to the surface once more, just in time to see Euribios wading toward me, uncaring of the hands that grab at him. Curiosity and want war for dominance on his features. This is a creature who will take and take and take.

The spirits yank at me, redoubling their efforts, and it's a struggle to keep my head above water.

"So defiant," the Thief says, drinking me in, his eyes shining brightly, "even now when you know fighting is hopeless."

I don't know whether he's referring to the ghosts pulling me down or the more general problem of me being his captive.

My lips slip beneath the surface once more.

Euribios grabs my shoulders. "Let me help you," he says, and I think for a moment he's going to draw me up.

But then—

"I anoint you in the waters of the dead."

I don't have time to suck in air before he plunges me down into the depths of this pool.

Beneath the surface, a thousand different souls howl, their faded magic sparking against my skin.

He holds us prisoner.

Centuries of unrest.

Never ending.

The spirits drag me deeper and deeper into the dark waters.

Need our tithe.

Give him to us.

They claw at my glowing skin.

"*I am going to kill him,*" I say into that cursed water. My voice rings true and clear, lilting eerily in the water.

I sense something sweep through the dead then, something besides their hunger and fury.

Excitement.

Their hold loosens on me just a bit.

Give him to us, they repeat.

The siren in me smiles.

"*I will.*"

Euribios jerks me to the surface once more. "Rise, my consort," he says.

I'm shaken. In those depths I heard the dead, and I felt them. All those who passed during the centuries he's ruled here; they're not supposed to be languishing here in this tiny pool.

The defunct ship I saw earlier now comes to mind. The vessel sits unused at the castle's dock, and beyond it, an entire ocean awaits. But the captain or ferryman or whoever moves souls on it is no longer doing so, and the fae who have died are suffering for it.

This must end.

The spirits have released me, but the Thief's hands are still on my skin, his eyes following his touch. The human in me wants to pull away from him, but the siren beckons him closer.

So very arrogant to linger in the water with a siren. So very arrogant…and reckless.

Save Des. Kill this monster. Those are the only two goals I have. Now that I know my glamour works on the Thief, these goals seem temptingly easy. But that's the same thought I had when I sought to ambush Galleghar on Barbos. No doubt there's a trap waiting for me here as well. Nothing is easy when it comes to the Thief.

There are two kinds of predators. One that chases after prey, and one that coaxes its prey to it.

A great god like Euribios must feel impervious to harm. He's too great, too powerful.

It will be his downfall.

But I can't be too hasty.

Let him think he has control of the situation. Beguile him softly.

I stare up at the Thief. "Am I the only one to be baptized?"

His eyes glitter. In response, he steps closer to me, his gaze fixed on my face. "You are…utterly singular. You always have been." He looks awed by the effect I have on him. "If you want to baptize me, siren, then simply give me the order."

He begs for death!

I take his hand. "Come, my captor king."

My blood stirs as I tug him deeper and deeper into the pool. I feel the ancient compulsion to draw my victim into the water.

Months ago, I thought about the origins of my kind. How sirens were known for luring sailors into the sea. That story never made sense: The perverse cruelty of it all. The seeming randomness of the victim and the manner of death.

But it's not random at all.

The water is hungry for blood.

I am hungry for blood.

Vengeance and lust and blood sport all call to me.

Have patience…

Maybe those sailors deserved their deaths. Maybe they didn't. But this god does.

I place my hands on Euribios's shoulders. He's watching my lips, waiting for my next order.

Patience…

"Let me anoint you in the waters of the dead."

My claw tips dig into his shoulders, pressing down. Slowly, he lowers himself.

Patience…

I lean in close, until only a breath separates my lips from his. "Drown," I breathe.

Our patience is gone.

The Thief laughs, looking disturbingly unfazed. "I warned you I had precautions put in place."

My stomach tightens with dread and disappointment.

Too hasty. Of course, it wouldn't be that easy.

The Thief's form flickers and fades.

An instant later, he reforms exactly where he last was.

421

When he does, something in his face changes. Maybe it's confusion; maybe it's surprise. Whatever it is, it's a dead giveaway that Euribios's precautions are not working as they should.

He glances at the dark corners of the room. "The shadows—" the Thief accuses.

"*Have betrayed you*," a familiar voice finishes.

I jolt, my eyes darting up toward the sound.

And there he is.

Des.

CHAPTER 44

Des.

My heart thumps painfully.

Dear God—*Des.*

He's right there, a stone's throw away.

The Night King drapes himself over Euribios's throne, his back leaning against one of the armrests, his legs propped on the other, lounging like he wasn't all but lost to me only moments ago.

My connection throbs, just as it has since the Thief exposed his true power and identity.

It must be a trick, a cruel, calculated trick. Euribios holds Des's life in the palm of his hand.

Only, the Thief is looking a bit startled too. He swivels to face the Bargainer, even as he still struggles against my command.

Never have I seen a creature withstand my glamour this long.

Des lifts his eyebrows. "Didn't expect the shadows to fuck you over, did you?"

The Night King hops off the throne and saunters to the pool. Briefly, his eyes touch on mine, and I see a thousand things in them. Most of all, I see yearning, so much yearning.

It matches my own.

My Bargainer.

I stare at him like he's an apparition. All that pain I was working on overcoming just to function—it's like the wound reopened. But now there's hope to accompany the pain. So much hope, I can barely breathe around it.

Maybe this *is* a trick…but perhaps I'm not the one being played.

The Thief fights against my glamour and the pull of the dead who still cling to him. It's now his turn to attempt to escape this pool, wading toward the edge.

"You're to stay in this pool, Euribios," I command from behind him, the full force of my glamour folded into my words.

Beyond him, Des sways a little toward me, even as he stares at Euribios. I can tell my mate is trying hard not to look in my direction. He's no longer immune to my glamour, and I'm no longer holding my powers in check.

Between us, the Thief's progress slows. He looks over his shoulder at me. "You will pay for this later," he says, his voice laced with venom.

The room around us darkens with Des's vengeance.

People like us are someone's nightmare.

I narrow my eyes on the Thief and smile a little. "I don't think so."

The King of Night comes to the edge of the pool and crouches, studying our foe. The Thief jerks against the incessant pull driving him downward.

"You might have power, Euribios," Des eventually says, "but there is one thing you never considered."

My heart beats faster. Somehow, Des orchestrated this.

"Loyalty."

Euribios's back is to me; what I would give to see this conniving monster's expression.

Des says, "For centuries, the shadows and I have been the closest of confidants."

The shadows speak to me, Des admitted back on earth. It was how he learned so many secrets.

"Do you think that means anything to them? To me?" the Thief says. "I existed before the dawn of day."

The shadows around us shiver and grow.

"Do you know what they told me?" Des says.

Euribios falls silent.

Des's face hardens. "Even shadows can deceive and gods can die."

Des looks at me then, and like a thunderclap, I feel that look down to my bones.

Love, love as endless as the night. That's all I see in his eyes.

"Now, my queen," the Night King says to me, "where were you?"

He's handing off the torch, letting me resume the insidious task I began. Slowly, a smile creeps along my face.

Vengeance at last.

I lift my chin. "Des, you are to ignore every command I give from this point forward."

His eyes flash with devilish delight. "As you wish, my sweet siren."

With that parting line, he vanishes, melting into the darkness as he has so many other times since I first met him. Our bond sings, and I feel him down the other end of it, sure and steady.

My gaze moves to the Thief, and my whole persona changes. For a minute, I set aside the knowledge that Des appears to be alive and well.

An entity needs to pay.

"Face me, Euribios."

Slowly, the god rotates, his expression incredulous. He's dominated others for so long that he can't possibly recognize the position he's now in.

"I will enjoy paying you back for this—" he vows.

"You will *not* threaten me," I say. "Nor will you use any of your magic on me or anyone else. Right now, you are *powerless*."

The Death King curves his mouth. "I will *never* be powerless, enchantress," he says, wading through the souls to get to me, still resisting my earlier command to drown. He doesn't look frightened—I don't think the Thief even knows what fear is; he's never had to fear a thing in his life.

As he moves toward me, he murmurs. His oily magic stirs, and I sense him redrawing his ward.

Too late, Death King. "Drown," I say, my voice hypnotic.

The Thief barks out a laugh, interrupting his work. "You cannot kill me—"

"I can do *whatever* I want. So come closer," I say, moving out into deeper water, souls slipping past me. "Find me beneath the waves. Feel my watery kiss. Drown in my arms. Die for me, my undying king."

Sinister. Seductive. Even death is tempting when a siren delivers it sweetly.

The Thief continues to wade toward me, only now his torso is disappearing beneath the water's surface.

"I cannot die."

"Yes," I breathe, "you can."

426

I move to the middle of the pool, feeling my magic in my veins and in the water. Euribios's eyes are locked on mine, longing shining bright in them. The water has nearly reached his shoulders. He murmurs once more.

"Meet me down in the water's depths," I say, coaxing, *coaxing*. "There's nothing to fear. Breathe it in. Drown."

My words strike like an anvil.

The Thief's breath catches, and a spark of something enters his eyes. It's not fear; he's too alien a creature for that. Shock, maybe—or betrayal.

Or maybe it's that, for all his dealings with death, this eternal thing can't conceive of it happening to him.

And now it is.

Whatever ward he's been casting, it sits in the air unfinished, and it's not clear that it would be useful at this point anyway. My eyes, my body, my magic—everything that I am beckons to him.

Join us down below.

It doesn't matter that he's a god and I'm not, nor does it matter that my power is infinitesimal next to his. I promise a dream, a beautiful, deadly dream, and what is more powerful than that? Dreams, desire—what *wouldn't* you do to have what you most want?

I slip beneath the lapping surface. All around me howling, phantom things grab and claw at the Thief.

They hadn't harmed me—I hadn't even thought they were capable of it—but they're harming Euribios, splitting his skin open. His blood looks like ink in the water before he heals over.

"Drown, drown, *drown*." Even down here I whisper it.

The waterline climbs up his neck, then his jaw.

I don't know whether he sinks the rest of the way himself

or if he stops fighting against the powers pulling at him, but all at once, his head sinks below the surface.

Drown.

The Thief—Euribios—opens his mouth and draws in water.

That's all it takes for the spirits to swarm him, descending on the god like ravenous beasts. If I thought they were hurting him before, it's nothing compared to their onslaught now. I see muscle and bone as they tear into him.

More disturbingly, the dead shove their way into his mouth.

The Thief's eyes are open, and the entire time, he stares at me, his eyes sharp with desire and alarm. Euribios reaches for me, either in want or in need, the water around his arm darkening with his shadowy blood.

But I never take that offered hand, and the spirits crowd in so thick that after several moments, the Thief disappears behind ephemeral bodies.

The moment the two of us lose eye contact, his screams start, the sound muffled by water and the spirits forcing their way into his mouth.

I linger underwater, my ears feasting on his dying cries. They grow fainter and fainter, until they eventually vanish altogether.

And then—

BOOM!

The Thief's magic detonates, rippling outward. It slams into me, throwing me back before blasting across the throne room.

In its wake, the spirits begin to fall away from the Thief. Only there's no more Thief. No body, no bones—just a few drops of inky blood. The last of his dark magic unfurls in the water then dissipates.

His death wasn't the sweet seduction I promised him it would be. It was painful, brutal. As it should've been.

He's gone.

The Thief is finally dead.

Maybe there will always be darkness and shadows and all those things that happen when the sun goes down. Maybe night will always be waiting to swallow up the earth, but today—

Darkness died.

CHAPTER 45

When I rise from the water, the dead cling to my clothes, not wanting to release me. Eventually—and reluctantly—they do. I gave them the blood they demanded after all.

They slip back into the pool where they wait for whatever it is the rulers of the Underworld do with the souls of the dead.

Now that the Thief is well and truly gone, his staggering magic lifts from the air, and the room around me brightens.

The siren's savage nature still rides me hard. I want to kiss and touch and taste and torment. I want it all so badly that my wings and claws throb.

I've only taken a step or two when Des appears several feet from me.

I stop, and I don't dare breathe. This feels like a spell, one that will be broken the moment I move.

We stare at each other for one beat, then two. And then the spell is broken.

Des disappears, only to reappear right in front of me.

The Night King crushes me to him, and it is everything I need.

I gather his shirt into my fists as his lips find mine. Suddenly, it feels like I can breathe again, like the world has colors and purpose and joy because Desmond Flynn, King of the Night, is alive and in my arms.

He tastes like magic and mayhem. I want to laugh; I'm sure I'm going to cry. Des is no dream, no apparition that will be swept away when the Thief has had his fun.

Somehow, he outwitted death.

When the kiss ends, I stare up at him. Those pale silver eyes, that softness right around his mouth, all those planes of his face that are so very heartbreaking—I didn't know I could miss anything so damn badly.

"You're real, right?" I whisper.

"I'm real." The Night King is giving me that gaze of his, the one that makes me feel like I'm worthy of worship.

"I thought I lost you—" My voice breaks.

He curves up the corner of his mouth, and he looks at me so tenderly. "There are many uncertainties in life, but this one thing holds true: I will always come back to you, cherub."

Des is not just darkness. He's moonlight and stardust; he's wishes and adventure and a love as vast as the night sky.

And he's here, *alive*.

He's alive.

A flash of anger flares through me, and I give him a light shove. "I thought you were *dead*."

He smiles, catching my wrist. "Awww, cherub," he says. "Don't be mad."

"Don't 'awww, cherub' me, Des," I say, yanking my wrist out of his grasp. "You can't even know what it was like," I say hoarsely. "You *can't*." I couldn't dream up a nightmare worse than that. Those hours I spent lamenting him.

Des closes the last of the space between us, his face turning somber. "I *can*, Callie. I almost lost you once." He pinches his eyes shut and gives his head a shake. "I'm so sorry," he says. Des opens his eyes, his gaze blazing. "For deceiving you and forcing you to experience that. There is *no* worse hell."

There really isn't.

"And I'm so sorry for making you face the Thief alone." He takes my hand and cups it between his. "Never again," he vows, his voice fierce.

I take a deep breath and pull myself together. Now that Des is alive and burning with his own brightness, my skin has finally started to dim, my wings and claws and scales disappearing.

"I want more than promises and apologies from you," I say.

When he realizes exactly what I'm asking, Des's eyes brighten and a corner of his mouth lifts.

He brings his wrist up in front of himself. As I watch, a strand of spider silk forms around it followed by a dull black bead.

"Is this fair?" he asks.

A deal. One *I* get to claim.

I give him a skeptical look. "One bead? I endured my soul mate's *death* and faced down a god, and all I have to show for it is one measly bead?"

"Demanding siren. Fine."

A second bead appears next to the first.

I give Des another light shove, a laugh slipping out of me. The laugh turns into a sob. And the sob…the sob gives way to ugly heaving tears.

And that's how this fearsome siren ends up sitting on the Bargainer's lap in the Death King's throne room, listening to the Bargainer sing her a fae lullaby, his head pressed to hers.

It was bound to happen. The last bit of my bravery was spent killing Euribios. I've got nothing left.

"I love you, cherub," Des murmurs. "More than any fairy has a right to love anything." He sweeps away my tears with his thumbs.

I nod against him.

"I'll add a whole row of black beads to the bracelet—several rows. Just please stop crying. I can't bear the sight of you sad." He punctuates the sentiment by taking my hand and kissing the base of my palm. And then he kisses each fingertip. The whole thing is so ridiculously sweet that I choke up again.

Closing my eyes, I take a few deep breaths. It's a physical thing, putting myself back together, but I eventually do it.

I open my eyes and cup Des's face. "I love you." I smile a little as I say it. Then I rise to my feet, pulling the Bargainer up after me. He still wears his crown, and he looks every bit the fairy king.

He squeezes my hand, and I think that's his way of seeing if I'm ready to leave this room, and God, am I ready, but before we go, I notice a discarded shirt several feet away. It's Euribios's shirt—he must've removed it right before he entered the pool.

After walking over to it, I pick the shirt up. Des eyes it curiously as I twist the cloth around and around, turning the shirt into a makeshift rope. I then slide the rope through my belt loops.

There's a box this belongs in, a box that sits in a house with sandy floors and chipped countertops. A box that all my most prized relics go in.

"It's a memento," I say, tying off the Thief's shirt.

Des's gaze turns capricious. "You may not live in the ocean, Callie, but you are every inch the siren."

I don't know much about sirens, other than the few lines I've found in dusty school textbooks and what I've learned myself, but collecting macabre mementos of my victims seems about right.

The Bargainer's gaze sweeps over the pool. The waters are still humming, the sound pricking my skin.

His eyes drop to me. "You've never been more fearsome than when you took down the Thief," he says.

I remember my magic singing through my veins and the thrill of watching my victim bend to my will, a god whose immortal life I stole because I ordered him to die.

"You were watching?" I ask.

Des should be frightened of me, not impressed. But I guess I'm overlooking the fact my husband is a cold-blooded killer.

"How could I not? I'm a terribly curious creature."

So he watched me kill. I wonder if he thinks of me differently.

People like us are someone's nightmare.

Then again, maybe he always thought of me this way; I just finally lived up to his dark imaginings.

The two of us leave the throne room before winding our way back through the palace.

Des's eyes study our surroundings. "So this is the Palace of Death and Deep Earth," he says. "I've got to admit, I was expecting a little more."

"A little more of what? Ghosts?" Because I saw *plenty*. Not going to get those little fuckers out of my head for a long while.

"My mother used to tell me tales of the monsters that lurked in the land of the dead."

I'd bet money the Thief hunted them all down for sport long ago.

"*Are* you going to tell me how you did it?" I ask, interrupting his reverie.

Des gives me a sly look. "How I tricked the Thief of Souls?"

"No, how you learned to whistle. Of course, how you tricked the Thief." Like pulling teeth with this one. I'm going to need every century of my newly long life to tease out this man's secrets.

His eyes spark with delight at my attitude; Des likes me best with my claws out.

"Now, cherub, you know these secrets are going to cost you."

"Des!"

He laughs. "Two words: kinky sex. If you agree to it, I'll sing like a choir boy and tell you everything."

We both nearly died—the whole world almost fell to the Thief—and this is what he's thinking about right now? Kinky sex?

I narrow my eyes.

"Promise you'll enjoy it, wife. I'm vividly imagining pressing you up against the side of our pool and licking that glowing water from between your—"

My skin is starting to glow, which is hugely embarrassing.

"*Fine*. But you're going to tell me everything."

———

"It began with Solstice."

The two of us have stopped walking so Des can explain himself.

435

"When I discovered the Thief of Souls—Euribios—had wanted you to drink the lilac wine so you'd be vulnerable to his magic, I learned three things: One, the Thief was a clever bastard. Two, he wanted you. And three, it seemed no fae was immune to his magic. He could put any of us to sleep the same way he had all those soldiers; the only thing holding him back was his own scheming."

My mind is racing, listening to this.

"I knew the Thief was waiting for the right moment to exact his plans—whatever they were—and I couldn't let that happen." Des's eyes fall heavily on mine. "Not when I knew he wanted you.

"So I devised a plan of my own, one that would save you and the Otherworld. I altered it as new information came in about the Thief. And once I discovered he was not just a god but *the* God of Darkness, I knew even my power was useless against him."

And yet, somehow, Euribios still died.

Des threads his fingers through mine. "I'm sorry I didn't confide in you, Callie. He was using shadows to watch us."

Of course. If Des had told me his plans, the Thief would've learned of them, and the element of surprise would've been lost.

"My father's prophecy—I knew the human it mentioned was you, so I knew that not only could Galleghar fall, but the Thief could be taken down with him."

My brows knit. "How could you be sure the prophecy was about me?" I ask.

The corner of Des's mouth curves up. "Shadows are not the only creatures who tell me secrets. There are pixies and diviners and all sorts of other fae with secrets to share."

So my mate learned I was destined to stop Galleghar.

That truth sits heavy in me. I was fated to be a killer centuries before I was even born. I try not to shudder at the thought.

"At some point, it came to me. How to truly stop Euribios." He pauses dramatically.

I give him a devastating look. "And?"

He laughs. "You're adorable when you're impatient." He pulls me close and wraps a lock of my hair around one finger. "I made two deals—one with the Thief of Souls and another with the shadows. With the Thief, I agreed to willingly become his prisoner so long as neither you nor I died."

The Thief hadn't been able to get his hands on Des until that deal. Not when the Night King made a habit of obliterating the fae the Thief controlled. So Des came to him and struck a deal that made my mate seem weak and desperate. And Euribios, in all his pride and power, believed it.

"With the shadows," Des continues, "I promised to rid them of Euribios once and for all if they were willing to deceive him."

The shadows that wouldn't speak of the Thief of Souls.

"That's a big promise," I say. "How did the shadows do it?"

"You mean, how did they trick the Thief?"

I nod.

"Power is sentient—it can make decisions for itself."

Des and I knew that better than most. It was what kept us apart for seven years.

"The shadows are part of that sentience," Des continues, "and they're what Euribios derives his power from—as do I.

"And that was the Thief's fatal mistake. The god forgot our power comes from the same source, a source with its own free will. So the shadows and I—we tricked him."

I raise my eyebrows.

"I spoke to the darkness during the only times I knew the Thief wasn't listening—when you dreamed of him."

All those sick dreams—Des couldn't stop them from happening, but he could use them against the Thief.

"The shadows told me everything I needed to know, and it was them who helped me strike the deal with Euribios. And when the time came, the shadows severed the Thief's hold on me."

He trusted the darkness with everything that mattered to him.

"Why do you think the shadows helped you?" I ask. For years they were unwilling to breathe a word against the Thief.

Des stares down at me, his gaze intense. "Even before I could really use my power, I spoke to the darkness. The shadows were my first friends."

I think of that lonely pale-haired boy who lived on Arestys, and my heart aches for him, even though that boy's struggles made him the man I love.

"Euribios brutalized them just as he brutalized the fae. He abused them into submission eons ago, until the God of Light defeated him and freed the shadows. But then my father unleashed Euribios, and the shadows were forced to cower before his power once more.

"It's not in the nature of shadows to be disloyal—even to terrible creatures—but they learned what it was like to exist outside of fear, and that's not something you can forget."

What Des doesn't add is that fear probably wasn't the only factor that swayed these shadows. Desmond Flynn is beloved by the darkness.

"And so, with your help," I say, "the shadows turned on their god."

Des squeezes my hand, his eyes flashing in a very fae way. "And so they did."

———————

We continue heading back through the palace. My thoughts are spinning a mile a minute from all Des has told me. Faked deaths, disloyal shadows, and the secrets that saved us all.

I only shake off these thoughts when the two of us enter the room I found Des in. The altar still rests where I last saw it, along with all those shelves of potions and medical instruments and books with gilded titles. On the floor are my discarded weapons and the shattered remains of the objects previously knocked from the shelves.

None of that, however, is what catches the Bargainer's attention.

His gaze locks on the slumped form on the other end of the room. In an instant he disappears from my side before reappearing—wings and all—next to the body of Galleghar Nyx.

I pace over to my discarded weapons and fasten them back on before I dare to creep closer to Des and his father. Part of me is fearful that Galleghar is still alive. Evil fathers have a way of defying death. In fact, this whole situation has the ring of déjà vu to it, only my and Des's roles are reversed.

The Bargainer kneels, his white-blond hair skimming his jawline as he stares down at the man who gave him life and death in equal measure.

"Is he dead?" I ask.

"Quite." Des's gaze travels over Galleghar. Then the Bargainer touches one of his father's chest wounds. He studies Galleghar's injuries for a long time before he finally glances up. "He was right to fear you. You did kill him in the end."

"That was the Thief."

"You killed the Thief, and with the Thief's death, the bond they shared broke. The Thief could no longer keep Galleghar's death at bay."

Birds, meet stone.

There are still so many questions I have—like why Euribios woke Galleghar when he did and why the old god decided to uphold his end of their bargain when he so obviously could've broken his oath—but I fear I won't get answers.

As we stare down at Des's dead father, a spectral hand separates itself from Galleghar's body, then an arm.

Oh geez, I forgot where we are for a moment.

The Thief was right about one thing: the dead don't ever *really* die if you're kicking it in the Kingdom of Death and Deep Earth. They just change form.

A chill runs over me. Is that what happened to the Thief? Did he just change form?

No, I refuse to believe that.

Des stands, grimacing down at the man. "I wonder if it's possible to beat the shit out of spirits…"

I take Des's hand as Galleghar's spirit separates from his body. "Leave your father to his fate." I'm sure the afterlife has its own form of punishment for the wicked.

With that, the two of us leave the room and Des's father behind.

———

Before we depart, we free the prisoners locked in the castle's dungeons. There are forty-four of them in total, all that remains of the prior ruling house.

Their bodies are scarred and emaciated, and their eyes

440

have lost that spark of hope. One look at them makes it clear the Thief won't be the last struggle this kingdom faces.

And yet, not an hour after they're released, several of them have moved to the dock, pointing at this or that section of the neglected ship. And the ferryman I saw earlier now wades through the Well of Resurrection, pulling out the spirits one by one. It's one of the strangest sights I've ever seen, and that's saying a lot at this point.

Des steps up to me, his fingers entwining with mine. "Much as I've enjoyed our revelries here, I do believe it's time to go, Callie."

God, I couldn't agree more.

We make our way through the castle and back out the front doors. Above us, the darkness has fled. There's a sun low on the horizon and cotton candy skies. Under the light, even the pale gardens look different—less ominous and more peaceful.

The two of us walk down the path that winds its way from the castle entrance to the archway I passed through earlier, only from this side, the doorway doesn't quite look the same.

We stop in front of it. On this side, two stone doors are fitted into the enormous archway. Extending from either side of them are massive stone walls that encircle the palace grounds.

I eye the barred gates in front of us. Just before I think we might have to smash into it, the doors creak open, revealing the inky darkness of the Pit beyond it.

"That was…easy," I say.

All the myths promised escape from the land of the dead was impossible. But what do I know? No one gave me a guidebook to this place.

"The hard part is coming up," Des says ominously.

The two of us walk through the gateway, and I only have to struggle a little against whatever enchantments have been placed on it.

When we enter the Pit, Des illuminates the space. He whistles at the sea of skeletons. "That's a lot of dead bodies."

It's a sad sight, but at least the fairy who drove these soldiers to their deaths has now been stopped.

Des comes over to me and wraps a hand around my waist. At his back, his talon-tipped wings shimmer into existence. "Hold on, cherub," he says.

"What are you—?"

He launches us up, and the rush of air steals my words.

Unlike the trip down, nothing touches either Des or me as we ascend. The creatures are either still under my glamour…or they know better than to harm their king.

We barrel upward for who knows how long before I start to feel it.

Magic.

It bears down on us, pressing against my skin, wanting us to stay in the land of the dead. The higher we climb, the heavier it is. And then it's not simply pushing down upon us but fighting inside us, clawing against our flesh. It feels like the time I flew on an airplane when I had a sinus infection. My ears are screaming at the pressure, and my skin stings.

We're never going to make it.

"There's no easy way to do this, cherub, but it'll be over soon," Des says against me.

You mean it's going to get worse?

The thought has hardly crossed my mind when it does in fact get worse. God, it does. My skin lights up as I moan. My entire body is getting crushed by the weight of the magic.

442

I'm just about to let loose the mother of all screams when—

BOOM!

The magic explodes around us, rippling over my skin.

And then we're through.

I sense it stitching itself back together beneath us. I glance down at the darkness, unnerved. It was so easy to enter the land of the dead, like easing into a tub, but near-impossible to escape it.

It's as I gaze below us that I see the glint of a pair of eyes, trapped on the other side of the magical barrier. They stare at me for a moment before plunging back into the inky shadows.

A shudder works its way through me. Good riddance.

We climb the last bit of the way up, and when we crest the ridge of the Pit, I catch sight of hundreds of fae who've have gathered around it.

News of my face-off with the King of Death and Deep Earth clearly spread.

And at the front of them is Temper, who looks immensely relieved.

As soon as the crowd sees us, they cheer, the night coming alive with claps and whistles and sparks of light.

We land in front of Temper, and she grabs me, hugging me tightly. "Thank God you're back," my best friend says. "You were gone for too long."

Des steps up to us, and Temper opens one of her arms. "You get in here too, Desmond. You're my brother now."

He steps in with a shy smile, letting my best friend crush him in our embrace.

"Did you kill that monster?" Temper asks, releasing us.

I meet her eyes. "What do you think?"

She stares at me for a moment, then lets out a laugh. "Ha ha, you badass. I hope you gave him my regards before you blew him to smithereens."

I shake my head, a whisper of a smile curling my lips.

Des breaks away from us to rise into the air.

The crowd, which had been murmuring upon our arrival, now quiets.

My mate's eyes move over the group of them. "For the past decade, our kingdom has been plagued by the Thief of Souls." Magic amplifies Des's voice, and it booms out into the night. "He kidnapped our soldiers, raped our people, and started a war in our world. He destroyed our peace and the sanctity of our kingdom.

"It was only recently that we discovered the Thief of Souls had raided the Kingdom of Death and Deep Earth and taken the throne by force. Days ago, he took me hostage and kept me prisoner in his castle.

"When all the world thought me lost, my soul mate— your queen—marched down to the gates of the Underworld and faced the Thief head-on."

No one speaks, though I feel all sorts of eyes move to me.

Des gestures for me to join him where he hovers in the sky. Reluctantly, I do.

Once I'm by his side, he stares at me. I can see an entire universe in his moonlit eyes.

"But Callypso Lillis, Queen of the Night, didn't just face any foe. The Thief of Souls was none other than Euribios, the primordial god of death and the dark."

There are intakes of breath throughout the gathered crowd, then thoughtful murmurs as they take me in.

"Your queen faced Euribios, and she *vanquished* him."

Gasps. I feel those gazes on me like the hands of the dead.

But it's the Bargainer's gaze that holds me rapt. He gives me a soft smile before announcing to the gathered crowd, "The Thief is no more."

Back in Somnia, the royal prison is suddenly full of very confused fae soldiers. Among them are Janus and Malaki.

"Has someone been naughty while I've been away?" Des asks from the other side of the bars.

"What is going on?" Janus demands as the iron door slides back.

"Callie killed one of your great and mighty gods," Temper says from where she stands next to me. "Not to be rude, but you all have some weak gods if this one can trounce them," she says, nudging me.

"Hey!"

"What?" the sorceress says. "I'm *kidding*."

"Temper." Malaki's deep voice has my friend sobering. He steps up to her, ignoring me and Des and every other individual swarming the halls of the dungeon. His eyes are fixed on Temper, and his wings—his wings are *out*.

He touches her cheek, and that's all it takes for my fiery friend to soften. She slips into Malaki's arms.

"Don't ever do that to me again," she says, "or I'll kill you myself."

Des's general holds Temper tightly, and it's a testament to whatever they've got going on that he doesn't take that threat the wrong way.

Janus looks between us. "Seriously, is anyone going to tell me *why* I'm in the Night Kingdom's dungeon?"

The Bargainer's eyes fall on me while he plays with the beads on his bracelet. "The queen and I would be delighted to fill you in," he says to Janus. "For a price, of course." He winks at me.

Eight years ago, this began with a dead man and a deal. And now, here we are, with a few more dead men and a few more deals under our belts.

I take Des's hand, and the two of us lead the group out of the dungeon.

The King of the Night brings our clasped hands to his lips and presses a kiss to the back of mine. His silver eyes gleam.

This man.

He's the Bargainer who saved my life over and over, and the king I ended up saving, a time or two.

He's a trickster, a secret keeper. He's the dark side of the moon. He's my beautiful, terrible mystery.

My friend. My soul mate.

From flame to ashes, dawn to dusk—until darkness dies. He's mine, and I'm his. *Always.*

EPILOGUE

7 years later

Des and I land in our backyard, our wings folding up behind us. Overhead, the stars glitter, and far below our yard, the Pacific crashes against the beach.

Twining my fingers through Des's, I start toward the house. My eyes go to the moss-lined shingles and the weathered exterior. The paint is peeling a little, but I'm hesitant to redo it. When I bought this house a decade ago, its imperfections were what I cherished most about it—well, that and the ocean in the backyard.

Our house on Catalina Island can be the pretty one. This is our homey bungalow.

I lead Des to the sliding glass door. With a *snick*, it opens, revealing our bedroom beyond.

The walls are covered in photographs of faraway cities. The only thing consistent about them is the smiling couple in each—Des's light features pressed closely to my dark ones.

Scattered among the photographs is the Bargainer's artwork—most depicting Otherworld cities we've been to that my camera conveniently can't capture. Of course, there are a few embarrassing sketches of me, a couple of which are borderline inappropriate.

That's what I get for still being a sucker who makes deals with the Bargainer.

And the rest of the room is filled with kitschy trinkets—some from this world, some from another. Most are the result of one of Des's rigged dares—like the enormous sombrero pinned on the wall that he got me to wear for an entire evening. But some, like the Cycladic figurine sitting on our bookshelf, are gifts we've given each other.

But all of it is a testament to the incredible life we live.

Ahead of us, the comforter slides back from the bed.

I give Des the side-eye. "*That's* a bit presumptuous."

"No, cherub. *This* is presumptuous."

The top button on my pants pops open, and my zipper slides down. My shirt tugs itself up.

My skin brightens with interest because even after all these years, my siren is still a hussy when it comes to Des.

The King of the Night laughs and scoops me up before tossing me lightly onto the bed. "Phew," he says. "I've still got it."

He drapes himself over the lower half of my body, his torso conveniently nestled between my legs.

Des smooths his hands down my inner thighs, his gaze caught on mine. I feel the cool brush of his bracelet against my skin. I wear its twin on my own wrist.

Favors we owe each other.

Des still moonlights as the Bargainer, and I join him on his deals probably more than I should, especially considering I still do part-time work with Temper at West Coast Investigations…and I help rule a kingdom.

I feel a brush of magic, and the Metallica shirt Des wears now slips off. My fingers trail over his tattoos. I trace the rosary of black beads twisting up his arms. If I took the time to count them all, I'd find 322 of them, the exact number of beads that first bound me to him.

"You owe me a few favors, cherub." He punctuates that declaration with a kiss to the hollow beneath my throat. His pelvis moves against me, and my core flares to life.

I thread my fingers through his white hair, tilting his head back so our gazes meet. "You owe me a few favors yourself."

He cocks an eyebrow. "Is that right?" I feel the faintest breath of his magic as my shirt melts off me. "Lucky for you, I think I know just the thing to clear me of my debts…"

The Bargainer moves down my torso, his lips skimming my skin. He kisses my belly button, and his hands glide to my hips before continuing down…

His breath fans across my flesh, and it raises goose bumps along my arms.

Too good to be true.

All that hoping and wishing and yearning. Life is never supposed to give you what you want, and if it does, best to not assume it's forever.

But if there's one thing I've learned about the Bargainer, about us, it's that we've paid our dues and then some. And now we get to have this for the rest of our very long lives.

Suddenly, Des pauses, his mouth poised in that tantalizing space between my abdomen and my pelvis.

He turns his head to the side, pressing his ear into my soft skin, as though my very flesh is whispering secrets to him.

His grip tightens on my hips. Ever so slowly, he lifts his head, his eyes meeting mine.

I can't read his expression. I can't read his expression, and I really, *really* want to know what's running through his mind because the look he's giving me is *not* normal.

"What?" I finally say, breaking the weird silence between us.

Des smiles, and it's so bright, so heart wrenchingly beautiful that it's physically hard to look at him.

He leans down and kisses my flesh.

"What?" I say again.

"I have a secret."

Author's Note

The end of a series always brings with it contradictory emotions. This one especially. The Bargainer series spans nearly five years of my life from its humble inception back in the spring of 2014—when *Rhapsodic* was originally slated to be *Moonlight Rhapsody*, a novella that was part of a paranormal romance anthology—to the series it is today..

My dear readers, thank you all for coming on this journey with me. This book belongs to every one of you. You were the ones who originally encouraged me to keep on with the story—even at the very beginning, when I'd only posted a few teasers and thought maybe I'd let this story slip through the cracks and collect dust on my computer—and you were the ones in the end who helped me wrap Des and Callie's story up.

To answer the question I get most often at the end of a series ("Will you ever write more books about Des and Callie?"): I'm a big fan of never saying never, but as of right now, I have no plans on any future books in this series.

That being said, I have many other stories slated to take place in the supernatural world(s) Des and Callie live in, so if you enjoy paranormal and fantasy reads (with romance! huzzah!), you're in luck. I'll be starting my next series in this world, and I won't reveal what it's about yet, but I will say that if you like enemies-to-lovers romances, this next series might be up your alley!

Thank you all again for your readership. Truly, I can never say that enough. I am continuously humbled that my stories mean something to you all. In a world full of instant entertainment, you who find yourselves lost in a book are rare gems. Thank you for letting my words be a part of your world.

Hugs and happy reading,

Laura

Keep a lookout for the first book in
Laura Thalassa's Four Horsemen series

PESTILENCE

PROLOGUE

They came with the storm.

The sky surged, great plumes of clouds tumbling and roiling together. The desert air thickened, feeling damp and smelling unusually ripe.

Lightning flashed.

BOOM!

The world lit up like it was on fire, and there they were—four great beasts of men astride their terrible steeds.

The monstrous mounts reared back, pawing the air as

their masters stared out at the world with foreign, fearsome eyes.

Pestilence, his crown perched upon his brow.

War, with his steel blade held high.

Famine, a scythe and scales at hand.

And Death, blighted Death, his dark wings folded at his back, a torch of bilious smoke tight in his grip.

The Four Horsemen of the Apocalypse, come to claim the earth and lay waste to the mortals that dwelled within it.

The sky darkened and the steeds charged, their hooves kicking up dust as they galloped.

North—

East—

South—

West—

The horsemen rode to the four corners of the world, and in their wake, machines broke, fuses blew. The internet crashed and computers died. Engines failed and planes fell from the sky.

Bit by bit, all the world's great innovations ceased to be, and the globe slid into darkness.

And so it was, and so it shall be, for the Age of Man is over, and the Age of the Horseman has begun.

They came to earth, and they came to end us all.

CHAPTER 1

Year 5 of the Horsemen

"We draw matches."

I level my hazel eyes on the tiny wooden sticks in Luke's fist. He strikes one against our rough-hewn table, the flame flaring bright for a second before he blows it out.

Around us, the fire station's overhead lights hum in that distressing way most electronics do nowadays, like at any moment they might sputter out.

Luke holds up the matchstick with the blackened tip. "Loser stays behind to see our plan through."

This was the painstaking decision we made. One person doomed to die, three more to live.

All so we could kill that ungodly sonuvabitch.

Luke folds the tip of the burnt match into his palm with the three unburnt ones, then dips his hands beneath the table to mix them up.

Outside, beyond one of our decommissioned fire trucks,

all our necessary belongings are packed, ready for a quick escape.

If, of course, we're one of the fortunate three.

Luke finally lifts his hand, the matchstick stems jutting from his closed fist.

Felix and Briggs, the other two firefighters, go first.

Felix draws a matchstick...

Red-tipped.

He lets out a breath. I can tell he wants to fall back in his seat; his relief is obvious. But he's both too macho and too aware of the rest of us to do so.

Briggs reaches for his...

Red-tipped.

Luke and I share a look.

One of us is going to die.

I can see Luke preparing himself to stay behind. I've only ever seen that expression on his face once before, when we were putting out a wildfire that had all but encircled us. The fire moved like the devil drove it, and Luke wore the expression of a walking dead man.

Both of us survived that experience. Perhaps we'd survive this devil too.

He holds his fist up to me. Two wooden sticks jut out. Fifty-fifty odds.

I don't overthink it. I grab one of the matchsticks.

It takes a second for the color to register.

Black.

Black means...black means death.

The air escapes my lungs.

I glance up at my teammates, who are all wearing various looks of pity and horror.

"We all have to die sometime, right?" I say.

"Sara…" This comes from Briggs, who I'm halfway positive likes me more than a colleague and friend ought to.

"I'll go instead," he says. Like his bravery counts for anything. You can't date a girl if you're dead.

I close my fist around the match in my hand. "No," I say, resolve settling in my bones. "We decided this already."

Staying behind. I'm staying behind.

Deep breath.

"When all of this is over," I say, "someone please tell my parents what happened."

I try not to think about my family, who evacuated with the rest of the town earlier this week. My mom, who used to cut the crusts off my sandwiches when I was little, and my father, who was so upset when I told him I volunteered to stay behind for the last shift. He looked at me then like I was a dead woman.

I was supposed to meet them at my grandfather's hunting lodge.

That's no longer going to happen.

Felix nods. "I got you, Burns."

I stand. No one else is moving.

"Go," I finally order, "he's going to be here in days." If not hours.

They must see I'm not dicking around because they don't bother arguing or lingering for long. One by one they give me tight hugs, pulling me in close.

"Should've been different," Briggs whispers in my ear, the last to let me go.

Should've, could've, would've. There's no use dwelling on this now. The whole world ought to be different. But it isn't, and that's what matters.

I watch through one of the large windows as the men

leave—Luke unhitching his horse from the garage, Briggs and Felix grabbing their bikes, their things strapped to the back.

I wait until they're long gone before I begin to gather my things. My eyes move over my pack, stuffed with all manner of survival gear—and a book of Edgar Allan Poe's best works—before landing on my grandfather's shotgun, the oiled metal looking particularly lethal.

No time for fear, not until the deed is done.

I might be doomed to die, but I'm taking that infernal fucker down with me.

CHAPTER 2

No one knows where the Four Horsemen came from, only that one day they appeared on their steeds, riding through cities and wildlands alike. And as they passed through town after town, human technology broke like waves upon the rocks.

No one knew what it meant. Especially when, all at once, the Four Horsemen disappeared just as suddenly as they had appeared.

Our electronics never recovered, but we began to rationalize the inexplicable events away: t was a solar flare. Terrorists. Synchronized EMP pulses. Forget that none of these explanations made any sense—they were more reasonable than some Biblical apocalypse, so we cringed and swallowed down those half-baked theories.

And then Pestilence reappeared.

———

I sit at our table for a long time after my teammates—*former* teammates—have left, running my fingers over the polished wood of my grandfather's shotgun, getting used to the feel of it in my hands.

Other than re-acquainting myself with the weapon over the last two weeks when I shot the crap out of some tin cans, it's been years since I handled a gun.

I've killed a sum total of one creature using this weapon (a pheasant whose death haunted my twelve-year-old dreams).

Going to have to use it again.

I get up, sparing another glance out the window. My bike and the trailer I jerry-rigged to the back of it sit across the way, my food, first aid kit, and other supplies strapped to the back. Beyond my bike, the Canadian wilderness perches on the hills that border our city of Whistler. Who would've thought a horseman would come here, to this lonely corner of the world?

On a whim, I head over to the fridge and grab a beer— the world might be ending but fuck it if there's no beer.

Popping the cap off, I cross over to the living room and click on the TV.

Nothing.

"Oh for fuck's sake." I'm going to die a horrible, shit-sucking death, and the TV decides that today is the day it stops working.

I slam a palm down on the top of it.

Still nothing.

Muttering oaths my grandfather would be proud of, I kick the good-for-nothing TV, more out of spite than anything else.

The screen sputters to life, and a grainy image of a newscaster appears, her face warped by the bands of color and contortions the TV makes.

"...appears to be moving through British Columbia...

heading towards the Pacific Ocean…" It's hard to make out the reporter's words under the static-y white noise. "…Reports of the Messianic Fever following in his wake…" Pestilence has only to ride through a city for it to be infected.

Researchers—those that remain dedicated to their work even after technology has fallen—still don't know much about this plague, only that it's shockingly contagious and the primary vector of transmission is *horseman*. But a name has been given for it all the same—the Messianic Fever, or simply the Fever. The name was cooked up by spooks, but that's what the world has come to—spooks and saints and sinners.

Turning off the TV, I grab my bag and gun and head out, whistling the *Indiana Jones* theme song. Perhaps if I pretend this is an adventure and I'm the hero, it will make me think less about what I'm going to have to do to save my town and the rest of the world.

I spend most of the day and a good part of the evening setting up camp off of the Sea to Sky Highway, the route he's likeliest to take. And dear God do I hope that the horseman will pass through while it's still light out. I have shit aim in broad daylight; at night I'm likelier to shoot myself than I am him.

Seeing how my luck's going today, there's a chance, a good chance, I'll fuck this up. Maybe Pestilence makes a detour, or decides to be clever and approach from another direction. Maybe he'll pass by without my ever noticing.

Maybe maybe maybe.

Or maybe even wild, frightening things have a pinch of logic to them.

I grab my gun and extra ammunition, creep close to the highway, and I settle in for the wait.

461

He comes with the first snow of the season.

The entire world is quiet the next morning as the powdery white flakes blanket the landscape and turn the road pearlescent. More snow flutters down, and it all looks so ridiculously beautiful.

Out of nowhere, the birds take flight from the trees. I startle as I see them all high above me, their bodies dark against the overcast sky.

Then, from a dozen different locations, wolves begin to howl, the sound sending a primordial shiver down my spine. It's like a warning call, and in its wake, the rest of the forest comes alive. Predators and prey alike flee past me. Raccoons, squirrels, hares, coyotes—they all rush by. I even see a mountain lion loping amongst them.

And then they're gone.

I exhale a shaky breath.

He's coming.

I crouch in the dim forest, shotgun clutched in my hands. I check the gun's chamber. Remove and reload the cartridges just to make sure that they're properly in place. Adjust and readjust my grip.

It's as I'm double checking the ammunition in my pocket that the hair on the back of my neck rises. Ever so slowly, I lift my head, my gaze fixed on the abandoned highway.

I hear him before I see him. The muffled clomp of his steed's hooves echoes in the chill morning, at first so quiet that I almost imagine it. But then it gets louder and louder, until he comes into view.

I waste precious seconds gaping at this…*thing*.

He's sheathed in golden armor and mounted on a white steed. At his back is a bow and quiver. His blond hair is pressed down by a crown of gold, and his face—his face is angelic, proud.

He's almost too much to look at. Too breathtaking, too noble, too ominous. I hadn't expected that. I hadn't expected to forget myself or my deadly task. I hadn't expected to feel...moved by him. Not with all this fear and hate churning in my stomach.

But I am utterly overwhelmed by him, the first horseman of the apocalypse.

Pestilence the Conqueror.

CHAPTER 3

No one knows why the horsemen arrived five years ago, or why they disappeared so soon afterwards, or why now Pestilence and only Pestilence has returned to wreak havoc on the living.

Of course, everyone and their Aunt Mary has their answer to these questions, most that are about as plausible as the tooth fairy, but no one has actually ever had a chance to corner one of these horsemen and pump them for answers.

So we can only guess.

What we do know is that one morning, seven months ago, the news bleated to life.

A horseman, spotted near the Florida Everglades. It took the better part of a week for the rest of the report to drift in. About how a strange sickness was taking the people of Miami by storm.

Then the first death was announced. They did a big spread on the woman, for the few hours she held the sole title of tragically deceased. But quickly the death count doubled, then doubled again. It grew exponentially, first wiping out Miami, then Fort Lauderdale, then Boca Raton. It moved up the East Coast of the United States, right along with the movements of this shadowy rider.

This time when the horseman passed through a city, it wasn't technology he destroyed, but *bodies*. That's when the world knew that Pestilence had returned.

Glossary

Arcane Forest: believed to be the place where the first trees took root; located in the Flora Kingdom; birthplace of the Green Man.

Arestys: a barren, rocky landmass belonging to the Kingdom of Night; known for its caves; smallest and poorest of the six floating islands located within the Kingdom of Night.

Avalon: also known as the City of the Sun and the Isle of Light; capital of the Day Kingdom.

Barbos: also known as the City of Thieves; the second largest of the floating islands located within the Kingdom of Night; has garnered a reputation for its gambling halls, gangs, smuggler coves, and taverns.

bog: a shadowy carnivorous Otherworld creature that eats its victims alive; feared for its ability to make its victims live out their worst nightmares as they die; native to the Night Kingdom.

Borderlands: area where day meets night; the border

between the Kingdom of Day and the Kingdom of Night; borders between fae kingdoms.

changeling: a child swapped at birth; can alternatively refer to a fae child raised on earth or a human child raised in the Otherworld.

co-bind: the process by which fae share and exchange magic.

dark fairy: a fairy who has forsaken the law.

Desmond Flynn: ruler of the Kingdom of Night; also known as the King of Night, Emperor of the Evening Stars, Lord of Secrets, Master of Shadows, King of the Night, and King of Chaos.

fae: a term denoting all creatures native to the Otherworld.

fairy: the most common fae in the Otherworld; can be identified by their pointed ears and, in most instances, wings; known for their trickery, secretive nature, and turbulent tempers.

gast: wraithlike creatures who feed on the life force of other fae; gasts burrow belowground but come to the surface to feed; native to Memnos.

glamour: magical hypnosis; renders the victim susceptible to verbal influence; considered a form of mind control; wielded by sirens; effective on all earthly beings; ineffective on creatures of other worlds; outlawed by the House of Keys because of its ability to strip an individual of their consent.

Green Man: king-consort of Mara Verdana, Queen of Flora.

House of Keys: the global governing body of the supernatural world; headquarters located in Castletown, Isle of Man.

Isle of Man: an island in the British Isles located between

Ireland to the west, and Wales, England and Scotland to the east; the epicenter of the supernatural world.

Janus Soleil: ruler of the Kingdom of Day; also known as the King of Day, Lord of Passages, King of Order, Truth Teller, and Bringer of Light.

Karnon Kaliphus: ruler of the Kingdom of Fauna; also known as the King of Fauna, Master of Animals, Lord of the Wild Heart, and King of Claws and Talons.

Kingdom of Day: Otherworld kingdom that presides over all things pertaining to day; transitory kingdom; travels around the Otherworld, dragging the day with it; located opposite the Kingdom of Night; the eleven floating islands within it are the only landmasses that can claim permanent residence within the Kingdom of Day.

Kingdom of Death and Deep Earth: Otherworld kingdom that presides over all things that have died; stationary kingdom located underground.

Kingdom of Fauna: Otherworld kingdom that presides over all animals; stationary kingdom.

Kingdom of Flora: Otherworld kingdom that presides over all plant life; stationary kingdom.

Kingdom of Mar: Otherworld kingdom that presides over all things that reside within bodies of water; stationary kingdom.

Kingdom of Night: Otherworld kingdom that presides over all things pertaining to night; transitory kingdom; travels around the Otherworld, dragging the night with it; located opposite of the Kingdom of Day; the six floating islands within it are the only landmasses that can claim permanent residence within the Kingdom of Night.

Lephys: also known as the City of Lovers; one of the six floating islands within the Kingdom of Day; believed to be one of the most romantic cities in the Otherworld.

ley line: magical roads within and between worlds that can be manipulated by certain supernatural creatures.

loi du royaume: Otherworld law that dictates all fae must submit to the rules of the kingdom they are in.

Mara Verdana: ruler of the Kingdom of Flora; also known as the Queen of Flora, Lady of Life, Mistress of the Harvest, and Queen of All that Grows.

mate challenge: a duel between two rivals for the hand of a mate; usually ritualistic as mate bonds cannot be transferred.

Otherworld: land of the fae; accessible from earth via ley lines; known for its vicious creatures and turbulent kingdoms.

Peel Academy: supernatural boarding school located on the Isle of Man.

Phyllia and Memnos: sister islands connected by bridge; located within the Kingdom of Night; also known as the Land of Dreams and Nightmares.

pixie: winged fae roughly the size of a human hand; like most fae, pixies are known for being nosy, secretive, and mischievous.

Politia: the supernatural police force; global jurisdiction.

portal: doorways or access points to ley lines; can overlap multiple worlds.

Sacred Seven: also known as the forbidden days; the seven days surrounding the full moon when shifters remove themselves from society; custom established due to shifters' inability to control their transformation from human to animal during the days closest to the full moon.

seer: a supernatural who can foresee the future.

shifter: a general term for all creatures that can change form.

siren: supernatural creature of extraordinary beauty; exclusively female; can glamour all earthly beings to do her bidding; prone to bad decision-making.

Somnia: capital of the Kingdom of Night; also known as the Land of Sleep and Small Death; biggest island in the kingdom.

supernatural community: a group that consists of every magical creature living on earth.

Thief of Souls: the individual responsible for the disappearances of fae warriors.

Well of Resurrection: body of water located in the throne room of the Palace of Death and Deep Earth that can hold the dead; used to baptize the Death Kingdom's ruling family.

werewolf: also known as a lycanthrope or shifter; a human who transforms into a wolf; ruled by the phases of the moon.

About the Author

Found in the forest when she was young, Laura Thalassa was raised by fairies, kidnapped by werewolves, and given over to vampires as repayment for a hundred-year debt. She's been brought back to life twice, and with a single kiss, she woke her true love from eternal sleep. She now lives happily ever after with her undead prince in a castle in the woods.

…or something like that anyway.

When not writing, Laura can be found scarfing down guacamole, hoarding chocolate for the apocalypse, or curled up on the couch with a good book.

You can find more news and updates on Laura Thalassa's books at laurathalassa.com.